FERN MICHAELS

EMILIE RICHARDS
SHERRYL WOODS

Maybe This Time

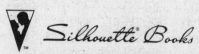
Silhouette Books

Published by Silhouette Books
America's Publisher of Contemporary Romance

SILHOUETTE BOOKS

MAYBE THIS TIME

Copyright © 2003 by Harlequin Books S.A.

ISBN 0-373-21898-2

The publisher acknowledges the copyright holders of the individual works as follows:

WHISPER MY NAME
Copyright © 1981 by Fern Michaels

ONE PERFECT ROSE
Copyright © 1992 by Emilie Richards McGee

DREAM MENDER
Copyright © 1992 by Sherryl Woods

Praise for these award-winning authors

FERN MICHAELS

This *New York Times* bestselling author has a passion for romance that stems from her passion for the other joys in her life—her family, animals and historic homes. She is usually found in New Jersey or South Carolina, where she is either tapping out stories on her computer or completing some kind of historical restoration. Legions of fans around the world thrill to the romantic stories Ms. Michaels creates in every one of her novels.

EMILIE RICHARDS

Award-winning author Emilie Richards believes that opposites attract, and her marriage is vivid proof. "When we met," the author says, "the only thing my husband and I could agree on was that we were very much in love. Fortunately, we haven't changed our minds about that in all the years we've been together." They have lived in eight states— as well as a brief, beloved sojourn in Australia— and now reside in Ohio. Though her first book was written in snatches with an infant on her lap, Emilie now writes full-time—unless the infant, now a teenager, reminds her that it's her turn to carpool. She loves writing about complex characters who make significant, positive changes in their lives. And she's a sucker for happy endings.

SHERRYL WOODS

has written more than seventy-five romances and mysteries in the past twenty years. She also operates her own bookstore, Potomac Sunrise, in Colonial Beach, Virginia, where readers from around the country stop by to discuss her favorite topic—books. If you can't visit Sherryl at her store, then be sure to drop her a note at P.O. Box 490326, Key Biscayne, FL 33149, or check out her Web site at www.sherrylwoods.com.

CONTENTS

WHISPER MY NAME

Fern Michaels

Chapter One

Washington, D.C., in autumn can be one of the most beautiful and exhilarating cities in the world, yet Samantha Blakely walked on lagging feet down Connecticut Avenue, oblivious to the bright gold and orange leaves that cast dappled shadows on the sidewalk. It was unseasonably warm and she felt itchy beneath her heavy sweater jacket, but she was too disheartened to remove it and carry it over her arm. Indian summer, she mused as she kicked at the dry, papery leaves. All Hallow's Eve was tomorrow, and tonight was Mischief Night, when all the neighborhood children would be out wreaking havoc.

Samantha grinned. How well she remembered her own youth and the bars of soap streaking windows and the eggs thrown with gay abandonment. It seemed so long ago, and everything had changed from those remembered nights in a New York neighborhood. Right now, she felt as old as Methuselah and as weary as Job.

She looked up and scanned the numbers on the row of houses and realized she was home at last—the basement apartment she rented from Gemini Delaney.

Samantha fished in her handbag for the bright gold key which hung from a Gucci chain and had been a gift from Gemini, who said that every girl who had her first apartment deserved a Gucci key chain. For some reason the sparkling gold always gave her such a lift, like now, when she was depressed. Gemini always had the answers.

At first Samantha thought she was at the wrong brownstone when she saw a huge orange pumpkin which leaned against a straw facsimile of a scarecrow that leaned beside her door. A giggle found its way to her lips. Gemini again. Gemini Delaney was the oldest little girl Samantha knew, getting her pleasures from the celebration of a second-rate holiday. Sam knew when she made her way to the old lady's door she would find a replica of her own decorations. Wonderful, thoughtful Gemini.

Sam's eye fell to the thin circlet on her wrist as she fit the key in the lock. She would have to hurry or Gemini would start to fret, and she shouldn't be upset, not with her precarious health. All Sam really needed was a quick splash of cold water on her face, a dab of perfume, and a fresh scarf around her neck, preferably one Gemini had given her, and she could skip next door and make it right on time.

Reverently, Sam placed her camera, a Hasselblad and her dearest possession, on the foyer table. Her cinnamon-colored eyes lingered for a moment on the worn case and a single tear formed in the corner of her eye. She wiped at it impatiently. The camera was all she had left of her father, who had been a photo-journalist for CBS News. When he had been killed by terrorists while on an assignment, the camera had been sent along to her by one of his associates. It was all she had left of the man she called Father and who had taught her everything she knew about photography. She couldn't think about that now. Now she had to shift into third gear and get over to Gemini's.

As Sam smoothed the towel over her creamy complexion, she wondered how her feisty but lovable old neighbor had fared with her physician's visit that she knew had taken place early that afternoon. As she ran the brush through her short cropped hair, she realized she had come to love the old woman and would grieve sadly when she was gone.

Don't think about that now, she cautioned herself. Think about how happy Gemini is going to be when the portrait of her nephew, Christian Delaney, was finished. Sam's eyes lightened at the thought and her somber mood lifted. The portrait of Delaney was a piece of her finest work, and she knew it. Running a close second to her love for photography, painting in oils was her most gratifying work. Tonight, after she returned to her own apartment, she would work on the background for a few hours. She hadn't exactly sloughed off working on the portrait, but job hunting was no easy feat, and she was so tired when she returned home at night that all she wanted to do was sleep. Most of the headway she had made on the portrait, which she was copying from a photograph, was done on the weekends. And Gemini had been a real gem about the whole thing. Gemini understood; she always understood.

Sam rummaged on her cluttered dressing table and found the bottle of Chanel No. 5 that had also been a gift from Gemini. She lavishly dabbed on the potent scent. Sam giggled again when she remembered how she and Gemini had been watching television one evening when the commercial came on for the famous perfume. Gemini had laughed uproariously and called the advertisement an obscenity. The next day Neiman-Marcus had delivered the square, elegant box of Chanel to Sam's doorstep. "I will feel this way forever." Sam giggled again, recalling the husky, sensual voice of the model in the ad as she exited her apartment and locked the door. But only if the male model emerging from the water was someone like Christian Delaney. He was the stuff dreams were made of—impossible dreams.

Before she had a chance to lift the heavy bronze knocker, the door was opened by Gemini's housekeeper. "Miz Delaney is waiting for you and has your cocktail all ready. She's a bit upset because her doctor told her she couldn't have a sherry before dinner. Right now she's in there sipping the cats' gin-and-tonic. She don't listen to me, Miss Blakely. Maybe you can talk to her."

Sam's eyebrows shot upward in alarm. "Esther, maybe it's just tonic water she's drinking. Gemini wouldn't disobey the doctor's orders. Where is she?"

Esther snorted indignantly. "It's gin, all right, and you can just forget about that tonic water. Them cats are both drunk as two skunks. She's been giving them sips in their water dishes. And I can smell gin a mile away. Miz Delaney is well on her way to getting looped, and I know it." With another snort Esther bobbed her spikey gray head and departed for her own domain—a brick and copper kitchen aromatic with spices and herbs. Sam blinked. She had never seen anyone except Esther who could actually swish an apron the way a stripper tossed her tassels.

If Gemini was drinking, that meant the doctor's news was bad. Gemini could handle anything, even a good drunk. Squaring her shoulders and pasting a smile on her pretty face, Sam bounded into the room and headed straight for the Queen Anne chair where the old lady sat. "Gemini, you are something, do you know that? A pumpkin and a scarecrow. It's perfect. What made you think of it? I love it. How in the world did you get them here?" She knew she was babbling, but she was unable to stop herself. "And that pumpkin is a perfect round ball. When I was a kid, they were always sort of lopsided and... Oh, darn it, Gemini, what did the doctor say?" Sam blurted out as she dropped to her knees at the old woman's feet.

Gemini Delaney straightened her back and patted her blue-white hair, which was carefully arranged down to the last strand. "That doctor is nothing but a spring pup; he's not even dry behind the ears," Gemini said testily, ignoring Sam's question. "For the life of me, I don't know why I put up with him."

"You put up with him because he's the best cardiologist in Washington, D.C., that's why," Sam said softly. "Now, tell me, what did he say?"

"Among other things, he said I was a vicious, cantankerous old woman who should have been put out of her misery ten years ago. What do you think of that?"

Sam forced a smile to her lips. "Did he, now? Or did he say you were a spirited, beautiful lady who should know better than to ignore a doctor's orders?"

Gemini slouched slightly in the yellow velvet chair and muttered, "It might have been something like that, but I really can't remember. This gin robs your brain; you know that. Just look at those stupid cats lying in the fireplace,'' the old lady snapped.

Sam laughed. ''I'd be lying in the fireplace, too, if I drank straight gin. What happened to the tonic water?'' she asked, sniffing the glass that rested next to Gemini's chair.

''That fool doctor said if I didn't go into the hospital for his triple bypass I wouldn't last out the week; those were his exact words. That means I have exactly four days left. It's funny how I can remember those words so exactly. Don't you think that's funny, Sam?''

''Hilarious,'' Sam said past the sob in her throat.

''But there is some good news,'' the old lady said brightly. ''Christian is on his way home. Speaking of Christian, how is the work going on the portrait?''

''Fine, just fine. When I go home tonight, I'm going to work on it. I think I landed a job today. They actually gave me a contract, and I wanted to talk to you about it. I don't know what to do. It's with *Daylight Magazine,* and I think the only reason they even considered me was because of my father.''

''Don't be such an upstart that you can't accept help, Sam,'' Gemini said shortly. ''You're an excellent photographer; I've seen your work. Almost as good as your father's. In time you'll be better. Take the job and prove your worth to them. Something else is bothering you. Tell me about it.''

Anything to divert the old lady from her grim thoughts, Sam thought worriedly. ''It seems to me this contract is tying me up pretty tight and the money they're paying isn't all that good. I know I can't demand or expect anything like the seasoned pros get, but this is barely a living wage. I thought *Daylight* paid well and...oh, Gemini, I don't know what I expected. Look, here's the contract; it's the last two paragraphs that concern me. What do you think?''

The pale, blue-veined hands that reached for the contract were steady, as were the bright, piercing blue eyes. Gemini scanned the printed words and then guffawed. ''You're right, child, this contract...''—she sought for just the right word and finally came up with it—''...stinks! Now, this is what you do. You tell them to take out...get me a pencil over there on the desk. Good girl. Now, have them take out paragraph four altogether; demand that paragraph six give you better splits; delete paragraphs nine and ten and..."—the pencil flew over the pages as Sam watched in awe—"...and this is the figure you ask for, and you tell them you won't take a penny less. You tell them that photographs by Orion, that unisex name you insist on using, is one day going to put *Daylight Magazine* right up there with *Time*. You have to be tough and you can't backwater. Tomorrow you march right in there and stand up like your father did. This is what you want. Then you tell him to take it or leave it. Leave your portfolio. Who gave you this contract, anyway?"

"A Mr. Jebard in personnel. Gemini, I don't know if I can do that," Sam said hesitantly.

"Do you believe in yourself, Sam, and in your work?" Gemini said testily.

"Of course. You know I do."

"Then you can do it. I don't want to hear another word. Call me tomorrow after you leave the office. Where's that Esther? She should have announced dinner half an hour ago."

"Here I am, and I didn't announce dinner 'cause I was waiting for you to dry out. You dried out now, Miz Delaney?"

"You old fool, I wasn't even wet," the old lady said fondly to her shiny-faced housekeeper. "Well, don't just stand there, help me get up."

"No, siree, Miz Delaney. The doctor said you was to eat off a tray, and that's exactly what you're going to do."

"And I pay her to torment me like this! Do you believe it?" Gemini sniffed, making no physical effort to move.

Sam smiled weakly, knowing what the light-hearted banter cost the old lady. Esther knew it, too, as she bustled around fluffing first one pillow and then another, finally placing a foot-stool at Gemini's feet.

"What do you want me to do with them dumb cats lying in the fireplace?" Esther demanded. "It's their dinner time."

"You'll be the death of me yet, Esther. Can't you see they're sleeping? They can eat anytime; leave them alone."

"They ain't sleeping; they're drunk, and when they wake up they're going to have a hangover and I'll have to walk them on a leash. No self-respecting black woman walks cats on a leash. I ain't going to do it, Miz Delaney," Esther muttered as she stomped from the room.

"I worry about her," Gemini said softly as she leaned her frail head back into the softness of the daffodil-colored velvet chair. "She doesn't know it yet, but she's leaving for Seattle. I made all the arrangements this afternoon. I don't want her here when I...when I...she needs a vacation," she said lamely.

Sam's throat constricted at the haunted eyes and the bluish tinge around Gemini's mouth. She forced herself to strive for a light tone. "What has Esther prepared for dinner? Do you know, Gemini?"

"Let's both ask her. Here she comes now with the trays. What have you cooked tonight?"

"The only thing you're allowed to have. Sliced lean chicken and a cup of Jell-O. For Miz Blakely, a sweet potato and a small steak with salad."

The old lady's voice was a shade firmer when she baited the housekeeper still again. "No imagination at all. I'm allowed to have an egg, and you know it. Why didn't you bring me a poached egg?"

"*You* said you could have an egg; the doctor didn't say so. No egg," the housekeeper said adamantly.

Sam's fork was poised midway to her mouth when the soft chime of the telephone bell permeated the room. "I'll get it, Gemini," she said, rising from the chair. "I have it, Esther," she repeated to the housekeeper, who had entered the room at a fast trot. "Hello. Yes, this is Gemini Delaney's residence. Who's calling, please?" Sam covered the receiver with the palm of her hand. Her cinnamon eyes asked a question, but all she said to Gemini was, "It's the overseas operator. Your nephew, Christian Delaney, is calling from Turkey."

The old woman's face lit up momentarily and then settled into grim lines. "Sam, tell him I'm sleeping and that I can't be disturbed. I'll get too emotional, and, right now, I can't handle that.'' Sam nodded.

"Go ahead, operator, I'll take the call.'' Sam's heart fluttered wildly. At last, after all these months of working on the portrait Gemini had commissioned, she was finally going to hear the man's voice. It would be deep and husky; she could almost feel it. "Aunt Gemmy, it's Chris here. I've been delayed... *squawk ... sputter ...—crackle ...* sometime toward ... what's that ... who is this ... *crackle ...*''

"This is Samantha Blakely. I live next door to your aunt.... Hello! Can you hear me ... ?''

"Sputter ... crackle ... squawk ... what man? Where's my ... *crackle ...* home ...''

"Try to get the operator back!'' Sam shouted into the crackling phone.

"*Squawk ...* When did you say she would be back?'' *Crackle ...* and the line was dead. Sam replaced the phone and shrugged her shoulders. "It was a very poor connection, Gemini. I could barely make out what he said. I think he's been delayed, but he is coming home. You heard my end. I'm sorry. Don't worry, he'll make it.''

Gemini waved a clawlike hand. "It's all right. Don't fret, Sam. I'm tired now and I think I'll retire for the night. Call Esther for me and have her help me. Her nose gets out of joint if I don't lean on her every so often. Tell her to bring the phone to my room and plug it in. I have several calls I have to make before I call it a night.''

Sam threw her arms around the thin woman and choked back her tears. "Not to worry, Gemini. He'll get here in time; I know it.''

"I know it, too, child. You finish your dinner and then run along and work on that portrait so you can have it done by the end of the week. Good night, Sam,'' she said, kissing the young girl's cheek.

"Gemini, thanks for the pumpkin.''

"Later you can make Christian a pie—when he gets here, that is.''

"Of course, I'll be glad to."

"It's his favorite," Gemini said wearily.

Sam obediently finished her dinner as Gemini had instructed. The food, so carefully prepared by Esther, was bland and tasteless on her tongue. As she ate and chewed methodically, Samantha reflected on the unknown well of courage that she had found in herself ever since the truth about Gemini's failing health had become known. Talking so matter-of-factly about death was one of the most difficult things Sam ever had to do. Yet, it was necessary. Gemini demanded it. Confident and pragmatic, Gemini reassured Samantha that death was also a part of living and that eighty-one years was more than enough time for any woman to accomplish a full, exciting life. Sam told herself that Gemini was right, but that didn't help to erase the pain she felt when she thought about the time that the wonderful old woman would no longer be there.

Thanking Esther for dinner, Samantha went back to her own apartment and changed her clothes in favor of a pair of faded old jeans that were streaked with vari-colored paint, and a comfortable, worn shirt. The portrait of Christian Delaney stood on an easel in the spare bedroom in the direct light of the track lamps she had installed. The handsome, intelligent face of Christian Delaney stared back at her from the canvas. The silvery-gray eyes looked out at her from beneath unruly, dark brows and, as always, Sam thought she detected a trace of humor in his otherwise formal and serious pose. Short-cropped hair that held a hint of a wave dipped over his broad brow, and his head was held arrogantly on the thick column of his neck.

Samantha shook herself. It had happened again. Sometimes, when she turned on the light and stood before the portrait of Gemini's nephew, the canvas seemed to breathe life. It was silly, really, for while her painting was true to life and closely followed the photo Gemini had given her, it certainly wasn't so lifelike that she should have these feelings.

Setting a tall stool before the easel and reaching for her palette and various tubes of paint, Sam prepared the quiet browns and umbers she needed for the background and remembered the long, quiet conversations she had shared with Gemini concerning the subject of Christian Delaney. It was possible that Gemini's descriptions of her nephew were so detailed that Samantha imagined she knew the subject of the portrait personally. Even more foolishly, Sam's dreams were more and more often concerned with the real flesh-and-blood Christian, and once or twice she had laughed at herself when she suddenly realized she was actually talking to the dabs of color and paint that created his image on the canvas.

"Stupid fantasies of an old maid," she chided herself as she dabbed and mixed her colors. Yet her gaze was drawn again and again to the eyes that stared back at her, and a tingle of anticipation raced down her spine as she thought that soon, very soon, she would be meeting the real Christian Delaney.

Brush poised in midair, Sam frowned. It wasn't possible…it just couldn't be possible that she was falling in love with the man in the portrait. True, Gemini had spoken so often of him that Sam had the impression that she actually knew him. But the rest was pure foolishness. No self-respecting, halfway intelligent girl who was trying to carve out a career in photo-journalism for herself right here in this day and age could become so mesmerized with a man in a painting that she felt she was falling in love with him!

Her eyes locked with those on the canvas and the anticipated tingle danced the length of her spine. "Foolish!" Samantha scolded herself as she slammed down her palette and concentrated on the background of the portrait, purposely refusing to permit her eyes to stray to the handsome, compelling features of her subject.

Chapter Two

The heavy portfolio tucked under her arm, Sam waited patiently for a bus at the corner that would drop her off at the *Daylight* door. Inside her purse, in the zipper compartment, was a neatly typed list of corrections for her new contract. Would the man called Mr. Conway be amenable to the changes she was going to request, or would he laugh and tell her to peddle her work somewhere else?

Sam settled back in her hard seat on the bus and willed herself to relax. She felt good and at this precise moment in time she felt she exuded confidence. For some strange reason she always felt that way after a few hours of work on Christian Delaney's portrait. The work last night had gone well, and Gemini would be pleased. Even Christian Delaney, if he ever saw the finished product, would find himself hard pressed to find fault with her work. What was he like? Gemini had said he stood well over six feet and had steel-gray eyes that saw through a person to the very soul. At Gemini's death he was to inherit the family-owned business, and at that time he would settle down and raise a family, or so Gemini hoped. Gemini had said he was strong willed, yet gentle and vulnerable, but she hadn't explained how or why he was vulnerable, but had said someday Samantha would find out for herself. It would be easy to fall in love with Christian Delaney, and if Samantha admitted the truth, even to herself, here on this noisy bus, she was already half in love with his likeness.

"K Street," the bus driver called loudly to be heard above the busy chattering.

Sam slid from her seat and walked to the middle of the bus and waited for the double doors to swish open. She held the portfolio tightly and settled her canvas shoulder bag more comfortably on her shoulder. She made the half-block in minutes and walked through the revolving door. "Mr. Conway, here I come, ready or not," she muttered, pressing the Up button. Her heart fluttered wildly when the elevator door opened and she squeezed past the departing occupants. She pressed number 16 and leaned weakly against the wall. Did she have the nerve? Could she do what Gemini told her to do? Of course she could. She had come this far, and besides, how would she ever explain her lack of courage to Gemini?

Sam's eyes did a slow once-over of the elaborate reception area and came to rest on a lacquered china doll-like woman sitting behind a desk with an intercom system at her fingertips. "I'd like to see Mr. Conway, please," Sam said in a voice she didn't recognize.

The receptionist spoke softly, her voice a musical chime. "May I ask your name?"

"Samantha Blakely. I'm a photographer and I work under the name Orion."

"You're Orion!" the tiny woman exclaimed. "May I say that I saw the pictures you took of the boat people and...and they were just...you captured... What can I say? I liked them."

Sam literally gasped. "Did you really like them? I always feel that I did well if just one person says so. Thank you, thank you so much for the compliment."

The other woman smiled. "Mr. Conway is busy, but I'll interrupt him. He's just putting in his office." She gave Sam a wicked wink and pressed a small white button. She spoke softly and motioned with her hand. "Just give him time to put away his golf club and get behind his desk," she whispered. Sam let her left eye close and walked slowly to a heavy oak door. At the receptionist's nod, she opened the door and then closed it softly behind her. *Here goes nothing,* she said silently as she walked forward to a monstrous desk.

A pink, balding-type man rose from behind the desk and held out his hand. "Charlie Conway," he said jovially, "and you're Orion. Sit down and take a load off your feet. What can I do for you?"

Samantha licked at dry lips and remembered Gemini's words. "Look, Mr. Conway, I'm a good photographer—not the best, but good. Your Mr. Jebard offered me a contract yesterday to work for this magazine. I led him to believe I would sign it, and I had every intention of signing it until I read it more thoroughly. What I'm trying to say is, it's not satisfactory. I'd like to tell you what I would like, and then perhaps we could compro— then perhaps we could come to terms. On second thought, Mr. Conway, I can't compromise or come to terms." Before the man behind the desk could utter another word, Sam was reading off her list of corrections to the contract. "Not a penny less, Mr. Conway. I'll be honest with you. I want this job more than I ever wanted anything, and I know I'll be an asset to your staff, but you have to be fair, too." Sam leaned back, a fine beading of perspiration dotting her forehead. She waited.

"You got it. Listen, kid, what do you do for an encore?"

"Got it? You mean you…you agree to my terms and I don't do an encore?"

"I don't think so. You shot your load the first time around. Look, kid, I knew your old man and I liked him. You've got the same kind of guts he had. There aren't too many people who would march in here and make demands, not even the seasoned pros. You've got guts, and I like that. Your old man and me, we went through some rough times back in the old days. I bunked with him for three solid months in Beirut, when neither one of us could take a bath in all that time. We remained friends, and let me tell you something. Your old man smelled about as raunchy as I did when we finally made our way home. I heard he died a couple of years ago. I'm sorry. He used to talk about you and that Brownie Hawkeye you had. He was proud of you, kid.''

Sam was stunned. "Mr. Conway, are you giving me the job just because you knew my father?"

"No! You said Jebard gave you the job yesterday. I just cleaned up his contract for him. What kind of camera are you using?"

"My dad's Hasselblad."

"Kid, that camera has a soul. Don't ever lose it. You using your dad's Leitz lenses?"

"Every last one of them." Sam smiled.

"Looks like we're in business, then. You can start work Monday morning. I'll see what's on the roster, and your first assignment will be ready whenever you are. Welcome aboard, Orion," he said, holding out his hand. "I'm glad you're using your old man's handle. Old cameramen never die, that kind of thing," Conway said sheepishly. "And, kid, call me Charlie. Oh, one other thing—if that's your portfolio, leave it here. Our new president will be in Monday, too, and I'm sure he's going to want to check over our newest addition. I'll give you a good buildup, kid."

"Mr. Con—Charlie, thank you, thank you for everything, but mostly, thanks for telling me about my dad. Maybe someday we can get together and swap stories. I'd really like to hear about some of your experiences."

"I'd like that, too, Orion."

Sam walked on air all the way back to her apartment. She felt good. Thank God for Gemini. She was supposed to call her from the office and let her know how she made out. Darn, she thought wretchedly, how could she have forgotten something so important? A taxi. She would take a taxi and get home as fast as she could and tell Gemini in person.

She was too late....

On the day of the funeral, it was fitting that it should rain. Complying with Gemini Delaney's wishes, the services were simple and private. Esther had been given the name of the law firm that handled the old woman's affairs, and the lawyers had taken it from there.

Flowers arrived at the funeral home, and notes of condolence came to Christian Delaney, who still had not returned home. When Samantha questioned Esther as to how Mr. Delaney could be reached, the dark-skinned woman shook her head and shrugged. "All I know, Miz Blakely, is that those lawyers are trying to reach him. But you know Miz Delaney never waited for no man. Her instructions were to have the funeral and get it over with quickly. She used to say that life was for the living, and that the dead don't deserve much more than a passing respect."

Sam smiled bleakly. How like Gemini that was. Never thinking of herself. Gemini was a giver, not a taker. Samantha was aware of the old woman's affection for her nephew and what a comfort his presence would have been during those last days. And yet Gemini hadn't summoned him home. Even though Gemini had been so forgiving concerning her nephew's lack of interest and understanding, Sam wasn't so certain she could.

At the yawning grave site, Samantha gave way to the tears that were building inside her. The rain slashed down unmercifully. The only other mourners present, as per Gemini's instructions for privacy, were Esther, several friends from the neighborhood where Gemini had lived for the past twenty years, and a wizened old gentleman in a shabby, black raincoat and a slouch hat whom Sam rightly suspected was one of Gemini's lawyers.

As the last prayers were murmured and silent goodbyes were said, Samantha found it increasingly difficult to choke back her tears. She knew she had to look forward, not backward. She would grieve for Gemini in private, late at night. For now, she had to carry on with her life just as Gemini expected. She mustn't betray the confidence that Gemini had had in her. She would give her best to *Daylight Magazine* and prove her own worth.

Esther and Samantha rode back to the brownstone together, each silent with her own thoughts. When they approached Connecticut Avenue, Esther dried her eyes on her handkerchief and blew her nose. "I'll be taking a late-afternoon plane to Seattle, Miz Blakely. I've written down my address." She dug in her handbag and withdrew a slip of paper. "If there's anything you need and I can help, that's where I'll be."

"Thank you, Esther," Sam said warmly, suddenly realizing how much she was going to miss the housekeeper's warm concern. "You've been a good friend, and I'm going to miss you."

"You won't have time to miss anybody, Miz Blakely. Those two cats Miz Delaney left to you are going to keep you busy enough. Why, you'll be working at your magazine just to keep those two devils in gin."

The two women laughed, each remembering Gemini's devotion to her cats.

"Tell me, Esther, did Gemini name them Gin and Tonic before or after she discovered their penchant for the drink?"

"Miz Blakely, just like everybody else who ever had anything to do with Miz Delaney, they just lived up to what she expected of them!"

Alone that evening, Sam automatically switched on the track lighting in the spare bedroom, intending to work on the portrait of Christian Delaney. Fresh tears stung her eyes as she realized that Gemini would never see the finished product. Still, Gemini had commissioned the portrait and, in fact, had paid her in advance. The money she had given Sam had gone for expenses while job hunting. That advance had meant that Samantha had been able to hold out for the best job she could land, instead of being forced by dwindling finances to grab the first thing that came along. Her commitment to Gemini had been to complete the portrait, and complete it she would. Then she would have it sent on to Christian Delaney with a note of explanation.

Lifting her eyes to the easel, her gaze fell on the face of Christian Delaney. She knew it was only her imagination, but there seemed to be a calculating look about the silver-gray eyes. Samantha bit her lip. The one person Gemini had loved more than anyone else in the world had been absent from the private funeral ceremonies.

Tonight was definitely not the right time to work on the portrait, she decided as she switched off the light, and she wondered if she was more disappointed for Gemini than angry. One of the cats snaked around her ankles and purred loudly. "All right, all right. I promised Gemini I would take care of you, and I will. Let's go into the kitchen, and I'll warm up some milk for the three of us."

Just as Sam was dressing for work on Monday morning, the doorbell shrilled. Startled, she laid down the hairbrush and raced to the door. Who could be ringing her bell so early on a Monday morning? She glanced at the sunburst clock in the living room as she opened the door. It was only seven-ten. "Registered letter for Sam Blakely," a tired-looking older man said quietly.

Sam frowned. Now, who would be sending her a registered letter? Please, God, don't let it be the magazine saying they had second thoughts. She scribbled her name and closed the door. Hmm. Hartford, Masterson, Quinlan, Jacobsen, and Zigenback, Attorneys at Law, followed by a prestigious address on Wisconsin Avenue. With trembling hands, Sam slit open the envelope and quickly scanned the contents. She was to be present in Addison Hartford's office at twelve noon for the reading of Gemini Delaney's will. Sam grinned. Gemini wasn't leaving anything to chance. The two cats, Gin and Tonic, were to come to her for care. Gemini was making it legal. It wasn't so bad; she could take a taxi and still be back in the office by one o'clock. She stuffed the crisp, crackling legal letter into her purse and resumed her dressing.

After setting a small bowl of water, a second of tonic water, *sans* gin, and a dish of cat food on the kitchen floor, Sam was ready to leave for her first day at her new job. She felt good and knew she looked just as good in her tailored navy pants suit. At the last minute she crushed a matching beret on her head, covering her short-cropped curls. Her camera case over one shoulder and a smart burgundy shoulder bag completed her outfit.

Her heart skipped a beat and then steadied as her eyes fell on the orange pumpkin. *Don't think of that now. Today is the first day of the rest of your life,* her mind mumbled over and over.

She reached the corner just as a bus pulled to a stop. She boarded and settled herself for the short ride downtown. No worries, no problems. She had given her word to Gemini, and she would keep it. The cats were hers and she would see to their proper care. She smiled as she remembered what they were doing when she left. Gin had found a spot in the clothes hamper and had managed to wrap himself in a bright scarlet towel, while Tonic had dragged her boots from a heavy box and settled herself half-in and half-out of her fur-lined left boot. They were making themselves right at home, but she promised herself that she was going to put both of them on the wagon and turn them into respectable cats if it was the last thing she did.

"K Street!" the bus driver shouted loudly. Sam followed the other debarking passengers and headed straight for the *Daylight* offices.

Her co-workers turned out to be a friendly group of people. Easygoing, willing to help, and an endless supply of stories to tell. By eleven o'clock she had had the grand tour, been assigned a cubbyhole of an office, been introduced to the supply room with wall-to-wall film supplies, and had been informed that her meeting with the publisher and president was set for two o'clock. A memo on her clean desk also informed her she was to report to Charlie Conway at three o'clock for her first assignment.

Sam busied herself for another forty-five minutes by hanging up some of her favorite shots on the small cork bulletin board that came with every cubbyhole. She stood back to admire her handiwork. Photos by Orion. It did have a ring to it. Dad would be proud if he could see her now.

If she half-raised herself from her chair and stretched her neck, she could just make out the bank of clocks hanging on the newsroom wall. She did both and then reset her watch. Time to leave for Hartford, Masterson, Quinlan, Jacobsen, and Zigenback.

Sam waited patiently in the dusty, fern-decorated room of the old, prestigious law firm. Eventually, a middle-aged secretary appeared and crooked her finger in Sam's direction, which she took to mean she was to follow. Monstrous double doors creaked shut on dry hinges as Sam crossed fifty feet of worn carpeting. She looked around. Old furniture, bookshelves filled with legal tomes, and a desk the size of a billiard table with a row of diamond-shaped windows took up one corner of the room. To the left of the heavy-looking bookcases were two leather chairs, one in burgundy cracked leather and the other black. A brass lamp and a spittoon ashtray rested on a dusty table. The only words Sam could think of were "old" and "dry," just like the aging man behind the desk. Sam stared down at the wizened gentleman with the sparse white hair and pince-nez and recognized him from the cemetery. She held out her hand, which he ignored. "I'm…"

"Sam Blakely," chirped a reedy voice. "Sit down and let me read you Mrs. Delaney's will. Mr. Delaney can't be here, so we might as well proceed. My eyes aren't what they used to be, and I can't seem to…I don't know where that infernal will is," the old man fretted. "It doesn't make any difference; I know what was in it. Someone will send you a letter confirming what I'm about to tell you. Settle back, Mr. Blakely, and…now, where did I…never mind."

"Mr. Hartford, it's not Mr. Blakely—I'm Ms. Blakely. Mr. Hartford, is your hearing aid turned on?" Sam asked as she noticed a braided wire that ran into his shirt collar.

The old man ignored her words and laced his fingers together. "If I recall rightly, what Gemini's will said was that you, Sam Blakely, are to receive the dividends from fifty-one percent of the family-owned stock for ninety days. After the ninety days an addendum to the will is to be read—if I can find it," the old man said peevishly. "It seems to me that you can't vote, but I'll have one of the younger men check that out and get back to you."

Sam gasped. "Mr. Hartford, are you sure you don't have me mixed up with someone else? I was supposed to get the cats—cats, Mr. Hartford. Mr. Hartford, what about the cats?" Sam shouted.

"Those drunken animals! It's a disgrace and a sin the way

Gemini turned them into alcoholics. There's no need for you to shout, Blakely. The battery in my hearing aid is low, but I assure you I can hear just fine. There was something about the cats in the will. A neighbor, I believe, was to be entrusted with their care, plus a cash annuity to pay for their alcoholic comfort. I'll have to check that out.''

"I'm that neighbor—I'm Samantha Blakely. Never mind, Mr. Hartford, just send me the letter. I have the cats and they're being well cared for," Sam said wearily as she watched the frail attorney fidget with the button in his ear.

"Oh, pish and tush, this infernal gadget never works when I want it to work," the old man muttered. "It's no never mind. May I say I admire that hat you're wearing, Mr. Blakely? I had one quite similar to it when I was a boy. Everything's gone now—the hat, my hearing, my eyesight. I'm retired, you know, and just came into the office today because Gemini and I were friends for sixty years. It was the least I could do. I'll keep in touch, Mr. Blakely.''

Should she protest again and hope to get through to the old man, or should she just leave? Sam shrugged. What was the use? Before she could button her jacket she heard loud snores permeate the room. No use at all. In the waiting room with the dusty ferns and threadbare carpet, Sam looked around. All the doors were closed and there was no sign of anyone. Probably taking a nap. She giggled as she tiptoed out of the office and hailed a cab.

There must be a mistake, and, hopefully, it would be righted in the form of a letter. Fond as Gemini was of her, she certainly wouldn't leave her a controlling interest in her business. After all, hadn't Gemini said that her nephew was the sole heir? And, come to think of it, just what was Gemini's business? She had never said, and Sam had never asked. Ninety days and then an addendum was to be read. What exactly did that mean? It was all a mistake, and one she couldn't worry about now. If she was lucky, she could catch a sandwich in the snack bar at the office and freshen up before she was to meet the new president of *Daylight Magazine*.

* * *

Sam knocked smartly on the door of the president's office promptly on the stroke of two o'clock. A terse, cold "Come" made her draw in her breath. He sounded like an ogre, an angry ogre. Squaring her shoulders, she entered the office and walked over to the desk where a man was shouting into the phone, the high back of his chair turned toward her. Impatiently, he waved a hand in the air, motioning for her to sit.

"Just what does that mean? Mr. Hartford, I have great respect for your age and your ability, but how in the name of heaven did you allow Gemini to be duped by some...some gigolo named...what was the name...? Sam Blakely? You were Aunt Gem's closest friend and should have seen to her last needs and wishes. Well, it won't hold water, I can tell you that. There is no such thing as an unbreakable will. I'll break it, and I'll break the neck of Sam-whatever-his-name-is. Find him, Mr. Hartford, and I'll show you a chiseler out to bilk old ladies. Gemini must not have been of sound mind. What do you mean, she drew up the will herself? Don't give me any sermons, Hartford, I want that will contested. I'm the heir, the only heir. No, I don't be-grudge Gemini's gifts, but I do intend to find that weasel, Sam Blakely, and wring his neck. Do you hear me, Hartford? Don't you pay out one cent of those dividends. Get it through your head I'm the heir—the *only* heir. No, not for later, for now. How old is this Sam Blakely, anyway? Twenty-three! What time was he in your office? You should have kept him there till I could get there! Hartford, I don't care what kind of hat he had on! I'm advising you now that I'm going to break that will long before the addendum is to be read. You're right I want to see a copy of the will!" Silence. "In that case, Mr. Hartford, I won't just break his neck—I'll kill him before I let him prey on some other poor, unsuspecting old lady. Of course I don't mean it. He'll never be the same, though, I can assure you of that. After work I'll stop by your home and pick up a copy. Do you still reside in Georgetown? Around seven, then."

Sam stifled a gasp. Good heavens, it wasn't possible, was it? He couldn't be...he was! The new president and publisher of

Daylight Magazine was Christian Delaney, Gemini's nephew. Sam's head reeled as she stared at her new boss. How could this happen to her? And why hadn't Gemini told her? Sam remembered the old woman telling her that Christian would inherit the family business when she passed on, but she hadn't known that publishing was their business. A lump formed first in the pit of her stomach and then worked its way up to her throat. And to think he actually thought she had bilked dear, sweet Gemini! Well, she would just tell him he was mistaken; that was all there was to it. Mr. Hartford was a different story, but this man wasn't wearing a hearing aid. Talk about your comedy of errors. How could a reasonably intelligent man like Christian Delaney jump to conclusions like this? He was going to turn around and she would tell him. Oh, how had she ever gotten into this mess? It was so simple, if this lump would just go away, she might be able to get the words out. Fifty-one percent of the stock was going to her, and that meant the man with his back to her only had forty-nine percent. Would it make a difference if she was male or female? He thought she was a gigolo. *Gemini, do you know what you did?*

The man turned abruptly, the phone clenched in his powerful-looking fist. Slowly, deliberately, he replaced it and spoke, his words chips of ice. "Orion, isn't it?" Not bothering to wait for her reply, he continued: "I must apologize for the conversation you just heard. It's a family problem and I allowed myself to get out of control for a few minutes. I've looked at your portfolio and I liked what I saw."

She was supposed to say something, acknowledge the compliment. "Thank...thank you," she said lamely.

"You're new, according to Charlie Conway, but then so am I—in the capacity of president, that is. Until recently, I've been in charge of foreign publications and keeping our diplomatic doors open overseas. We should get along fine since we're both starting out at the same time. You bear with me and I'll bear with you. What do you say?"

His eyes were just as beautiful as in the photograph.

"That...th-that would be fi-fine." Fifty-one percent, fifty-one percent, fifty-one percent! her mind shrieked silently.

"I wanted to spend some time with you and go over your portfolio, but I have some personal business I must take care of starting right now. How would you like to have dinner with me? I have an evening appointment, but I think instead I'll take care of the matter now, before I get any hotter under the collar. Let's say Jour et Nuit. Are you familiar with it? No? M Street at Thirtieth in Georgetown. You'll like it—fireside dining, and the food is served Continental style. Very impressive wine list. I guarantee it. Well," he said abruptly, "will you have dinner with me?"

Sam's mind raced. "Of...of c-course."

"Do you always stutter?" Christian Delaney asked, frowning.

"Well...I...I...this is my...my first day...and...and I never met a president before."

Christian Delaney laughed, a deep, rich baritone. She knew, she just knew he would laugh like that. "I have news for you; I've never been a president before, either, and I'm not all that sure I'll be any good at the job."

"Of course you will. You look just the way a president should look," Sam babbled and then was instantly embarrassed at her words. She flushed.

"Amazing! Absolutely amazing!" Christian said in a voice that resembled awe. "A woman today who can still blush. I like that, Orion. You've got yourself a date with a president." The steel-gray eyes were merry and showed just a shade of devilment. Did presidents do things like "that." If the president was a man, he did. The flush darkened, to Christian Delaney's amusement. "Look, do you think you could meet me at the restaurant? I don't usually make my dates do this, but I'm going to be running late, and...and I want to get to know you better."

Before or after you kill me? her whirling brain questioned. "I don't mind, Mr. Delaney."

"I think I'm going to like you, Orion. A woman who stutters because I'm a president and who can still blush and who says she doesn't mind meeting me at the restaurant. Do you even check the prices on the menu?''

An invisible broom handle stiffened Sam's spine. "As a matter of fact, I do. And," she said airily, "I don't eat much."

"Seven o'clock. And I was complimenting you, whether you know it or not. I appreciate promptness."

Was he mocking her? "I'll be on time."

"Are you one of those women who dawdle and pick at their food, or do you eat to enjoy?"

"I know what fork to use and I've never been known to use my fingers. I usually eat fast because I'm hungry and my dad taught me never to leave anything on my plate. Did I leave anything out?" she asked, a cutting edge to her voice. "And," she said, holding up her hand, "I do not pick up the check."

The silvery-gray eyes narrowed to slits. "We'll discuss that over dinner. That's a smart-looking outfit you're wearing. More than suitable for the restaurant."

"Yes, I know. I've been to a restaurant before, Mr. Delaney. I won't embarrass you."

Christian Delaney inclined his head slightly as Sam left the office. At the door Sam turned and almost missed the speculative look in Christian Delaney's eyes. Those gray eyes that stared back at her every day from the portrait. She said nothing, but merely closed the door quietly behind her.

Once again Sam craned her neck to stare at the clock. Another half-hour till her meeting with Charlie Conway and her first assignment. Where would it be, and what would it be? Might as well go to the supply room and stock up on film and other supplies while she was waiting. But first she would get a cup of the rancid coffee the cameramen called ambrosia and think a little. She really had to decide what she was going to do. Christian Delaney was no fool. Gemini was right—he saw straight through to your soul. She didn't like the thought and felt frightened. What would he do when he found out Orion was Sam Blakely? Would Charlie Conway tell him before she could? Not likely; nor would the other cameramen and newsmen. They were introduced to her as Orion, and first names held. As far as they were concerned, that was her handle and they cared nothing for her legal name; and, if by some chance someone mentioned it, they would promptly forget it; it was the nature of the trade.

Why was she so edgy, so frightened? She hadn't done anything wrong. A mistake had been made, and as long as she didn't accept any money from Gemini's estate, she was in the clear. A sinking feeling gripped her innards. She had every reason to be frightened. Christian Delaney was ruthless and without sentiment. Business always came first. Hadn't he proved this by putting business ahead of being with Gemini in her last hours? Europe was only ten or eleven hours away by air. He hadn't even come to the funeral. Gemini's estate was business of the first order. Why should she expect him to be any less ruthless and understand the mistake that had been made? Surely, Christian Delaney wouldn't want the alcoholic cats. That issue she would fight him on simply because she and Gemini had many discussions and she had given the old lady her word that she would care for the animals. She would honor her promise no matter what.

Gemini—kind, gentle, feisty Gemini, owning *Daylight Magazine*. It was unbelievable. No wonder Gemini had known what to tell her to ask for in the contract. "Don't be such an upstart that you can't accept help." Those were Gemini's words. So what if she used the unisex name? So what if Gemini helped her with the contract? And so what if Gemini put in a good word for her? She was a darned good photographer, and she would prove it or die trying. There was no way she would let Gemini down, not now, not ever.

Sam stretched her neck. Five minutes to three and she hadn't gotten any coffee, after all. Her musings had taken up a good twenty-five minutes. Now it was time to meet with Charlie Conway and see what she would be doing and where she was going.

Evil, blue-gray smoke as thick as marshmallows greeted Sam as she rapped smartly on Charlie Conway's door and entered. Coughing and sputtering, Sam collapsed against the wall and burst into laughter as she waved her arms to ward off the obnoxious fumes. "Now I know where my dad caught his habit. I didn't think there were two people in the whole world who would find the same cigar and actually smoke it."

"Let me tell you something, kid," Charlie said, working the fat, brown cylinder between his teeth. "These cee-gars were the only thing that kept me and your old man sane during some darned fool uprising in South America. We decided early on that if we were meant to be killed, it wasn't going to be by some guerrilla, but by a fifteen-cent cee-gar. They're up to thirty cents now. Would you believe it? You can open the window if you want," Charlie said generously.

"I wouldn't think of it," Sam retorted as she dabbed at her watering eyes.

Charlie worked the cigar to the side of his mouth and fished around his cluttered desk for a sheaf of official-looking papers. "Okay, Orion, you're going to partner with Ramon Gill. In case you don't know it, he's got the fastest pencil in the east. He's a good man—lascivious, but good. You can handle it. If he gets out of hand, threaten to take a shot of his left profile; he hates that. You're going to California tonight. Here's your plane ticket, along with some expense money. Right now, that fire raging in the canyon is nothing more than a brush affair, but in another twelve hours it's going to be the biggest bonfire you ever saw. I want you and Ramon to be the first ones there."

Sam nodded. It never occurred to her to ask the man seated behind the desk how he knew the brush fire was going to rage. He was a newsman, and if he said it was going to go, then it was going to go. Newsmen had a sixth sense, and that was good enough for her.

"I want you and Ramon right there in the front. Don't be afraid of a little soot and ash. Just get me good footage. You got that?" Sam nodded. "And don't let some jackass try to ward you off because you're a woman. Around here you're Orion, cameraperson. Is that clear?" Sam nodded. "Well, what are you waiting for?"

Sam grimaced. "I was sort of hoping for a 'good luck' or 'take care' or something."

"You make your own luck, and if you have any brains, you'll

take care of yourself. My wishing you anything isn't going to make a bit of difference. Hang in there, kid, and I'll see you back here in three days, give or take a few either way."

Before she left the office, Sam phoned Ramon Gill and arranged to meet him at National Airport at eleven o'clock. They would take the "red-eye" together, getting in to Los Angeles in the wee hours of the morning.

She took another taxi she couldn't afford back to the apartment to pick up the cats for boarding. Time for a quick shower and time to pack a duffel. Then dinner with Christian Delaney. Sometime between the appetizer and dessert she would tell him *she* was the Sam Blakely mentioned in Gemini's will. With a little luck she could run out of the restaurant before he fired her, and she could at least get one assignment for *Daylight* under her belt. She had to make it perfectly clear to him that she had known nothing about the will. Also, she'd make him understand she never knew Gemini owned *Daylight Magazine.* Her heart pounded all through the taxi ride and only returned to normal when she exited at her doorstep.

Her hand trembled as she fit the gold key into the lock. The phone in the living room was shrilling as she closed the door and threw the dead bolt. She raced across the room only to hear the dial tone as she placed the receiver to her ear. Whoever it was would call back if it was important.

First things first. She stripped down, showered and redressed. Makeup went on sparingly, as did a dab of perfume. She packed heavy twill pants and sweat shirts along with a week's change of underwear. Toilet articles in a leather case were next, along with a pair of hiking boots. In this business you traveled light and smelled a lot.

Now the cats. She called them and, as usual, they ignored her. She'd have to do what Gemini did. Craftily, she bent down to the liquor cabinet in the corner and managed to clink the gin bottle and tonic water at the same time. One cat was on her shoulder, and the other twined himself around her leg. "Look, guys, this was a fake. There isn't enough in either bottle for a shot. You're a disgrace. The vet isn't going to cater to your problems, so let's go on the wagon right now. A few days of milk will do you both a lot of good." Both cats looked at her disdainfully and swept out of the room, their lush tails straight out to show their disapproval. "Come on, now, you have to get into your basket," she said, chasing them and scooping both up at the same time. "I don't want to hear a peep out of either one of you. You're sober now and you're going to stay that way." Both cats hissed their anger as she snapped the lid of the carryall and lugged it to the front door. Now, where was the vet Gemini had used for the cats? Quickly, she flipped through her address book till she found the name of the animal hospital. Rockville! A fast look at the sunburst clock told her if she avoided the rush-hour traffic, she might make it. She still had the keys to Gemini's vintage Mercedes. As much as she disliked doing it, she would have to use the car.

The cats hissed and clawed at the wicker as she lugged them to the garage at the rear of the brownstone. She slid open the doors and placed the cats on the floor in the back of the car. A yowl of outrage made the fine hairs on the back of her neck stand on end. "Both of you be quiet. I can't drive with all that screeching," she called over her shoulder as she maneuvered the heavy car down the alley and onto Connecticut Avenue. Sam drove fast, her eyes glued to the rearview mirror for any sign of the city's finest. Walter Reed Medical Center on the right. She was making progress.

Sam popped a stale mint into her mouth as she swung north on Georgia Avenue and made her way to the Capital Beltway. The Interstate green read: NORTHERN VIRGINIA. Sam took the second right, looping back to merge westbound with Interstate Maryland 495. Noticing a gap in the middle lane, Sam pushed down on the directional lever and eased into the slow-moving traffic. She heard the snap of the wicker lid as her eyes sighted the Mormon Temple. To Sam's eye it looked like a glacial cathedral sculpted from a massive chunk of ice. The cats were loose and hopping onto the front seat. Playfully, they hissed and scratched at the plush seats to celebrate their freedom.

Twenty minutes later Sam stood at the reception desk in the

vet's office, the heavy basket next to her on the countertop. Loud hisses and snarls swept through the office. Quickly, Sam explained who she was and the situation with the cats.

"Miss Blakely," the receptionist said, a look of panic on her face, "the doctor can't treat Mrs. Delaney's cats. He simply refuses. The last time they were here we all had to go on tranquilizers. They're disruptive. We couldn't determine what their problem was and decided they were just riddled with neuroses. I'm sorry, really sorry."

It was Sam's turn to panic. They had to take the cats. "If I tell you what's wrong with these cats, will you take them?"

The receptionist inched away from the counter. Her eyes were shifty as she stared at the noisy basket. "Well, that depends on whether the condition is treatable. I'm Dr. Barstow's wife, and I can't have my husband upset with those animals like the last time. What is it?" she asked fearfully.

"They're alcoholics."

"Alcoholics?" Mrs. Barstow said stupidly.

"Yes. I've got them on the wagon, but I can see now that I'll have to wait till I get back to dry them out. Just give them some gin and tonic and they're as docile as two kittens. Believe me," Sam pleaded as she made her way to the door, hoping against hope that the woman wouldn't call her back and demand she take the hissing cats with her. "I'll pick them up in a week, sooner if I get back before then. Thank you, thank you so much," she babbled as she ran from the office.

If she didn't hit traffic, she could make her seven o'clock appointment for dinner with Christian Delaney right on schedule. She prayed silently all the way back to the city and didn't draw a safe breath till she hit Wisconsin Avenue. She drove through Rock Creek Park, admiring the rich colors of late autumn, silently congratulating herself on a job well done. The cats were safe, for the moment, and she had Gemini's car back, secure in its space in the double garage. Carefully, she locked the garage and slipped the keys into her purse. Along with her confession, she would turn the keys over to Christian Delaney. Surely, he wouldn't mind that she had used his aunt's car for the trip to Rockville. After all, it was for the cats, not a joy ride.

She raced around the corner to her apartment. She dialed and waited for the crackly voice of the taxi dispatcher to tell her how long she would have to wait for a cab. "Three minutes," she was told.

Sam heard the phone ring as she locked the door behind her. Should she go back and answer? She was saved the decision when a blue and white cab slid up to the curb. Whoever it was would have to call back later. A lot later.

The cab ground to a smooth stop in front of the restaurant just as a yellow Jaguar cut in front of it. Christian Delaney emerged from the low-slung sports car just as Sam paid the driver.

Christian Delaney eyed the worn duffel bag and the heavy camera case. Sam explained and was surprised to see her escort frown. "It's no problem; you can check both of them at the cloakroom."

"You're wrong. I'll check the duffel, but this camera never leaves my side."

"It must make a cold bedfellow." Christian grinned as the maître d' showed them to a cozy table near the monstrous fireplace. "What will you have to drink, Orion?"

"Scotch on the rocks." Sam watched as Christian's eyebrows shot up in surprise. What did he think she was going to order, a Shirley Temple? He ordered the same thing for himself and then lit a cigarette. "That's the second time I've surprised you in the space of a few minutes. Why?"

Christian answered bluntly, "I was surprised that Conway assigned you to cover the pictorial side of the fire, and I didn't expect you to order Scotch—it's a man's drink."

"Two sexist remarks in one sentence." Sam grinned. "I don't see what my gender has to do with my ability to photograph a fire, and I happen to like Scotch."

"Well said." Christian grinned, showing a flash of strong white teeth. "What time does your plane leave? Who's the journalist? Normally, I would know all about this assignment, but as I told you, I had family business to take care of this afternoon and didn't go back to the office after lunch.''

Sam was glad she had both hands around the squat glass in front of her. She blinked and felt her heart resume its normal beat. ''And did you settle your family business?'' Was that calm, casual voice hers?

''No, I didn't.'' Christian's tone was vehement. ''If there's one thing I cannot and will not abide, it is professional, slick con artists who prey on defenseless old ladies. Tomorrow, I'm hiring the best private detective firm in the city to track down that slick weasel, and when I find him I'm going to...'' Sam gulped and wished she could drown herself in the amber fluid she was holding. Now. She should tell him now! Samantha opened her mouth, forcing the words to her lips. But before she could utter a sound, he interrupted.

''I'm sorry. That's the second time I allowed family matters to intrude. Pleasantries only from now on. Tell me how you came to be a photo-journalist.''

Sam relaxed. This was familiar ground and she was comfortable. What seemed like hours later she glanced at her watch, dreading to see what numbers the hands rested on. Soon it would be time to go; and, suddenly, she didn't want to leave this man's presence—not now, not ever. She must tell him now, before she left. She couldn't continue playing this game of hide-and-seek. In essence, she was deceiving him, and that deceit was making everything a lie—her job, the assignment, this dinner, even the way Christian's eyes were smiling into hers. Her confession would change everything. Samantha gulped, feeling a shudder run through her. Taking a deep breath, she began: ''Christian, I must tell...''

Christian's voice was cool, almost mocking when he interrupted: ''That's the third time I've seen you glance at your watch. Am I boring you?''

Sam stared at the man across from her and flushed a deep crimson. ''On...on the contrary. I just...just realized that...that it's getting late and I'm going to...to have to leave...soon. I'm having such a good time I don't...I don't want to leave,'' she said honestly and could have bitten her tongue the minute the words were out. "But before I do, I have to tell…"

Christian leaned across the table and took both of her hands in his, stifling her determination to tell him about his aunt's will. "Then don't go. Stay here with me. I'll call Charlie Conway and tell him to get another photographer. I like you, Orion, and I don't want you to leave, either."

"Christian, there's nothing I would like better, but I can't do that. I gave my word, and as much as I want to stay, that's how much I want to cover this story. Please understand. Photography is part of my life. I can't just…just throw it in on a whim." At the look on Christian's face, she added hastily, "Not that this is a whim, it's just that I have to tell…" Not knowing what else to say, she sat miserably in her chair.

"Believe it or not, I understand. There will be other days and other nights," he said meaningfully.

Sam forced a chilling note into her tone when she replied, "Mr. Delaney, I think I should tell you that I do not sleep around, nor would I be any good at one-night stands. I have a tendency to lock into situations. Now, if you would like to revise that last statement of yours to read, 'there will be other days and other evenings,' I can go away on this assignment with a clear head and have something to look forward to on my return. I do like you and I want to see you again, but I also don't want you to get the wrong idea or later say that I misled you. That's why I want you to know…"

"I do know. And you could never mislead me, Orion." Was she mistaken, or was his face registering shocked disbelief at her words? Had she really said those things aloud? Evidently. Up front. Always be up front with everyone, Gemini had said. People always respected honesty and forthrightness. Sure they did, Sam thought cynically. *I think you blew it that time, Gemini.*

"I have to leave now," Sam said, looking at the circlet on her wrist. "But before I do…"

"I'll drive you to the airport, I can't let you take a taxi. What would you think of me?"

Exasperated, Sam tossed her napkin onto the table. Would this man never let her speak? If she wanted to make her plane on time, she'd have to give it up as hopeless. The first thing she would do on her return would be to sit him down and tell it like it was. A minuscule twinge of guilt nipped her conscience. Had she really done her best to tell him, or was this assignment more important than the truth? "It's not necessary to take me to the airport, but I would like it, if you're serious," she was astonished to hear herself say in a smooth voice.

"Orion, you have no idea just how serious I am. This probably sounds a little corny, but I enjoyed that little speech of yours a minute ago. I hope we do have many days and evenings together. Let's pick up your duffel and get out of here."

Sam walked on air out to the yellow sports car and was in seventh heaven all the way to the airport. At least it was seventh heaven as long as she didn't allow herself to think about what a coward she was for not revealing to Christian that she was the Sam Blakely he was seeking—seeking to wring his neck, she reminded herself. It was all a mistake; she was certain of it. As soon as that doddering old lawyer looked into the matter, everything would straighten itself out. Gemini couldn't have left her anything besides the two cats. It was unthinkable. All Gemini had ever said was that the two cats were going to be Sam's responsibility, and Samantha had assumed that taking the cats would somehow repay Gemini for the countless kindnesses the old woman had shown her. Besides, this was no time to be revealing anything to the publisher and president of the magazine that was giving her the first big break at becoming a successful photo-journalist. She couldn't take the chance of having Christian become so angry that he took the brush fire assignment away from her.

To Sam's surprise, instead of dropping her off at the terminal, Christian parked his car and escorted her to the ticket counter. Ramon Gill was standing just beyond the ticket line, sporting his *Daylight* press badge so she would recognize him. Ramon's Latin eyes flicked over her appraisingly. "So, you're Orion. Somehow, I wasn't expecting someone as pretty as you."

Sam's trigger had been pulled, and she almost bristled with a stinging retort about how being a female photographer didn't necessarily mean you had to look like a dragon. But she thought better of it. If she was to work successfully with Ramon Gill, that would mean they had to be on good terms. Instead of giving him a sharp retort, she smiled a coy thanks for his compliment.

"Ramon, have you met our president? Mr. Christian Delaney."

Gill's eyebrows raised in surprise. "Yeah, I've heard there was somebody new in the front office. How do you do, Mr. Delaney? I've followed your work on the foreign market, and as a journalist, I appreciate it. You've gotten our reporters into some newsfronts where even *Time* magazine was unwelcome."

"I did my best," Christian answered, shaking Ramon's hand firmly. "Listen, why don't you go and grab a cup of coffee? There's still time before the takeoff. Orion and I have a few things to discuss."

"Yeah, sure," Ramon agreed affably. "Say, Orion, want me to take your duffel with me? It's good to see a woman who can pack sensibly. I was sort of worried that you'd come with fifty-nine suitcases and that we'd have to wait all night for the baggage. I always travel with carry-on bags myself."

Sam handed Ramon her duffel. "I appreciate it." As Ramon reached for her camera and gadget bag, Sam stepped backward. "These stay with me, always."

"Sure." Gill shrugged. "I know all about it. I ought to. I've been working with you camera people long enough. The camera never leaves your side, right?"

"Right."

"Okay. See you at the boarding gate." With a nod to Christian, Ramon hefted his own duffel plus Sam's and headed for the coffee shop.

"You handled that very well." Christian smiled down at her. "I could see that you were just ripping to straighten out Ramon's thinking about female photographers. Restraint and discretion are the better part of valor."

Sam laughed. "Am I that transparent?"

Christian looked down into her upturned face, a long, penetrating look that seemed to steal her breath away. "Come on," he prodded. "You're going to get a proper sendoff."

"And what is that?"

"A beer in the V.I.P. lounge and then a very sound kiss just before you board."

All the while they conversed over their beers in the softly lit V.I.P. lounge, Sam's thoughts were focused ahead on the kiss he promised her just before she boarded the plane. The conversation was lighthearted and she joined Christian in some teasing banter, but all the while her eyes drank in the familiar planes of his face, the tiny cleft in his chin, the lines around his eyes that said he had spent a good deal of time in a hot, sunny climate, the slight salting of gray near his temples, and, most of all, the lights that glowed from the depths of his silvery-gray eyes.

She liked the way the corners of his mouth lifted when he smiled. The slight tilt at the end of his nose hinted at his Irish heritage. His heavy, almost unruly, brows added a sternness to his features that was waylaid by the humor in his smile. Fleetingly, she wondered if anyone, even a great artist, could capture this man's vitality and masculinity on canvas. Now, to her discerning eye, she realized how flat and inaccurate the portrait in her spare bedroom really was. It was the image of this man, not the great personality and charm he exuded.

Christian glanced at his watch. "I'd better get you down to the gate now, or I'll just sweep you up and refuse to let you leave me. You're very beautiful, you know. And I like the way your eyes flash when you laugh. You have a very nice laugh, Orion, and I intend to hear it often when you get back from your forest fire." His tone was deep and husky; the expression in his eyes excited her.

They ran, hand in hand, toward the gate where her plane was waiting and had just arrived when the flight was announced over the public address system. Sam's heart beat like a trip-hammer at the thought of his promised kiss. She wanted that kiss, needed it, and shamelessly knew that she was anticipating it.

Her hand shook slightly as she handed her boarding pass to the flight attendant. Suddenly, Christian had wrapped his arms around her and drew her close into his embrace. For a long moment he gazed down into her eyes before he lowered his head and pressed his lips to her mouth.

The touch was light, fleeting, teasing. His strong arms held her, refusing to allow her to escape. Again, he looked down into her eyes, an expression of surprise glowing in the depths of his own. The room seemed to spin; all sound was muted; only the drumbeat of her heart sounded in her ears. And when again his head lowered to hers, his mouth possessed hers, demanding an answering response, giving a promise of things to come.

"Sir. Sir!" the flight attendant insisted. "Sir, you are hampering the other passengers from boarding the plane. Sir!"

Reluctantly, Christian released Sam. Bewilderment and surprise were struck on his features. "Orion..."

"Please, sir, you are blocking traffic!"

"Off you go, Orion. I'll be waiting," he murmured huskily. "Get going before I steal you away," he added gruffly.

In a trance, Samantha hurried down the corridor to the plane. Dazedly, she found her seat beside Ramon and fastened her seatbelt. Her lips were still tingling with the touch of Christian's kiss. Her body felt the hot imprint of where his arms had held her. Shaken, she pushed her camera bag beneath the seat and tried to control her rising emotions. She was almost looking forward to the long flight to California. She needed time. Time to think.

Ramon stirred beside her. "That was quite a little scene you and Delaney performed out there. And, by the way, it's nice to know there are still some girls who can blush."

Chapter Three

Tired, giddy with success, Sam stopped dead in her tracks in the middle of the airport parking lot and stared at her companion, Ramon Gill. A surge of laughter overcame her, and she wiped tears away with the back of a grimy hand. "You should only see what you look like! I swear, Ramon, there's a decided odor of singed hair and charcoal wafting this way."

"Ha!" Ramon snapped. "They'll never place you on the ten best-dressed list. And that isn't exactly Arpege clinging to you. I'd sell my soul for a shower and a fresh change of clothes right now. The least you could have done was to make a later flight reservation so we could have showered. You in a hurry or something?" he asked, unlocking the door of his Corvette.

"Or something." Samantha grinned. "If I never smell smoke again, I'll be just as happy." Jackknifing herself into the Corvette, she settled herself and leaned back against the seat.

"That's it, sleep," Ramon chided as he slipped the key into the ignition. "You women are all alike. Here I am, wounded in battle and just as exhausted as you, and yet I have to drive. Where to, lady? And it better not be Maryland."

Sam smiled. "Wounded, are you? Since when do they give the Purple Heart for singed eyebrows?"

Ramon returned her smile. They had formed a mutual appreciation for one another during the assignment of following the forest fire. Together, they had discovered that they were both unyielding when it came to covering the news story to the best of their ability. Instinctively, they had assisted one another, falling into an easy rapport. Ramon put the words on the paper, and Orion's photographs brought them to life.

"I repeat, Orion, where to?" he asked as he paid the parking fee at the booth near the edge of the lot. "In other words, where do you live?"

Sam was instantly awake, her mind racing. She had forgotten. How could she go back to her apartment? Christian Delaney said he was hiring private detectives to track down the "gigolo" who had befriended his Aunt Gemini. If she went back to the brownstone before she could make her explanations to Christian, she would be spotted and then the fur would fly. She was too tired for confrontations, for explanations, and there was no way she could face Christian at the moment. For now, at least, evasion would be the best tactic. And it might continue to be until she could straighten out this mess. With any luck at all, the ancient lawyer would have discovered his error by now concerning the fifty-one percent of the stock being left in her name.

Samantha drew a deep breath and exhaled slowly. "Actually, Ramon," she said airily, "I was thinking that perhaps you could drop me off at the airport Holiday Inn. It won't be out of your way. I'm just too tired to go back to my apartment and wait for the water to get hot and for the heat to come on. All I want is a shower and sleep. Just drop me off." Before Ramon could answer, Sam had taken her duffel bag from the back seat and had her camera slung over her shoulder.

Ramon glanced at his companion suspiciously. "If Holiday Inns are your thing, it's okay with me. I'm going to stop by the magazine. Do you have any messages to deliver?"

"I'll call Charlie after I take a shower and brush my teeth. Do you think it's possible to have cinders and soot in your teeth?"

"Anything is possible," Ramon muttered as he swung the

Corvette down the ramp to pull alongside the entrance to the Holiday Inn.

"Thanks for the ride, Ramon." Sam grinned at the journalist's second suspicious look and waited on the curb for the sports car to swing onto Jefferson Davis Highway. The second the fast-moving car was out of sight, Sam hefted the duffel over her shoulder and headed for the Crystal Underground Shopping Center. An hour later she was laden with two burgeoning shopping bags, compliments of her American Express and Visa cards. She had to have clothes, and since she had decided not to go back to her apartment for the time being, she had no other choice but to buy new clothing from the skin out.

The motel room's door double-locked and the chain in place, Sam turned the shower on full blast and stripped down. She stood under the needle-sharp spray, letting the tiny beads of water wash away the top layer of soot and grime that had worked their way through her clothes. She lathered her silky skin twice and managed to shampoo her hair at the same time. What seemed like forever later to her, she stepped from the cascading water and wrapped herself in the skimpy motel towels.

First things first. How much had she charged with her plastic money? Recklessly, she rummaged through the shopping bags until she had a neat pile of receipts in her hand. Mentally, she tallied them up and gulped. Cash—how much cash did she have? With one eye closed to ward off disappointment, she peered at the thin sheaf of bills in her wallet. A grand total of sixty-three dollars. Darn, why did she feel like such a criminal? She hadn't done anything except be nice to an old lady of whom she had genuinely been fond. Another one-eyed look in her checkbook told her she wouldn't be able to camp out in a motel much longer, not at forty-two dollars a day plus food. She would have to face Christian Delaney, and soon.

Sam returned both the checkbook and credit slips to her purse. She popped a crystal mint into her mouth and dialed the main number at the magazine. The switchboard operator put her on hold. Sam leaned back against the propped-up pillows and was instantly asleep, the squawking phone in her hand.

Sam awoke refreshed, the alarm beeping on her digital watch, at eight a.m. She vaguely remembered waking up once during the night to total darkness and also vaguely remembered hanging up the phone. She opened the drapes and peered out at the tall building on top of the Crystal Underground from her fourth-floor room. It was difficult to tell exactly what kind of day it was. It looked cold, and here she was with nothing more than a heavy sweater purchased at the shopping center. She had to get her own clothes or she would freeze to death.

She showered, taking her time, and then called down for room service and was informed that all meals were served on disposable plates with plastic implements. She had time for a leisurely breakfast and the ride into the city. The first day back after an assignment was always a slow day to catch up. It was either a congratulation or gripe-and-complaint day. Either way, it was still slow.

A drab gray light filtered through the window at her cubbyhole office at *Daylight Magazine* and directed Sam's attention to a small stack of mail which rested on her desk. Before she could begin to open the vari-sized envelopes, Charlie Conway slouched into the office. "You did a good job, kid. The lighting on those pics is some of the best I've ever seen. Just in case you're interested, the front office asked for a complete set of photos. I expect you'll get some praise from on high. You did a good job, and Ramon had only good things to say about the way you work, and coming from him, that's the best."

Sam smiled happily. "Ramon actually said that?"

Charlie rolled his cigar around in his mouth a couple of times and grinned. "Actually, what he said was you were okay but weird, and you had this thing about motels. Oh, yeah, he said you forgot where you lived."

Sam flushed and then laughed. "I was so tired, Charlie, and what with the jet lag, I just didn't have the stamina to go all the way back into town. I tried calling you, but the girl put me on hold and I fell asleep and didn't wake up till this morning."

"You're forgiven. I'll forgive anything you do if you keep

giving me pics like the ones of the fire. You got a lunch date? I'd like to hear about the fire.''

"No, I don't have a lunch date, but I have to run a few errands. I can stop by your office later if you want and we could have a cup of coffee and talk about it, unless you have another assignment for me.''

"You're on call. It's a date, then. Any time this afternoon is okay; the rag has been put to bed.''

"Didn't Ramon fill you in?'' Sam asked inquisitively.

"Ramon told me to read about it in the magazine. He's like a superstitious old gypsy. He'll talk my ear off once the rag hits the street, but not one second before.''

Sam watched the old editor as he exited the office, an ominous, billowing cloud of foul gray smoke in his wake. She fanned furiously at the air and was startled to see Christian Delaney standing in the doorway. "Welcome back, Orion.'' He smiled from ear to ear.

Sam felt her heart begin to thud. It seemed to have some kind of bongo rhythm all its own as she stared at the handsome man in the doorway. "Th-thank you. It's good to be back.'' She waited, uncertain if she should get up and hold out her hand, or if she should stay seated behind the rough, scarred desk. You didn't shake hands with a man you kissed, not if you kissed him the way she had, anyway. Throwing caution to the winds and ignoring her fast-beating heart, she rose and walked over to the publisher. She grinned and said, "Come in, said the spider to the fly.'' Christian Delaney needed no second urging.

"The question is: Who's the spider and who's the fly?'' He grinned back as he drew her to him.

"Hmm, does it matter?'' Sam murmured as she nuzzled her head against his chest.

"Not to me, it doesn't,'' Christian said huskily as his mouth met hers. The kiss was butterfly soft, yet demanding in its intensity.

Sam moved slightly and stared deeply into Christian's eyes. "I liked that. Kiss me again,'' she said boldly.

They were both shaking when Christian released her and held

her away from him at arm's length. Sam stared back, knowing her feelings were revealed in her shaky gaze. She swallowed hard. She couldn't have uttered a word if her life depended on it. Apparently, Christian felt the same way, for he kissed her lightly on the cheek and opened the door. "Dinner," he said gruffly. "After work, around six." Sam nodded.

"How...how di-did you like the pictures?" Sam blurted. Suddenly, she couldn't bear for him to leave her office. From this moment on, she knew she was going to love this small, confining space with a passion unequaled.

"Pictures? What pictures? Oh, those pictures! Good, very good. I liked them." He turned, his face serious, the silvery-gray eyes hooded. "You're some kind of woman, Orion! Did anyone ever tell you that?"

Sam grinned. It was okay for him to leave now. "Only my dad, and I'm not sure that counts."

"Let's keep it that way," Christian said over his shoulder as he strode briskly down the corridor.

A silly look on her face, Sam slumped in the creaking swivel chair. It was a beautiful cubbyhole, and it smelled just as beautiful as she sniffed at the faint, almost elusive, scent of the publisher's cologne. She had to find out what it was and buy a gallon of it. She would spritz it all around. "I'm in love!" she chortled happily. Her happiness was short-lived when she remembered how she was duping Gemini's nephew. She had to tell him. Tonight, she would tell him, after dinner, when he took her home.

Don't think about that now. Why not? her mind questioned. *There isn't anything else to do.* "Yes, there is," she said aloud. "I didn't open my mail." Quickly, she sifted through the mail and sorted it into piles. Circulars, sale flyers from various department stores, bills, two letters from college friends who insisted on keeping in touch, and a legal-looking envelope from the Women's Bank. Her bank. She slit open the envelope and withdrew a pale green check attached to a letter. One short paragraph that said Sam Blakely was due the enclosed third-quarter dividend check from the Delaney stocks. Beyond realizing that the amount was in six figures, she couldn't comprehend the actual sum. She had no basis for comprehending money in such large amounts. Sam lowered her eyes at the slip of paper she was holding. She gagged and the check fluttered and fell to the floor. Transfixed, unable to move, her eyes followed the square of paper. She gagged again and covered her mouth with both her hands. It couldn't be! There was a dreadful mistake! There just wasn't that much money in the whole world! And they sent it in the mail, she thought in horror. Oh, God! Oh, God, what was she going to do? Pick it up, of course. You didn't leave $667,395.42 laying on the floor. Gingerly, she picked up the check and stared at it again. Did one fold a check for this amount? Was it one of those that you did not fold, spindle, or mutilate? Quickly, she opened her top desk drawer and dropped the check onto a pile of blank paper. She slammed the drawer closed with shaking hands and held it in place. Slowly, she inched the drawer open a fraction. It was still there. Oh, God, it was still there! She would give it back to Christian tonight when she told him who she was. He would know what to do with it. That's what she would do.

Gemini, how could you do this to me? she wailed silently. *He's never going to understand. I can feel it.* Blind panic covered her like a mantle and then coursed through her veins, leaving her weak-kneed and trembling. There had to be a way out of this; she just had to find it. She would put herself in Christian Delaney's place and try to react the way he would. Now, let's see, first she would explain and then hand him the check. He would say something magnanimous like, "Why thank you, Ms. Blakely. There aren't too many people in the world who would return a check for $667,395.42. Believe me, I understand perfectly why you're returning it. You're returning it because it's a mere drop in the bucket compared to what you would get from our relationship if we married. Even the lowliest copy runner at the magazine knows I'm the heir to the Delaney publishing fortune. When you compare $667,395.42 to a fortune, it doesn't take much imagination to know which one you'll pick." A squeal of pure agony escaped her tight lips. She *couldn't* tell

him! She *had* to tell him! She would compromise. She would
tell him later, much later. For now, she wanted more time with
him, more time to feel his lips and arms around her, so when
she was in the dark days to come, she would at least have memories. Gemini had lived on her memories for the last forty years.
She would have memories and $667,395.42. And this was just
the third quarter. If she were to take that amount and multiply
it times four, she would have... Oh, God! She had to give it
back. Perhaps what she should do was to send it anonymously
to the bank president. She was a woman; she'd understand.

An unseen devil perched itself on Sam's shoulder and whispered, "It's yours; Gemini saw to it. It's all legal. You don't
really have to give it back. Why not take a 'wait and see' attitude? If Delaney finds out who you are, see how he handles it
before you return the money. You could find yourself out in the
cold without a job, an apartment. That dividend check will buy
a lot of warmth."

"Not the kind of warmth I'm looking for," Sam snarled at
the invisible devil. "I won't do it. I'm giving it back!"

A copy boy stuck his head in the door and yelled, "Catch!"
And he tossed her a heavy manila envelope. "Charlie wants you
to go over Ramon Gill's story and space the pics."

Sam nodded and flipped open the envelope. Thank heaven for
work. Thank heaven for anything that would take her mind off
the slip of paper in her desk drawer.

Working industriously for the next several hours, Sam managed to finish up her work a few minutes before six. Time for a
quick spruce-up and a dab of fresh makeup and she would be
ready to meet Christian for dinner. Her heart fluttered wildly at
the thought and then thumped heavily in her chest. What was
she going to do with the check? She couldn't carry it with her;
you just didn't carry that kind of check around. She couldn't
leave it in the office drawer. The safe. She would ask Charlie
Conway to put it in his safe. Too late; he was gone. Vaguely,
she remembered smelling his cigar as he walked by the office
and said something about seeing her in the morning. Now what
was she going to do? The first thing she should do was put the

green slip in another envelope. *Hide it!* her mind screamed. *Where?* She answered herself. The only place left—Christian Delaney's safe. What better place. She would seal it, scribble her name on the envelope, and forget about it. Ha! How did a person who had $889.88 to her name forget about a small green piece of paper bearing her name and the sum of $667,395.42. One didn't forget; what one did was ignore it. Immediately, she felt better and she felt positively light-headed once the check was safe inside a manila envelope. Carefully, she sealed the metal hook beneath three layers of Scotch tape. Her hands were trembling so badly she tangled the tape around her fingers and finally ended up pulling the sticky tape apart with her teeth. The matter tended to, she literally fell into the swivel chair and collapsed. She wasn't meant to have money, not if it did this to her. Disgust washed through her as she stared at the square envelope in front of her. Disgust gave way to pity for herself as she continued to stare at the fateful envelope. *Gemini, you shouldn't have done this. Whatever possessed you to do such a thing?* Finding no answers, Sam mentally affixed an invisible ramrod to her spine and stood up. Before she could think twice, she picked up the envelope and marched down the hall to Christian Delaney's office. The door stood open and she knocked lightly before entering.

The scene was an exact replica of the first time played out in the publisher's office. The handsome publisher stood with his back to her, shouting into the phone. Sam blanched at the words and dropped the manila square she was holding. She didn't want to listen, didn't want to hear more ways the man was going to kill her. She should leave, run as fast as her slim legs would carry her, but she couldn't. Not yet. She would punish herself and listen.

The words were ice cold and the harshest she had ever heard. "It's been seven days! What do you mean you have one lead and you aren't even sure of that? Fine, if money is your problem, then put more men on the case. I told you before I didn't care what it costs. Find Sam Blakely! Did you check with the postman? His mail was being held at the post office and was picked up today. Right, it was picked up today! Do you want to know why it was picked up today? I'll tell you why!'' Christian Delaney thundered into the phone. ''The dividend checks went out in the mail this week for the third quarter. Right now, this minute, he's probably winging his way to the Mediterranean intent on bilking some other old lady. Check the airlines. Now that that weasel has money to burn, he's apt to go first class. Gigolos do that. What do you mean, how do I know that? I just know. What about the Division of Motor Vehicles? He doesn't own a car. It figures. Try the rental agencies. I understand you can rent a Mercedes for a very small down payment. My aunt would never ride in anything but a Mercedes or a Checker cab. I'm certain you never thought of that,'' Christian said sarcastically.

Christian turned and motioned for Sam to sit down. He rolled his eyes in apology and again turned to face the panoramic view of the nation's Capitol. ''I can't wait to hear your lead. Let's have it. A man named Sam Blakely. What street? Spell it; Kilbourne Place, off Mount Pleasant Avenue. Do you have a number? Amazing! Second floor, number 1755. I have it. You're right I'm going up there, and right now. When was he seen last? Of course I'm edgy. And I'll stay edgy until he's behind bars or I have my hands around his neck. I'll call you later.''

Sam's brain was working double time and her fingers were fidgeting with the shoulder strap of her heavy canvas bag. When Christian turned to her and smiled, her heart melted and she wanted to leap up and throw her arms around him. He must have felt the same way, because he crooked his finger slightly, beckoning her to him. She fell into his arms and sighed deeply. Gently, Christian stroked her soft curls and held her close. ''If I kiss you now,'' he whispered huskily, ''we'll never get around to dinner.''

Sam moved slightly from his embrace and smiled. ''Charlie Conway is gone and I want to put this in the safe. Will you do it for me?''

Christian reached for the envelope and turned it over, looking at both sides. ''You didn't put your name on it.'' Not waiting for her to answer, he picked up a black grease pencil and scrawled "Orion" across the front. "It doesn't feel as though there's anything in it."

Sam forced another weak smile and remained silent.

Christian twirled the dial on the wall safe and then deposited the envelope. Locking the safe, he smacked his hands together. "Okay, let's get out of this place. I have a stop to make before we go to dinner. I hope you don't mind, but it really can't wait. I'm sure you heard my end of the conversation, so you know what's been going on. By God, the nerve of that weasel!"

"What...what weasel?" Sam gulped.

"The weasel who duped my Aunt Gemini and the weasel we're on our way to see. That weasel!"

"Oh," Sam said inanely, "that weasel."

"He's the one. When I'm finished with him, he'll never prey on another poor, unsuspecting old lady again."

"Is that wise?" Sam asked hesitantly. "What I mean is, you can get yourself into a lot of trouble taking this matter into your own hands. Besides, perhaps there's been a mistake..."

"If there's one thing I can't stand, it's deceit," Christian interrupted through clenched teeth. "I despise lies and trickery. I may have been born into money, but it's meant nothing to me. I receive a salary just like everyone else here at Delaney Enterprises. My parents saw to it that I worked my way through life. At the age of twelve I had two paper routes because I wanted a new bicycle. I worked summers.... What I've done, I've done myself. The money that's come to me through the family has barely been touched. I don't live the life of a playboy. As for the shares my poor misguided aunt left to that Sam Blakely, just let it suffice to say that I want it back. All of it. This has been a family-owned business, and as far as I'm concerned, it will always be. Fifty-one percent of the stock is the controlling interest. How can I ensure the growth of this company if the controlling stock is owned by a Sam Blakely? There's a lot at stake, and I intend to settle it—immediately!"

Sam was stunned. Why was he telling her this? Was this his way of making his threats known? Could it be he already suspected that she was Sam Blakely? Oh, if ever there was a time to bare her soul, this was it. Swallowing hard, she forced her tongue to working order and managed a garbled, "Christian, there's something I think…what I mean is, I'd like to talk to you…"

"Darling, remember what you were going to say. We've got to get moving. Tell me over dinner."

She knew she should have insisted. Allowing him to cut her off was too easy. Now was the time, before things went too far, before it was impossible to tell him, and then he would find out sooner or later and hate her for it. But it was not to be. Christian took her by the arm and led her out of the office.

As Christian drove along the unfamiliar streets, he turned to Samantha. "I left my driving glasses back at the office. Watch for Mount Pleasant Avenue. This is Seventeenth Street, isn't it?" Sam craned her neck backward and managed a jerky nod. "It should be along about here. It's been years since I've been in this area. If the trolley tracks were still here, it would be a breeze. There's something about streetcar tracks that make me melancholy."

"Turn left, Christian. There's Mount Pleasant Avenue," Sam said quietly. What had she been thinking of? She had actually been going to tell him. If she had, he never would have called her "darling." She meant something to him. She was certain of it. And he certainly meant something to her; just how much, she was afraid to even measure. "Kilbourne Place on your left. What number are you looking for?"

"End of the block, number 1755, second-floor apartment!"

Christian guided the car to the curb and sat for a moment. "I shouldn't have brought you with me. This doesn't look like the kind of neighborhood that's safe to walk around in after dark. I'm not even sure the car will still be here once we come out of the building."

Sam looked at the grimy brick building and winced. Venetian blinds that held years of dirt were hanging lopsidedly on the cracked windows. One window on the second floor was being propped open with a portable television set. A tattered blue curtain fluttered wildly. A sudden gust of wind came up, and dry leaves hurtled through the open window. What if some thug lived inside and he attacked them both?

"Lock your door, Orion, and hold on to my arm," Christian said, holding open the door for Sam.

Clutching Christian's muscular arm, Sam walked with him up the brick steps into a filthy hallway that reeked of years of stale food and other nauseating odors. Cautiously, they made their way to the top of the rickety steps with the aid of a fifteen-watt bulb that hung precariously from a frayed electrical wire.

Christian rapped loudly on the door and then stepped back, pulling Sam with him. No answer. He rapped again and kicked at the bottom of the door at the same time. "Yeah, whatcha want this time?" a whining voice demanded. Sam felt faint at the sight of the wizened old man who opened the door.

Christian stepped back another step and asked forcefully. "Is your name Sam Blakely?"

"And what if it is. My old mum gave me that name seventy-two years ago, and I'm still using it, so what business is it of yours?"

Christian ignored the question and asked another. "How long have you lived here?"

"As long as the cockroaches—and that's forever. Who are you, anyway?"

"Did you know Gemini Delaney?" Christian demanded in an angry tone.

"Don't know no Gemini anyone. Crazy name if you ask me. I ain't into that star stuff myself. Matter of fact, I just got out of the hospital today. Was in there for a whole month. I had pneumonia," the old man said proudly. "'Course, I was in the charity ward, but they took care of me just like everyone else, and they even called me Mr. Blakely. It's important for a man not to lose his identity. I was born Sam Blakely, and I'm gonna die Sam Blakely. Say, now, what you gonna pay me for answering all these questions? Listen, you ain't from one of them there TV shows, are you—you know, the hidden camera one?"

"No," Christian said disgustedly. "Look, I'm sorry to have bothered you. Here," he said, handing the old man a twenty-dollar bill. "Buy yourself a good steak and some vegetables and see to it that all the good they did for you in the hospital doesn't go to waste."

"That's mighty nice of you, Mister. You sure you ain't from one of them TV shows and they're going to come here and take this money from me after they turn off the cameras?"

"I'm sure," Christian said over his shoulder as he guided Sam down the dim stairway. "Don't touch anything, Orion."

Outside in the fresh air Sam gulped and swallowed hard. Poor Christian. She had to tell him; she couldn't allow him to keep searching like this. He looked so defeated.

Inside the car with the doors locked, Christian drove through Rock Creek Park. He was silent for so long Sam began to feel apprehensive. She should say something to break his mood. She should tell him now before this charade went much further.

"Orion, I'm sorry. This was a beastly thing to subject you to. All I can do is apologize. This business with my aunt has me caught up in a whirlwind. No more unpleasantries. I've been looking forward to this evening since you left for California. This is our evening and I don't want anything to spoil it."

The husky, intimate tone of his voice sent tingles up her spine. She felt herself drawn to him, losing herself in him. When he looked at her that way, with a crinkle of a smile in the corners of his eyes, she was reduced to Silly Putty. All reason escaped her; all determination to confess her true identity evaporated. To keep herself from melting beneath his silver gaze, she struggled to find conversation. "Is anyone at the magazine taking up a collection or planning a party of some sort for Ramon Gill? He's getting married next month," she blurted.

"No. I didn't know. I'll speak to Charlie about having a luncheon or something. Gill has been with the magazine for a long time. It's the least we can do. You're a romantic, are you?"

"All women are romantics." Sam grinned in the darkness. "Are you a romantic, Christian?" she teased.

"Of the first order. But if you tell anyone, I'll deny it. How would it look to my staff if they found out I was all mush inside?"

Sam laughed and the tension was relieved. They were both relaxed now, with a long evening ahead of them. She would tell him tomorrow that the Sam Blakely he was seeking was right here—under his nose. Right now, she needed this man who claimed he was a romantic. She needed to feel him beside her, needed his comforting words, and, at the same time, perhaps she could give him something in return. *I can't fall in love with him; I just can't.* A tiny, niggling voice warned that it was too late. She was already in love with Christian Delaney.

Christian had made reservations at a marvelous German restaurant in downtown Washington. Beer was served in lagers, and hearty pork sausages and cabbage were the main fare. All through dinner, Tyrolean musicians played their wind instruments and strolled among the tables. Samantha was mesmerized. It was immediately apparent that Christian was a familiar patron from the way he was greeted by the waiters and maître d'. The service was impeccable and the atmosphere conducive to quiet conversation. Throughout dinner, Christian kept up a cheerful banter, never once mentioning his search for one Sam Blakely. Time and again Samantha would find herself looking into his silvery-gray eyes and feeling as though she would drown in his warm, lingering looks. His gaze touched her face, her hair, her eyes, her mouth, and ignited a flurry of strange yearnings and excitement that she had never known. Reaching across the table, he touched her hand, holding it, fondling it, possessing it, as though he would never let her go.

Sam wished that dinner would never end. She preened in his attention, became breathless under his sultry glances and in the promise that was in his eyes.

Christian was just suggesting a ride along the Potomac when the pager he wore on his belt beeped insistently. His tone was full of disappointment when he excused himself to phone the office.

Sam watched his retreating back as he made his way to the phones. Suddenly, as though coming out of a dream, she began to panic. The evening was almost over! Christian would be wanting to take her home! It was hopeless. She would not lie to him or, at best, evade the truth again! She would face his rage and fury and tell him who she was. She would pray he would understand. She respected him too much to deceive him any longer. And, heaven help her, she loved him.

As she was pondering her problem and mourning over the fact that she would lose both the man she loved and the job she wanted in one stroke, he reappeared at the table. "Penny for your thoughts. Orion, something's come up at the office. I've got to go back there. It's an important break in the Mideast story. It couldn't come at a worse time!"

"Time and news wait for no man, Christian," Sam murmured regretfully, secretly relieved that once again the decision to confess all was taken from her hands.

"Come on, I'll get you home before I go back to the office," he said as he signed the check.

"You don't have to worry about me. I can take a cab home. It's all right, really." She had to tell him, but she needed his undivided attention, and this was not the time, nor the place. Or was this line of thinking another indication of her cowardice? she wondered, disgusted with herself.

"No, it's not all right. I'll take you home and then I'll go to the office," he insisted as he took her arm and led her out of the restaurant.

As they waited for the attendant to bring his car around to the front, Samantha became rigid. "This is really silly, Christian. I can take a cab right from here to my doorstep. Really. I'll be fine."

"If you're certain," Christian compromised. "Tell you what, I'll leave my car here and send for it in the morning. I'll ride in the taxi with you as far as the magazine, and I'll make sure the driver gets you home safely."

Christian climbed into the cab beside her. "I'll make this up to you, I promise—as soon as possible."

Samantha smiled reassuringly. "I don't mind, not really. There's always a next time."

Christian pulled Sam into his arms. "There's no time like the present," he whispered against her ear. And when his mouth came crashing down on hers, she felt the earth move beneath her feet. It was a long, lingering kiss, a kiss that dreams were made of. It was a kiss that held promises and soft words. Words like love, and eternity....

Breathlessly, she pulled out of his embrace and leaned her cheek against his shoulder. "God, I hate to leave you. I could hold you like this forever. I've never felt this..."

"Sh!" She silenced him by pressing her finger to his lips. The panic was rising in her breast again. She couldn't let him declare his feelings for her until she confessed her relationship with his aunt. To do otherwise would be unfair, and he would hate her for it.

Chapter Four

Sam looked at her wrist for the third time in less than five minutes. She had to do it. She had to tell Christian Delaney that she was the Sam Blakely in question. He had to understand. And if he didn't, she would have to work double time to make him aware that she had nothing to do with Gemini's bequest, that she had been completely in the dark until the day the letter arrived from the lawyer.

A quick look in her tiny pocket mirror told her her face was on straight; nothing was smudged. She was glad now that she had chosen the raspberry silk dress and Halston perfume. She looked her best, and right now that feeling was paramount. Would Christian understand? Finding no answers to her tormenting questions, Sam took a deep breath and marched down the long, narrow hallway to the publisher's office. Blunt. She would tell him straight out and not mince words. Up front. No lies, no deceit. She would say it like it was and take whatever was coming to her.

Sam moistened dry lips and tapped quietly on the heavy door. "Come in."

Sam's eyes closed momentarily and then she squared her

shoulders. She was Daniel going into the lion's den. No, she was Samantha Blakely going into…

"Orion! What a pleasant surprise, and one with which I would like to start every day." How husky his voice was. How sensual his voice was. Yes, he was handsome. He was coming around the desk, ready to take her into his arms. He would kiss her and then she would tell him. No, she had to tell him first. She moved slightly out of his reach and then turned to stare at him for a brief second.

"There's something I have to talk to you about, Christian. It really can't wait another moment." Why was her voice cracking like this? *Because I care,* she answered herself.

"You sound so serious, Orion," Christian said in mock severity.

"I am serious, very serious. I tried to tell you several times, and you would always interrupt me, and then I finally lost my nerve and took the easy way out. I don't want you to do that again until I tell you what I have to…to…to say to you."

Christian's tone, as well as his expression, was both amused and indulgent. "Orion, you have my undivided attention. You may proceed. Look, I'm going to sit down so I won't tower over you."

Sam jammed her hands into the side pockets of the colorful dress so the publisher couldn't see how they were trembling. She took a deep breath and squared her shoulders. "Christian, I know that you will understand what I'm going to say because you are a man of…of…compassion. I know that you will understand that I tried on several occasions to tell you, but…what I mean is…you may at first think I was trying to…but…I wasn't…I am Sam Blakely," she finished lamely.

Christian Delaney neither moved nor spoke.

Sam rushed on. "I'm that…that dastardly person who owns fifty-one percent of this…this company. I didn't know until I got the letter from the lawyer! Say something! Please, you can't blame me! I didn't know! I don't want the fifty-one percent! I tried to tell you in the restaurant before I left for the West Coast, but you kept interrupting me. I wanted to tell you when I got back, but...I didn't mean to deceive you. It was just that things got out of hand and...and..."

Silvery-gray eyes stared at her and through her. How cold and dead they looked. There was no need for words on the publisher's part. His eyes said it all. As far as he was concerned, she, Sam Blakely, ceased to exist.

"It's not the way it seems, and I did try to explain, but you kept interrupting me," Sam said in a shaky voice. "You must believe me! I don't want this magazine or your aunt's money! I don't know why she did what she did. I'm telling you the truth. Why won't you believe me? Please," she pleaded, "don't look at me that way. I thought—I hoped—that you would be fair and understand." What was the use? He was listening to her, but he didn't hear a thing she said. It was over. She turned to leave, her legs like fresh Jell-O, barely holding her erect.

Christian's words, when they finally came, shocked her. "You'll never see a penny of my aunt's money. I'll fight you in every court in the land. Liars make poor showings in a courtroom. So be prepared."

Sam's shoulders drooped. She wasn't a liar. She wasn't. She had tried to tell him. She had wanted to tell him from the very beginning. And now, because of her willy-nilly procrastination, it was all over between the two of them. How he must hate her. Scalding tears burned her eyes as she closed the door softly behind her. How final, how terminal the small sound was. You closed a door and part of your life was left behind.

Shoulders slumped, feet dragging, Samantha faced the long, seemingly endless corridor back to her office. Her heart was choked in her throat and the world around her seemed dark and without life. Suddenly, someone was holding her arm, shaking it.

"Orion, Orion, have you heard what's going on?" It was Ramon, and from the look of him, he was excited.

Samantha dragged herself back into the world of the living. Sudden sounds of clacking typewriters bounced into her awareness. Noise and confusion made her blink. What was going on? From the look of things, something important. Efficient secretaries were ripping papers from their machines with the speed of sound. Sam glanced around for Charlie Conway, but he was nowhere in sight. Milling reporters huddled into groups, talking excitedly.

"C'mon, Orion, get with it! Haven't you heard? Guess not. Word just came in over the teletype. Break in the Mideast crisis," Ramon told her. "I think I'm going. Cross your fingers. I missed out when it happened, and Conway told me this would be my turn."

Instantly, comprehension dawned upon Samantha. This would be the story of the decade.

Ramon, seeing the fervor shining in her face, prodded, "Get in there, Orion. See if you can get Conway to let you come along. As long as you keep your mouth shut and click your shutter the way you did in California, you can tag along with me anywhere. If I were you, I'd go in there right now and plead your case."

Sam was stunned. It was the answer to her unasked prayer. She could go away and try to forget Christian Delaney. Lose herself in her work. When she got back, things might be straightened out. When he had time to think, Christian might decide… Oh, what was the use of tormenting herself like this? This, for now, just might be her answer. "Ramon, do you think Charlie will assign me?" she asked, a note of desperation in her voice.

"No. But it will make you feel better. Lizzie is the one who's making the travel arrangements. I've already put in a good word for you. Everyone around here knows Lizzie runs this company."

Sam looked puzzled. "Lizzie is just a secretary."

Ramon shrugged. "So? She runs this company. Even Delaney does what she says. She's one of those people who's never wrong. And Delaney inherited her when he took over. Some say she was old man Delaney's mistress, and others say she was just a platonic friend. All I know is if Lizzie books a flight for you, you go. You'll learn, Orion."

"Have you seen Charlie?"

"He's getting the roster ready. Go on, Orion. What have you got to lose?"

What did she have to lose? Nothing. Without Christian there was nothing left. This assignment could mean her emotional survival, and it was suddenly the most important thing in the world. She wanted to go, needed to go. "Ramon, are you sure? About my tagging along with you, I mean."

"Orion, you make me look good. I'm no fool. I saw your pics, and with my story that makes us a winning team. And"— he grinned, lasciviously—"you aren't half-bad to look at, either."

"Gee, thanks."

"Your turn." The journalist grinned.

"Well, you aren't half-bad yourself. I like the way you dead-dog a story. Of course, that Latin charm goes a long way with the ladies, and they're the ones who spill to you."

"It's the teeth, Orion. They flash like a beacon in the night. Gets them right here," he said, pounding his chest. "Get going before Conway thinks you aren't interested."

Sam inched her way between the milling journalists and photographers and finally made it to Charlie Conway's office with one bruised elbow and a skinned shin. Cautiously, she opened the door a crack and then walked in hesitantly. "Charlie...oh, Charlie! I want to go!" she said adamantly.

"So does everyone on the magazine. I want to go myself. Heck, I'd drop all of this in a minute, but they tell me I'm too old. How do you like that? I'm too old! Seasoned, maybe, but old—never! Those young pups out there, think they know everything. I'll let you know, Orion, at the same time everyone else knows. If it's any consolation to you, Gill was in here three times pleading your case. You're late," he snapped.

"I just got here. I really want to go, Charlie."

"Check it out with Lizzie," Charlie said, relighting his stubby cigar.

"Does she really run this magazine?" Sam asked curiously.

"I think so. She sure tells me what to do. This roster is a farce. The real story is who she's making the travel arrangements for. It's a game we play around here. When the smoke clears, we match up our lists just to see how close I came to hers. It's a stupid way of doing business, but, she hasn't goofed once in all the years I've known her. Go on, see if she's got your name on the list. Get out of here. Can't you see I have work to do?'' the old man said gruffly.

Sam watched Conway pick up a dart and throw it at a penciled likeness of Lizzie that was tacked to the door. ''Ha! Right on the nose!'' Charlie chortled as the dart found its mark.

Lizzie was built like a dowager queen and that was how she reigned in the front reception area. Sam made her way to the marble foyer and stood staring at the woman behind the desk. Her pencil was flying over a sheaf of papers, making notes and canceling out other notes. She peered over the top of her glasses and picked out a pencil from her top knot of spiky gray curls.

''You got a problem, Orion, or do you just naturally stare at people?'' she asked in a gravelly voice.

''Both, I guess. Am I on your list, Lizzie?''

''Did Gill send you in here?''

Sam nodded. ''I just found out you run this place. I thought Mr. Delaney was…''

''He is. I am. I'll get back to you. Run along now, I'm busy. Ah, by the way, did the dart hit my nose or my top lip?''

Sam watched in horror as the old lady whipped out a dart and aimed it at a faded newspaper clipping of Charlie Conway. Peals of scratchy laughter erupted from the receptionist as the dart found its mark.

Panic gripped Sam's stomach muscles. Had that been a look of pity in Lizzie's eyes when she posed her question? Or was she becoming paranoid about everything? What had she been asked? Whatever it was, the woman was obviously waiting for an answer. ''Yes,'' Sam muttered weakly as she walked back toward Ramon.

''Well?'' Ramon snapped, clutching at her arm.

''She said she would get back to me. I have a gut feeling I'm not going to go, so be prepared. The gods aren't looking on me too favorably right now,'' Sam said morosely.

They waited for over an hour before Christian Delaney made his appearance in the newsroom.

Lizzie and Charlie stood behind Christian, each holding a slip of paper. First Charlie handed the publisher his, and then Lizzie held hers out. Sam watched, holding her breath, as Christian compared both slips of paper. "It's a tie." His eyes narrowed as he scanned the list a second time. "I want to say, here and now, that I am the one who has final approval of this list, and there are one or two changes I think should be made." Sam's heart thudded, knowing what was coming.

"According to this, Orion is the only woman selected. It's too dangerous, Lizzie. Charlie, what about Mac Williams? Orion hasn't been in the Mideast. Take her off the list."

Sam's spirits fell to her shoes. How could he do this to her in front of a room full of people? Tears stung her eyes as the journalists and photographers dropped their eyes to avoid seeing her humiliation and hurt. This was a deliberate slap in the face, his way of getting back at her. How could he do this to her! How dare he!

Sam stared at Christian Delaney, hardly believing his words. How could he humiliate her this way? And then another feeling coursed through her—that alien feeling she had come to know so well. She was hurt, hurt to the core of her being. Did he really think she wasn't good enough to go with the others? Was he really denying her the chance to go along because she was a woman, or was he getting even with her because he hated her? Tears of self-pity flooded her eyes and she gulped back a threatened sob. Her shoulders squared imperceptibly. She couldn't let him know how she felt. She was a professional, and professionals didn't weep and wail when something wasn't to their liking. She had to put on a good face and make out the best she could. Maybe he thought he was fooling the others, but she knew why she wasn't being permitted to go.

The looks on the men's faces told her all she needed to know. She was on her own. You didn't cross the boss or ever tell him what to do. It was part of their code. Christian Delaney was the publisher and president. He was supposed to know what he was doing; that's why he was a boss. Ramon Gill shrugged and walked away, the others following.

Sam's throat constricted. She had to say something. How could she just walk back to her cubbyhole office without making a fight of it? She couldn't. Her voice, when she spoke, surprised her; it was even and calm, belying the turmoil she felt. "I think I'm good enough to go with the others. It saddens me that, as my employer, you feel I'm lacking in ability…and other things, as well. I know that…"

"Spare me, Orion, whatever philosophy you're about to spiel off." Sam was stunned at the cold, arrogant look of the man as he towered over her. He was so close she could smell the faint minty aroma of his breath. "My decision stands; you remain behind. You may own fifty-one percent of this magazine, but I am still president and publisher."

"It was a mistake. I don't really own the controlling interest," Sam said, a note of panic creeping into her voice.

A muscle twitched in Christian Delaney's cheek; and, if possible, his voice was even more chilling, his eyes more steely, his stance more arrogant when he spoke. "Oh, there's no mistake; you own the controlling interest, all right. Even if you owned ninety-nine and eight-tenths percent of the stock, you still wouldn't be permitted to go with the others. It's not safe; you'd hinder the others. Regardless of what you say or think, a woman is a woman, and all the men would feel responsible for you. Get it through that air head of yours—E.R.A. hasn't caught up over there. My orders stand. Now, get back to work before I decide to dock your pay."

Sam was mortified beyond words. She stared a moment at the publisher's retreating back and then ran to her office and slammed the door shut. Great choking sobs tore at her throat. Air head! He had called her an air head! He had added insult to injury. The slender shoulders shook with the intensity of her sobs. All of this was happening to her because of Gemini's generosity. Why couldn't he realize it was all a mistake? That fifty-one percent was going to make trouble for her in more ways than one. What hurt most of all was he didn't believe her; he sincerely believed that she had duped his aunt into leaving her the controlling interest in *Daylight Magazine*. He was so wrong. Why wouldn't he listen to her? Did he really hate her so much?

"I didn't do anything wrong," Sam whimpered to the empty office. "The only thing I'm guilty of is falling in love with him. I love him, I love him," she sobbed heartbrokenly. She sniffed and dabbed at her eyes and then blew her nose lustily. "I'll show him. I'll show him that I don't care about the assignment. I'll make him understand, somehow, that I don't want or need his aunt's legacy. If it takes me the rest of my life, I'll make him understand." It was a hopeless thought, and Sam knew it in her heart. Christian Delaney hated her. A chill washed over her when she remembered his steely eyes and his icy words.

One weary day after another passed. Sam's eyes hungered for a glimpse of the publisher as she went about the mundane chores that Charlie Conway assigned her. Once she had literally collided with him at the water cooler. She wasn't sure if she imagined it or not, but he had appeared shaken at her nearness, and for a brief second she thought he was going to reach out and take her into his arms. Instead, he had nodded curtly and strode off down the long corridor. Her heart had fluttered wildly all day long.

Sam finished her sandwich and tossed the waxed paper and half a deli pickle into the trash can when Charlie Conway's voice shouted for her attention. "Orion, do me a favor, will you? I can't seem to locate that confounded office boy. Take Mr. Delaney's lunch in to him and set it up."

"Charlie, isn't there someone else…? What I mean is, I can't do…go…in there…Lizzie—can't Lizzie do it?" She felt like a rabbit caught suddenly in a snare. She wanted desperately to see the handsome publisher, wanted desperately to… "I can't do it, Charlie!" Sam bleated.

"Guts, Orion. You can do it. You *will* do it. That's an order. Now, move it!"

Sam picked up the plastic tray with Christian Delaney's lunch on it and carried it precariously down the long corridor that led to his office. The door was partially open and she debated a second before kicking lightly with the toe of her shoe to announce her arrival.

Christian Delaney's back was to Sam as she placed the tray on the neat, uncluttered desk. She was just removing the napkin from the sandwich tray when he swiveled abruptly and knocked her off balance. The ham and rye and the two halves of the kosher pickle slid across the desk. In her attempt to reach for them, she leaned too close and fell into Christian's lap. This couldn't be happening to her. It was. Strong arms held her close, too close.

"This is one way of announcing your arrival. A simple 'Here's your lunch' would have worked just as well." The voice was controlled, with no hint of amusement in it.

Sam felt herself drain of all color. Why did she feel so weak, so...trapped? The vise-like hold on her arms hadn't lessened. Her senses reeled with the scent of the man holding her. This was what she wanted, what she needed—to be near him, to have him hold her and whisper sweet words. Evidently, he was expecting her to make some comment or he would have released her. "You moved...I wasn't expecting...Charlie said there...I'm sorry," Sam muttered. In her agitation in trying to defend herself, she found herself cheek to cheek with the man holding her.

Silvery-gray eyes stared into hers, drawing her into their depths. Sam waited, wild anticipation coursing through her like a riptide. She knew he was going to kiss her, and she made no move to extricate herself from his strong hold. His lips were feather light upon her own and she responded in kind. It was Christian who withdrew first, his eyes blazing into her own. Before she could draw a breath, his lips seared hers, sending fire through her veins. When he released her a second time, she was shaken to her very being. He must care for her; otherwise, how could he kiss her like this? Her heart soared and then plummeted when she heard his next words as he somehow thrust her from him, still keeping his hold on her arm. His voice was cold and clipped. "That was a mistake, and I apologize. Have the office boy get me another sandwich." She was dismissed.

Sam shook her head slightly to clear it. Her eyes narrowed.

He had done it to her again. He had humiliated her and, worse yet, he had taken advantage of her by kissing her. Never mind that she had wanted him to kiss her, even willed it. An angry retort rose to her lips. His cold eyes were mocking her as she turned on her heel. "Yes sir, Mr. Delaney, sir." At the door she clicked her heels and snapped a salute.

The publisher's deep, mocking laugh followed her all the way back to her office. It wasn't till an hour later that she remembered to order him another sandwich. Christian Delaney wouldn't starve—he ate people alive, especially photo-journalists.

Her desk cleared for the day, Sam spent the remaining minutes watching the hands on the wall clock creep toward the five and twelve. Soon it would be time to go home and spend another lonely evening watching television. She knew she could work on the painting of Christian, but all the life seemed to have gone out of the project. The plain and simple truth of the matter was she couldn't bear to even pick up a brush.

Christian Delaney's voice thundered over the partition. "There must be someone around here. Where's the assignment sheet? Lizzie," he roared, "where's Matowskie? Where's Blandenberg? And what happened to Jefferies and Arbeiter? Well?"

Sam rose and stood in the doorway. If the angry publisher thought he was cowing Lizzie, he was mistaken. His arrogant, insufferable attitude only worked on dimwits like herself. The man hadn't been born who could cow Lizzie.

"Matowskie is in Seattle. You sent him yourself three days ago. Blandenberg is in Israel on vacation. You approved it yourself three weeks ago. Jefferies and Arbeiter are covering an assignment in Venezuela. If you're looking for a photographer, there's one standing right behind you." Lizzie's tone was saccharine sweet, yet firm. She ran the company, and no upstart like Christian Delaney was going to intimidate her. Besides, she was sixty-nine years old, and rank did have its privileges.

Sam's heart started to pound and then she started to bristle. Just let him ignore her this time. Now she was angry. Whatever the assignment was, she wanted it. How could he turn her down this time? He couldn't. If she was all there was, he had to use her. It never occurred to her to even wonder what and where the assignment was.

The publisher's eyes went from Lizzie to Charlie Conway to Sam. He didn't bother with more than a cursory glance in her direction before he locked in with Charlie Conway. "Order the Lear jet to be made ready. The board decided that with the feedback coming in so steadily from the Mideast, we're going to take a crack at the energy problem from here. The destination is the Southwest. You're it, Orion."

Lizzie answered for her. "That's what she's here for. Two hours, Orion. Be at the airport."

"Who…who's going with me?" Sam stammered. Not that she cared. She didn't care about anything except that Christian Delaney had said she could go, that he was giving her the assignment, and Lizzie, God bless her, approved. If Christian assigned her to cover Dracula's castle, she couldn't have cared less.

"Me," came the curt reply.

Sam swallowed hard and then she grinned from ear to ear. "You got it, Mr. Delaney." Now let him make whatever he wanted out of that statement. She was going to the Southwest with him. Together, in one plane. They would be working side by side. Truth was truth. She was going to have him all to herself, and by some stroke of luck she just might be able to convince him of a few things. Whatever, she had a fighting chance now, and she was going to make the most of it.

Lizzie favored Sam with a heavy-lidded wink, and Charlie Conway shifted his evil-smelling stogie to the left side of his mouth.

Chapter Five

Sam hadn't really known what to expect when she arrived at the private airstrip on the outskirts of Baltimore, where she was to meet Christian Delaney to embark on their assignment of American energy resources, but the shining Lear jet, with its engines whining in warm-up, certainly wasn't it. And when she lugged her camera equipment and duffel bag out to the winged machine and curiously looked into the cockpit for a glimpse of the pilot, Christian answered her unspoken question.

"I'm a qualified pilot, Orion. This little beauty is all mine. Personal property; not an asset of Delaney Enterprises."

Samantha felt herself flush with anger. She wanted this assignment, but at what price? Was he going to be caustic and riddle her with his sarcasm during the entire trip? Holding back a tart reply, she threw her duffel up the gangplank and into the plane. Forcing a smile to her lips, she turned to meet his stare. "She is a beauty, Mr. Delaney, and I have every confidence in your ability as a pilot."

"Good. Then you won't mind sitting up front with me." His eyes watched her, daring her to demur.

Sam's spirits sank lower. She wanted nothing more at this point than to hide away somewhere near the tail of the plane, far away from this man who created such conflicting emotions in her. This job would necessitate working very closely with him to complete the assignment. Was she prepared to be so near him, close enough to touch, and yet, at the same time, recoiling from his presence? Inhaling deeply, as though breathing in the courage she would need, Sam reminded herself that this very same man who held such a great attraction for her was the one and the same who refused to believe her innocence concerning Gemini's will.

"I'd enjoy sitting up front," she heard herself say lightly, refusing to meet his eyes, fearful that the lie would show itself there in the windows of her soul.

"Good. Got everything? We won't be anywhere near a drugstore where you can buy flash bulbs or anything else."

Samantha bristled in spite of her resolve not to allow him to get to her. "Mr. Delaney, I'm a professional. I assure you I've got everything I need."

Her sharp tone seemed to go unnoticed. "Great. Climb aboard."

The silvery wings reflected the gold of the sun as they leveled off at twenty thousand feet. Christian's command of the Lear was impressive, just as Sam knew it would be. Everything Christian did was with an inborn confidence and certain ability. His hands on the instruments and controls were steady and knowledgeable, and his voice was crisp and authoritative when he called in to the control tower far below.

Their first destination was a uranium mining plant in southwestern Arizona. Hours alone with Christian Delaney.

"There's a coffee maker in the back. Want to try your hand at it?"

Wordlessly, Sam unhitched herself from the seatbelt and, stooping slightly, made her way into the body of the plane and to a small counter near the tail section. Everything she needed was readily available, including coffee cream in the small refrigerator beneath the shiny counter.

As she waited for the coffee to brew, Sam sat and chewed at

her thumbnail, realizing a sense of tension drain out of her. Just being near Christian set her teeth on edge. There was a sorrow that settled somewhere between her second and third rib because he believed she was a fortune hunter of the worst kind. There was nothing to say and nothing she could do to convince him that she hadn't preyed upon an old woman's sentiments.

The coffee maker gurgled and indicated its cycle was completed. She prepared two mugs, remembering Christian preferred cream, no sugar. Cautiously, she made her way forward again and handed him the steaming mug. For an instant their fingers touched, and Sam felt a bolt of electricity shoot through her. How long had it been since he had touched her? How long since he had taken her in his arms and claimed her mouth for his own? Ages. Centuries past a lifetime.

Slowly, she sipped her coffee, covertly watching Christian's every movement. She realized his casual expertise in handling the plane. How confident he was. How masterful. It was little wonder that he had come to loathe her. This was an open, straightforward man who was used to taking up the reins of responsibility. Lies and deceit had no place in his life. He would never believe that she had tried to tell him the truth about her identity time and time again. And now, she had begun to wonder just how hard she had tried. Was it possible that she had unconsciously allowed him to interrupt her every time she was about to tell him that she was Sam Blakely? Had she been so greedy for his kisses that it had jeopardized her own honesty?

For what was beginning to seem like a lifetime, Samantha sat beside Christian Delaney while their plane headed due West, and the plains of America rolled beneath them. The publisher's silence was deafening. He hated her, she was certain of it. There was no use trying to explain her relationship with his Aunt Gemini and the fact that she hadn't even realized the old woman's connection with Delaney Enterprises, much less connived to dupe her into writing her into the will.

If Samantha had somehow hoped that this time alone with Christian would be an opportunity to mend the wounds, she knew now how wrong she had been. She knew if Christian would turn to look at her his eyes would be shards of steel and his face would be a mask of granite.

She surveyed his uncompromising concentration out the windshield and toward the horizon. Could this be the same man who had swept her off her feet—the same man who possessed her lips with his own? Who had promised her tender moments with his eyes and offered her shelter and a loving haven with his arms?

Why didn't he say something? Anything! How could he expect to complete an assignment under these circumstances? Silently, she willed him to turn and speak to her. Instead, he fixed his steely gray eyes straight ahead and his mouth into a thin, forbidding line. He held her in contempt, and now that same contempt was filling the cockpit and choking off her air.

Sam massaged her temples, warding off a migraine. She watched Christian's every movement and saw his casual expertise in handling the plane. Samantha found it impossible to tear her eyes away from him. She memorized his profile, the arrogant set of his head above broad shoulders and powerful body. She knew every nuance of his features. Knew them and loved them. She had loved this man long before she ever knew him. Long, patient hours of working on his portrait into the lonely hours of the night when only she and his likeness shared the solitude.

She loved him. Didn't he know that? Couldn't he sense it? Feel it? How could he be so stupid and insensitive? Did he think only of the fact that Gemini Delaney had made a ridiculous gesture by willing her that large interest in the family business?

Guilty tears stung her eyes. She had had opportunities to confess to him that she was the Sam Blakely he was seeking. But she had let them go by. And now, when she had finally told him, it was too late. She had made him feel like a fool for not having known much sooner. Little wonder he thought she was a fortune hunter.

A sudden jolt shook Samantha out of her reverie. Her eyes flew to the left wing, where the engine was issuing a cloud of black smoke. Her stomach lurched warningly. She sought Chris-

tian with her eyes; panic welled within her. She saw the tense-
ness in his shoulders and neck and the hard set of his mouth.

"Christian! What's wrong?"

"How do I know?" he growled from between clenched teeth.
"But if we're going to crash, it's not going to be from twenty
thousand feet up. Hold on, I'm taking her down."

Samantha felt the pressure in her ears as the craft descended
and the ground below came closer and closer. "Where are we?"
she gulped, looking for the gray skyline of a city.

"We've been out over the desert for the past hour. That's
California straight ahead, Arizona below.

"Better hold on tight, Orion. Take the flotation cushion from
under your seat and put it in your lap. Get your head down, way
down!" His tone compelled her into immediate action.

She heard Christian try to make radio contact and send a May
Day signal. It was all happening so fast, as fast as the rush of
air against the windshield as the Lear plummeted toward the
earth. She heard Christian swear, trying again and again to make
contact, muttering something about an electrical burnout in the
instrument panel. "Hold on, Orion, we're going down!"

Long moments. Eternity. Pressure in the cockpit dropped. Her
ears popped. A lifetime of prayers skated through her mind, and
every one of them included Christian.

She felt the aircraft's speed decrease until she thought they
must be hovering in midair. Suddenly, she felt as though the
floorboards beneath her feet were rattling, shaking, grinding
against something. The wheels touched the ground and the plane
seemed to skid through the whirling dust as it swooshed and
careened wildly. Samantha's heart was in her mouth as she
pressed her head down and felt the safety belt dig into her ab-
domen, holding her back against the seat when the momentum
was hurling her forward.

A terrible wrenching sound filled her world as the Lear tilted
crazily to one side. She heard Christian swear again under his
breath and the thunderous noise in her ears subsided as he cut
the engines.

Cautiously, incredulously, Samantha raised her head from the cushion. They were on the ground, and although they were tilted to one side, all forward motion had ceased. They were safe!

"This is your captain speaking." Christian laughed with wild relief from where he slumped back against his seat. "At this time I'd like to thank you for flying blind, and *Daylight Magazine* thanks you and hopes your stay in the Arizona desert will be enjoyable. I'd like to say, at this time, that the temperature is a pleasant one hundred ten degrees. Be certain to gather all your belongings and check the overhead racks so nothing is left behind."

Sam unsnapped the seatbelt and crawled across the cockpit, throwing her arms around Christian. "I knew you could do it! I knew it! I prayed for both of us!" she cried, planting a wet kiss on his cheek, his nose, his eyes, and finally his mouth.

Hard hands closed around her arms, pushing her away. "Am I really to believe you prayed for the both of us, or just yourself, Orion? Think how much simpler it would be to take over Delaney Enterprises if I wasn't around to stop you!"

This couldn't be happening to her. She must be having a nightmare. When she awakened, all would be well. No, it wouldn't. Nothing was ever going to be right again. An invisible ramrod stiffened in her spine and she locked glares with her accuser. "No matter what I say or how I explain, you aren't going to believe me. I don't have to defend myself, Christian—not to you or to anyone else. You've already judged and found me guilty. I'm sorry for both of us that whatever it was we had wasn't strong enough to weather this." Was that cool, positive voice really hers? Now, when the end of her world was looming before her? The ramrod in her spine slipped beneath Christian's silvery, unblinking stare.

"Get your gear together, Orion. We can't stay here. As the captain of this plane, consider that an order. This is not time for hysterics." His voice was controlled, but there was a thinly veiled note of venom beneath it. Clearly, she had no choice but to follow his orders.

Christian hefted himself from his awkward position in the crazily lopsided cockpit and literally had to crawl through the hatch to the rear of the plane. Silently, he emptied the small refrigerator of soft drinks and a small supply of canned goods. He searched the compartment over the seats and found the one containing the first-aid kit and flashlight.

Red-faced, Sam watched him, knowing that she herself would have set out into the desert without a thought to the supplies to be found aboard the aircraft. Even in crisis, Christian kept his head. And now, here alone in the wilderness, it suddenly dawned upon her that she was completely dependent upon him. Somehow, the thought was not comforting.

The heat was oppressive. By shading her eyes, Sam could see Christian striding ahead in the distance. Her heart thudded and then was still. If she wanted to catch up and not lose sight of him, she was going to have to pick up her pace. And, she told herself, he had the food and drinks, not to mention the compass she had seen him discover in the first-aid kit.

Quickening her steps over the hard-packed sand, Sam seemed to be gaining on Christian's retreating figure. Keeping up that long-legged stride might have tired him. Or else he was deliberately slowing down so she could catch up with him. She only wanted to keep him in sight; she didn't want to walk beside him.

Sam's pace slackened as she wiped the perspiration from her brow and dabbed at her neck with the tail of her shirt. This heat was worse than anything she had ever experienced. Her mouth was full of cotton balls and gritty sand. The minuscule grains were in her eyebrows and her hair, and her skin itched. She wished for a drink but would die before asking him for one of the sodas he had taken from the plane.

Suddenly, Sam's heart thumped madly as she saw Christian turn to glance at her over his shoulder. He stopped and faced her, concern written on his features. Coming abreast of him, Sam shaded her eyes against the golden glare of the sun.

"Give me your duffel, Orion." Obediently, she handed him the soft-sided bag. Dropping to one knee, she watched him rifle through it, withdrawing a spare shirt. "Here, wrap this around your head to protect you from the sun."

Clumsily, Sam struggled with the shirt, finding it impossible to do as he ordered. "You've already had too much sun," he said solemnly, taking the garment from her and doing it for her.

"I'd like to offer you something to drink, but we have to conserve whatever we have. Here, take this." He stooped to pick up a smooth pebble from near her feet, wiped it off on his shirt, and offered it to her. "Put this in your mouth. It's an old Indian trick to fool the salivary glands and bring moisture to the mouth." Sam did as ordered and, while it didn't produce the hoped-for results, her mouth didn't feel so parched.

"We'll stop now and rest. We'll continue for a few hours when the sun begins to set. Since I'm responsible for you, you'll do as I instruct. Understood?"

Samantha nodded in agreement, grateful for the opportunity to get off her burning feet. The heat was coming off the sand and penetrating her hiking boots, and she wished for a cool pool of water to put them in.

Christian led her over to a bone-dry, scrubby-looking bush of indistinct genus and faced her away from the sun. He placed the duffel under her head and ordered her to stay put. Then, taking himself to the opposite side of the bush, he settled himself down.

Tired though she was, she hesitated lying back and succumbing to sleep. She wasn't certain that Christian wouldn't leave without her, and she admitted to herself that she was afraid he might. What would she do if he took it into his head that she was more trouble than she was worth, and he left her here alone? She couldn't sleep—she didn't dare.

Back home, when she couldn't sleep, she would get out of bed and work in her darkroom or go through the stacks of old pictures she had collected. Or work on Christian's portrait, she reminded herself bleakly. Quietly, she withdrew the prized camera and squinted into the sun. Why not? There was nothing else to do, and she had a generous supply of film in her gadget bag. Why not take pictures of the desert? When she looked at them in years to come, she would remember. It wasn't fair. How could this be happening to her? There he was, mighty male animal, sleeping like a baby, and she had to stay awake because she was afraid he would leave her.

Sam focused the lens and adjusted her f-stop. She moved slowly, striving for the correct light. She turned, her intention being to snap a picture of the sleeping publisher. His features were relaxed in sleep, making him look vulnerable. Only she knew what kind of lurking monster was hidden behind those handsome features. Quickly, she snapped again and again. In those years to come she could quietly torture herself by staring at his likeness. Tears burned her eyes unexpectedly. Her feelings were too raw, too injured, to make logical thought possible.

Feeling her eyes upon him, Christian woke up with a start. He glared at her and kept his silence. Samantha felt compelled to explain. "You looked so vulnerable, so peaceful...I only wanted to capture it on film."

"A likely excuse. What you probably meant to do was bash me over the head and then you'd meet little resistance to holding on to that fifty-one percent," Christian snarled. "Well, I have news for you, Miss Photographer, you won't get rid of me that easily."

"Is that what you think? Of all the stupid, insufferable... you're detestable! I can't even look at you!" she shot back.

"You have that a little backward. It's you who's detestable. Imagine, taking advantage of a little old lady. It's criminal, do you know that? Criminal!"

"Think whatever you like. As long as I know I didn't do anything, I can live with myself and that fifty-one percent!" she cried savagely. "The only thing I was guilty of is...was...not explaining the mixup in the first place. Change that to the only *stupid* thing I was guilty of. I grant you the whole situation appears decidedly suspicious, but you won't give me a chance to explain."

"Explain! No thank you," Christian said sourly. "I've had enough lies to last me a lifetime. Besides, I know my Aunt Gemini was nobody's fool, yet you seemed to have managed to talk her out of the controlling interest in the family business. Heaven only knows what you'd try to talk me out of before this trek through the desert is over.''

Sam backed off a step, hardly believing what she had heard. She flinched as though she had been physically struck. She wouldn't cry; she refused to give him that satisfaction. Besides, when you were dead inside, everything stopped working, even tears.

Christian Delaney wasn't finished upbraiding her. ''And when we get back to Washington, consider yourself dismissed. Don't even bother coming into the office. You're through!''

The words and his anger vibrated along Sam's nerve endings and she felt her fingers curl into claws. The invisible ramrod in her spine stiffened. ''You can't fire me! I didn't do anything! I'm good at what I do, and you know it!''

He leaped to his feet and stared down at her, his mouth fixed into an implacable line of fury. ''I don't know any such thing. It's my magazine, and I don't want you to have any part of it.'' His voice had dropped two octaves and held a barely controlled rage. He was an imposing figure, glaring down at her: tall, lean, powerful.

''I have an unbreakable contract. Gemini saw to that. You try to fire me and I go to court. I'll charge you with sexual harassment!'' What was she saying? Was she crazy? At the malevolent expression on his face, Sam stepped backward.

Christian blanched. His fury was barely controlled. His white knuckled fist reached down and picked up his canvas bag and slung it over his shoulder. Turning away from her, he stomped off, dark head lowered over hunched shoulders.

Following behind at a safe distance, Sam seethed inwardly. Had she really said all those things? From the expression on his face, she had not only said them, but he had believed her. As if she would ever do any such thing. She didn't want his company or his money. She had lashed out in self-defense, aiming to stun him, hurt him. Any mean and hateful thought that had flown into her head, she had spit out through her mouth. It was one thing to defend herself, to hurt someone, but it had been totally unnecessary to keep sticking in the knife and twisting it for emphasis.

"There's one other thing, Mr. Delaney," she called to his retreating back. "I want to go on record as saying that I detest people who have the power to shatter other people's dreams and then actually go ahead and do it. You are one of those people! First, you let Gemini down by putting your business first instead of being there at the end when she needed you. And now you suspect the worst about me and refuse to listen to any explanation."

Even as she watched him, he stopped dead in his tracks. Every muscle in his body tensed and he was ready to spring like a wild jungle cat. Fear balled up in her throat, choking off all air. She had gone too far. Reminding him that he hadn't been home in time for Gemini's last days and then her funeral had been a low blow, and it didn't appear he was going to take it lying down.

Paralyzed with terror, she saw him turn. He placed one foot in front of the other, stalking her. Unable to move, unable to think, she was mesmerized by his approach. Threatening, lethal, determined, he closed the distance between them. Powerful, potent and ruthless, he sighted his quarry and hypnotized her with the predatory glare in his silver-gray eyes as though she were a jackrabbit paralyzed by oncoming headlights.

Samantha gasped for breath and felt the shock of motion return to her limbs. She turned and ran, throwing one leg in front of the other, escaping, scrambling away as though a hound of hell were on her heels. And he was.

Her feet slipped in the sand; her breath came in ragged gasps. Her duffel and camera bag banged against her legs in an unrelenting rhythm. Just when she thought that her heart would burst, she felt herself being pulled backward and her legs sprawling out at awkward angles.

Together they rolled over the shifting sands. He bore his weight on top of her, stilling her struggles. She was locked against his heaving chest, feeling his labored breaths against the side of her face.

She felt him draw away, felt his gaze upon her. Panic tearing through her, she cautioned a glance at his face. His eyes were burning through her to her very core. Fear subsided; there was no menace in his silver-shadowed glance now. Instead, there was something else there, something she didn't dare put a name to.

With a force that was almost violent in its intent, he covered her body with his own. Pressing down, bearing down, stilling her struggles and kicks, he held her, dragging her arms upward over her head to prevent her from tearing at his face. Her breathing came in pants and ended in an inconsolable groan of hopelessness.

Deliberately, with barely concealed menace, Christian glared down at his prey. He studied her face for a long, unendurably long moment. Their eyes locked—hers with trepidation, and his with victory. He lowered his head, aware that she was incapable of movement, and his mouth came crashing down upon hers.

The desert sand shifted beneath her weight, and Christian shifted his length to hold her captive. His lips possessed hers and awakened her already heightened senses. Samantha's world became full of Christian. The taste of him, the feel of him, the power of him—they all assaulted her awareness. His sensual demands excited and aroused and ignited her passions.

The heat of the sun was dimmed by the desire that blazed between them. His intimate exploration of her mouth sent tingles of pleasure down her spine. His hands released her arms, allowing them to wind around his neck, holding embracing, answering his.

The touch of his hands aroused and inspired a slow curl of heat that emanated from her offered body and consumed them. He tasted her flesh, where her shirt revealed it, all the way down to the soft swell of her heaving breasts.

His excursion of the smooth curves of her body was sure and designed to please, as though they had roamed and discovered many times before this. The fires licked at Samantha's senses, tearing down her defenses, allowing her to forget all else besides being here, this minute, with Christian, loving Christian.

She had never felt so alive, so vibrant, as she did when she was in his arms, and she knew with a certainty that the only death that would ever exist for her was to be separated from this man who could sizzle her passions and awaken her desires.

His fingers were in her hair, on her throat, teasing the pleasure points beneath her ear. Each of his movements was created and drafted to overwhelm her and to ensure his complete and total possession. A tide of desire ebbed over her objections. There were no objections. There was nothing—only Christian, the man she loved and wanted.

Her back arched, her arms held him close, her lips answered his, and when she felt him draw back and roll over, pulling her with him, she gladly followed. Their legs tangled, their breath mingled, and with a wanton abandonment she undid the buttons of her shirt, allowing him complete access to the heated flesh beneath. With authority his fingers wound through the silky strands of her hair, pulling her head back while his lips made a heady progression along her throat to the valley between her breasts.

Desire became a fire, white-hot and searing them together in a wild and lusty experimentation of lips and hands. On top of him as she was, she was aware of his lean, muscular body between her knees. She felt the sun burn into the newly exposed skin of her back, matched only by the even hotter touch of Christian's lips on her breasts.

Samantha looked down into his eyes, feeling as though she was bathed in molten silver and golden sands. A hidden spring of emotion bubbled to the surface as she whispered, "I never knew love could be like this."

Suddenly, she felt him stiffen beneath her. His hands ceased their tender excursion of her flesh, and his mouth, pressed against hers, became hard and unyielding. Pulling away, staring down into his face, she saw his gray eyes harden and become like forged steel.

"Love, Orion? I thought you called it sexual harassment!"

Sam pulled away from him and struggled to her knees. Wounded beyond belief, she fumbled with the buttons of her shirt, covering herself from his scrutiny. How could she have been so stupid? Did she want this man so much that she could forget her own self-respect?

Christian narrowed his eyes to slits. She watched his lips tighten into a grim, white line. "Why were you taking pictures of me?" he demanded.

A sob rose to Sam's throat. If she answered him, he would know how close to tears she was. She turned her face to the side and clenched her hands into tiny fists.

"I asked you a question. Answer me!" Christian thundered.

Through superhuman effort she submerged a sob. If she could only stop her body from trembling. Her mind raced; she would not, not ever, admit to this man that she had wanted his picture so she could remember him when he was most vulnerable.

Christian lunged suddenly, reaching out a long arm and pulling her against his massive chest. Samantha's face was within a hair's breadth of his. Fascinated, she watched a muscle twitch in his cheek. He was holding her much too tight—too tight to breathe. Her breath was coming in short, ragged gasps as Christian cupped her head, with its tousled hair, in his big hand, forcing it back at an awkward angle. His voice was soft and full of menace as he stared down into her tear-moistened eyes.

"You would have allowed me to make love to you a moment ago," he said huskily. He thrust her from him; his voice was tight and bitter. "It won't work, Orion. If you don't believe or accept anything else, believe that I will never permit you to take control of Delaney Enterprises."

Anger and humiliation ripped through Samantha. She didn't deserve this treatment, but she had no defense. He would never believe her, no matter what she said or what she did. She wanted to lash out at him, tell him that she would have given herself to him because she loved him. Not money or his publishing empire. Only Christian. The words never found their way to her lips. She could only stand there with her eyes cast down at the dry, arid ground, and only sheer determination helped her choke back the tears.

A long moment of silence crept between them as he waited for her answer. His eyes bore through her expectantly, and when

Samantha found the courage to meet them, she was surprised to find a dark yearning in his gaze. But it was fleeting, and when he decided she had no reasonable answer for her actions, he turned away.

Tears were flowing wildly down Sam's cheeks as she stuffed the camera into its case. She was careful to keep her back to Christian so he wouldn't see how vulnerable she really was. She couldn't allow him to find her with her defenses down again. The hurt was too great, too crippling.

Sam's tears and stuffy nose were replaced with hiccups as she trudged behind Christian. The only thing that made the trek bearable was the pleasure she was going to have when she handed over the sealed envelope in the publisher's own safe. She'd tear the check up before his very eyes. Then she would tear up her contract with *Daylight Magazine*. If Christian Delaney didn't want her, then she didn't want him, either! Even as she thought it, a fresh wave of hiccups seized her, punishing her for the lie. She would spend her life wanting Christian Delaney, and she knew it.

Chapter Six

Samantha was surprised how chill and cold the nights in the desert could become after the broiling heat of the day. She and Christian were camped for the night beside a rare outcropping of ancient rocks that still managed, somehow, to hold a little of the sun's heat. They both knew it was a temporary state of affairs since the sun had only gone down a little over an hour ago, and soon those same rocks would be clammy and cold—as cold as the stars that were beginning to twinkle in the velvet blackness of the night.

Her scanty knowledge of outdoor living seemed grossly inadequate now, when it was really being put to the test. Thank goodness for Christian. He, at least, had had the foresight to realize they would need a fire for warmth, if not for the light. So, during their interminable walk he had instructed her to gather dried vegetation when it was available. Their northeast journey had taken them closer to the foothills where the terrain had given way from loose sand to a rocky foundation. There was much more protection from winds and an ample supply of dried, scrubby bushes whose underbrush snapped off easily in the hand.

Working together, they gathered rocks to make a fire ring, and with the cigarette lighter from his pocket, they ignited the brush, feeding the fire from time to time to maintain it.

She was silent as she watched Christian work, and she wondered if he felt she was foolish because she didn't think of this small comfort herself. Out of his duffel he withdrew several packages of cheese crackers and an already-opened can of soda. It was tonic water, and the bitter liquid was more refreshing to their thirst than the sweeter soda that Christian had also taken from the plane's small refrigerator.

Sam settled down on the far side of the fire and after a moment Christian brought her the first-aid kit he had retrieved from the compartment over the seats. "Poke through this, will you, Orion? I've already taken the compass out, and that's what we've been following. Maybe there's something else we could use." Sam looked up, surprised by the almost friendly tone of his voice. Maybe, just maybe, if there was nothing else they could salvage of their relationship, they could develop a camaraderie and help each other through this uncertain situation of being stranded in the desert, miles away from anywhere.

Her hopes were dashed when Christian spoke again. "That's woman's stuff; I don't know a bandage from a snake-bite kit."

Angrily, Sam snapped open the metal lid. Of all the chauvinistic…just because she had long hair and wore lipstick didn't signify that all she was good for was "woman's work"!

First of all, there was a second compass. Wordlessly, she tossed it over to Christian, who immediately checked it against the one in his pocket and nodded his head confidently. Next, Sam dug out a first-aid cream for small cuts. Happily, she opened the plastic tube and smeared the soothing lotion on her weather-dried face, satisfied with the immediate results. Since they had suffered no injuries, not even minor scratches, she had no immediate use for the various ointments and iodines and bandages. But at the bottom, folded into a flat rectangle, enclosed in an envelope of clear plastic, was a shock blanket—a thin, aluminum-gray nylon sheet designed to keep in thermal body heat. It would appear the nights wouldn't be so cold, after all. Happily, she displayed her find to Christian. "You take it," he told her. "I'll make do with the extra clothes in my duffel."

The extra shirts and light jacket which were stowed in her duffel bag were further protection against the cold. She may have to go to sleep hungry and tired, but she wouldn't be cold. As Christian banked the fire, Sam wearily made a pillow of her duffel bag and tried to assume a comfortable position to sleep. The shock blanket was light, but within a few minutes she happily admitted that it lived up to its purpose. Turning on her side, she was soon fast asleep.

Sometime during the early morning hours, when the sun was just creeping over the horizon, Samantha awoke with a start. Something was holding her and preventing her from rolling over onto her back. Christian. Apparently, the cold night air had had its effect on him, and he decided to share the shock blanket with her.

His arm was flung carelessly around her in sleep, the tips of his fingers just resting on the swell of her breasts. His body had molded itself around her in sleep, and they were nested together like two spoons. His breath feathered against her cheek, and she realized that somehow, during the night, in their exhausted sleep, he had slipped his arm beneath her head and she was resting on his shoulder. For a long, glorious moment, Samantha knew the joy of awakening in the arms of the man she loved. *Did love,* she corrected. She couldn't, wouldn't allow her defenses to slip now. Knowing what being devastatingly hurt by Christian's unrelenting suspicions could do to her, she was not going to put herself in that position again. To contradict the adage, once was certainly enough!

Christian seemed to sense her wakefulness, or had he already been awake and watching her sleep. The thought was disconcerting and Sam flushed as she thought of how his fingertips had rested so close to her breasts.

"Rise and shine, Orion. We've got a long day ahead of us."

Obediently, she hauled herself out from under the shock blanket and away from his embrace. Immediately, the morning air felt chill and hostile. Or was it just because she had moved away from this man whose masterful confidence in even the most precarious of situations could make her feel protected and secure?

They decided to save a few remaining packages of crackers and cheese for later and broke camp to travel while the air was still cool. Mile after mile, Sam trudged along behind Christian. His tall, straight back became a directional for her, a beacon in the vastness of the desert. She found she was capable of losing all track of time. Glancing at her watch time and again, she realized how slowly the minutes passed when one was miserable and exhausted. She rolled the smooth pebble around in her mouth—having decided it did help—and thought about the two remaining cans of warm soda in his duffel.

The sun had reached its apex, and Christian was searching for a spot of shade where they could rest through the worst heat of the day. He was less than successful, finding only a low stand of sun-burned, leafless trees that had probably been around since the time of Christ.

"This will have to do. Take something out of that duffel and cover your head." He had already stripped off his shirt and draped it, Arab fashion, over his own head.

Following instructions, Samantha then dropped to the ground and lay down with her arm over her eyes. The thought of the wonderfully wet soda was becoming an obsession. After a few minutes she sat up, knowing her sudden movement was noticed by Christian. Working fast and furiously, she dug through her duffel and withdrew the shock blanket and the first-aid kit.

Reading her thoughts, Christian jumped to his feet, and together they carefully laid the blanket over the stunted trees, securing it at the corners with gauze bandage. Sam noted how well they worked together in an amiable silence. Once or twice their hands touched, and Samantha felt as though she'd been jolted by an electric charge. Whatever she felt for this man, it definitely was not indifference.

Settled close together in the shade they had created, they shared a few sips of the precious soda. It didn't quench their thirst, but it was wet.

They continued their march through the coolest part of the

day, when the reds and golds of the sun slanted across the ground, making long, dark shadows of every bush and rock. When the sun dipped below the horizon, and it became too dark to walk safely, they again set up camp. This time, Christian gathered the rocks to make a fire circle while Sam scrounged for dry wood.

When Sam was digging through the duffel, the unmistakable sound of metal against metal clinked.

That night they felt as though they'd feasted like kings: half a can of soda, a package of crackers, and half a can of deviled ham. The icy stars twinkled down on them, seeming friendlier than the night before.

Once again, Christian banked the fire so it would burn slowly throughout the night. Sam settled herself down, and placing her head on the duffel, she lay back and threw the thin shock blanket over her.

A moment later Christian crawled in beside her and, back to back, they drifted off to sleep.

Sometime during the night Sam awakened to find her head nestled on Christian's broad shoulder and her arm thrown carelessly over his chest. Her right leg was cradled between both of his, and he held her lightly in an embrace. It was dark, too dark to see him. The fire had almost completely gone out, and the desert night air on her face was cool in contrast to the warmth they generated beneath the blanket. But she knew somehow that Christian was not asleep. She sensed his awareness as though it were a tangible thing.

"You sleeping?" she heard him whisper. She remained silent, pretending sleep. If she admitted she was awake, she would have to move, have to take her arm from around him and take her head from his chest. She listened, hearing the thump of his heart, hearing the slow intake of his breath.

It was peaceful, so peaceful, and they cuddled together beneath the blanket as though they'd slept together for every night of their lives.

Tenderly, he turned to face her; she could feel his breath upon her cheek. Softly, softer than the night air, he grazed her cheek with his lips.

More than anything, she wanted to turn, capture his lips with her own, taste his kiss and feel his arms tighten around her. But the thought of him accusing her of seducing him, of trapping him, of making love to him and making him love her just to get her hands on his money and the Delaney empire was too great. Her humiliation would be beyond bearing.

Still feigning sleep, Samantha sighed deeply and turned over on her side, facing away from Christian. In the darkness, she squeezed her eyes shut and a single tear of regret escaped from behind her long, upswept lashes.

Christian stirred, turning toward her, snuggling close, his body pressed against hers, spoon fashion. His arm wrapped around her and she relished the comforting warmth, the gentle gesture. Long into the night, to the first break of dawn, Samantha lay quietly, determined to remember this gentle truce into the long, dark future.

Four more days passed and the quiet truce between Samantha and Christian continued. But just beneath the surface, lying like a tiger stalking its prey, were the differences between them. Samantha had surrendered the need to explain about Gemini, and Christian didn't mention it.

The Hasselblad camera she had inherited from her father became part of a game they played. During the day whenever an interesting ground formation or light study came to Samantha's attention, she stopped, took out the camera, and snapped away. She took several pictures of Christian as their journey progressed and he had come to the point where he even good-naturedly posed for her. He had sprouted a scrubby beard, and his hair was unkempt, as were his clothes. But he now sported a wonderful bronze tan that resembled newly minted copper.

Samantha herself had traded her long-sleeved khaki shirt and slacks for a brief costume of halter top and shorts for an hour or so each morning, and Christian's tan was rivaled only by her own.

The first-aid cream she had found in the kit was a wonderful protection against the drying heat of the sun as far as her face was concerned. She was determined not to return to Washington dried out like a prune, with only her hands and face kissed by the sun. She supposed she was being foolish, and Christian called her a sun worshipper, but vanity won out.

Several times when they stopped at noonday, she had entrusted her camera to Christian and he snapped pictures of her while she posed for him. They laughed that when they finally returned to D.C. and looked at the pictures, it would seem as though they had shared a vacation in the sun. Samantha fleetingly wondered if his casual statement meant that the wounds between them were healing.

Chapter Seven

Early morning stars were still visible in the sky when Christian awakened her. Dragging herself from sleep, Samantha was forced to leave the warmth of the thin blanket. While Christian went about covering the fire with loose earth, she quickly ran a brush through her hair and straightened her clothing.

"If I'm correct," Christian said, breaking the silence, "we should be out of this wilderness within the next two days. California should be right over those hills in the distance."

His words should have been encouraging; instead, they filled Sam with a sense of dread. Civilization and home didn't hold the promise she had wished for at the beginning of this adventure when the plane had gone down. Civilization and home now meant being away from Christian. Their camaraderie had developed out of a mutual dependence on one another. Once back home, that relationship would end and Christian would send her out of his life forever.

As they packed their belongings into the two duffels, Christian shook a soft-drink can experimentally, a frown creasing his face. It had taken all their willpower to refrain from emptying the can of its last few sips of liquid. The scowl on his face communicated to Samantha the seriousness of their situation. The distant hills seemed so far away, too far and too long to be without water or some other liquid to ward off total dehydration.

Glancing in her direction and realizing that he had transmitted his worst fears, Christian soothed, "Come on, now, it's not as bad as all that. We're well into the foothills now. There's bound to be a water source, no matter how small."

Samantha smiled weakly, running her tongue over cracked, dry lips. How would they ever find water in this huge, vast wilderness? The out-croppings of rock were so numerous that they could climb right past a tiny spring and never notice it. It seemed Christian wasn't going to allow her time to worry. He helped her load her duffel, slung her precious camera case over his own shoulder, and pointed her off along the trail they had been following for the past two days.

Hours passed; the sun climbed the sky in a wide, pepper-dry arc. With each hour the trek became more unbearably hot. Even the wind that stirred the dust and threw it in their faces was dry and hot. Still Christian encouraged her to go on. She knew without a doubt that without his strength she could have given up hope days ago, out beneath the burning sun, brain scorched, helpless.

When they stopped to rest later in the afternoon and when they had consumed the last of the too-sweet, flat, nevertheless wet, soda remaining in the last can, Christian pulled his navigating map out of his duffel. As he studied it for the umpteenth time, Samantha saw him look upward, searching the sky. She knew he couldn't be looking for a search plane. That possibility had already been discussed and discarded. The itinerary had been indefinite, and waiting for someone at *Daylight Magazine* to become concerned about their whereabouts and begin a search would be foolish. And deadly.

"What are you looking for, Christian?" she asked as his eyes once again scanned the bright blue sky.

"Birds."

"Birds? You...you don't mean vultures...do you?" she finished weakly.

"No, birds. They need water, too, you know, and some of the

bigger ones feed on rabbits and woodchucks, which also need water. Usually, birds roost near a water supply, and in late afternoon they usually head home.'' Even as he spoke, a clutch of high-flying figures dotted the sky.

''I've been watching them for some time. According to my map, the treeline of these foothills is just a little way off. Get it, Orion? Trees. Birds?''

''Let's go, then,'' Sam said as she struggled to her feet. ''We still have a couple of hours of daylight to search.''

''Atta girl,'' Christian praised as he helped her sling her duffel over her shoulder. ''Say a prayer and keep your eye on those birds.''

The trek had become more difficult now that their trail took them on an incline. Soon Sam was able to see a line of scrubby trees and the underbrush looked thicker, more plush, somehow. Christian kept his vigil on the sky, leading Sam upward and to the right, to the west.

By some miracle that Samantha was never able to fathom later, she found herself at the top of a rise, leaning heavily upon Christian's arm, and below her, barely visible in the thicket surrounding it, was a beautiful clear rivulet of water that reflected the sun's fading red-gold rays.

Samantha sat across from Christian, feeling better than she had in days. The tiny rivulet had quenched their thirst and had miraculously replaced itself from a water source that fed it before spilling over onto rocks and disappearing into the earth.

Handing Samantha a handkerchief that had been dipped in the water and wrung out, Christian smiled. ''Tomorrow morning, we'll follow the direction of the water. It's my guess that farther up in the hills there's a wonderful spring, and perhaps even a little waterfall.''

''You mean we might even be able to bathe?'' Samantha asked hopefully.

''That's my bet.''

When Sam fell asleep that night, before exhaustion overcame her, she dreamed of the spring and prayed for a waterfall.

In the morning, before the sun had barely skipped over the horizon, both Sam and Christian were eagerly on their way to discover the mother stream. There were times when the little river went underground and became difficult to follow. Other times, they could actually measure it growing in size.

Shortly after noon, they found it. Water. In all its glory. The sun danced over it, creating millions of shimmering lights in its dark blue depths. There was even the prayed-for waterfall, although it was only a few feet in height and was hardly more than a trickle.

"What did I tell you?" Christian laughed triumphantly. "The lady ordered a waterfall, and there it is."

"Somehow, I think I should have made my requirements more specific," Sam teased, already pulling off her shoes for the anticipated plunge into the shimmering pool.

Heedless of Christian's presence, she stripped down to her bra and bikini panties and leaped into the pool. The water was cool, actually cold, and took her breath away. After diving below the blue surface once again, she came up for air, giggling in delight.

"Do you sleep with your socks on, too?" Christian laughed, calling her attention to himself.

It was then that she saw he had already discarded his socks and boots, stripped off his shirt, and was unbuckling his pants.

"What are you doing?"

"Same as you, only with less."

Squealing with embarrassment, Samantha dove once again and came up on the far side of the pool. When she surfaced she saw that Christian was already up to his waist in the water, and the pile of clothing on the bank attested to the fact that he was naked.

"Why so embarrassed?" He laughed. "Listen, Orion, I'll make a deal with you. You wash my back and I'll wash yours."

"Ha! A likely story. You must think I'm pretty dumb to fall for a deal like that!"

Christian laughed. "Why not? Things got to be pretty nice between us out there on the desert. As a matter of fact, there were some nights there when you were pretty darned friendly."

Sam flushed. His manner was only half-teasing; his eyes were telling her something else altogether. "Christian, I expect you to behave like a gentleman. You keep to your side of the pool and I'll keep to mine."

"Talk about likely stories," he said, advancing on her. "More likely you'll take over fifty-one percent."

Staggering beneath the weight of his words, Samantha stepped backward. It had been so long since Christian had accused her of duping Gemini out of his inheritance that she had almost forgotten that the argument existed. The careless sting of his words and the decreasing distance Christian was putting between them sent a spur of panic into her chest. She stood, wading toward the far side of the pool where the water was more shallow. Beneath the sheer material of her bra, which was even more revealing when wet, Samantha's breasts were firm, and the rosy crests were erect from the coolness of the water. She saw Christian's eyes drift to them, his pleasure evidenced by his sultry look.

Still he advanced on her, closing the distance between them. In defense, not in play, she splashed him, heaving quantities of water at his head. He bent, grasping her knees, and pulled her down, the water closing over her head. Whooping for revenge, Samantha splashed and tormented him by threatening to run from the pool and steal his clothing. "Then see what kind of macho image you create running through the desert stark, staring naked!"

Laughing, Christian captured her and threatened to dip her under again. Screaming for mercy, Sam clung fiercely to him, her arms locked around his neck, her face pressed close to his.

Suddenly, it seemed as though time ceased to tick. Nothing, no one, existed in the whole world, only the two of them. Gently, he embraced her, cradling her head in one hand and supporting her back with the other. Backward, back, he dipped her and into her line of vision swept the sky and the scudding clouds. Slowly, deliberately, he bent his head, beads of water shining on his dark hair. Closer and closer his mouth came to hers.

Samantha gave her lips without reservation. She knew she would always give herself to this man, knowing with her whole heart and soul that he truly loved her. If only he would admit it—to her, to himself. She knew with that one, gentle kiss that she could never belong to another.

Christian lifted his head, questions in his silvery-gray eyes, his brows furled together over the bridge of his nose. He disengaged her arms from around his neck and stepped away from her.

"The water's getting cold," he growled, making her wonder if he was half as angry with her as he was with himself.

Late that afternoon, Samantha began to gather their freshly washed clothing from the surrounding bushes on which she had placed them to dry. She glanced over at Christian, who was busy gathering firewood with which to roast a small rabbit that he had successfully trapped earlier. When Sam had first seen the pathetic, limp little carcass before Christian skinned and dressed it, she swore she wouldn't touch a bite of it. Now, with her stomach complaining with hunger, she knew she would set her squeamishness aside.

As they had gone about their chores to make a comfortable camp for the night, there had been little communication between them. Christian seemed to be pondering his own thoughts and she was still remembering his remark about taking over of fifty-one percent of the pool. Money. Why did everything have to come down to money? *Gemini,* Sam said to herself, *you don't know what a curse that legacy has been. Why, for heaven's sake, did you do it? You must have had a reason, but for the life of me I can't think what it could have been.*

When the first stars were shining in the velvet-black sky, and the little fire was sputtering into glowing embers, Samantha rested against the rocks and patted her midsection. Much as she hated to admit it, the roasted rabbit was the best meal she could remember ever eating.

"I was afraid you'd be too squeamish to eat." The sudden sound of his voice in the still night startled her.

"Only my sensibilities are squeamish. My stomach had other ideas." She tried to keep her voice light while measuring his mood. There were times that to say Christian's moods were mercurial was an understatement.

"Orion, I've been thinking. Do you really mean what you say—that you never wanted and still don't want your inheritance of Delaney Enterprises?"

Sam's eyes widened. "Of course. I know I've never had a right to that inheritance. I still don't know why Gemini did that. It certainly had nothing to do with her feelings for you. She adored you; you know that."

"Well, I've got my own ideas about Aunt Gemini. However, if you listened closely to the terms of the will, there's an addendum to be read in the near future. Also, it forbids you to either sell your shares or to sign them away."

Now Sam's interest was definitely piqued. "I remember something to that effect."

"Now, before you go off the deep end, Orion, hear me out. If my calculations, and also my navigational skills, are correct, right over that ridge is California. If you're sincere about the inheritance, you'll marry me there. Community property laws would relieve you of twenty-five and one-half percent of Delaney Enterprises, still leaving you a rich woman, but putting the family business back into my control."

Stunned, Samantha leaped to her feet. "What are you trying to do? Test me? I've already told you I don't want it—*any* of it! Take it! Take it all!"

Christian's hands grabbed her arms painfully. "I can't take it, Orion. And you can't give it to me. You can't even sell it to me. This is the only way."

Samantha looked up into his face. There was a shadow in his eyes, a shadow she was certain wasn't created by the moonlight. There was an urgency in his voice she had never heard there before, and as the full reality of his proposal dawned on her, she thought her heart would break. Marry him? She would have cheerfully followed him to the end of the earth just to hear him say he loved her. Now, the thing she had wanted most ever since the first moment she had set her eyes on Christian Delaney had been made a mockery. A sham. Lowering her head so he couldn't read the pain in her eyes, she nodded, unable to hold back the biting words that she threw up in defense of her emotions. "As you say, I'd still be a rich woman. I'll go to sleep tonight dreaming of how I'll spend all that money—if we ever get out of this predicament alive, that is." Even to her own ears, her voice was dead sounding and unconvincing.

"Oh, we'll get out of this alive, all right," Christian said positively. "Come over here. I want to show you something." Unceremoniously, he led her to the top of the rise where he had been gathering firewood. Off in the distance, in the direction he was pointing, he told her to watch. After what seemed an endless moment, a sharp light appeared in the distance and swept across the horizon.

Not comprehending what she was seeing, Sam looked baffled.

"It's the highway, Orion. It's the road back to civilization!"

That night, while Christian slept, Samantha lay awake, huge silent tears dropping onto her cheeks.

Chapter Eight

Los Angeles Airport was a hub of confusion, and Samantha followed closely behind her new husband as they struggled through the crowd of businessmen and tourists. The confusion surrounding her was insignificant compared to the bewilderment she was feeling. So much had happened in the past three days that she believed she would never again gain a firm grip on reality.

Christian led her to a seat near Gate 53, where they would board their plane taking them back to Washington, D.C., and then murmured something about picking up a few magazines.

As he walked away, Samantha sat amidst the flurry of arrivals and departures as she reflected over the events that had led to her becoming Mrs. Christian Delaney. After trekking out of the hills and hitching a ride on the highway, they had found themselves in the little California town of Primo. While she had sat by, Christian had called the offices of *Daylight Magazine* and made several other quick phone calls. A quick shopping trip through Primo's minuscule business district and then a visit to the City Hall where they applied for their marriage license. Then Christian had taken her to the town's medical clinic, where she had stayed for rest and treatment from their desert ordeal. That was the last she had seen of Christian until he had checked her out of the clinic and then taken her to the magistrate's office, where they were married. Next was a chartered plane flight to Los Angeles and the airport.

A rapid machine-gun fire of events that were fuddled and baffling had brought her to the here and now. Mrs. Christian Delaney. A marriage of convenience. A marriage to prove that she wasn't the gold digger he accused her of being. A marriage that was a sham.

Aboard the jetliner that would take them back east, Samantha watched Christian and she saw that it wasn't until they were airborne that he relaxed. She hadn't realized just how uptight he had been. And he looked so tired. Drawn and fatigued. Suddenly, she wanted to cradle his head to her breast and whisper comforting words. She wanted to tell him she loved him and please not to contemplate divorce once they were back in Washington.

If sleep were the order of the day, she might as well do as Christian was doing. She slept fitfully, her dreams invaded by Christian Delaney chasing her across the desert. His sun-bronzed face was contorted in rage as he shouted angry words at her. Tripping and falling, she raced through the sand, screaming and yelling, begging him to believe her. *Let me explain!* she shouted over and over. *At least hear me out!* He was gaining on her, faster, faster. Her heart thundered as she fell in the sand, unable to get to her feet to escape him. *You don't understand. I had nothing to do with Gemini's will! I didn't even know about it. Listen to me! Why won't you believe me? Please, please love me!*

Samantha shuddered and woke up to see Christian leaning over her, a strange look on his weary face. "You were having a nightmare," he explained.

She felt disoriented, shaken, remembering the vivid dream. Had she cried out? "I'm sorry if I woke you up," she said quietly, trying to fathom the expression in his eyes.

"You didn't wake me up. Are you all right now?"

Was that concern she heard in his voice? Instead of answering him, she closed her eyes again, feigning sleep. From beneath her

heavily fringed lashes, she watched as he settled himself in the
seat. She had never actually seen a man's shoulders slump before, indicative of defeat. She must be wrong, she told herself.
It was merely fatigue. Men like Christian Delaney were never
defeated.

Now that she was married, her life was bound to be different
somehow. Even though her marriage would never be consum-
mated. Even though it would quickly end with divorce. When
they arrived back in Washington, she would go her way and he
would go his. Lawyers would handle everything. There would
be no chance meetings, no pounding hearts, no tears for what
might have been.

In the *Daylight Magazine* offices the marriage between Christian Delaney and resident photographer Orion was completely
misinterpreted and met with overwhelming good wishes and con-
gratulatory handshakes. Neither Christian nor Samantha explained that the real reason behind the marriage was to relieve
Samantha of the twenty-five and one-half percent of Delaney
stock in order to return a controlling interest to the publisher.

Sam deduced that Christian must have made the announcement of their nuptials by phone from California because Lizzy
and Charlie seemed to have planned the whole shebang. There
were canapés and champagne and well wishes all around. When
a toast was made to the new bride and groom, Christian pleased
his staff by planting a kiss on Samantha's lips.

It was with relief that Sam noticed Charlie pull Christian away
from the festivities on urgent office business. Seizing the opportunity to escape the festivities, Sam gathered up her camera case
and slung it over her shoulder. It was time to go home. She
frowned. Where exactly was home? Home was the basement
apartment next door to Gemini's where she paid the rent. And
then she must make arrangements to have the cats returned to
her. They were, after all, still her responsibility until the respec-
tive attorneys settled the question of their custody.

Sam laid the camera case on the nearest chair. How could she
have forgotten? Christian Delaney said she was fired. That meant

she had to clean out her desk and take her belongings with her. She might as well do it now and be done with it. This way she wouldn't have to make another trip back to the office and chance a stray meeting with her publisher husband. It would be clean and quick. Forget all those brave, indignant things she had said and thought about on the long plane ride home. If he didn't want her working for his company, she wouldn't. The day would never come when she would force herself on an employer or a man. The fifty-one percent could rot for all she cared. For now, all she wanted was to pick up the pieces of her life and get on with it the best way she knew how.

Her task took all of ten minutes. She would have to hurry or the taxi would leave without her. Two manila envelopes full of pictures, a spare makeup case, and her camera under her arms, she left the tiny cubbyhole that had been her short-lived office. She didn't look back; she couldn't.

Inside her own small apartment she very carefully locked the door, shot the dead bolt, and then slid the chain into place. Even a SWAT team couldn't break down this door with its grille over the paned glass. She was safe. But who was she safe from? Christian Delaney?

Sam walked around the small apartment, touching this and that. Her personal things that she had left behind held meaning only for her. Something was bothering her, and then it hit full force. She really was stupid. Coming back to this apartment was the most stupid thing she could have done. Hadn't he told her that he was taking over Gemini's apartment? Right now, this very minute, he could be upstairs. Her heart began its wild fluttering. Why had she done such a stupid thing? *Because,* a niggling voice said quietly, subconsciously, *you knew he would be there and you wanted to be as close to him as possible.*

Dejectedly, Sam sat down on the sofa and let the tears flow. It was true. She did want to be near Christian, in the hopes that he would come to her and say the past was past and he did truly love her. Would she ever hear him say those words to her?

Panicking with the turn her thoughts were taking, Sam looked around for something to do. The cats. A quick call placed to the vet's and the cats would find their way home in a taxi. Then a shower—a long, cold shower. And an aspirin. Two of them!

An hour later the cats, Gin and Tonic, were stretched out under the cocktail table. "I really feel sorry for you guys, the way you've been shifted from pillar to post. I have some chicken livers in the freezer along with a few gizzards. And I'm going to cook them for you right now. Now that I'm a married lady, I suddenly feel very domestic." Gin nipped at Tonic, who, in turn, snarled his revenge by way of a clout with his paw on Gin's head. Gin's back arched and he spat his anger, which Tonic ignored. "Go to it, guys. Get it out of your system, because you aren't getting high on me. This is a dry house as far as you're concerned."

Sam added a few onions and a little salt and pepper to the livers and gizzards and decided they would be wasted on the cats; besides, she was hungry herself. She quickly plucked a package of cat food from beneath the sink and filled two small bowls. She poured milk into a medium-sized dish and added a drop of rum flavoring as an inducement and then whistled for the cats. As always, they ignored her. "So starve," she muttered, spooning the chicken livers and gizzards onto a dinner plate.

The hours crawled by, and to Sam's disgust there was no visit or even a phone call from Christian Delaney. The least he could have done was make some sort of overture so she could reject him. This should have been her honeymoon. She was spending her honeymoon with two reformed alcoholic cats. "This is the pits," she snapped at the cats as she crawled into bed.

The first thing she did the following morning was call the Women's Bank to ask an officer to recommend a woman attorney. She scribbled down the number and called for an appointment. She circled a date a week into the future and then stared at the calendar.

She should start thinking about her future and what she was going to do. Should she take a trip to the unemployment office? Was she fired or had she quit? And what about the name change? Already she was getting a headache and it was only mid-morning. She had to do something constructive like shower and dress. Then she'd make a trip to the market for some food and stop at the post office to pick up her mail. She would buy a few newspapers and see what the job market was offering for un-employed photographers. That should take care of her time till early afternoon. Then she could do some laundry, prepare a little dinner, watch some television, and go to bed. ''Some honey-moon,'' she grimaced. Was she really legally married?

Sam completed her errands and was back in front of the tele-vision screen in time to catch the four-thirty movie. A Chinese TV dinner was heating in the oven. The cats were napping con-tentedly. She kicked off her shoes and propped her slim ankles on the edge of the cocktail table as she sorted through the mail. A sale flyer from Woody's, an American Express bill, the utility bill, scads of letters addressed to Occupant or Resident, and a legal-looking letter from Gemini's lawyer. The most important first. She decided she could live with owing American Express $123.46. She would have to pass up Woody's sale and write out a check for the utility company or have her power cut off. The stiff, crackling, legal paper informed her that she was to be in the attorney's office on Monday, the seventeenth, for the reading of the addendum to Gemini's will. The meeting was to take place at ten-thirty in the morning. Did she have to go? Probably not, she answered herself. After all, she was engaging her own at-torney to handle matters. Still, perhaps she should go so that when she met with her private lawyer she would have more knowledge about the current state of affairs. She would go and demand copies of everything in triplicate. Gemini had always said to get everything in triplicate. They can fool you once, even twice, but three times? That was another story. She wouldn't sign anything unless it was in triplicate.

Sam stared at the sleeping cats and then her eye fell on the silent phone. Why couldn't it ring? Why couldn't Christian call her to see if she was all right? New husbands shouldn't be so…blasé about…about their wives.

The timer on the stove buzzed. The TV dinner was done. She peeled back the foil from the tray and stared at the messy-looking concoction. Yuk! She couldn't eat this…this mess. She had to eat something. The refrigerator yielded little in the way of food: a mushy apple, some cheese that was stiff and hard around the edges, and some grape jam. She should have bought real food when she stopped by the neighborhood deli. A stale breadstick in the breadbox did nothing to enhance her appetite. She was back to square one and the TV dinner. Morosely, she picked at the steamy, stringy chow mein and chewed on the barely visible rubbery shrimp.

It took her less than five minutes to straighten out the kitchen and replenish the cats' dishes with canned milk. Listlessly, she walked back to the living room and the noisy television. Whatever Woody Allen was doing, it must be funny. She decided if the Allen movie couldn't distract her, nothing could. Irritably, she switched off the set.

Time was laying heavily on her hands. Samantha needed to interest herself in something, yet she admitted that she found she would pause, stand stock-still, and listen for some movement upstairs—footsteps, the clatter of a pot, something that would tell her Christian was upstairs in Gemini's apartment. She fully realized the need to feel close to him.

As she wandered through her apartment, she entered the spare bedroom where she had spent so many hours working on Christian's portrait. She would probably never finish it now. How could she? Every line of his face had become dear to her. She would have tried to breathe life into that painting, wishing it could become the man she had come to know so well.

Her lazy gaze fell on the camera and gadget bag, the same ones she had carried through the desert. Suddenly spurred to action, she hefted the bag and carried it to the portion of the spare bedroom off the bathroom where she had set up a darkroom. Her blood tingled and her interest sparked. The film, the pictures that she and Christian had snapped of one another throughout their time in the Southwest.

Working quickly, but deftly and untiringly, she developed the twelve rolls of film that held the memories and images of those seemingly long-ago days when Christian had been within reach of her fingertips.

The long strips of positives and negatives hung from a make-shift clothesline to dry. Finally, admitting her exhaustion, she crept to her bed, to sleep, to dream, to relive her adventure with the man she loved. She had worked blindly, her hands going through the motions. She hadn't dared to pause and dwell on the pictures developing before her eyes. She had to sleep, and that wouldn't be possible if she studied the photographs. The memory was too fresh, too new. Soon, hopefully, she would be strong enough to look at them, cherish them. But for now, she would escape her pain and sleep.

When the phone rang shortly after noon the next day, it sounded like an alarm. Sam stared at the phone a moment before she realized it wasn't ringing. The alarming sound had been the doorbell. Was it Christian? If it was, what was she going to say to him? What was there to say? Nothing, she grimaced as she released the chain and slid the dead bolt. Before she opened the door, she asked, "Who is it?"

"Barbara Matthews from the *Post.* I'd like to talk to you, Mrs. Delaney."

Mrs. Delaney! She was Mrs. Delaney. "Why?" Sam demanded through the door.

"I think my readers might be interested in your new marriage to one of the most eligible bachelors in the country. I want to do it for the Sunday section. I'll only take up an hour of your time."

How could she refuse? She knew how hard journalists worked and how difficult it was sometimes to fill space. Why not? What did she have to lose? Sam opened the door to admit a vivacious, sparkling redhead who was at first glance a sizzling size three. Sam hated her on sight. "Come in," she said graciously. She motioned for the petite reporter to sit on the sofa and then sat down across from her in a shabby leather chair.

Barbara settled herself comfortably and flipped her notebook to a clean page. "I'll ask the questions, and if you have something you want to interject, feel free to interrupt me. First of all,'' she said in a lilting, musical voice, "tell me, how does it feel to be Mrs. Christian Delaney?"

This was a mistake. She must have been out of her mind to agree to this interview. "Well…I…it's…"

"There's no way to describe it, right?" Barbara said, making squiggly marks on her pad. "My readers will understand that. All that money! You'll be able to go anywhere, do anything. How have you handled that?"

What's to handle? Sam thought huffily. "I personally think…actually…you see…"

"It's mind-boggling. I understand, and my readers will certainly relate to that. Wishful thinking, if you know what I mean. How do you think you'll like having servants to wait on you and cater to your every need? You *were* a working girl like the rest of us."

"I've always been…been rather in-independent and…"

"You'll handle it like you were born to it, right? Good, good answer; my readers will identify. Now, tell me,'' Barbara said, leaning over and whispering confidentially, "is he as romantic as the tabloids make him out to be? Does he really have steely eyes that can cut you to ribbons, or do they go all soft and melting, making your head swoon?"

"That's…that's a…a fair…"

"I knew I was right, I just knew it!" Barbara chortled, making a quick row of scratches on her pad. "He'd make a perfect Adonis!" she all but squealed. "Gifts. Has your new husband showered you with gifts yet?"

"Well, actually…you see, it's been such a short…what I mean is…"

"You don't have to say another word. I understand perfectly. He'll do the showering when you leave for your honeymoon. By the way, where is that to take place?" the reporter inquired.

Would the reporter believe her if she told her she was honeymooning alone? Not likely. Sam flushed a bright crimson. "I don't think Chris… Listen, you don't understand. I really shouldn't be talking to you. You've got it all wrong…"

"But of course, I understand. It's a secret, right? I don't blame you for one minute. It's just that my poor readers are so starved for romance that they eat this sort of thing right up and beg for more. I'm sure a round-the-world cruise is not out of the question, right?"

"Right," Sam squealed. She had to get this girl out of here before she suffered a nervous breakdown.

Barbara Matthews coughed to clear her throat. Holding her hand over her mouth, she complained, "Too much talking. Gets me right here." She coughed again.

"Can I offer you something? A drink? Coffee?"

"I would like a drink if you don't mind. Bourbon, straight up," she said firmly.

That was good. No ice in the drink. The cats would continue to sleep. Once they heard the clink of ice or the opening of a bottle, it would be all over. Deftly, Sam poured the bourbon into a squat glass, one eye on the snoozing cats. She extended the drink to her guest and let her breath out in a deep sigh. The cats hadn't noticed.

The petite Miss Matthews downed her drink neatly and immediately asked another question. "Now, Mrs. Delaney, for the record and for my more liberated readers, tell me what you're going to do about your job. Do you plan to continue with your work, or are you going to become, how shall I say it"—she pursed her mouth, seeking the right word and finally came up with it—"domesticated?"

I wonder what she would think if I told her I'm applying for unemployment compensation tomorrow? Sam mused. "I haven't decided exactly…I think what I'll do is…"

"Play the housewife bit for a while. Perfectly understandable. I'd do the same thing myself. Children…what about children? Do you see any in your immediate future?"

Sam's neck was beginning to perspire. "At least a dozen," she said bluntly.

Barbara Matthews scribbled furiously. "Mrs. Delaney, when can I meet Mr. Delaney? I would like a few good quotes from him. I guess he isn't home from the office yet. I really have to get back to my paper and get started on this. Listen, what do you say we fudge a little?''

Sam blinked, not quite understanding what the reporter meant.

Barbara Matthews continued. ''What I mean is, if I were to ask Mr. Delaney if he was madly in love with you, he would naturally say yes, right? And if I asked him if he was going to show you the world and shower you with presents, he'd tell me yes to that, too. So, why don't I just say that and this way I won't have to hang around and wait for him and spoil your evening? By the way, why are you still here? Oh, never mind. I know, you're getting a few things together. Sometimes,'' she said, throwing her hands in the air, ''I get so flighty, I don't know what I'm doing. But don't you worry about a thing. I'm really going to knock myself out on this interview. Did you by any chance see the piece I did on the two pandas at the zoo?''

''No, I guess I missed it,'' Sam said defensively.

''Not to worry. I'll send you a copy. Say, would you mind if I used your powder room?''

''No...no...it's right through there.'' Sam pointed. Anything, anything at all to be rid of this woman.

Barbara Matthews went into the bathroom through the spare bedroom and Sam tapped her fingertips impatiently on the arm of the chair. Her eye fell on the empty glass that had held the bourbon the reporter had downed in one gulp. Quickly, she picked up the glass and brought it out to the kitchen before the girl could suggest another drink to whet her whistle. Sam wanted Miss Matthews out of her apartment—as soon as possible!

When Sam returned to the living room, she had expected to find the reporter waiting for her. Instead, after a few minutes, Miss Matthews exited from the spare bedroom. Somehow, imperceptibly, her attitude was altered.

''Thank you so much for your time, Mrs. Delaney.'' She winked slyly. ''I do so envy you. You really did snare yourself some hunk. Every woman in the country is going to hate you with a passion for taking Christian Delaney out of circulation.'' If anything, Barbara Matthews' speech was even more rapid than before. For some reason, Sam felt that the reporter wanted to leave the apartment even more desperately than she wanted to be rid of her.

"Don't you worry about being envied, Mrs. Delaney," the reporter chattered while she slipped into her coat. "You just take it in your stride. Once the women of America get to know you as I have, they'll all take you to their hearts. 'Poor little working girl marries super-rich tycoon.' I'm going to do a fabulous piece of work on this one. Thanks again and much happiness." The girl literally lunged for the door. In the space of an instant, she was gone.

Samantha leaned against the door. What in the world was going on here? A dizzy reporter from the *Post* shows up and harasses her into an interview and then takes off out of the apartment as though the hounds of hell were on her heels.

Chapter Nine

Three days passed without Christian Delaney getting in touch with her. Sam sat down on the couch, her mind racing. Today was Sunday; tomorrow was the reading of the addendum to the will. Today was also the day the article Barbara Matthews was working on would appear in the special section of the Sunday paper.

Sam glanced at her watch. She had all day to get through before her meeting tomorrow at the attorney's office. Tomorrow she would see Christian. Still, she had to get through the rest of the day. The zoo! She would go to the zoo and see the pandas herself. She would stop at the deli and ask them to pack her up a picnic lunch, and she would spend the day wandering around the zoo. No decisions to be made today. Tomorrow it would be all over.

Donning warm clothing, Sam left the apartment, stopping at the deli for her lunch and a copy of the Sunday paper. Her eye fell on the left hand corner of the newspaper and a square box with a Santa climbing down a chimney. It was a reminder that there were only eight more shopping days till Christmas. Sam was appalled. Eight days! Where had the time gone?

Her purchases intact, Sam left the corner store and walked up Woodley Road on her way to the zoo.

She tramped through the zoo, getting colder by the minute. Lately, it seemed that all she did was make mistakes. She really didn't feel like roaming around looking at animals in cages. She admitted that the steamy, smelly birdhouse would do nothing for her except possibly curb her appetite. It was only three-thirty, but it would be dark soon. And if she wasn't mistaken, it felt like snow. A sudden wind whipped up, blowing her coat collar high around her neck. Sam clutched at it and buttoned the toggle securely and huddled down into the warmth the heavy coat provided. She wished she had a hat, something to keep her ears warm.

Sam started the uphill climb to the exit, holding on to the iron rail. She raised her head slightly as she felt something wet hit her nose. It was snowing. How she loved the first snowfall of the year! She might as well go home now. She hitched the heavy Sunday paper and her paper bag, holding the lunch she hadn't gotten around to eating, more firmly under her arm. Small children laughing and giggling raced ahead of her as the giant clock at the entrance sounded the time. She smiled as she listened to the tune. The wind was stronger now and the snow seemed to be falling a bit more heavily. She was surprised to see a soft carpet of the white stuff covering the ground already. And she had been oblivious to it all afternoon. It certainly didn't say much for her state of mind.

Inside her snug apartment Sam dropped the soggy Sunday newspaper onto the cocktail table and removed her coat. She'd make herself some soup and have crackers with it for dinner, take a warm bath, and then read the paper. After that she would sort out her thoughts and make plans for what she was going to do with the rest of her life after her visit to Gemini's lawyer tomorrow. There were no two ways about it; she had to get on with her life, without or with Christian Delaney.

Her light dinner finished, her bath completed, Sam powdered herself lavishly with Esther's last birthday present to her—Zen bath powder. She wrinkled her nose appreciatively; she loved the sweet, intoxicating scent. She slipped into a scarlet velour robe and tied the sash.

Wind whistled outside the grilled windows and Sam shivered. The small bedroom was drafty. Her eyes traveled to the free-standing fireplace in the corner of the bedroom, the main reason she had rented the apartment from Gemini. A quick-burning Duraflame log and she was set. Was it her imagination, or did she feel warmer already? Power of suggestion, she mused.

Settling herself comfortably beneath the floral comforter, Sam snuggled back against a mound of pillows. She felt rather like a bird in a nest. Deftly, she tossed aside the first three sections of the heavy, wet newspaper and searched for Barbara Matthews' article. She found it on page two of the Living section.

What she saw shocked her as though she'd stuck her finger in an electrical socket. Pictures! Her pictures! The pictures she and Christian had taken of one another with her father's Hasselblad during their trek in the desert!

Throwing back the comforter, stumbling on it as it caught around her legs, she leaped for the spare bedroom. Those were *her* pictures! The ones she had developed and had left hanging from the clothesline in the darkroom. How…how had Barbara Matthews gotten her hands on them?

Switching on the light in the spare bedroom, her eyes first fell on the easel holding Christian's portrait and saw it was still covered with the paint-stained old sheet she had thrown over it. Almost fearfully, hoping against hope, she looked toward the end of the room where she had created the darkroom. The long strips of negatives still hung there, but the positives were gone. And she knew who had taken them!

"No, no, no!" she heard herself cry aloud as she rushed over to them. Quickly examining them, she saw with her own eyes the figures in the negatives were one and the same with the pictures in the Sunday paper.

Her mind snapped back to Barbara Matthews' visit. The reporter must have taken them when Samantha had allowed her to use the bathroom. That was why she had seemed in such a hurry to get out of the apartment.

Samantha felt her knees buckle under her. It was a dirty, low-down trick. But there was no help for it now. The damage had been done. Christian would either see the article or, at the very least, hear about it. Whatever, the end result would be the same. He would think she had maliciously offered the snapshots to the reporter, and he would hate her with a passion!

In a flurry of panic, Samantha rushed back to where she had dropped the paper. She was compelled to read it, to examine the photos. Somewhere in the article they would have to give credit for the photos. Somehow, she felt she couldn't believe what was happening to her until she saw her name in print. It was just a bad dream, she repeated over and over in her mind.

Diving for the paper, her eyes tried to take it all in at once. Disciplining her attention, she slowed and looked more carefully. Christian would think she had selected them to make him appear foolish. There was one of him looking over his shoulder at the camera, a silly wink and a silly smile on his face. Another taken by an outcropping of rocks…sitting beside the campfire…and one in which they had used the delayed timing and both were in the shot together, sitting close, the campfire casting shadows and light on their features and making them look incredibly romantic. There were eleven photos, each more compromising than the one before.

Sam's eyes raked the column of print. It appeared the reporter was big on pictures and small on words. Sam's eyes widened as she read the text and she gasped. She had said no such things!

Good heavens! Where had the reporter gotten such an idea? This was beyond belief! People were actually going to read this and believe it! Correction: it was an early edition of the paper; people had already read it. Christian must have seen it. Oh, no! She whimpered into the pillow. She would sue; that's what she would do, the first thing in the morning. It must be libelous; it had to be. She hadn't said anything like this. Where did that stupid reporter get such ideas? She would never be able to face Christian Delaney again. This couldn't be happening to her; it just couldn't. A bright flush stained her fresh-scrubbed face. Even her ears felt hot. She felt ashamed, mortified, and darned indignant. Tears welled in her eyes at her predicament. Now, what was she going to do?

The blue-white flame from the fireplace blurred her vision as she stared into the flickering flames. She had to do something about a rebuttal. A letter—she would write a letter to the paper and one to Christian Delaney denying...denying what? She had to get her thoughts together and think this through, and she had to do it before the meeting tomorrow morning.

Sam tossed back the covers and walked over to the shuttered window. She opened the louvers and stared at the whiteness beyond the pane of glass. It looked like a winter wonderland in the mellow glow of the streetlight. The wind was strong and she could hear it shrieking in the trees near the curb as the branches dripped and swayed with their mantle of whiteness. It had been a long time since she had seen snow like this in Washington. It would be a white Christmas, after all. The thought depressed her.

The slim girl shivered in the draft from the window. She closed the louvers and looked longingly at the warm bed she had just left. A cup of tea would do her good right now, she decided, and she really should also change the litter box. It would give her something to do while she thought about the interview in the Sunday paper.

Sam had just tossed the tea bag into the trash container when the doorbell sounded. She frowned and looked at the kitchen clock. It was eight-fifty. Who could be visiting her on such a night? She walked hesitantly to the front door and peeked through the tiny peephole. Christian Delaney! Sam swallowed hard. What did he want? The doorbell chimed a second time. He had read the paper! Oh, no! She swallowed again and released the chain. Her shaking hands slid the dead bolt and then the regular lock. She moistened her dry lips and swung open the door, her face impassive. "Yes?" she asked quietly.

"May I come in? It's rather blustery out here, as you can see." Sam said nothing but stood aside for him to enter. She watched as he shook the snow from his tweed jacket and brushed at his hair. She was surprised that he wore no overcoat, then remembered that he only had to come from as far away as next door, which meant walking down two flights of stairs. She closed the door but made no move toward the living room. She waited, her heart pounding in her chest. Suddenly, she was aware, acutely aware, of her shiny scrubbed face with its layer of cold cream and even more acutely aware of her naked body beneath the scarlet robe.

Christian Delaney stared at her and then walked into the living room. She had to follow him if she wanted to find out what he wanted. She waited till he sat down on the sofa and then she perched herself on the arm of the wing chair across from him. Still, she said nothing, waiting to see why he was here.

"I came to congratulate you on the article in the *Post*. I had no idea that you were so...so articulate or that you cared so much." Sam felt a chill wash over her at the sarcastic tone. Would he believe her if she explained? And why did she have to explain? Let him believe whatever he wanted. She shrugged and remained mute. Christian frowned.

"Did you read the article?" he asked nonchalantly. Sam nodded. "I was more than a little surprised to see the photographs. Somehow, I hadn't expected you would sell them to the *Post*. *Time* would have been my guess." His voice was quiet, dangerously quiet, and his face betrayed no hint of what he was truly feeling. If anything, he seemed faintly amused.

"I...I didn't sell them..."

"No? Foolish girl. *Time* would have paid you a small fortune for them. Oh, that's right, I almost forgot." He snapped his fingers. "You don't need money, do you? Not with what Aunt Gemini left you. So, why did you do it? Spite?"

"No, you don't understand. I developed those photos the other night, and when that reporter asked to use the bathroom... Oh, what's the use? You'll never believe she stole them."

"Try me," he said, a strange, soft note coming into his voice. His silvery gaze penetrated her, beseeching her to make him believe her.

"It's just as I told you. I let her use the bathroom. She went in through the spare bedroom. I never thought..." Samantha drew herself to full height and squared her shoulders. "Barbara Matthews *stole* those photos from this apartment! That is the truth. I would never, could never, be so low-down as to publish them. They were ours, Christian." A sob rose in her throat. "They belonged to us, and I'm angrier than a hornet to think that they've been made public!''

Christian moved close to her, making her dizzy with his mere presence. "At one time in the desert you threatened to publish the photos.''

"I'd never do it. It was only a threat. I wanted to rile you.''

"That you did, most successfully.'' A slow smile crept onto his face, softening his features and bringing humor to his mysterious silver-gray eyes. "The one I liked best was the one of you with your shirt wrapped around your head. And that silly one of you washing our clothes in the spring like an old Indian woman.'' He laughed, relaxing, believing her.

"It would be nice if you offered me a drink—a celebration, so to speak.''

If she fixed him a drink, she would have to move, and she knew her shaking legs and trembling hands would give away her emotions. "Help yourself,'' she said, motioning to the small cabinet holding the liquor. Christian stared at her a moment, then rose to make his own drink. He carried a bottle of liquor and a glass to the cocktail table and set them down. He frowned a second time as he removed the cap from the vodka and poured a drink. "Ice would be nice,'' he said quietly.

Sam blinked. Both cats were on the cocktail table in a second, clawing and spitting in their quest for the liquor. "Stop them!'' Sam screeched. "Don't let them have any liquor! I'm drying them out!'' Feverishly, she reached for Gin, who leaped out of her way and landed on Christian's lap, clawing at his jacket. "Now, look what you've done!'' Sam cried as she tried to wipe up the spilled liquor with the hem of her robe, revealing a shapely, satiny leg and thigh.

"What the…?'' Christian sputtered as he saw the vodka bottle topple as Gin fought Tonic for the aromatic spirits.

"Do you know what you just did? Why couldn't you pour the drink over the cabinet? Oh, no, you had to bring it over here, and now see what happened? I've had those cats on the wagon for a long time, and you just undid all my good work. Well, they're your responsibility now, and you can just take them with you when you leave here. They're all yours," Sam said angrily.

"The least you could do is help me clean it up." Frantically, she ran to the kitchen for a dish cloth and tried to wipe up the spilled liquor. Once her eyes met Christian's as she mopped at the table. The scarlet robe had parted and an expanse of creamy bosom was visible to his sleepy, silvery gaze. Hastily, she dropped the cloth and drew the robe tighter around her. A dull flush worked its way up her throat and into her cheeks.

"I'm sorry," Christian said huskily. "I had no idea the cats were still boozing it up. You should have warned me. I can see now that we have to do something about them."

"Not we! *You* have to do something about them! I'm giving them back to you—now!" Deftly, she scooped up the drunken cats and placed them in their basket. "Here's your cats and there's the door."

Christian grinned. "Would you really turn me and those poor, defenseless cats out on a night like this? According to that article I read today, you are a hopeless romantic. I refuse to leave!" he said adamantly.

"Well, you aren't staying here," Sam shot back.

"Of course I am. We're married, and those cats are both our responsibilities. I think," he said, grinning widely, "the best thing to do right now is let them sleep it off, and we should turn in ourselves."

Sam blanched. "As far as *I'm* concerned, we're not married! The whole idea was to legally transfer the Delaney stock to you. A marriage of convenience."

"You told the whole world, via the *Post,* that we were married and wanted dozens of children. I'm here to make that wish come true. In the eyes of the *Washington Post,* we're married, and that's good enough for me," he said in an amused voice. "Are you ready?"

Sam pretended ignorance. "Ready for what?" As if she didn't know. One moment she was spitting and hissing at him with her eyes, and the next she was pinned in his strong arms. He held her firmly, diminishing her struggles and overpowering her gasped objections. His lips were on the soft skin beneath her ear; his face was buried in the soft curls that clung to her neck. Insistent, persuasive, his mouth explored her skin, finding and pursuing the pleasure points that sent shudders through her body and made her weak. In spite of herself, Samantha clung to him, relishing this one heady moment, expecting it to be ripped away from her, leaving her bereft and alone and missing him.

Tenderly, he held her head in his hands, lifting her face for his kiss, touching her lips with his in a way that was both familiar and exciting. His hands traveled the length of her body, molding it and pressing it closer to his. She strained toward him, allowing him to hold her this way, loving it, loving him. Softly, so softly that at first she thought she imagined it, his voice rumbled deep in his chest and he whispered her name, "Samantha." A whisper so soft, so poignant, it fed the fires of her desire and echoed in her heart. Again, he whispered her name, telling her the things that lovers say, whispering them for her, words she had given up all hope of ever hearing from Christian.

He gathered her up in his arms, carrying her to the bedroom, taking her from the light into the dark, taking her with him into a world filled with the sound of his voice and the feel of his arms. A safe world, a place where his arms sheltered her and his lips worshipped her. Together they tumbled down the endless corridors created by their love. Together they found the hidden springs of their desires and the gardens of trust and belonging.

Christian was tender; he was forceful. He was all things for all times, and she responded to him, loving him, knowing that he loved her. He made her his own; he turned back the pages of her girlhood and introduced her to the fulfilled future of a woman. And always, he loved her.

For a thousand times his lips touched hers. For an eternity his hands possessed her. He touched her body and evoked an answering cry in her soul. Her heart belonged to Christian, for now, forever. And later, a short eternity later, when the fire had died down to low embers and lit the room with a faint orange glow, it was Christian who looked down at her with wonder in his eyes, softening their silvery hardness to molten pewter. And when he spoke, it was to whisper her name.

Chapter Ten

Sam woke up slowly, a feeling of contentment in every pore of her body. A slow, happy smile worked its way around the corners of her mouth. It wasn't a dream. It had been real, every single minute of the long night. She stretched luxuriously, deliberately postponing the moment when she would open her eyes and then touch her husband, lying beside her. She wanted to savor each second until she could no longer struggle against the need to feel his warm, hard body against hers. She couldn't stand it another moment. Squeezing her eyes tighter, she reached out and groped beneath the covers. A sinking feeling settled in her stomach. He was gone! "Christian!" she cried softly, thinking he was in the bathroom. There was no answer.

A sob gathered in her throat as she rolled over on the bed and pummeled the pillows with clenched hands. He was gone. How could he do this to her? How could he go off and leave her without saying something? Anything, even a goodbye, would be better than waking up with this cold, dead feeling. "I hate him! I hate him!" she cried, over and over, as tears soaked the pillow beneath her face, feeling used and foolish.

Crying and making herself sick wasn't going to help. She had to get up and shower. A note. Perhaps he didn't want to wake her up and had left a note. He was considerate. Surely, he had left a note. There was nothing.

Her tears long dried, she sat on the sofa, and it wasn't until both cats staggered to the cocktail table and began licking at the sticky surface that anger rose in her, threatening to choke the life from her body. He had left the cats! Just who did he think he was, barging into her apartment and giving the cats liquor and plying her with soft words and taking her to bed to exercise his matrimonial rights? And she had let him! What a fool she was! Now, she had to go to the lawyer's office and face him.

Sam managed somehow to get through her morning ritual of showering and dressing by habit. Everything she did was automatic, with no thought beyond the moment and what she was doing.

Opening the drapes, she was stunned to see the monstrous accumulation of snow that greeted her gaze. It was a known fact that the District of Columbia fell apart when snow had the audacity to accumulate more than an inch. This looked to her unpracticed eyes like a good eight inches. There would be no buses, and cabs would be at a premium. If she wanted to reach the lawyer's office, she would have to walk. And she would have to start out as soon as possible if she wanted to make the appointment any way near on time.

Sam rummaged in her closet for a heavy sheepskin jacket and also dug out a fur-lined hat from a box in the corner. Bright orange mittens, a gift from Norma Jean back in college days, completed her outfit. She looked down at her serviceable boots and prayed that the manufacturer's label proclaiming them to be waterproof was accurate.

If she hadn't been so miserable, she would have enjoyed her trek to the lawyer's office. People were scattered everywhere, cheerfully digging out cars and helping one another as playful children pelted one and all with snowballs that dissolved on impact. She trudged on, dodging the flying snowballs, careful to watch her footing. If there was one thing she didn't need, it was a broken bone of any kind.

Exactly one hour and forty minutes later she stomped her way into the lobby of the law offices. The blast of warm air made her blink and wish she was back outside in the clear brisk air. Shaking the snow from her jacket, she walked to the elevator and waited.

The ferns were still intact, as was the smell of lemon polish on the furniture. It was still as dry and dusty as before. Sam wrinkled her nose, fighting off a sneeze. She looked around and was surprised to see a handsome young man advance in her direction. He held out his hand and smiled. "David Carpenter. You must be Samantha Blakely. Follow me. I'll be conducting this meeting. Your aunt's attorney, my uncle, is home in bed with the flu. I'm a junior partner of the firm. I hope you don't have any objections to my handling the affairs."

"Of course not," Sam muttered as she followed David Carpenter's long-legged stride down the corridor. Anything was an improvement over Gemini's age-old friend.

While the young attorney gathered his papers together, Sam looked around the office and liked what she saw. The brown and beige plaid drapes were partially closed to ward off the intense glare from the white world outside. The low-slung beige leather chairs were comfortable and matched the thick pile of the cocoa carpeting. It was a room whose atmosphere was restful and masculine. The rich pecan of the paneled walls reminded Sam of Gemini's library, as did the copper bowls full of daisies and ferns. Her inspection of the room completed, Sam turned her gaze to the lawyer and waited for him to speak.

David Carpenter cleared his throat and then leaned back in his swivel chair. "Back there in the hallway I referred to you as Samantha Blakely. I apologize. I should have called you by your newly married name, Mrs. Delaney. It's just that I've been working on this case for so long, and Sam Blakely has become engraved on my brain. In the beginning I made the same mistake my uncle made in thinking you were a man. Your husband, as you know, was most upset. However, rest assured that he and I both spent several hours this morning going over matters, and he understands his Aunt Gemini's intentions."

"Mr. Carpenter, where is…my…hus—… Where is Christian?" Sam asked hesitantly.

"He left here thirty minutes ago. He said he had pressing business at the office. He left a message for you, though. Now, let me see, where did I put it? Oh, yes, here it is. 'I'll be home for dinner, and make my steak rare.'"

Sam's heart soared and took wing. Christian would be home for dinner! She was going to cook for him, and he liked his steak rare. Her smile, when she turned it on the young attorney, was as dazzling as the brightness outside the plaid-covered windows. "Thank you for telling me."

"No problem. Now, let me see. Yes, here it is. This is a letter addressed to you, written by Gemini Delaney shortly before her death. You were only to receive it if you were married to Mr. Delaney. Otherwise, it was to be destroyed." Rifling through his papers, he withdrew an envelope that was addressed to Mrs. Samantha Delaney.

Sam extended her shaking fingers to accept the stiff bond paper. Seeing Gemini's scratchy handwriting renewed a pang of grief. Fighting back tears, she forced herself to open the envelope and read Gemini's last message to her:

Dearest Samantha,

Forgive an old woman's meddling, but the very fact you are reading this letter means my nasty little scheme has ended with you being married to my nephew, Christian. Let it suffice to say that the end has justified the means.

I have made no secret of my deepest regard for you or of my loving fondness for Christian. My problem was in seeing the two of you find each other. I knew you were the girl for him from the moment I set eyes on you. The difficulty existed in having Christian discover this for himself.

It was a simple matter of having him notice you, and I could think of no better way of assuring this than having him think you were the beneficiary of the controlling interest in Delaney Enterprises. I'll bet *that* made him sit up and take notice!

Now the time has come to have the original stock revert to its rightful owner, Christian. Other provisions have been made for you, Samantha, and, needless to say, you are now a very wealthy woman.

Thank you, dear girl, for caring for an old woman. Let your first daughter carry my name.

Remember me,
Gemini

When Samantha looked up through her tears, it was to see the lawyer smiling fondly down at her. "It seems the old match-maker has had her way."

"Yes, Mr. Carpenter. Gemini Delaney was a wise and wily lady."

"I can see you're not in the mood to have me read the entire addendum to you," he said kindly, offering her a tissue to dry her eyes. "We can go over it at your convenience. By the way, the dividends for the stock that you've already received are yours to keep. I hope you invest them wisely."

"Well, actually, Mr. Carpenter, I didn't cash the check. I gave it to Mr. Delaney in a manila envelope to hold in his office safe. Perhaps you should call him and tell him I'm returning it. I never had any intention of keeping the money. I know Gemini meant well, but I really can't accept it. I tried to explain all of this to your uncle, but he kept getting me confused with a man, and he has a definite hearing problem. I gave up trying to explain, think-ing it would all work out. I don't want a cent from the estate. I want you to tell Christian that for me, and I want you to do it today."

"Are you saying what I think you're saying?" the young law-yer asked incredulously. "Don't you think you should be the one to tell Mr. Delaney? After all, he is your husband."

"I want it to come from you, and I want you to explain the mixup."

"Mrs. Delaney, this is very unorthodox. First, your husband comes in here and tells me he wants things one way, and then you come in and tell me you want it another way. Do you think you could get together and arrive at some sort of mutual agreement so I'm not forced to do double work? We're rather short-staffed here right now.''

"What did Christian tell you to do?'' Sam asked fearfully. Maybe she wasn't going to get the chance to broil that rare steak, after all.

"To make a long story short, he wants you to have half—fifty percent—of the Delaney estate. Half of everything. Now, you tell me you want nothing, not even the dividends.''

"That is it, exactly. And I want you to make Mr. Delaney aware of my intentions before he comes home to dinner tonight.''

"I'll certainly do my best, Mrs. Delaney, but your husband has a mind of his own, and he was most adamant this morning when he told me his wishes.''

"Thank you for your time,'' Sam said, rising and holding out her hand.

"Goodbye, Mrs. Delaney, and I also want to thank you for braving that white stuff out there. How did you get here?''

"I walked.'' Sam smiled.

"I'll get on this right away, and perhaps by the time your husband gets home tonight, we'll have it all settled to your satisfaction.''

"Is there anything else, Mr. Carpenter?'' Sam asked hesitantly.

"David. Call me David. As a matter of fact, there is. I hope you'll include my name on the guest list for the wedding.''

"Wedding?'' Sam asked, puzzled.

"Yes. Mr. Delaney and I discussed it at great length this morning.'' The lawyer paused to smile, a hint of a flush reddening his ears. "To quote your husband, Mrs. Delaney, he wants to do everything up right, twice, to make sure you don't get away.''

Sam gasped, "Christian said that!'' Her heart was beating trip-hammer fast. All the love she had locked away in a tiny part of her breast swelled and grew and burst forth, shining in her eyes.

"I seem to be missing something here,'' David Carpenter

murmured quietly, a frown on his face. "I hope I haven't let any cats out of the bag."

"Cats! Cats!" Sam laughed. "All because of the cats!"

"I beg your pardon, Mrs. Delaney, I'm afraid I don't understand…"

"I'm having trouble with it myself, David," Sam called over her shoulder as she sailed out of the lawyer's office, her feet barely touching the floor.

Her first stop was a supermarket where she picked out the biggest steak she could find. Ingredients for a salad and some baking potatoes. Something for dessert, and an apron. If there was one thing a new bride needed besides perfume, it was an apron, and not necessarily in that order.

It was mid-afternoon before Sam made it back to her apartment, slipping and sliding, carrying two full bags of groceries.

She hung her coat in the tiny closet and immediately set about cleaning the apartment. She cleaned out the grate and added two logs to the fireplace. With machine-gun speed she whipped off the bed sheets and replaced them with fresh ones. A quick once-over in the bathroom and a new bath mat and her house was in order. While the tub filled with luxurious, scented steam, she retreated to the kitchen and began her preparations for dinner. The porterhouse steak was thick and a beautiful beefy-red. Deftly, she added a little tenderizer and sprinkled on a few spices. She set the broiler pan on top of the stove and moved on to the baking potatoes, which were long and perfectly shaped. The vegetables were perfection as she rinsed them under cold water. Her only cop out had been the frozen deep-dish apple pie made by the renowned Mrs. Smith. The pie could bake along with the potatoes, and at the last minute she would slip the steaks under the broiler.

She was married, really married. Her hands trembled as she slid the frozen pie onto a cookie sheet. This would be the first meal she cooked for her husband. "Gemini, you fox, this was what you angled for from the beginning. Wherever you are, I hope you know that your plan worked. And I really wouldn't have given him the cats. I just said that because I was angry. I said I would take care of them, and I will.''

Sam fished around in the market bag and withdrew the apron she had purchased in the dime store. At best, it was useless. As big as a handkerchief and sheer as gossamer. A delicate ruffle around the edges led into the tie that was of bonbon proportions. She just knew Christian would love it.

The clock in her sunshine kitchen of yellow and orange read six-forty-five. The table was set to perfection; the candle was waiting to be lighted. At precisely, six-fifty-eight her doorbell chimed. Quickly, she patted at the ridiculous apron—no not ridiculous; sexy—and raced to the door. She flung open the door and fell into Christian's arms. This was where she wanted to be, where she belonged. For now, forever.

''Hey, it's cold out here and it's snowing! Can I come in?'' Christian said huskily. Without loosening his hold on her, he managed to slip out of his heavy jacket. ''I like your apron.'' He grinned.

''I knew you would; that's why I bought it!''

''Come here,'' he said, drawing her closer.

Sam buried her head against his broad chest, burrowing against him. ''I have to put the steak under the broiler. Everything else is ready,'' she sighed.

''Steak?'' Christian said in a nonplussed tone.

''David Carpenter said you wanted a steak and that you liked it rare. That's what I'm making for dinner. Did you change your mind? Did David make a mistake?'' Sam asked anxiously, not wanting anything to spoil this first dinner for the two of them.

''No! I did say that, but the last thing I want to do right now is eat. Right now, all I want is to make love to you. All through the night until I know every inch of you. And you can start pleasing me by taking off that apron.''

Sam giggled. ''But what about the steak? I paid seven dollars and forty-three cents for that piece of meat,'' she whispered against his ear.

''Orion, there are some things more important than eating— and this is one of them.'' Deftly, he picked her up and headed for the kitchen. Sam wiggled and reached down to turn off the broiler.

"See that pie I baked for you? I was going to lie and say I spent all afternoon slaving over a hot oven. It was one of those frozen creations that are supposed to mesmerize a man."

"What am I going to do with you? Didn't anyone ever tell you that women are supposed to be a mystery to men? You've given away all of your secrets, and this is only the second day we've been together as husband and wife. What am I going to do with you?"

"For starters," Sam said softly, "you can whisper my name the way you did last night, and then we'll think of something after that."

ONE PERFECT ROSE
Emilie Richards

Chapter One

There were a lot of things a man couldn't do with frozen fingers. Work, for one thing. Shave or comb his hair, for another. There were a host of things he couldn't do to a woman—and a host she wouldn't allow him to do, even if he could.

Right now, the thing that Jason Millington's fingers refused to do was lift a mug off the counter of a downtown coffee shop and bring it to his lips.

"Sumpthin' wrong with the coffee, bud?"

Bleary-eyed, Jase stared at the proprietor. He was short and fat, a balding turnip of a man with the unlikely name of Red. The coffee shop was Red's Place. "Just taking my time."

"A lot of time."

Jase looked from side to side, although he already knew that he and Red were two of the six people in a room that could hold forty. "Don't exactly need the seat, do you?"

"We got laws against loitering."

"We've probably got laws against harassing paying customers, too."

"Ain't seen no money."

Jase gouged his pants pocket with his index icicle and heard the reassuring clank of change. He had recycled enough aluminum that evening to afford a sandwich, too. But he wasn't going to buy it from Red. Jase had a long night ahead and more stops to make. If he timed those stops right, he could stay out of the cold until dawn's early light.

He stood and bent his fingers just far enough to hook three quarters and slide them across the counter. Red mumbled, but he left. Jase went back to warming his hands over his cup.

Cleveland's winters were the flip side of hell. No one moved to the city because of the weather. The symphony, maybe, or the art museum. Even the lakeshore in summer or the colorful ethnic festivals. But no one made a home here—or attempted to make a home—because he liked January's wind straight off Lake Erie or February's treacherous blizzards.

The optimistic viewed March as a prelude to April. Tonight Jase wasn't optimistic. The temperature outside was thirty-eight degrees, and he had little protection. His coat had been given to him by his sister, and it had more holes than the frost-heaved city streets. What was left of the pile lining had a bad case of mange, and the sleeves were three inches too short. Pamela had never had much of an eye for size.

Jase's coat branded him, as did jeans with the knees and seat worn to a shine and cardboard-lined shoes with no shine at all. There were dozens of men on the streets tonight with the same inadequate clothing, the same minimal change in patched pockets, the same listless expression. Lack of good food and sleep made anybody listless, even the strongest and brightest.

The coffee shop door opened with a bang. Two men who made Jase look like an *Esquire* model, blew in on a gust of Lake Erie wind. One had a greasy ponytail and what looked like a brass curtain ring hanging from an ear. The other man had an angelic, toothless smile.

Red was at the door before it had banged shut. "I told you a million times, I don't want you in here. Get out."

"Ah, Red, what're we hurting?" asked the toothless one. "We got money for dinner tonight."

"Don't look good for business, you in here. Looks like a home for derelicts."

Jase listened to them argue. By the time the two men gave up and left, he figured his own minutes were numbered. He managed to wrap his hands around the cup and lift it to his lips.

Just as Red turned in Jase's direction, the door banged again. Jase followed the sound with his eyes, grateful for the reprieve. He hoped this argument would last long enough for him to finish his coffee.

A woman stood in the doorway this time. From across the room Jase could see she was shivering. She wore a coat of unattractive rat-brown wool, but no gloves, hat or scarf. Her legs looked bare, too, and he hoped to God that at least she was wearing panty hose.

"Mr. Dewayne?" She stepped forward, aiming herself at Red. "I'm Becca Hanks. I came by last night about a job, but the man behind the counter said I should come back tonight and talk to you."

She held out her hand. Jase gave an involuntary wince as Red grudgingly crunched it in his own. Shaking hands was something else at which frozen fingers did not excel.

If she was in pain, she didn't show it. She had a small chin, rounded and delicate, but she lifted it until it was the most prominent part of her face. "I'm sorry I'm here so late, but I had car trouble, and I walked the last mile." She reached inside a large plastic handbag, retrieved a piece of paper and held it out to Red.

Red looked as if she were giving him a dirty tissue. He took it as if it was one, too, his thumb and forefinger pinched at one corner as if to avoid disease. He held the paper away from his face and scanned it. Then he handed it back.

"Don't see a phone number or a real address. Just a postal box. Can't call you at the post office."

"I know. I'm sorry. But I'm new in town, and I'm—I'm staying with friends until I get a place of my own."

"Friends got a phone?"

"I couldn't bother them with my calls. But if you think you might be hiring, I can stop by as often as you say."

Jase listened to the husky twang of Appalachia in the woman's speech. She put words together as if she'd had a certain amount of education, but no one had educated the mountains out of her accent.

She wasn't pretty. From what little he could glimpse of her body, she was much too thin. Her light brown hair was long, and the ends were ragged, as if someone had chopped at them with dull scissors. The weight was pulled off her face with a rubber band, neat but unflattering, and the style exposed a face chapped with cold. There wasn't anything wrong with her features, but there was a lack of vitality, maybe even a lack of hope in her expression that canceled everything else.

She coughed, politely turning her head and covering her mouth, but the cough, deep and wrenching, seemed the final straw for Red.

"Hah. Don't bother coming back. I can't use you."

She looked as if he'd hit her, but only for a moment. Her chin lifted again. "I'd work hard. No one would work any harder or faster."

"You don't even have a real place to live. How do I know you're not passing through? I gotta train my help. I'd just get you trained and you'd be gone."

"Oh, no, I'll be staying. I—"

"How're you going to buy a uniform? Shoes? How're you going to keep them clean while you're waiting for a paycheck? Huh? Tips here don't count for nuthin', not on this shift, anyway. Less you got money to start off, you can't make it two weeks. And I don't give no advances."

Red didn't give her time to answer—although by then Jase doubted she was going to, anyway. Wiping his hands on his apron, Red went back behind the counter and disappeared through a swinging door.

Jase wanted to shift his gaze, to give the thoroughly defeated young woman the balm of privacy, but as he started to do just that, he realized she was coughing again. The cough was a racking spasm that shook her frail body until her legs no longer seemed able to hold her. As he watched, her knees began to fold.

He was off his seat and across the room before he knew he

had moved. He did not want to get involved. He had his own brutal night to get through; he did not need a complication. Cold, hunger and no place to sleep were complications enough. But a stranger named Becca Hanks was collapsing in front of his eyes, and that made her problems more compelling than his.

He had his arms around her in a moment. "Lean on me," he ordered. "I won't let you fall."

She seemed to have no choice. She swayed against him. He bore the burden of her weight as wave after wave of coughing tore through her. She weighed as little as a child. In robust good health she would probably still be light, but now there was room on her small-boned frame for another twenty pounds.

"I can't—I can't—"

"Don't try to talk. Concentrate on breathing." Jase held her tighter.

Becca gasped, fueling more coughs.

"I'm going to get you to a table. Hold on. Sitting might help." He searched for the closest refuge, then, half dragging her, he encouraged her in that direction.

"What are you doing?"

Jase looked up and saw Red bearing down on them. "What's it look like?"

"Looks like you're not on your way out the door."

"You're a bright man, Red."

"I want you both out of here."

"When she's feeling better."

"Now!"

Jase succeeded in getting Becca to the table. He urged her into a chair. She doubled over and gasped. Jase watched all the color the wind had whipped into her cheeks fade away. "Get her a glass of water." He squatted beside her chair and patted her gently on the back.

"I'm not—"

His head snapped up, and his eyes narrowed. "Red," he said quietly, "you get that water now, or so help me God, your name's going to be Black and Blue."

Red started to reply. Jase got to his feet in one fluid motion, towering over the sputtering man. Red made a split second assessment and disappeared behind the counter. He returned with the water.

"You've got the milk of human kindness in your soul." Jase took the water and squatted beside Becca. "Here you go, honey. Take small sips. Don't gulp. Hold it in your mouth for a few seconds if you can and warm it before you swallow."

She reached for the glass, but her hand was trembling too hard to hold it. Jase held the glass to her lips, and she took a sip.

"Good. Great."

"I want you out of here." Red seemed to feel braver with Jase crouching beside the chair. But he backed away as he added, "You'll scare away my customers."

"Don't worry. Anybody who'd eat in this dump is too stupid to be scared."

There was noise from the chair that didn't sound like a cough. Jase wasn't sure whether it was a laugh or a stifled sob. He wondered if this woman had anything in her life to laugh about.

He held the water to her lips, and she took another sip, then another. The coughing eased until she was able to manage the water by herself. Finally she lifted her head and stared at him.

"Thank you kindly."

"I didn't do anything."

"I'd be...a heap on the floor."

"A very small heap."

"This place could use...some decorating."

"You'd be wasted here."

Becca tried to smile, but a new round of coughing ensued instead. She turned her face away from his.

Jase stood. One of the men who had been at the other end of the counter was coming toward him. He was old and obviously poor, but there was nothing about him to suggest he was homeless, probably just one of the many elderly who lived in one-room apartments in the vicinity. "I just want to warn you," he said in low tones. "Red's calling the cops. I could hear him from my seat."

Jase nodded his thanks. He and Becca had done nothing illegal, but there were an array of charges Red could threaten them with. A little intervention could actually help Becca, who, with the right kind of luck, might end up in a hospital for the night. But Jase was in no position to explain himself to the Cleveland cops.

The old man shuffled back to his seat. Jase lowered his head so Becca could hear him. "Can you walk now?"

"I think so."

He gripped her elbow and helped her to her feet. She was unsteady, but as he watched, she struggled to regain her balance.

He told her what the old man had said. "You could stay here. They'll just ask you a few questions."

"No!" She coughed again, but the spasms had lessened a little. "Let's make tracks out of here."

"It's bitter cold out there."

"I'll be okay. Thanks. Go on."

He didn't loosen his grip on her elbow. "We'll go together. No argument," he added when she tried to protest. "You collapse on the floor, I'll still be here when the cops come."

She obviously didn't have the strength to resist. She let him lead her to the door.

"Your dinner," she said as his hand went to the doorknob. "Weren't you eating when I came in?"

"No. I was just having coffee." He turned and looked longingly over his shoulder toward the counter. He thought he could see steam rising from what was still nearly a full cup.

"I'm sorry you can't finish it," she said.

"It was just coffee." He opened the door and guided her out into the cold.

Becca didn't know when the cough had begun. It had been with her for so long now that it seemed an integral part of her, like her eyelashes or her feet. She supposed it had gotten worse. The episode in the coffee shop was the most frightening she could remember. There had been seconds piled on seconds when she could not draw a breath. Breathing was one of those things she had always taken for granted, like a place to live or enough food to eat. She wondered if breathing, too, was going to become a struggle.

The wind howled past her bare ears. She reached inside her coat pocket and pulled out a scarf. Moth-eaten and faded, it had not been appropriate to wear on a job interview, but now, with trembling fingers, she wrapped it around her head and throat. As she did, she looked at the man who had rescued her.

Captain Kidd or Bluebeard had probably looked gentler. A pirate's red bandanna covered his dark hair, and half a week's growth of beard shaded his face. He was dressed much like the other homeless men she had encountered, clothes so old someone else had discarded them, shoes with soles that were marginally attached. Thankfully he was cleaner than most; even his clothes were clean.

He seemed either too young or too old to be on the streets. She guessed he was a year or two on her side of thirty, the right age to be holding down a job and earning his way. Not that age was the only requirement for finding a job. She was the right age, too, and she had been unsuccessful. Once the downward spiral began, jobs moved farther and farther out of reach.

"We probably ought to move down the block," he said. "I don't think the cops will be looking for us, but there's no point in waiting for them to show up."

"I'm Becca." She held out her hand.

He grasped it gingerly. "Jase."

"Thank you." She shoved her hands into her pockets to keep them warm. "I guess I'd better get back…to my friends' apartment. They'll wonder what happened to me."

Jase knew the truth when he heard it. He knew a lie, too. Becca didn't lie well, as if she'd had little practice, or as if it went against her basic nature. "I heard you say you were having car trouble."

"It just died." She began to cough. The change from the heated coffee shop to the cold wind seemed to compress her lungs. She leaned against a wall and forced herself to breathe through her nose.

"A mile away?"

She nodded.

Jase knew the section of town they were in. Draw a circle with a one mile radius, and there was no safe place inside it for a woman walking alone. "You can't make it a mile."

"I did once tonight. I'll do it again."

"And what if your car doesn't start?"

"It probably just needed a rest."

"Like you."

She looked up. He had clear green eyes under thick dark brows. She read concern in them. "Thanks for worrying. But I'll be fine."

"I'm walking you to your car."

"I don't need your help. You've helped enough."

"I'm walking you to your car."

She would have argued if there had been even one ounce of fight left in her. But she needed all her fight to control her cough. She didn't need another attack like the one she'd just endured. Collapsing on the street was far more dangerous than collapsing in the coffee shop.

She started walking, and Jase walked beside her. He didn't seem to think that talking was necessary, and she was glad. She had no strength for conversation. Each step was torture. A gale-force wind whipped between buildings and almost knocked her flat. Her bare legs were frozen, and she longed for the jeans packed in the trunk of her car.

They'd covered five blocks before he spoke. "Do you really have a place to stay?"

"I told you I did."

"There's a woman's shelter not too far from here, and they usually have beds for emergencies."

"I'm not an emergency."

They'd covered five more blocks before he spoke again. "I'm guessing you're from West Virginia."

"Kentucky."

"You're a long way from home."

"This is home now."

"Why Cleveland?"

She gave a bitter laugh, and for a moment she was consumed by another fit of coughing. She stopped until she had recovered. "Because there are jobs here," she said as she continued walking. "I'd heard...there were plenty of jobs."

"The country's in a recession."

"It's always in a recession for people like me."

"People like you?"

She didn't answer, and he didn't push.

They turned onto a short residential street lined with old, ramshackle houses and vacant lots littered with trash where houses had been torn down. They walked its length, avoiding a small pack of dogs, before they turned onto a main avenue. Half a block down a city tow truck was fastening a chain to the bumper of a rusty old Chevrolet.

Becca gave a small cry.

Immediately Jase knew why. "Your car?"

She managed a nod, but she was coughing again.

"We could try to stop them, but it won't do any good. Now that it's hooked up, they'll tow it no matter what. You'll have to go down to the city impound lot and pay the fine to get it back."

She straightened enough to watch, and as she did, the tow truck driver got into his cab and started his engine. In a moment the truck and Becca's car were gone.

There was a church on the corner just behind them, a brick monument to Cleveland's immigrant past. Becca lowered herself to the third step and put her head in her hands. "That was my place to stay."

"There were better choices for a front yard than a no parking zone."

"It stalled there."

"The friends? The apartment? Lies?"

"I had to tell Red something. No one hires a waitress who lives in a car."

"Do you have money to get the car back?"

"I don't have money for a piece of gum." She looked up at him. "But I will. I'll find a way."

"Not tonight you won't."

She rested her head in her hands again. "Maybe not tonight."

Jase was torn about what to do. His plans had not included taking care of someone else. Yet what could he do? She was already sick. A night on the streets could kill her. A glance at the digital thermometer at a bank they'd passed had confirmed his hunch that the night was getting colder. She could not spend it outside without protection. Even her car could have been a death trap.

"There's a mission not too far away," he told her. "I heard about it from another man this evening. They serve soup if you go to their service first."

"I'm not hungry."

"Look, you don't have to feel like you're taking charity. From what I hear, the soup's payment for listening to the preacher's wife sing."

"You go on. Thanks…for everything you've done, but I want to be left alone," she managed, before another cough began. He sat quietly until she looked up from her coughing spasm. "You're still here."

"I'm not leaving until you're warm and fed."

"Go on and get out of here."

"If I was sensible, would I be out on the streets in the first place?"

She stared at him. "Why are you doing this?"

"Because apparently you're too tired and too sick to make a good decision by yourself."

"I can do anything by myself! Nobody has to help me!" She began to cough again. When she had stopped, she put her face in her hands.

"Becca, you'll die out here."

She realized that this stranger, who didn't seem to have his own life in order, might be right about hers. Fear curled inside her, more powerful than the pain and the despair. She had reasons, two of them, to keep on living. "Okay. I'll go. But it's my decision."

"Sure." He stood. "We'll walk slow."

She followed the pace he set. The route was an unfamiliar tangle of rights and lefts, but she stopped caring immediately. She no longer had a car she had to get back to. Anywhere was as good as anywhere else. There was no feeling in her feet or her fingers by the time she saw a blinking neon cross at the end of a block of dingy storefronts.

Jase stopped and pointed. He wasn't sure if she'd seen the mission or not. He wasn't even sure she would make it that far. "That's it. Think you can sit through the service? It should be starting pretty soon."

She tried to rally. "I can do anything I have to."

"Good girl."

There were two lines spreading down the mission steps and onto the sidewalk. They were divided by gender. Becca joined one, Jase the other. The lines were moving slowly, and when Jase was halfway to the steps, he saw why. Each person underwent a brief search before he was allowed inside.

"What are you looking for?" he asked when it was his turn.

"Drugs, knives." The old man doing the honors gave him a quick smile. "You're clean. Welcome, Brother."

Jason nodded. Becca was waiting for him inside, and they found a seat in the chapel. Throughout the drawn-out service he kept an eye on her. Her eyes stayed closed after prayers. When she stood for hymns, she swayed on her feet. Even the relative warmth of the barny old chapel seemed to have little effect on her coughing. More times than not, Jase couldn't even hear the preacher—which was its own kind of blessing.

When the service had finally ended, the hundred or so who had gathered filed into a large dining hall. They stood in line for a bowl of soup and a plate of bread. Jase gave Becca his bread and carried the soup. He knew there wouldn't have been a drop left if she had been forced to carry it herself.

The soup looked watery and the bread dry. After they were seated at a long table, he crumbled his bread in his soup, solving both problems. He had rarely tasted anything better. He watched Becca choke down half a dozen bites. "How long since you've eaten?" he asked.

"I don't know."

He believed her. He already knew she wasn't the kind of woman who dwelled on her misery. "Keep eating slow. You'll fill up too fast if you haven't eaten in a while."

"I'm already full." She lifted her spoon to her mouth, anyway, and he guessed she wasn't going to waste a drop, full or not.

"They have beds here," Jase told her.

"Fifty beds," the man next to him said. He was clean and shaven. The only thing to identify him as poor was the disrepair of his clothing. "The first fifty in the door, twenty-five men, twenty-five women, get 'em. They stamp your hand?"

Jase looked at Becca. She shook her head.

"You won't sleep here, then," the man said philosophically. "Have to find another place."

"You're sick. Maybe they'll make an exception," Jase told her.

"I couldn't ask for someone else's spot."

He wanted to shake her. What did she have to prove, anyway? And to whom? She was nothing more than a homeless waif, and nobody, nobody, cared if she had pride or not. "Suit yourself," he said. "But before you die from exposure, be sure you leave a note telling the city you plan to pay for your own funeral…just as soon as St. Peter hands over your paycheck."

"What I do's none of your business," Becca told Jase. "If I didn't do what I thought was right, I wouldn't be any better than a critter."

"You'd be alive." Jase put down his spoon. Without her coat, he could see that Becca was as thin as he had guessed. Her cheeks were rosy again, but not from the wind. This time he was sure the cause was fever. She was in her early twenties, give or take a year or two, but she looked like she'd seen a hundred years of bad luck. "Proud and dead is nothing to brag about. You've got to sleep somewhere warm tonight."

"I'll find a place."

He had learned long ago not to waste his time. He finished his soup and waited for the plastic cup of pudding that volunteers were passing out. Then, when he and Becca were finished, he followed her to the door.

The preacher and his wife were waiting there to speak to each person as he or she passed through. The preacher frowned when Becca began to cough. "You're sick," he said. He touched her forehead with the palm of his hand. "You've got a fever, Sister."

"Couldn't she stay the night?" Jase asked.

"I'm not taking anybody else's bed," Becca said between coughs.

"Her best bet is an emergency room, anyway." The preacher named two hospitals in the vicinity. "One of them may admit her. And even if they don't, the emergency room will be warm and safe. As sick as she is, no one will make her leave before morning."

"Thanks," she said.

Outside Jase took one look at her and knew that, grateful or not, Becca was going to ignore the preacher's advice. He attempted some himself. "I meant what I said about the women's shelter. I know someone on staff. I'm sure they'll find a place for you. They can help you get back on your feet."

"I don't want charity! I'll take care of myself."

Jase realized he was stuck with Becca for the night. Every attempt he had made to foist her off on someone else had been in vain. She was too full of spirit. She would harm herself rather than let anyone help. Reluctantly, he admired her as he considered what to do.

"Are you looking for a job?"

The question surprised him. He wasn't, and he couldn't think fast enough to concoct a good lie. "No."

"Well, I'm not going to stop until I find something!"

"More power to you, but right now, let's just find you a place to sleep tonight."

"I'm fine."

"There's a construction site not far from here, and the basement level is completed. It won't be as warm as a shelter, but it's out of the wind. We'll go there."

"I'm not going anywhere with you. You've done enough."

He clamped fingers that were already growing numb again over her shoulder. "You're coming with me. I'll hound you all night until you do."

For a moment she wondered if he intended her harm. So far he had been nothing but kind. She met his gaze and tried to read his motives.

"I'm not going to let anything happen to you," he promised. "Let me do this much. Okay? I just want to get you out of the cold and the wind. And I want some sleep."

What choice did she have? She knew she was sinking fast. She couldn't make herself say the words, but she nodded.

He smiled a little. "Good."

By the time they reached the site of what was obviously going to be a new landmark for Cleveland's skyline, she knew she had no strength left. Jase seemed no worse for the eight block hike, but Becca's knees were shaking. She followed him along the side of the building, shivering as wind blasted around the corner. He seemed to know exactly where to go, and she guessed he had slept here before.

"There's a security force," he said. "Don't worry about them. They usually let people sleep inside on cold nights."

She thought that very odd, but she was too exhausted to comment. She followed slowly, her lips in a grim, determined line. They wound their way through construction debris and makeshift plywood tunnels. Finally he led her to some steps. "Can you make it?"

She nodded. He held out his hand, and she took it, afraid that if she fell, she would be a real burden. The stairwell was dark, and she was momentarily frightened, but he squeezed her hand as if he knew. "We're almost there."

At the bottom of the stairwell they stepped through a doorway. There was some light from the street lamps filtering through the unfinished panels of the floor above, but the basement resembled a huge, dank cave. She couldn't go on.

"There's a room at the back with some light from above. The last time I was here there was a kerosene heater for warmth."

"I don't like this."

"I don't blame you."

She began to cough. Jase put his arm around her to help keep her on her feet. She was shivering.

"You'll be safe. I promise. Would a maniac try so hard to get you to go to a women's shelter?"

"Let's go."

He guided her carefully. He knew the whole floor like the back of his hand, but the eerie mottled light distorted everything. Halfway across he looked up and saw a man with a flashlight in his hand. Jase blocked Becca's view. The beam traced the contours of his face. He waved it away. The man melted into the shadows.

"Jase?" she asked.

"It's all right. I told you, they don't mind us sleeping here. They've seen me before."

"They really don't." She was amazed.

"Let's go."

The room in the back was just as he had described it. And the heater took only a moment to light. She stood next to it to warm her hands. Jase watched her for a moment. When he was sure she wouldn't bolt, he went to the door. "I know where there are tarps and pads we can sleep on. I'll be back in a minute."

He was back before she had time to be frightened. "This isn't going to be terribly comfortable, but it will be better than sleeping in an alley somewhere." He spread a tarp on the floor and covered it with two pads that until a moment ago had protected some of the thousands of dollars worth of equipment stored in the next room. He rolled one into a pillow and saved two for cover. "There." He stood. "See what you think."

"You've done so much."

"Do me a favor in return. Get some sleep. I'll stand guard."

"But you have to sleep, too."

"I sleep in the daytime," he lied.

"What do you do at night?"

"Look for ways to stay out of trouble."

"You seem so..."

He watched her search for a word. "Normal?" he supplied.

"No. Efficient. I bet there are a lot of things you could do."

"Go to sleep, Becca. We can talk in the morning."

She went to the makeshift pallet and lowered herself to the floor. He watched her curl up on one side, her hands under her cheek. Her handbag was nestled against her chest, less from fear of theft, he supposed, than for the comfort of having something she owned close by. She didn't move for a moment; then she sat up and fished around inside it.

He wondered what she was looking for.

She pulled out a scrap of paper. From his limited perspective, it looked like a photograph.

She stared at it, as if it could give her solace. His curiosity was already racing full speed. She was young and probably attractive when she was well and well-fed. What had brought her here, and what had put her on the streets?

"Can I show you something?" she asked.

He was surprised. "Sure." He joined her on the pad, kneeling beside her. "What is it?"

She held out the photograph. He squinted in the darkness, just able to make out two shapes. Two small, pigtailed shapes in pink overalls. "Who are they?"

"They're mine."

"Where are they?"

Becca shook her head. The photograph disappeared back into her handbag. She lay down again and clasped it to her chest.

She wasn't sure why she had shown the photograph to Jase. It was her most precious belonging. If it had been in the car when they'd towed it away...

She shuddered. Then she shuddered again. The heater might warm the air eventually, but she was afraid the cold seeping through the tarp and pads was never going to go away.

She felt a hand on her shoulder. "You're freezing," Jase said.

She was as close to tears as she had come in a year. She was as close to giving up as she had ever been in her life. "I'm all right."

She wasn't all right, and he could only think of one more

thing she might accept from him. "I'm getting under the covers. I have no intention of forcing myself on you. Shivering, coughing women have never been an interest of mine." He lay down under the cover. Then he inched toward her until her back curved against him. Surprisingly, she didn't move away. "You'll warm up faster this way," he said against her hair.

She lay in the circle of a ragged stranger's arms and thought of all the things that had brought her to this place and moment. The last man to sleep beside her had been her husband. Tears tickled her eyelids, but she was too exhausted and the pain was too old to make her cry.

The man beside her was not her husband, but he was kindness and strength. She had almost forgotten that either of those things existed. "Why are you being so nice?" she asked.

He had been called many things in his life, but nice had rarely been one of them. His arms tightened a little. "Because you deserve to have someone be nice to you."

"I…we shouldn't be here."

"It's okay. Tomorrow we'll go somewhere else."

She thought about tomorrow. For once there was no small surge of hope that tomorrow would be better. She couldn't expect anything from the future. The best she could do was think about the present moment and a stranger's kindness.

She placed her hands on his arm. All thoughts faded, and in a moment she was asleep.

Jase stroked her hair. It smelled like soap, not shampoo, but soap, inexpensive and unadorned. He wondered if she had washed her hair in a public restroom somewhere. She would have, rather than be dirty. He knew that much about her already. Tomorrow morning he planned to discover more, right before he told her who he was and what had brought him to the streets.

She coughed, but she didn't wake up.

Tomorrow he would get her to a hospital. Tomorrow he would be sure her pride took a backseat to her health.

Tomorrow. He finally fell asleep thinking of tomorrow.

Chapter Two

"I don't care if it's bad business. Yes, you heard me right, I don't care if I take a loss." Jason Millington switched the telephone receiver to his left ear to give his right one a break. This was his fourth call in fifteen minutes. "I can afford to take a loss. Get me the coffee shop like a good boy, and be sure my old buddy Red doesn't come out of it with anything. Yes, I know he's a bastard. But I'm a bigger one."

Jase hung up with a flourish. At the same moment the door to his office, a door that was as solid and stately as his mahogany desk, banged into the wall. The three Winslow Homers artfully grouped a distance away from it danced uncertainly.

He didn't even look up. "Pamela, I presume."

"Your new secretary was going to announce me. I told her we don't announce family. Now she's cowering at her desk."

He gave her a look that would have made the bravest man uneasy. "I don't raise my voice to her. She has no reason to cower."

"Everybody's afraid of you."

"Except you, apparently."

Pamela crossed the room, bent low and kissed him. "I'm terrified."

"Don't be. You beat me up when we were ten."

"We were eleven. I was taller than you." Pamela found a seat and kicked off her shoes. She was not taller than her twin brother now. He was six foot, and she was six inches shorter, but there was still a strong resemblance between them. Her short hair was as dark as his, her eyes just as green. They both had the stubborn Millington jaw, although Pamela's was a more delicate version.

Jase knew what men thought of his sister. Twenty minutes after she had entered a room filled with more beautiful women, the men gravitated to Pamela. Her eyes sparkled with vitality; her features were mobile and expressive. But best of all, she was never afraid to say exactly what she thought. And Pamela never stopped thinking.

Now she gestured toward the stellar view of a Cleveland April outside Jase's twelfth-story window. "Someday you'll own it all, won't you, Jase? Own it all and change every bit of it to suit yourself."

Since that, or something similar, was her usual opening gambit, Jase ignored it. "Why are you here?"

"Not for your money."

He picked up a pen and tapped Morse code on his desktop. Pamela had said the same thing to him one day in March, and now the words brought back that day as clearly as if he were living it again.

The afternoon had been much like this one. He had been in the middle of a telephone business deal when Pamela walked in, and things had not been going his way. More irritable than usual, he had pulled out a checkbook, but she had waved it away.

"You know, Jase," she'd said, "all the world's problems can't be solved with money. It's so easy for you to write a check. Your funds are virtually limitless. Heck, your pen is worth more than three rooms of furniture at The Greenhouse. When I walk out that door, you won't miss the money. You probably won't even remember you gave it."

"So what *do* you want?" He had shoved his hands into his pockets and gone to the window. The Cleveland he saw was a growing city, rich with potential and energy. Pamela was right;

he rarely thought about the other Cleveland, the one where children went hungry, and men and women roamed the streets looking for shelter. That was Pamela's Cleveland. As a social worker at The Greenhouse, a refuge for homeless and battered women, it was the Cleveland she came up against every day.

"I think I want you to escape your narrow little world." She joined him at the window. "I want you to understand, just once, what it's like to be poor. What it's like to be hungry, to have no home to go to. Your money helps now, but maybe if you understood what it's like to have no hope, you could give the kind of help we really need."

"I'm sick of this conversation. I'm sick of you harping at me. I'm not the problem. You grew up with money, and the guilt's eating you up. Millingtons have always given generously to good causes. We have nothing to be ashamed of."

"You don't understand a word I'm saying."

He stared at the street below. Directly under his window there was a man shoving a shopping cart in front of him, one shuffling step at a time. "I don't understand," he conceded. "I don't understand why more people don't help themselves. There are jobs everywhere. Maybe some of those jobs aren't great, but they're jobs. I know some people can't work. They're too sick, or addicted or crazy. But what about others?"

"What about them? Maybe you should find out firsthand."

"How? Work in a soup kitchen for a night or two?"

"No. *Go* to a soup kitchen for a night or two. Yeah. That's what it would take, Jase. You'll never really understand what it's like to be without hope, but you could try it for a while. You might understand a little better."

He had learned to understand a little better, all right. After their conversation, he had taken her suggestion—or, more accurately, her dare—and lived on the streets for two nights and a day in between. Now, of course, he realized that he had pretended to be homeless as much for the novelty as to get Pamela off his back. Maybe there had been a little guilt mixed in, too. Everything had always been easy for him. He had been born into a family with assets ranging from steel mills to corporate farms and cattle ranches. He had been a superior, popular student and later, a superior, if not popular businessman. Millington Development was his own creation, and last year the company's financial statement had been solid gold.

But nothing of what he was, of what he had been born to, had mattered for two nights in March. He had learned quickly that one homeless man was the same as another. He had skulked around corners, avoiding places where he might be recognized and picking through trash that others had missed. And on the second and final night, he had met a woman named Becca Hanks.

The Morse code ceased abruptly. It was April again, and Pamela was waiting for his question. "I guess you'd tell me if you'd heard anything about Becca?"

She looked at him with sympathy. "No one named Becca Hanks has turned up anywhere. For a month now I've checked and rechecked every agency she might have gone to, every clinic, every mission or shelter. She just doesn't seem to exist."

"She exists. Or she did." He leaned back in his chair. "She slept with me in the basement of my new building down on 4th Street. She was sick and proud, and when I woke up the next morning, she was gone."

"I know. I'm sorry." Pamela reached over and put her hand on his. "But so many people pass through the city. They struggle to stay alive while they're here. If this Becca made it through the winter, she'll be safer now that the weather is warming up. Maybe she found a job and a place to stay, or she's just gone back where she came from."

"She never claimed her car. I've made arrangements to be called if she tries to."

"You've changed."

"Not at all."

"You've changed. You're softer around the edges these days. I like you better."

"You liked me all right before."

"I adore you. I survived childhood because of you."

He met her eyes. "We had a good childhood, Pamela."

"We had a rotten childhood, but we had each other."

He ignored that. "Why are you here if you don't have any news and you don't want money?"

"To take you to dinner. At The Greenhouse." She held up her hands. "Don't say no."

"You want me to take food from the mouths of people who need every calorie?"

"Somebody gave us a huge sucker of a ham, and the kids are practicing a play to entertain everyone afterward. It's a festive occasion, and you know you're always welcome there. You practically own the place."

"You'd be surprised if I said yes, wouldn't you?"

She grinned. "Truthfully?"

"I'll be happy to come. I've got something to talk to you and Shareen about, anyway."

Her grin widened. "Much softer around the edges."

"Tell Red that."

"Red?"

"Just a man I know who's going to wish like hell that he never met me."

The Greenhouse was not green. It was a rambling white Victorian with pink and yellow trim and a picket fence that was missing one of every six pickets. The house itself was in a constant state of disrepair. Shutters flapped in the breeze, and pieces of rotting gingerbread fell to the wide front porch every time the breeze turned into a strong wind.

One of the other residents had told Becca that Pamela Millington's brother sent a work crew for repairs every time there was a lull in one of his other projects. Little by little his crew had painted and nailed and shingled until the house was basically sound. Apparently the fence was next on the list, and new gingerbread was on order from a company that specialized in reproductions. Already the house outshone its neighbors, but the renovation had encouraged some other residents of the block to show more pride. Two houses down, new paint sparkled. Four houses down, someone was planting pansies.

Pansies were great, but Becca was in the backyard of The

Greenhouse planting peas. The first crop had been planted two weeks before, along with the lettuce. That was a little late, but in March, when she should have been making a garden, lettuce and peas hadn't been on her mind.

"Ma-ar-ry!"

April had been a surprisingly dry month. The black soil crumbled in Becca's hands, rich in humus and earthworms. The soil in Blackwater had not been nearly so rich. To have a garden there, she had hauled rocks and hoed until her back ached. But she'd made a garden, a big flourishing garden. Now, choked by weeds, the asparagus would just be nudging its way through the warming soil. Asparagus never quit.

The Greenhouse needed an asparagus patch.

"Mary!"

She turned, startled. "Shareen. You scared me to death!"

"I've been calling and calling you! Where's your ears at?"

"Glued on the side of my head, same as yours."

"You didn't answer."

"When I'm digging, I'm digging. Nothing gets through to me."

Shareen plopped cross-legged on the grass beside Becca. "What's that?"

"Lettuce. I planted two kinds. That's Black-seeded Simpson, and that's Oak Leaf."

"What's growing next to the fence?"

"Peas."

Shareen made a face, and Becca laughed. "I put in spinach, too."

"Girl, you trying to poison us?"

"I'm trying to save you money. If The Greenhouse grows some of its own food, that's less we have to buy."

"I know what you're trying to do. It's your choices!" Shareen stood and brushed grass off her jeans. The lawn had been mowed for the first time that morning. "Did you know we're having a party tonight?"

"A party?" Becca smiled. Just weeks ago she had wondered

if life would ever hold anything for her again. "What kind of party?"

"Doesn't have to be any kind. Just a party. Ham, sweet potatoes, my mama's vinegar pies."

"Is your mama coming?"

"She's bringing the pies. I'm going to talk her into staying. Pamela's trying to get her brother to come, too."

Becca loved Shareen's mother. Dorey Moore was a tiny woman with snapping black eyes and a mouth that could cut the most arrogant down to size. Shareen had more polish, but no less guts. Pamela and Shareen had nurtured Becca during her first week at The Greenhouse as gently and tenderly as she was nurturing her garden. Rarely in the last years had anyone been as kind to her.

Except one homeless man named Jase, who had probably kept her from dying.

"So you got to put on your dancing shoes," Shareen said.

"Are we getting dressed up?" Becca asked.

"Might be nice."

"I found the prettiest dress in one of the boxes of clothes we washed today. I can't imagine why anyone ever gave it away."

"Probably didn't fit them. Did it fit you?"

"It's a little big."

"Everything's a little big for you, except doll clothes. You eat double portions of that ham tonight. And Mama says one of the pies has your name on it."

Becca coughed, but the cough was no more than a tickle now. Weeks of intravenous antibiotics had seen to that. "I bet your mama eats peas."

"You're working too hard."

"This isn't work. It's pleasure."

"Will you go in now? Take a shower and lie down for a while before it's time to change into that dress?"

"I was going to help with dinner."

"No way."

Becca understood strong wills. She stood. "Then I'll help serve."

"Maybe." Shareen slung her arm over Becca's shoulder and gave her a squeeze. "Now, you go take care of yourself. That's the only job you gotta do here."

Becca owed Shareen too much to argue. But Shareen was wrong. Becca had to take care of herself, it was true. But she also had to find a way to pay back the people who had reached out to her and led her, one step at a time, back to some kind of a life. The garden was one way to contribute. In the weeks that were left to her at The Greenhouse, she would find others.

She wished there was some way to find Jase and do something for him, too. She wondered where he was now. Was his life going to be one of these dead-ends that made the papers from time to time? Homeless man found dead in cardboard box? He had told her he wasn't looking for work. What *was* he looking for? Whatever it was, she hoped that he found it.

Jase made a mental note that The Greenhouse fence still hadn't been fixed. The house was looking better, though. He stood in front of it and tried to figure out exactly why.

"No, you may not build a skyscraper here," Pamela said.

"I'm trying to figure out what's different."

"It does look better, doesn't it?"

"Lots better." He realized what had changed. "Who's been doing the landscaping?"

"Nothing gets by you, does it? It's our new resident. Mary Smith."

"Mary Smith?" He glanced at Pamela. "For real?"

"We don't ask too many questions."

"She's quite a gardener. What are the beds along the fence for?"

"Flowers. She's started seeds in the basement under an old fluorescent light."

"I wouldn't have guessed the shrubs could be saved. But she's tamed them."

"Come see what she's done in back." Pamela led Jase through the gate to a flat area behind the garage. "Vegetables."

"She's a paragon."

"She works too hard."

"Is that possible?"

She laughed. "You wouldn't understand."

"Well, if she works this hard, you shouldn't have too much trouble finding a job for her before she has to leave."

"I hope not. But she's like a lot of the others. She doesn't have much education, though she's smart as a whip. Unfortunately, IQ isn't as important as B.A."

Three little girls launched themselves out the back door and headed straight for Pamela. She laughed, delighted, and held out her arms.

"A fan club?" Jase asked.

"One of my compensations." Pamela dragged her clinging friends toward the back door. "Do you want me to find Shareen now for that talk you mentioned?"

"If we've got time before we eat."

"Why don't you wait in the parlor?" She left, walking as normally as anyone could with a child attached to each leg.

The parlor was a hodgepodge of old furniture and unusual, graceful touches. The Greenhouse received donations almost every day from church and civic groups. Some of the residents arrived with no more than the clothes on their backs, but they always left with a complete wardrobe. What furniture wasn't needed in the house went to individual residents setting up their own apartments.

Whimsy and fantasy were in short supply for the women in the house, but the parlor fulfilled some of those needs. There were overstuffed chairs covered in English floral prints, hand-crocheted doilies on polished wood surfaces, silk flower arrangements in vases. No matter that the prints didn't coordinate, the woods ranged from pine to mahogany, and the vases would never hold water again. There was an old Victrola and a supply of 78s for entertainment, and two bookshelves filled with hard-cover novels. The children were only allowed here if accompanied by adults, and even then they were required to be on their best behavior.

Jase felt uncomfortable in the parlor. If he had to play along with the Victorian theme, he would much have preferred a room paneled in mahogany and furnished with leather. He paced the small space until Shareen and Pamela arrived.

"The lion in his cage." Shareen went to him and gave him a kiss on the cheek. Like Pamela, she found nothing about Jase frightening.

He admired her, as he always did. She was tiny, with curves in all the right places and a smile that welcomed the world. The smile could change in a moment, though, if she thought anyone or anything about The Greenhouse was threatened. As a black woman growing up in inner city Cleveland, she had bounded over her own share of hurdles. The facts of life she had been forced to learn made her the ideal director for The Greenhouse.

"We're glad you came," Shareen told him. "We like having you here. But I know there's got to be a better reason than ham and sweet potatoes."

One of the things Jase liked best about Shareen was that she never beat around the bush. One of the reasons The Greenhouse continued to survive was Shareen's unswerving, unflinching devotion. "I've bought an old factory not too far from the Flats. The section's not fashionable, and the building's a mess."

"You want condolences?" Pamela asked.

"I want to convert it into apartments. The potential's there. The building will stand forever if someone doesn't take a wrecking ball to it. There's nothing wrong with it that can't be fixed. Right now it's heaped with debris. The windows are all broken, and it's a barn inside. But the floors are solid maple, and the space can be divided any way we want."

Shareen perked up. "We?"

"I could hang on to the property for a few years. I'm betting that there'll be renovation in that area by then, and more buildings will be turned into apartments. It's a gamble, but I win more of those than I lose."

"Modesty becomes you, Jase." Pamela dusted a cabinet top with the hem of her blazer. "What does this have to do with us?"

"I could wait, or I could turn the property into apartments

now. Not the same kind, obviously. I wouldn't be aiming for affluent professionals. If I do it now, I do it for people like the women coming out of The Greenhouse, people who are just getting back on their feet and need a place to start. There's money available to provide shelter for the homeless, not a lot of it, God knows, but a little. I'll donate the building and whatever supplies and workmen I can afford. The government will pick up some more of the tab. The rest will have to come from the community.''

"You're pushing all the right buttons. You know that," Shareen said. "The hardest thing we have to do is find decent housing for our ladies after they leave here."

"I know."

"What do you mean, the community has to come up with the rest?" Pamela moved on to the Victrola. "How much, and how do we get them to do it?"

"A lot. And getting them to do it is your baby."

"Committees? Fund-raisers?"

"Mother." Jase saw Pamela grimace. "It's right up her alley," he reminded her.

"I suppose."

"Mrs. Millington would be willing to raise the money?" Shareen asked.

"Mother thrives on committees. Jase is right. We'd need someone like her to head this up. She knows all the right people, and they all owe her favors. She sees to it."

"You're just going to give us this building, free and clear?" Shareen asked Jase. "How come?"

Jase smiled. "Ask Pamela."

"A blinding light on the road to Damascus," Pamela said. "He's been converted to good works." She reached out and touched his arm.

He felt her pride, and it embarrassed him. "I'm doing it because it needs to be done. The building's just sitting there. I hate waste."

"Well, whatever the reason, I'm sure glad you thought of us," Shareen said. "We'll do whatever we have to. I know our board will help, and there are some influential folks on it. They'll work with your mama. Maybe we can call some attention to problems while we're at it. The publicity can't hurt."

There was a knock on the parlor door, and a little girl in a green jumper opened it a crack. "Dinner's ready," she lisped.

"We're done?" Shareen asked. "For now?"

"Done."

Shareen scooped the child up and settled her on one hip. Then she led the way into the dining room.

Jase felt the party atmosphere immediately. Shareen and Pamela believed that joy was one of the things the women and children in the house had to be reintroduced to, along with good food and a safe place to stay. There was no occasion too small for a celebration, and crepe paper streamers and balloons were usually part of The Greenhouse decor.

Today the streamers were yellow and the balloons red. There was an arrangement of funereal white lilies on the pine sideboard, but the room was perfumed by the reason for the celebration.

"This ham," Pamela said, "must be fifteen pounds, and Gina studded it with cloves and pineapple. Doesn't it smell fantastic?"

Jase noted the sign on the wall, scrawled and decorated by a child. "I yam happy about ham?" he asked.

"We're happy about the sweet potatoes, too."

The china was mismatched garage sale variety, but it sparkled like the mismatched glassware. There were cloth napkins, and the same child who had made the sign had also turned her talents to name cards at each place.

He really didn't want to be touched. He was not a sentimental man, but he felt something catch in his throat when he realized his place was at the head of the long table. Shareen's mother arrived, pies in hand, and bussed his cheek on the way to the kitchen to deliver them.

He stood politely until she came back and almost everyone was seated. There were still two places vacant when Pamela, who was at his right, ordered him to sit.

"Those belong to Gina and Mary," she said. "They'll be serving."

He winked at a little boy who was missing his two front teeth and sat. They were the only males in the room. "You've got a full house these days."

"We turned away a woman with two children this morning. The city would close us down if we took in even one more person."

"Where did she go?"

Pamela didn't answer.

"Pamela?"

"I'd rather not say."

He put his hand on her arm. "Did you take her in?"

"Well, she's just staying at my place for a few days." She spoke so softly he could hardly hear her. "She has a sister from California who's driving out to get her and take her home."

"And what does Shareen say about that?"

"She didn't ask, and I didn't volunteer the information." She met his eyes. "And you're not going to volunteer, either. Got it?"

"You can't take in the whole world."

"And you can't buy it, but you'll keep on trying, won't you? Even if it's just so you can give it away again."

"Don't get any ideas. The factory is just one building, and I took a liking to it, so I had to think of some way to use it."

She leaned forward. "This Becca person changed you, Jase. You'll never admit it, but she did."

He leaned forward, too, and missed the entrance of the ham until he heard the round of spontaneous applause.

The applause covered the gasp of the woman holding the platter. When Jase finally did look up, he saw her, lips gently parted, eyes greatly wounded. His hand clenched Pamela's arm. Becca stared at him.

Then, as he watched speechlessly, she set the ham on the sideboard and disappeared back into the kitchen.

Chapter Three

The row that would hold carrots had to be double spaded. First the topsoil had to be carefully removed; then the subsoil had to be broken up and mixed with humus before the topsoil was restored. Becca had found an old leaf pile at a nearby vacant lot and hauled wagon after wagon of composted leaves back to the garden. This morning she intended to work them into the carrot row.

Everybody loved carrots, didn't they? Even the pickiest child could be tempted to eat a raw carrot, particularly if she had helped pull it from the garden. When Becca was no longer at The Greenhouse, her carrots would still be growing, nourishing the latest crop of Greenhouse children. For a moment she pictured herself as a New Age Johnny Appleseed, traversing the country, leaving asparagus and carrots in her wake. Johnny had been a homeless wanderer, too, but that hadn't stopped him from making his mark.

She dug the first spadeful of topsoil, but her heart wasn't in it. She felt well enough. If she took frequent rest breaks she would be able to plant carrots today and still have the energy to finish trimming the hedge along the back fence. She had the energy, but not the enthusiasm. Jason Millington, millionaire developer and brother of Pamela Millington, had stripped her of enthusiasm just as surely as Jase, compassionate, homeless man, had saved her life.

She dug the second spadeful of topsoil. What kind of game had Jase been playing that night? Did slumming give him some sort of thrill? Maybe he had been investigating some kind of financial deal, sleuthing for millions at Red's Place. Maybe Red's Place was going to be the site of a new downtown luxury hotel, and he'd been scouting out potential clientele.

She wanted to laugh, but it was tears that clutched at her throat. Tears, and she hadn't cried in years, not since everything that mattered had been taken away from her. Tears watered down her determination to make a new life for herself and her babies. There was no point in crying when there was so much work to be done. And there was no point in crying about a man who had pretended to be something he was not. She should be happy that he wasn't dining out of garbage cans and sleeping in doorways.

The third spadeful joined the others, but she couldn't stop herself from remembering last night's dinner. She had worn the new dress, a lilac floral print with a lace collar that had only needed a little mending. One of the children had tied a purple ribbon in her hair, and she had shined a pair of black pumps that almost fit. The kitchen had smelled heavenly, like Gramma's kitchen had always smelled at Easter, and she had known she was really on the road to recovery when her stomach had rumbled with hunger. It was funny how quickly she had learned to convince herself she didn't need food, how quickly she had learned to ignore her body's signals until one day they hadn't been there anymore. But all her signals had worked again last night. The party had made her happy; the ham had made her hungry.

And seeing Jason Millington in a suit that cost as much as six months' rent had made her feel like a fool.

She was sure he had recognized her. She hadn't changed as much as he had, after all. Her hair was different, and she had gained a little weight, but she was essentially the same.

He was nothing like the man who had gotten her through a

frigid March night. He was a sleek, elegant panther, while that man had been an embattled alley cat. Jason Millington the developer had all that alley cat's power and presence, and he had the clout to use it. She found it no wonder that he had made millions rearranging Cleveland to suit his fancy.

She had nothing but a high school diploma, and hardly that, but it hadn't taken her more than seconds to see the truth and seconds more to act. She had retreated into the kitchen and out the back door. Then she had gone for a long, long walk. She had returned to questions, but not to Jason Millington. He had been gone by then, worried, she supposed, that she might reveal his silly little secret.

There was a small pile of topsoil beside the row, but she was already exhausted. She hadn't slept well. Every time she had shut her eyes, she had seen Jason Millington's face. Every darned time.

"I could do that for you."

She knew who had spoken before she looked up. That voice had stayed with her during her weeks in the hospital. Sometimes she had heard that voice coaxing her to get better, insisting that she fight to stay alive. Twice she had even dreamed that Jase had come to see her and promised he would take her somewhere so they could both make a new start. Crazy, humiliating dreams.

"I'll do it myself, thanks," she said. She raised her head— and her chin. "I don't need your help. I never did."

"Well, the hair's different, and the clothes fit snugger. But the woman's the same."

"Funny thing. The man's not, is he?"

Jase didn't smile. He felt like a fraud, like a voyeur caught in the act. "Same man. Different clothes."

"They say clothes make the man. Even ignorant country folk have heard that one."

"I don't blame you for being angry."

"Angry? Why should I be angry, Mr. Millington? Just because you made me feel like a fool? You sure weren't the first, and you probably won't be the last."

She was angry, and despite his discomfort Jase couldn't help but admire the effect. Her cheeks bloomed with it; her brown eyes sparkled. He hadn't remembered the color of her eyes, but now he saw they were a rich coffee-brown, an interesting contrast to hair that was blond in the sunlight. Someone had cut her hair to her shoulders, and there were bangs caressing her forehead. The simplicity of the style suited her, emphasizing strong bones and a full bottom lip that was not about to curve into a smile.

"Will you give me a chance to explain?"

"I'd love to hear an explanation. My imagination's taken flight."

"I pretended to be homeless because someone close to me—"

"Pamela?"

He refused to implicate his sister. "Because someone close to me suggested that I needed to do more about the world's problems than write checks. So I decided I wasn't going to understand what it was like to be homeless unless I was homeless myself for a few nights."

"How lucky we are! Just think, you could have taken the environment or world peace as your pet charity. Instead you chose to slink around alleys with a bunch of bums."

"I don't deserve that."

"I worried about you! Didn't you even guess when you were playing bum that somebody might just think of you as real? That somebody might care a little or worry a little? You don't know how many times I've wondered what happened to you! I even said a few prayers, and I haven't prayed in a long time!"

Her impassioned speech had taken more out of her than she realized. She began to cough, but when he stepped toward her, she waved him away. "Leave me alone!"

"You're still sick."

"No, I'm not. I'm just not well yet."

While he waited for her to catch her breath, he thought about everything she had said. Life was a chess game to him, a game he always won. Becca had started her chess game with nothing but a pawn or two, but she was still playing hard. For the first time he felt something very close to shame.

"Look," he said when she seemed to be breathing normally again. "I'm sorry. I really am. I was going to tell you who I was the morning after we met, but you left before I could. I would have told you that night, but I knew if I did, you wouldn't have let me help you. And you desperately needed help. I was afraid you were going to go off into the night and die in some miserable corner of the city."

"I trusted you, and you were playing with me."

"I never meant to play with anybody. For my whole life I've had everything my way. I just wanted to see what it would be like if I didn't have anything."

"So what did you learn?"

"I learned what it means to be lucky."

"People make their own luck."

"Not always. Look at you. What did you ever do to deserve what you've been handed?"

"You'd be surprised." She lifted her shovel again and started to dig.

He wanted to jerk the shovel out of her hands and force her to rest, but he held himself back. "If you trusted me, Becca, why did you leave without saying goodbye?"

She wasn't going to tell him it had been pride mixed with a large dose of femininity. She had awakened snuggled tightly against his chest, and she had known that in the light of day neither she nor Jase were going to stand up under scrutiny. She had been dirty, ill, as close to defeated as she had ever come— even though she and defeat were old buddies—and she had not had the courage to face him and let him see the woman he had held in his arms all night.

"I was afraid somebody might find us."

"Where did you go?"

She turned over two more shovelfuls of soil. With the third she decided not to spare him. "It was still dark outside. I was going to sit on a bench somewhere until it was light; then I was going to start making the rounds of coffee shops, looking for work. I picked the wrong bench." She tried to lift the shovel and realized Jase was gripping it so that she couldn't. She stared into compassionate green eyes. "Two fellows jumped me and grabbed my purse. When I tried to follow, one of them knocked me to the ground. I woke up in the hospital."

"Becca."

Her expression didn't change, even though she couldn't remember anyone saying her name quite that way before. "I was there for weeks. For a while a machine did my breathing. When I could do my own again, they told me they wouldn't let me out unless I promised to come here while I mended. I didn't have a choice."

He touched her shoulder. Gently. So gently. "You are one pigheaded woman."

"I guess if I weren't, I'd be dead."

"And Mary Smith? How did she come into the picture?"

"I didn't have any identification. Becca Hanks had three strikes against her. When I woke up I thought maybe somebody might throw a woman named Mary Smith a ball or two."

"I'm so sorry."

"For what? For lying to me? For knowing somebody whose life is as messed up as mine? Don't be."

"I wasn't lying when I tried to help you. I wanted to do it. It didn't matter who I was. I wanted to help."

"You and your sister are two of a kind. And don't think I don't appreciate it." She pulled the shovel from his grasp. "You were kind to me. Maybe you even saved my life. I owe you thanks for that. But I don't want anything except a chance to make my own way. The people here are great, but I've got to leave. And I'm going to, just as soon as I pay them back for everything they've done."

Jase couldn't find the words to tell her that The Greenhouse didn't operate that way. And where were the words to tell her to slow down, to let someone else share her burden? She had gained a little weight and a little healthy color in her cheeks, but she was still a long way from well.

"It's all right to take care of yourself. Stay here until you're ready to face the world again. Let The Greenhouse help you. Let me help."

"You?" She frowned. "Do you own another floor I can sleep on? I'm guessing you owned that one."

"Becca."

"Why would you want to help me?"

"Because I can. Easily. Let me help you make a new start."

She wondered how many people said no to Jase Millington. He was dressed casually today, dark slacks, a green shirt that made his eyes glow like emeralds. But casual or not, he stood like a man who was used to people throwing themselves at his feet. He held himself with supreme confidence, his broad shoulders thrown back, his head cocked. He was a man any woman would feel drawn to.

She had liked him better, so much better, on a dark March night when he had been in trouble, too. "No." She tried the word out slowly, watching for its effect. "No, Jason Millington, the Whatever-You-Are, Third, Fifth, Tenth? I don't care. I've said thank-you for your help, and I'll say thanks for the offer of more. But I don't want anything given to me. Nothing. Not from anybody."

"Why in hell are you so stubborn?"

She thrust the shovel into the ground and whacked the top of it with her foot. Pain shot through her leg, but she didn't care. "Because stubborn is who I am! It's the one thing I've got that nobody can take away from me! The only thing!"

She was almost to the end of the row before he left. She didn't hear him go; she didn't watch him. But she knew when he was gone. Funniest thing, but she knew when he was gone.

Jase and Pamela's parents, Jason Millington the Third and his wife Dorothea, lived in a rambling eighteen-room house looking over five acres of manicured grass and evergreens in Hunting Valley, east of Cleveland. Dorothea suffered from allergies and disliked bees, so every flowering shrub and tree that had once bloomed on the property had been removed the week the Millingtons moved in. Pamela called her parents' estate Sing-Sing. They called it their little country cottage.

Jase seldom visited his parents at home. His work schedule

left little free time, and the drive to Hunting Valley annoyed him. He usually met them for drinks or dinner in Cleveland. He liked the city, the smells, the bustle, the energy, the rumble of traffic. He was never certain what his parents had needed to escape from by their move. Their home in Cleveland Heights had been spacious and perfect for the extensive entertaining that they still did. He could only guess that Cleveland Heights, with its mixture of rich and not-so, had become too much like the real world for them to feel comfortable.

On the Saturday evening after his talk with Becca, Jase found himself driving out of the city for his mother's birthday dinner. Pamela had insisted on meeting him there. Even though she had pleaded that a hair appointment was going to make her late, he knew the real reason why she hadn't driven with him. Pamela would not visit their parents unless she had her own car to make an escape in.

By the time he wound his way up the tree-shaded driveway, Pamela was already there. She was minutely examining newly planted juniper when he joined her.

"Have you been inside?"

"Not yet. I was just fascinated to see what new things Mother had allowed in her yard."

"How long have you been out here?"

"A little while."

"In other words, they don't know you've arrived?"

"Probably not."

"You couldn't face them alone?"

"Did I say that? Juniper fascinates me. The variety of plants Mother can find that don't flower or bear fruit fascinates me." She put one arm around Jase's waist. She was clutching a gift in her other. "Let's go."

"It's a party, Pamela. A celebration."

"Yeah. Someone might crack a smile."

"They're not that bad."

"They're worse." She put her finger on her lips to forestall any more discussion. "I'll be good."

"You'd better be."

He rang the bell. He had never lived in this house, so he didn't have a key or want one. Surprisingly, it was his father who opened the door.

"We were beginning to wonder if you were coming." Mr. Millington moved back to let them pass.

"Would we miss one of your wonderful parties?" Pamela asked.

Jase shot her a warning glance, but there was nothing except goodwill visible on Pamela's face. They exchanged minimal small talk before following their father into the garden room.

Dorothea Millington was watering a towering palm when they entered. She was a tall, thin woman with dark hair that she had not allowed to go gray, and hands whose hardest work was holding still for a manicure twice weekly. Her husband was even taller, broad-shouldered like his son and lean from regular workouts at a private gym. They would always be a striking couple.

"I was just about to tell Gladys to hold dinner," she said. She finished watering before she turned. "I do wish you'd let your hair grow out a little, Pamela. It's so wash and wear."

"Practical hair for a working woman. Happy Birthday, Mother." Pamela walked just close enough to hand her mother the gift. "No one will believe you're fifty-eight."

Jase got closer, but his mother was surrounded by a no-man's land into which one didn't intrude. He knew the boundaries. "Happy Birthday." He presented her with his gift. She leaned forward, and he kissed her cheek.

"I'll open these later. Gladys has already set out hors d'oeuvres, and your father made Manhattans."

Neither Jase nor Pamela drank Manhattans, but there was nothing to be gained from pointing that out again. Once Jase had wondered if his parents made Manhattans and graceless comments out of hostility. Now he realized their lack of tact was nothing more than self-absorption. Their world was narrow and comfortable. They had been born into affluence, and they had never balked at it the way he and Pamela had. They did not understand, could not understand, that there were others, most particularly their own children, who viewed the world differently.

He and Pamela accepted the Manhattans and exchanged more small talk. By the time they went into dinner, Pamela had been chided for not attending a benefit dinner for the Opera Society and he for allowing himself to be written up in the city magazine as one of Cleveland's most eligible bachelors.

Dinner was more pleasant, although Jase could not help comparing it to the party the night before at The Greenhouse. Here there were no streamers or balloons, and the dining room wasn't perfumed by the evening's menu. There was beef Wellington and steamed broccoli, and for dessert a chocolate almond torte purchased from an east side bakery. His mother ate only a few bites and looked askance at Pamela's seconds, although she refrained from comment.

They opened presents in the garden room over coffee. Jase's was an onyx brooch with a tiny spray of pearls, expensive, but not expensive enough to be considered in bad taste—the Millingtons didn't flaunt their wealth. Pamela's was an elegant black and white scarf from a Beachwood boutique. As usual, he and Pamela had not coordinated their gifts, but their gifts complemented each other perfectly. One year he had bought perfume and Pamela a crystal bottle to put it in. Another he had bought a blue cashmere cardigan, and Pamela had shown up with a silk shell of the same color to wear beneath it. They did not examine the phenomenon too closely.

"My children buy wonderful gifts," Dorothea said.

"Your children wish you the happiest birthday," Jase answered. He got to his feet, and Pamela joined him. "But I'm afraid I have to go now."

"Don't tell me you're working tomorrow."

"I am."

"It's Sunday, Jase. Neither you nor Pamela should be working on Sunday."

Jase knew his mother's comment stemmed less from religious fervor than from her dislike of her childrens' chosen professions. "Sometimes business can't wait."

"And people are still homeless on Sundays," Pamela said.

"It would be different if you needed these jobs."

"I need to do what I do, Mother," Pamela said. "And that reminds me, I need you to do something, too." Briefly, she outlined Jase's plan for turning the downtown factory into apartments. "Jase and I both think you would be the perfect person to head up our fund-raising committee. You know everybody in the city, and half of them owe you favors. You could make the difference between success and failure."

Dorothea's face was creased by unfamiliar wrinkles. "You want me?"

"Who better?"

"But I'm not even sure I approve of this project."

For one moment Pamela's face showed all her frustration, her hurt; then it smoothed into the expression that Jase had begun to think of as her family mask. Her voice was cold. "I suppose it's asking a lot to accept the fact that Jase is so flamboyantly successful that he can donate entire buildings on a whim, or that I'm mired up to my ears in trying to help people you'd rather I didn't even know, but that's what we are, Mother. And we'd like you to be with us on this. I hope you'll give it some thought."

Their father looked as if he thought he ought to object to Pamela's speech but wasn't quite sure why.

"What Pamela means," Jase said, smoothing the waters, "is that this is important to us, and we'd like to share it with you. But if you're not interested, maybe you can think of someone who might help."

"I don't know."

He nodded and took Pamela's arm. Firmly. "Don't worry. Just think about it." He said enough goodbyes to cover for Pamela's silence, then steered her through the house. At the door he kissed his mother's cheek and clapped his father on the shoulder.

He took Pamela to her car after the door had closed behind them. "Well, you almost got through the whole evening without a scene."

"You think that was a scene?"

"I know it wasn't the one you wanted to make. You're improving."

"I really don't hate them, you know. I just can't understand them! There's as much warmth in that house as in a North Pole igloo."

He watched her struggle for control. He had come to terms with his parents long ago, but he had been luckier than Pamela. As a boy, he had been granted more freedom. He had thrown himself into activities that took him away from home. Pamela had been kept on a tighter rein, and she had been exposed to her parents' rules and expectations until she had been forced to rebel or shrivel and die.

On the surface, their lives had been perfect, but the surface had been all there was.

He put his arms around her now. "It doesn't matter, does it?"

"No. Not unless I'm exposed to them for too long. Then the old longings start. Crazy, huh? I do therapy. I'm not supposed to need it."

"You just need a hug."

"And here you are giving it to me because they can't, and because there's no man in my life to do it. Both you and I are so afraid that if we meet someone and fall in love, we'll end up with a marriage like theirs."

He rejected the on-the-spot analysis, but in the same instant he thought of Becca. Why, he didn't know. "I'm not married because I don't have time."

"You're not married because you're afraid you'll go home to something like that. Both of us compensate all the time. I give other people the warmth and love I didn't get, and you reshape the world to your liking." She shook her head. "Don't listen to me. It's been a long, rotten day, and I'm wiped."

"Anything happen at The Greenhouse?"

"One of the residents' husbands drove back and forth for an hour and shouted obscenities until the police chased him away."

"Not...Mary's?"

"As far as I know, Mary doesn't have a husband." She paused. "Are you going to tell me your connection to Mary?"

He leaned against her car. "Mary Smith is Becca."

She sighed. "I figured that out last night when she took off after she saw you."

"I came to the house this morning to see her. She said she changed her name because Becca Hanks had three strikes against her."

"Do you know what that means?"

"I'd guess she has something to hide." He thought of the photograph of two little girls in pink overalls and wondered if they were part of what she was keeping secret. He had never mentioned the photograph to Pamela, and he didn't now. Becca had shared it in an unguarded moment, and she, like everyone in the world, was entitled to her privacy.

"Did she tell you she almost died in the hospital?" Pamela asked.

Something clenched inside him. "No. But she told me enough that I guessed."

"It was touch and go for a week. She had pneumonia, a particularly nasty variety. She was anemic, malnourished, dehydrated. You name it. She's a lovely person, Jase. I can see why you couldn't forget her. And so proud."

"That she is."

"We're having trouble getting her to rest and take care of herself."

"What can I do?"

Pamela joined him against the car. She folded her arms just as he had folded his. "She won't take anything from anybody."

"She's made that abundantly clear."

"What about a job?"

"What about one?"

"Do you have a job in Millington Development that she could do?"

He considered. Many of the jobs were highly technical, and many more required strength and stamina Becca just didn't possess. He could create a position in his office, but somehow he knew she would realize she wasn't really needed and decline. "I can't think of anything," he said. "And I think it has to be something she knows she's qualified to do, or she won't take it.''

"You're probably right.''

"Even if I found a way to hire her in a low level position, I don't know how she could afford housing.'' He wished the factory were already renovated. An apartment there would be the perfect start.

"She needs a live-in position. A job that comes with a place to stay.''

"I don't need a housekeeper. I'm never home.''

"Jase, what about Kathryn's house?''

Their grandmother's house was a subject Jase and Pamela usually didn't discuss. Kathryn Millington had been an eccentric, opinionated old woman, the heaviest cross their parents had been forced to bear. She had castigated her son for his stuffiness and choice of spouse until he had stopped allowing her in his home. Then, from a distance, she had taken her twin grandchildren under her wing and given them everything their parents had forbidden. She had greatly enlivened their childhood.

On her death, Kathryn had left Jase her home in Shaker Heights, a century-old Tudor with walls as thick as a fortress and two acres of elaborate gardens. Pamela had inherited Kathryn's summer home on Lake Erie in nearby Vermillion. Pamela lived there year round, one of the few privileges of wealth that she allowed herself to enjoy.

"What about the house?'' Jase asked.

"Don't you think it's time to fix it up and move in? You've been promising you would for three years now.''

Jase understood Pamela's attachment to the house. It had been a place of refuge. He was less attached, but still unwilling to sell it. He wasn't sure what the house represented to him, but it was more than an investment. "I'm happy where I am, and I haven't had time to do anything about renovations. What does this have to do with Becca?''

"Becca could supervise the renovations. She could live in the caretaker's cottage. And she could do the landscaping! The place is a jungle, but you've seen what she's done at The Greenhouse. What better recommendation do you need?''

Jase was only surprised that the idea hadn't occurred to him first. The cottage was four rooms, Tudor-style like the house, and quaint, to say the least. Through the years it had been used for guests or household staff, but it had always been called the caretaker's cottage. While the house would not be livable while it was undergoing restoration, the cottage would be more than comfortable.

He realized that if he said yes, he was making more than a commitment to help Becca. Once the house was fixed up, he would have to move in or sell. ''Do you think she'd agree to do it?''

''I think she might. It would be something she can really do, and she knows we know it. It's nothing like charity. That's what she's afraid of.''

He thought about having Becca so close by, so within reach. He could supervise her recovery, assure himself that she was really going to be all right. He didn't know why that was so important to him. Usually he left those sorts of commitments to Pamela. But this was one commitment he wanted to watch over himself.

''It would only be temporary,'' he warned. ''There's a lot to be done, but it won't take longer than the summer.''

''She'll be well by then, more able to cope.''

''Can she handle it? Is she well enough?''

''She can handle it better than what the world has in store for her.'' Pamela faced him. ''What do you think?''

''I think we've got a plan.''

''You know this isn't like you, don't you? It's very personal, Jase. You'll be seeing her frequently. She'll be hard to ignore.''

''Impossible,'' he amended.

''She's not like the women you know. You can't lose interest and write her off.''

''This is hardly the same thing.''

She looked at him as if she wondered. ''Just tell me why you're doing it.''

"Because I hate to see potential going to waste."

"She's not a city block you can level and replace with something new and flashy."

"Go home, Pamela."

She did, and he did, too. But on the way to his penthouse looking over the lake, he wondered what changes both he and Becca had in store for them.

Chapter Four

Among Kathryn Millington's eccentricities had been a reluctance to throw anything away. The house in Shaker Heights was still piled high with books and magazines. Every piece of first-class mail she had received was packed neatly in boxes. Every dress she had worn, every umbrella that had sheltered her gray head, every slipper that her five dogs had chewed, was still somewhere in the house. Each of the fourteen rooms held four times the amount of furniture it should, and when the house started bursting at the seams, she had begun to store things in the cottage.

When Jase unlocked the cottage door for the first time in the three years since his grandmother's death, he thought he was ready for what he would find. He had hired a cleaning service to dust and vacuum regularly, but there was only so much even the most conscientious could do when faced with total disarray. His work crew took one look at what awaited them and went for another pickup to supplement the one they'd driven there.

A day passed before the cottage floor and walls were visible, and two more before the most basic repairs had been made. It was a week before new paint graced the walls and cabinets, and another three days before new floors had been installed in the kitchen and bathroom. Not until that point did Jase feel that he could even bring Becca to see the house.

This time when he got to The Greenhouse, he didn't find her in the garden. She was in the kitchen by herself, working on a stew that looked to be nine-tenths potatoes, carrots and onions. It still smelled heavenly.

From the doorway he watched her work. She was humming as she stirred. Her hair was pulled into a tidy French braid, and she was wearing jeans and a man's flannel shirt. There was nothing boyish about the figure the jeans were molded to. The weight she had gained filled out all the right seams.

"I can see it's going to be hard to get you to leave that stew and go out to dinner with me."

She turned. The hand holding the spoon made slow, steady circles as she examined him. Finally she smiled. The smile disappeared quicker than it had come, but not quick enough to shortcut the leap in his heart rate. "I wondered if you'd come back."

"You didn't scare me away."

"I'll bet nothing scares you."

"I get scared when I think a woman is going to turn down a date."

"I'll bet you've never been turned down."

"There could be a first time."

"Sure could." She turned back to her stew. "This is my gramma's recipe. Only they're fresh out of rabbit and squirrel in these parts, so I had to make do with chicken."

"A pity." He moved closer, encouraged by that fleeting smile. "It smells good."

"You've never eaten stew in your life."

"Sure I have. Stew's not a have or have not issue. I've eaten everything. Name something I haven't eaten."

"Grass."

"Have you?"

"Close. Dandelion greens, poke salad, lamb's-quarter."

"My grandmother cooked dandelion greens with bacon."

"Expect me to believe that?"

"You'll believe it by the end of the night if you let me take you out for dinner and a short drive." He leaned against the counter beside the stove so he could see her face.

The rhythm of her stirring didn't change, but she was completely aware of him. Tonight he was the successful businessman who had come to dinner, the man who had almost made her drop a fifteen pound ham on the dining room floor. He was dressed in a dark suit, but he had removed his tie, perhaps to pretend he was "just folks."

He wasn't just folks. Since their last meeting she had learned everything she needed to know about him. Jase Millington was old money and brand new ambition. He was a ruthless businessman with one chink in his armor. He loved his sister unconditionally, and if Pamela told him to give money to The Greenhouse, he gave. If she told him to send a work crew, he sent. And if she told him to dress up like a homeless man to see how a growing minority of the population was forced to live, he dressed up.

Not without a fuss, she guessed. And not without some feeling that Pamela might be on to something. No one ordered this man to do anything he didn't believe in, not even his beloved sister.

She took her time answering him, because his invitation had caught her off guard. She had also learned he was good at that.

"Now, I'm from the country. You can tell that, I know. I didn't get a lot of education, and some that I got wasn't too good. But my daddy didn't raise any stupid young'uns. And he taught me real early to ask myself why a man was being nice to me."

"What answer do you get this time?"

"Not the usual. Usually a man wants something I'm not inclined to give out. I'm sure you, in particular, have no trouble getting that in other places."

"Are we discussing my sex life?"

"No. We're discussing what you want from me. You want me to make you feel good. You want to do something for me so you can feel better about yourself. You feel sorry for me, and you don't want to."

"All those deep, dark motives behind a simple invitation to dinner and a drive?"

"Well?"

He took the spoon out of her hand and set it on the stove. Then he took her hand in his. "I do feel sorry for you. What kind of bastard would I be if I didn't?" He squeezed her hand when she started to interrupt. "No, let me finish. I feel sorry for the things you've had to go through, but I don't pity you. You'll find a way to make your life better with or without me. I don't know much about you, but I know that. The thing is, I could make that process a lot easier."

She pulled her hand away. "Thank you kindly. But I don't want your help."

He went on as if he hadn't been interrupted. "I could make your struggle easier, and at the same time you could make *my* life easier, too."

"How?"

"I think you'll have to see for yourself, so you'll know I'm not making any of this up. But I do need your help, Becca."

She couldn't imagine what Jase Millington needed from her. But he had found the one sure ticket into her life. He and his sister had already helped her immeasurably. If he even remotely needed something she could give him, she had to agree.

She picked up the spoon. "What kind of dinner are we talking about?"

He shrugged. "Whatever you'd like."

"I won't go anywhere fancy. I don't want you spending money on me."

"I'm not eating fast-food hamburgers just because you're too stubborn for anything else."

She held out the spoon. "Then think of a compromise while I change my clothes."

She was gone before he realized that he had been left with a kettle of stew to nurture.

Upstairs Becca found Shareen and told her where she would be going. Then she considered what to wear. Her new wardrobe was small, but attractive. As a child she had learned to quilt, as a teenager to sew her own clothes. She could take anything apart, cut it down to size and reassemble it so that it looked like a new outfit. The Greenhouse had a sewing machine, and she had altered donated clothes for herself and some of the other women. In exchange one of them had cut her hair and another, who had worked for years in a department store, had given her advice on the colors she should wear and the kinds of clothes that looked best on her.

Now she chose a plain peach sweater and a patterned turquoise skirt. The outfit was simple and attractive, but not nice enough for the kind of restaurant Jase Millington would normally frequent. She chose her low-heeled shoes to make certain she wouldn't look dressed up.

He was still stirring when she came back downstairs. For a moment she let herself admire him. He looked at home at the stove as only a perfectly confident man could. She couldn't imagine what would ever diminish Jase's masculinity. Even when she had believed him to be a drifter, even when she had been too ill to make sense of a senseless night, she had recognized his strength and allowed him to take control of her life.

She couldn't allow that again. She wasn't ill now, and he wasn't a drifter. He was a man with much of the world at his fingertips. If she let him, he would choose a corner of the world for her, and there would be nothing wrong with his choice. She already knew he would be more than fair. But she had to find her own corner, and she had to get there under her own steam.

"Did you think of a place?" she asked.

He turned. She watched his gaze drift from her newly brushed hair to her shoes. She felt a tingle at the wholly masculine assessment. Once men had thought her pretty. Dewey Hanks had chosen her to be his wife because she was the prettiest girl in Blackwater. Of course, there hadn't been a whole heck of a lot of competition.

By the time Jase's eyes were level with hers again, she knew he approved of her choice of clothing and possibly of more.

"Becca, you look very nice."

"Thank you. But what you see is what you're taking with

you, so I hope you've come up with someplace where I'll feel at home.''

"I thought we could give old Red another try." He smiled as her eyes narrowed. "A joke. Besides, I've heard Red sold his place. And not for much."

"I might work up some sympathy. In the next century."

"I'm never sympathetic on an empty stomach. Let's go."

She crossed the room and turned off the burner. Then she followed him outside to his car.

She wasn't sure what she had expected Jase to drive, but it wasn't the dark blue sedan he led her to. His car was Japanese, not European, and although it was top of the line, she guessed it was half the price of a more prestigious model. He opened her door, and she relaxed against the leather seats. They were as soft as butter, contoured for every curve of her body. She shut her eyes and cuddled in as Jase backed out of the driveway.

Jase didn't speak until he had wound his way through the maze of residential side streets and onto a main road. Then he glanced at Becca. "Do you like Greek food?"

Her eyes were shut, as if she were enjoying the quiet purr of the engine. When she didn't answer, he realized she was enjoying something else. Sleep.

She didn't rest enough. Pamela had warned him. Here she was, sound asleep the moment she sat down. He gripped the wheel and turned his eyes back to the road. Since Pamela had suggested putting Becca in charge of the renovations and landscaping at the Shaker Heights house, he had given little thought to his decision to do so. Now he wondered. Certainly the job was a better possibility than many. If she was waiting on tables or helping in a child care center, she would be on her feet most of the day. At his house she could rest whenever she felt tired. But would she? Or would she work so hard at any job that she would work herself right back into the hospital? Or worse?

He glanced at her again and shook his head. When she was sleeping she looked young, impossibly so. She looked defense-less and sweet and malleable—which proved the adage that looks could be deceiving.

She slept for the entire twenty minutes it took to get to Constantine's. He had parked and turned off the engine before she stirred. When she opened her eyes she didn't apologize or make excuses. "Where I come from, getting a girl this relaxed is the beginning of a locker-room fairy story."

"What if the girl's been sick and still isn't well?"

"Easier prey."

"When are you going to start taking better care of yourself?"

"Do you make a habit out of worrying about everybody you come across? How on earth do you stay rich? How do you sock it to people like Red?"

"How do you know I socked it to Red?"

"I didn't. Not until just now. You've got a great poker face. It's hard to tell what you're thinking. But there's this little hint of a smile sometimes when you're pleased with yourself." She searched his features. "And there it is. What did you do to the poor man?"

"Poor man?"

"I bet he's a poor man now."

"Not poor. Just not as rich as he might have been if he'd used his head. Red thought he was getting a great deal, but Red didn't do his research."

"And you did?"

"I made it my business to research his block."

"And?"

"When the office building next door decides to build a new parking garage, Red's Place will be sitting smack in the middle of it, unless I get the price I want."

"How do you know they're planning one?"

"I don't. They don't, in fact. But a little research proves they need one badly, and the only likely location is Red's. And since the same corporation also owns a nice little piece of property over on Euclid that I've been itching to own for two years now, I believe a trade will be in order."

"And you knew this when you went after Red?"

He opened his door. "No."

"You went after him just because of the way he treated you?"

He got out, but not before she heard his answer. "No, because of the way he treated you."

She was still mulling that over as he held the restaurant door open for her. Constantine's was red-checked tablecloths and starched white café curtains in the windows. There was a blackboard with the night's specials, and Chianti bottles at each table with well-dripped candlewax decorating the sides. The atmosphere was someone's version of Italian bistro, the piped-in music was appropriate for dancing the Russian bear, and a brief glance at the blackboard testified that Greek or plain old Midwestern American was the cuisine of choice. A glance at the right-hand column on the blackboard reassured Becca that Jase had taken her caution seriously.

"Come on and meet Constantine and Mama."

"Mama?"

"She has a name that no one can pronounce, and she likes Mama better, anyway."

Together Constantine and Mama weighed as much as a Thanksgiving turkey without the stuffing. They fussed over Jase as if he were their first-born son and seated him at the best table in the house, one looking directly over the parking lot.

"Mama likes you. Good," Jase said when Mama had left them to choose from the hand-scrawled menu.

"How can you tell?"

"She'd call you 'Miss' if she didn't. I've seen her do it before. Freezes a woman dead in her tracks."

"I risked that?"

"Mama has good taste."

She favored him with her second smile of the night. She was charmed by Mama and his choice of restaurant. She had already gathered that he ate lunch here often, and that much of the nitty-gritty business of Millington Development was conducted at this very table.

Without waiting for an order, Mama brought them each a Greek salad large enough to qualify as an entrée. "I'm not even growing enough lettuce to fill this salad bowl," Becca said when Mama was gone.

"Save some room for Mama's moussaka."

"You said there was something I could do for you."

Jase was only surprised that she had waited this long to remind him. "I'll show you after dinner. I promise." He watched her toy with a Greek olive. "Should I order you something else?"

"I just hate to eat it. It's so pretty."

He realized she was serious. He wondered when he had stopped paying attention to simple pleasures. "Mama's an artiste with feta cheese and tomatoes."

"You probably think I'm silly."

"No."

"It's just that..." She couldn't think of the right words to explain her feelings. Not in a way that wouldn't remind him of what she had endured. "Well, I guess I just appreciate food," she said, because she had to say something.

He was immediately aware of how little he appreciated it. "It tastes as good as it looks."

She sighed and dug in.

She was halfway through before Jase spoke again. "Becca, I had Pamela looking for you after you disappeared that morning. When you recognized me at The Greenhouse, she figured out who you were. She knows your real name."

"I know. We talked. Shareen knows it now, too."

"There's nothing that would shock them. Nothing they wouldn't try to help you with."

"Is this why you brought me here?"

"No. I'm just concerned."

"Don't be."

"You showed me a photograph. Remember?"

She remembered too well. The photograph was gone now, taken from her along with her purse. She had almost lost her life, as well, and for a few days it had hardly mattered to her. "I don't want to talk about that."

"I wish you'd let me help."

"I know you do. What I don't know is why. Why does this matter to you? I'm nothing. Nobody. Just somebody who drifted through your life once."

"You're Becca Hanks. Not Mary Smith, classic nobody."

"I'm Becca. And Becca has to figure out who she is and where she's going. And she has to do it on her own."

"On her own and alone are two different things."

"Maybe."

He realized she had left the door to her life cracked, but just barely. If he tried to storm his way through, the door would slam and never open again.

They talked about The Greenhouse until the moussaka came. Becca promptly asked for half of hers to be packed to take home. Mama refused, promising it was so good, Becca would find room for it somehow. She did, but there was absolutely no way she could manage the devil's food cake that was meant to finish the meal. That, Mama packed up. By that time, she and Becca were firm friends.

"She made me promise to bring you back again," Jase told Becca on their way to the car.

"Speaking of promises, is this where I find out what you want me to do for you?"

"I've never met anyone with less patience."

"Jase…"

He opened her door. "This is where you find out. Just give me a few minutes to get you there."

She was silent as they drove toward Shaker Heights. She didn't know much about Cleveland. When she'd still had her car, gas had been too expensive for sight-seeing tours. She had stayed away from the city's better residential sections because there had been no jobs there for someone like her. She knew they were headed for one of those sections now. The streets were wide and tree-shaded, the lawns as green as Jase's eyes, and the houses were stately.

"Do you live here?" she asked at last.

"Not yet."

"You're planning to?"

"I'm planning to live right here." He pulled into a driveway that ended well away from the street.

"This is a mansion."

"Not at all. It's a big old house that needs more work than it's worth."

"That's not possible." She got out of the car without waiting for Jase to come around to her door. "It's a castle."

"Well, it's Tudor design, but that's as close as it gets to being royal."

Becca wasn't sure where to look first. Even though the sun had set, she could see how wonderfully substantial the house was and how individual. This was not one house of many in an upscale development, constructed of particle board and decorative two-by-fours. It was built of stone and brick, with recessed windows of tiny diamond-shaped panes. There were four chimneys pointed toward heaven, and the heavy timbers gracing the upper story obviously had a purpose.

The house was surrounded by trees she wouldn't be able to stretch her arms around. Branches badly in need of pruning scraped the slate roof. The lawn had been mowed, but no one had adequately tamed the shrubbery—and there seemed to be acres of it—for a very long time. The house did not look abandoned; it looked as if no one loved it.

"You want to buy it to save it." She faced Jase, and she was smiling. "You saw it and realized how badly neglected it had been. So you want to buy it to save it. Who'd let a house like this one go? There should be people living here, kids laughing, dogs running through the yard, yappy little lap dogs with squashed-in faces." She gestured to one side. "There ought to be a garden over there. Probably is already, only somebody has to find it again. Can't you see it? Roses and lilacs and iron tables with pitchers of lemonade? And croquet? This is a yard for croquet."

He realized that this was the longest speech she had ever made. "Croquet?"

"Don't sound so disgusted. It's a perfectly good game. We used to play it at church picnics and pie suppers when I was a little girl."

He grimaced. He ran three miles a day and played tennis or

racquet ball whenever he had time. But croquet was a game from another solar system. "Would you like to see the inside?"

"Do you have the key?"

"I own the key."

"Then you've already bought the house?"

Jase rarely felt guilty. He was too busy for guilt, and he had a core of beliefs he rarely strayed from, making guilt unnecessary. Why, then, had he begun examining his life so minutely since Becca had appeared in it? Why was he uncomfortable telling her the truth, that he had owned this house for years now and hadn't done a thing to it? That he hadn't bought the house to save it, but had been given the house on a silver platter and paid very little attention to the gift?

"I didn't buy it, Becca. It's my grandmother's house, or was. She left it to me some time ago, and I couldn't decide what to do about it. But I've decided to fix it up and move in."

He hadn't been sure about the last part until he said the words. The house had to be fixed up even if he sold it. Now he'd made a commitment to keep the house, and he wasn't quite sure why.

"You mean it's been standing empty?"

"Yes."

"How many rooms does it have?"

"Fourteen or so."

"Fourteen rooms. Standing empty." She turned away from him and stared up at the house.

He owned an empty fourteen-room house while people slept in alleys and bus stations. He could see her thoughts just as clearly as if she were scrawling them on Constantine's blackboard. "Come on, I'll show you the inside."

She followed him, but he stopped at the brick walkway and held out his arm. "The path has to be leveled and redone. Hold on to me so you don't stumble."

She contemplated the arm, as sturdy and strong an arm as anyone had ever offered her. The man it was attached to was as strong a man as she had ever known. And his strength could be her undoing.

She took his arm and looked up at him, trying to read his expression. "Why are you showing me the house?"

"Give me a chance to explain. First, take a good look." Her fingers were so light against his arm that he could hardly feel them, but Jase knew they were there. He hadn't been this close to her since he had held her in his arms and felt her body convulse with coughing. He had slept an endless night with this woman, but they were still strangers.

"What am I supposed to be looking for?"

"Possibilities."

"I'm not sure I'm the best person for that. I've always believed everything was possible, and look where it's gotten me."

"It's gotten you here. Let's see where else it can take you." He started up the path. At the door she moved away from him, and he felt something very much like disappointment.

Inside he turned on the lights downstairs as Becca followed him. He said nothing, letting her form her own opinions. There were very few places to walk. Paths were cleared through each room, but furniture draped in plastic lined every wall and jutted out into the rooms. Boxes were piled in corners, some towering almost as high as the twelve-foot ceilings.

"Kathryn believed firmly in the waste not, want not, philosophy of life," he said when they reached the kitchen.

"Kathryn?"

"My grandmother. She detested titles. She was always Kathryn to us."

"There's enough furniture here to furnish three more houses like The Greenhouse."

"Some of it's priceless. Some of it I'll have to pay somebody to haul away."

"Can you tell the difference?"

"I'll have to hire somebody."

"Why haven't you done that before now?"

"I really don't know." And he didn't. Even now, talking about getting rid of Kathryn's things made him uneasy. "Do you want to see the upstairs? It's more of the same. Six bedrooms—

seven, if you count the nursery—and plumbing so old I could sell it to the Smithsonian."

"Is the upstairs piled high, too?"

"Higher."

She leaned against a linoleum counter that had skipped kitchen redecoration fads as it gracefully flaked and peeled. "So why are we here?"

"If I'm going to renovate—and I am—I have to hire somebody to oversee the job. I'm not talking about the actual work. I'll use people I trust, and I'll check up on them from time to time. But somebody has to be here to be sure things get done, to answer phone calls, unlock doors, run errands if need be. Somebody's got to consult with the decorator, take messages, be sure I'm getting what I pay for. Up to that point, I just need a warm body with a brain and a finger to punch buttons on the phone. Beyond that point, I need someone who can help oversee the outdoor work, supervise landscaping crews—"

"Landscaping crews? Are you kidding, Jase? You're talking about those companies with the trucks filled with chemicals to kill everything in sight? I know what they'll do. They'll take one look at that jungle out there and pull out their chainsaws. You'll be left with some new seedlings they cart in from who knows where, and the yard will look like somebody scalped it!"

"Well, what do you suggest?"

"You don't need new landscaping. I didn't get to see everything—"

"You're right. You didn't. There are over two acres exactly as overgrown as what you've seen."

"That's even better. Somebody had a plan for this house. I could see that, even though it's dark outside. Somebody loved that yard. Under all those shrubs and vines and ground cover are gardens. They don't need a chainsaw. They just need a loving hand."

"Will you be my loving hand?"

She didn't speak for a moment. She'd had an inkling he was going to propose that she be the warm body with the button-punching finger and the brain, but she had gotten too worked up to realize he was leading up to asking her to do the landscaping, too.

The soil here would be rich and black. There would be lily of the valley. She just knew there would. And lilacs and mock orange, hydrangeas and rhododendrons. There would be perennial beds with day lilies and bleeding hearts and daisies. There would be places for annuals, and maybe even a vegetable garden with decade-old plantings of rhubarb and raspberries. Somewhere there would be a sturdy clematis vine twining its star-shaped purple flowers round a trellis. All hers to guide and design.

"Why?"

Jase knew the most decisive moment had come. Becca could not be fooled. If he was not perfectly honest with her, she would know, and she would refuse. If he *was* perfectly honest with her, she might still refuse.

"I'm trying to think of something to convince you," he said.

"How about the truth?"

"You need a job, preferably one that includes room and board. I need someone like you to live here and help get this property in shape. I could find someone else, but I don't see why I should bother. You're perfect for the job, and I trust you. If you let pride stand in your way, you'll be doing us both a disservice. But if you have another reason for not wanting it, just say no and I won't bother you again."

"Did you make up this job for me?"

He hesitated for a moment. "I don't know how to answer that. I was wishing I had a job for you, and Pamela suggested this. She's wanted me to fix up the house and move in since Kathryn died. I've put it off. I'm comfortable where I am."

"Where are you?"

"I have a condo on the lake. It's very different. Modern, efficient. Chrome and leather." She made a face, but he was encouraged. "Will you do it?"

"Where would I stay? In one of the bedrooms upstairs?"

"Nobody can live here while the renovations are going on. The house hasn't been painted in years, and I know the paint's lead-based. There'll be lead contamination when they scrape to repaint. And that's just for openers. It'll be dusty and dirty and inconvenient. Luckily there's an alternative. Would you like to see it?''

A few minutes later she stood in the newly painted living room of the cottage. She turned around slowly, taking in the stone fireplace and cherry mantel, the diamond-paned windows with the wide sills, perfect for African violets.

She thought of all the nights she had lived in her car and the endless nights she had lived in a worse place. With its antique furniture and floral print curtains, the little cottage was a slice of heaven. The room smelled of fresh paint and fresher air, and for a moment she was aware of a lump in her throat.

"You would more than earn what I pay you," Jase said. "And if I have to look for somebody else, it will take me longer to move in. The house shouldn't stand empty any longer."

The man knew how to push all the right buttons. "I can see why you're such a walloping success," she said.

"Will you do it?"

"You forgot to mention the chainsaws again."

"You're right. I'm manipulative, and I suffer from tunnel vision. When I want something, I go for it until it's mine." His gaze didn't leave her face.

For just a moment she wondered what Jase was like if it was a woman he wanted. The thought rippled down her spine.

"I'll do it," she said at last. "Soon as I'm done at The Greenhouse, and soon as I've trained someone there to watch over the garden. But only because I know there's no one who can do this better. I'm going to earn every penny you pay me." She paused. "What are you paying me, by the way?"

He named a sum that was more than fair, but she knew she was going to be worth it. "Okay. But when the job is finished, I leave. You can only invent so many things for me to do."

Since he knew that even the best work crews could find reasons to delay, he wasn't worried. The renovation was going to take just as long as it needed to. The house would be ready when Becca was well, and not a minute before.

He drove her back to The Greenhouse, but only after she'd had a moonlight tour of the grounds. He left her on the front steps talking to Shareen, but it was a moon-speckled wraith kneeling on the ground at the house in Shaker Heights that he thought of as he drove home. As he'd watched her, Becca had pushed aside a thick mat of vegetation and peered into the darkness with a practiced eye. "Peonies," she'd said. "Peonies, Jase. And they'll bloom again once I've trimmed everything back so they get some sun. Imagine these peonies here all this time, just waiting to be reborn."

Chapter Five

Cara Preston had legs no company had enough assets to insure and breasts as perfect as a plastic surgeon's dream. She also had a breathy, quicksilver laugh she timed with the precision of a stand-up comic's punch line. Tonight the laugh was getting on Jase's nerves.

Cara's apartment looked over the lake with a view much like the one from his own. He had spent many pleasurable hours here. He had known Cara for two years, and he admired more than her impeccably constructed body parts. She was intelligent and ambitious, the vice-president and marketing manager of a Cleveland-based catalog company. Cara's plan for her life did not include a husband, at least not right away and not one rooted in the Midwest. She planned to serve out her time in Ohio, then move east to New York or Boston, where she would settle down to real success. In the meantime, she was content to enjoy a more-than-casual-but-not-truly-intimate relationship with him.

That arrangement had been more than satisfactory for Jase, too. They both saw other people. Sometimes they didn't see each other for a month or more, and he was hardly aware so much time had passed. When they were together they shared mutual interests and friends, but rarely their feelings.

Tonight Jase stood on Cara's balcony, a drink in one hand and Cara's hip in the other. They had gone out to dinner and shared a perfectly grilled rack of lamb and a lemon soufflé. Then they had gone to Severance Hall to hear the symphony. If the night followed classic lines, he would finish his drink, then Cara would lead him to her bedroom. He would leave her apartment in the early hours of the morning and finish the night's sleep in his own bed.

"You seem far away," she said.

"Do I?"

"You have all night."

"I guess it's been a busy week."

She moved away to freshen her drink. "You haven't said anything about your house. How is it coming?"

"Fine, I'm told. I haven't found the time to get by there often. I spent one afternoon going over the furniture with the appraisers."

"Didn't you say you're selling most of it?"

"That's what I'd planned, but now it looks like I'm keeping a houseful."

"Why? Was it worth more than you'd thought?"

"In a way." He thought of the afternoon he had spent with Becca and the appraisers. It had been one of those surprisingly warm spring days that sometimes occurred right on the tail of a frost. Becca had worn shorts, revealing legs that rivaled Cara's. He couldn't remember what she'd worn with them, but the shorts had definitely made an impression.

Ten minutes into the furniture tour, the appraisers were ignoring him and consulting Becca. He had hired a simple country girl to oversee his renovations—or so he'd thought—but the woman he had gotten knew volumes about antiques. More important, Becca had a feel for each piece, as if she had personally collected it. He'd had the strangest sense that Kathryn was in the room, nodding in satisfaction as Becca pointed out how perfectly a table fit into a nook or cranny, how wonderfully well a shelf fit in front of a window.

Of course, Becca had a ruthless streak that Kathryn had never had. By the time the appraisers arrived she had already cleared the house of much of its rubbish. Clothes, slippers and umbrellas had been given to The Greenhouse or thrown away, depending on condition. Phone books and magazines dating from the forties had also been culled. Kathryn's personal memorabilia had been sorted and boxed. Becca had saved all his grandmother's letters and thrown away all bills and junk mail. Now there was a manageable amount for him to go through with Pamela.

He still wasn't sure why he had given in to sentiment and refused to sell so much of the furniture. Without junk filling every corner, he had seen the majestic lines of the antiques, the patina from age and years of loving care, the tasteful beauty of the dark and light woods. Some he had sent to be refinished. Some he had just shifted into areas of the house that would be the last to be renovated. Perhaps the decision was only good sense. His collection of chrome and leather would be as out of place in the old Tudor home as a woman like Cara.

He glanced up at her and realized where his thoughts had led him. "Do you like antiques, Cara?"

She wrinkled her delicate nose. "I'm a tomorrow person. Not a yesterday."

"What would you do if someone left you an old house that needed thousands of dollars' worth of work?"

"Sell it to the highest bidder, contents included. Invest the profit in high-yield bonds."

"What if you were sentimentally attached to it?"

She laughed, and he felt another twinge of annoyance. "Not possible, dear. Don't you know me better than that?"

He did know Cara. He didn't know Becca. There was still much about her that had never been revealed. But he did know how Becca valued the past. He had watched her touch his grandmother's furniture, watched her discuss the merits of each piece with the appraisers. Briefly he wondered what Cara would do if she suddenly found herself penniless, with no place to live and no job to go to. Would she show Becca's courage and determination to succeed on her own?

He didn't know Becca, but she occupied his thoughts more

and more. And Cara and the other women he knew occupied them less.

Cara put down her drink and slipped her arms around his waist. "I always thought we were two of a kind, Jason. But maybe I don't know you as well as I thought. Sentimentally attached? The man I thought I knew didn't have an ounce of sentiment anywhere in his body."

He set his drink down, too, and put his arms around her. "Not an ounce? You don't think I'm sentimentally attached to you?"

"Truth?"

"Truth."

"I think when I move to New York, you'll forget you ever knew me."

He pulled her closer and laid his cheek against her dark hair. But when Cara suggested they go inside, he remembered that he had an early appointment in Toledo the next day. The evening ended sooner than either of them had planned, and Jase, at least, didn't regret it.

Among other things, Becca's car needed a new transmission, brake pads, four new tires and a body job. Jase's mechanic went over the car thoroughly and grumbled when Jase didn't take his advice to sell it for scrap.

Becca didn't know that Jase had paid her fines, and he didn't plan to tell her until the work on the car was completed. So far she had shopped for necessities by bus and on foot, but he knew that not having a car was a major inconvenience. If she had waited until she could afford the fines and the work herself, it would have been months before she had transportation.

The afternoon the car was ready, he drove it to Shaker Heights himself. It sputtered a little, almost as if it was surprised to be moving again, but halfway there it settled down to burning oil and guzzling gas. He parked on the street in front of the house. He planned to gently ease Becca into the subject of her car, then inch her toward the street. He doubted she would make a scene in public.

Two weeks of concentrated man—and woman—hours hadn't

made too many changes in the exterior of the house, but the yard was already showing signs of Becca's efforts. She had deigned to allow an arborist and crew to prune trees and large shrubs, but she had directed every swipe of the saw and clippers. There were signs that beds were being cleared and edged, also under her direction. The result was a pleasing trim and not the military crew cut that had so worried her.

Inside the changes were more evident. In the front of the house, floors had been sanded and sealed, new wiring installed and walls scraped and replastered. There were still sections where woodwork had been removed for refinishing, but the rooms were taking shape. He talked to a man who was repairing the fireplace and another who was removing a chandelier. The mystery of where the rest of the crew had gone was solved by a third man who was heading out the kitchen door toward the cottage. Jase followed him.

He heard laughter when he was still twenty yards away. The cottage door was open, but he heard men's voices. He stopped in the kitchen doorway and watched four men get the scolding of their lives as Becca poured them coffee.

"Now I'm telling you good gentlemen, I might not know much about wiring walls or putting in a floor, but I do know that buying lottery tickets with your hard-earned money is no way to get rich quick!"

"Come on, Becca," a man Jase knew as Roy said as he held out his cup for more. "We're each putting in ten dollars. That's not our life savings. Besides, with six of us doing it, that gives us sixty chances at the pot each week. This week the pot's twelve mill. Split twelve million six ways, and that's still a whole lot of cash."

"More likely a whole lot of nothing. You're throwing your money away. If you put ten dollars into the bank every week, you'd have over five hundred dollars in a year's time. That's a couple of weekends away from the young'uns with your wife."

"You haven't seen my wife." Roy held up his hands. "Okay, okay. But I'm a gambling man. If it's not the lottery, it's the races or betting on the ball game. I'm going to hit it big some-day. I know I am.''

"Don't be handing in your resignation too quickly," Jase said. "Jobs where you can sit and gab all day don't come along too often, even when you've won the lottery.''

The men grumbled, but they stood, snatching pieces of coffee cake from a plate in the middle of the table before they filed past Jase on the way back to the house. They were all gone by the time Becca spoke.

"They weren't goofing off. They work hard. I'm a terrible hard taskmaster. This was the first break they've had all day.''

"I've heard what a taskmaster you are. Word filters up to the top."

"They grumble a lot, and sometimes they get fresh. But they keep on coming back every day.''

Jase reached for a piece of cake and took Roy's seat. Becca had coffee in front of him before he could ask for it. "I hear you won't let them cuss.''

"I sure won't.''

"I hear you climb ladders when they're done to inspect every little detail.''

"I pretend. Half the time I couldn't tell bad work from good.''

He sipped his coffee. It was the best he'd had all day, includ-ing a cup in one of the city's finest restaurants. "I hear they're telling you the stories of their lives.''

"They've had interesting lives.''

"They've gotten a lot done. You've gotten a lot done." He studied her. She was dressed in pale green, just a T-shirt and skirt, but she looked as fresh as spring. As the sun tanned her face and arms, it bleached her hair to the color of wheat. She no longer looked tired or drawn. He realized that he hadn't heard her cough since the day he'd confronted her at The Greenhouse.

"I haven't gotten nearly enough done, Jase. I work and work, but this is a major project.''

"I don't want you to work and work. I'm not paying you to slave. Take your time. I haven't even put my condo on the mar-ket yet. I'm not in any hurry to move.''

"I don't want to take advantage of you."

"I'm taking advantage of you. Can't you tell the difference?" She poured herself a cup of coffee and sat down across from him. "I've been thinking about what you said last time you were here."

He admired the curve of her wrist as she lifted the cup to her lips. There was nothing studied about Becca's movements. There was none of Cara's languid grace, nothing to indicate she had ever thought about what a man might find attractive. She moved with purpose, each gesture the shortest distance between two points, yet watching her gave him a deep satisfaction.

"Jase?"

"What did I say?"

"About the yard. What you wanted me to do."

He tried to remember that conversation. "I wanted it to be practical, easy to keep up."

"That's right."

"And?"

"Well, if I give you what you asked for, I'll have to dig out everything your gramma spent her life planting and start all over again."

"As a master at using guilt, I recognize it when I hear it."

"Lord, I'm not trying to make you feel guilty. It's your house, even if it did used to be your gramma's heart and soul. And so what if a whole lot of thought and work went into it? If all you're interested in is a yard that a lawn service can mow and edge and maybe trim twice a year, you can sure have it. Only I can't give it to you."

"You can't?"

"No. I've tried. The first day I had a chance to work in the yard I walked over to that bed of peonies we found, and I told them they had to go because they were going to bloom, and Jase Millington the Whatever doesn't want flowers."

"I don't?"

"Don't you?"

He had a fleeting vision of his parents' house. "I never said that."

"Well, you said easy upkeep, didn't you? Flowers take work, Jase. No lawn service is going to do flowers. You'd have to have a gardener come in, or you'd have to get your own hands dirty."

He backtracked. "Just what did the peonies say when you told them?"

"They said thank you, but they'd been there a lot longer than you have, and they weren't going to move out. I reasoned, but by the time I'd weeded a little, they'd convinced me."

"They sound persuasive."

"Little red shoots coming up all over and not a thing I could do about it." She got up to refill his cup.

Becca always seemed to be in motion. He liked the way her skirt skimmed her hips and backside. All that purpose gave her the nicest little wiggle. "I guess the peonies will have to stay," he said.

"See, the problem is they started a rebellion. They've got all the perennials on their side."

He liked the way she said "p'rennyawls." He was beginning to wish he had spent more time in Kentucky. "A rebellion?"

"I tried to dig up one of your gramma's perennial beds. Same thing happened."

"One of the beds?"

"There are a mountain of them, Jase. Your gramma was fond of perennials. See, I think she liked things that lasted, things that she could pass on to the people she loved."

"When you're done with this job, I'm going to give you a new one collecting all the money I'm owed."

"I'm not trying to change your mind. I'm just reporting."

"Let's hear it all."

"Do you like the cake?"

He hadn't had a chance for a bite. Now he ate a piece while she watched him intently. It was wonderful, sweet and sour with a flavor that was vaguely familiar. "What is it?"

"Rhubarb cake. And guess where I got the rhubarb?"

He supposed it hadn't been at the store. "Kathryn did grow rhubarb. I remember it now. And she made pies, or rather, someone made them for her. Whenever we could sneak over here in the spring, she'd feed us rhubarb pies.''

''Sneak?''

''My parents thought Kathryn wasn't good for us. Rhubarb, either. It needed too much sugar to make it edible.''

''Why, that's terrible! Family not good for you?''

''What about your family, Becca?''

''All dead.'' She toyed with a fork, the first time she had purposely looked away from him since he'd sat down at the table.

His stomach clenched. ''The little girls in the picture, too?''

''I meant the family I came from. Parents, grandparents. I had an older brother killed in a fire on a navy ship and another in Beirut. The service was their ticket out of…the town where we grew up.''

The knot in his stomach eased, but he knew better than to ask about the children again. ''What did you find besides rhubarb?''

''Raspberries.''

''Kathryn made jelly. We were only allowed to eat it here.''

''And asparagus.''

''I refused to eat it. She rolled it in sugar once to make me taste it.''

''Do you like it now?''

''If I say yes, am I going to inherit an asparagus patch?''

''You did inherit one. You just have to decide if you're going to sow it over with worthless old grass seed.''

''What else?''

''Well, just the most important thing of all.'' She stood again and took his cup, although it was half full.

He leaned back in his chair and watched her clean up the other cups and take them to the sink. She ran water in a dishpan and added detergent and dishes instead of stacking the dishwasher. He had never found dishwashing intriguing before. She was much more fun to watch than a machine.

''You use guilt like a pro, and now you've added suspense to your repertoire,'' he said when she was almost finished.

''And you're a waiting champion.''

"I can wait forever if I have to, but I never have to."

"Have you always gotten everything you wanted?"

"No. I can't get you to take it easy and stop buzzing around here like a workaholic bee."

"Then maybe we've both met our match." She was silent for a moment, as if she were listening to her own words. "I mean, in terms of stubborn."

He couldn't see her face, but he could almost swear she was blushing. She *sounded* like she was blushing. "I have no match. You're a beginner compared to me."

She dried her hands on a dishtowel and faced him. If she had been blushing there were no traces. "Let me show you what stubborn is, Jase."

"You can try."

She favored him with one of her rare smiles and nearly bowled him over. She smiled so seldom that each time he noticed just what a cataclysmic experience it was. She was a pretty woman, but when she smiled, damn it, when she smiled she was absolutely radiant. He had the strangest feeling he didn't know her at all.

"You might get your feet wet and your hands dirty," she taunted, still smiling.

"My butler and valet will clean me off when I get home."

"You don't have a butler. Nobody in the whole U. S. of A. has a valet. Except when they park."

"How do you know?"

"My vast acquaintance with rich folks." She threw the towel on the counter. "Ready?"

"For anything."

Anything was the side of the house that had inspired visions of yappy little dogs and endless croquet games. Becca and Jase passed under a weeping willow tree that Jase had fallen out of once at age eight and through a slim gap in a newly clipped boxwood hedge. "What do you see?" Becca asked before Jase had even made it to the other side.

"More yard. A buildable lot or two. If I had a mind to do it and it was zoned accordingly, I could probably put two houses here.''

"Don't even think about it!''

He didn't point out the irony of her response. If anyone understood how desperately housing was needed, Becca should. On the other hand, anything he would build in this neighborhood was not going to help the homeless. "What was I supposed to see?''

"Look around.''

There were very few people he would waste so much time for. But this was Becca asking. He shook his head as he skirted the area. At the border of his property he found a deep, wide bed, newly weeded and layered with cypress chips. Thorny shrubs clipped a foot or two above ground level were beginning to sprout branches and leaves. "This?''

She slapped her hands on her hips. "Don't you know what they are?''

He tried to remember what Kathryn had grown here. There had been a swing in the corner by the boxwood, an old-fashioned porch swing hanging from a wooden frame. And there had been a table to hold lemonade and picture books. Once a bee had stung him. There had always been swarms of bees because of the roses.

"Roses.''

"Good for you.'' She came to his side. "Jase, I can't dig these up. I really can't. Regular roses take a lot of work. I know they do. They have to be babied to grow, fertilized and sprayed for bugs and leaf spot and mold. But these aren't regular roses. They're the old-fashioned kind, the kind that grew in gardens all over the world for centuries before somebody started dickering around to make them bigger or prettier.''

"How do you know? They're sticks in the ground right now. Sticks with thorns, the worst kind.''

"Because they're still here. Nothing's still here that wasn't hardy. Your gramma's been dead for three years now. And all anyone's done to this yard is cut the grass and cut off a branch or two that hung too low. That's it. Anything that needed care is gone now. But the roses are still here. Nobody fertilized or sprayed. They made it through the winters without being mulched or protected. I pruned them back a lot, because they were going wild, but look how they're taking off again. They'll be beautiful when they bloom, Jase, the centerpiece of the yard if you don't dig them up.''

He sensed more than just a passion for gardening in her plea. ''Where did you learn so much, Becca?''

She turned back to the roses, squatting to smooth the mulch. ''My gramma had old roses, too. Some of them came over to this country with her grandmother, from England. She tended them like they were her babies, only they don't need much tending, so mostly she just talked to them because she loved them so much. She told me stories about them.''

''What kind of stories?''

''There was one I remember, a poem, about a man, Sweet William, and the woman, Fair Margaret, who loved him. William married another woman, and it broke Margaret's heart. On his wedding night she appeared to him in a terrible dream, and he, being sure it was a bad omen, went to her house and found her dead.''

''I hope this ends happily.''

''Mercy no. He was so sorry for what he'd done that he lay down and died from it. He was buried beside Margaret.''

''I thought this was about roses?''

''It is. The story says that out of Margaret's breast sprang a rose, and out of William's, a briar. I still remember the next part exactly. 'They grew till they grew unto the church top, And then they could grow no higher; And there they tied in a true lovers' knot, Which made all the people admire.' ''

''There have to be happier stories.''

''There are. But even better I remember a little game we played. Every summer I'd go to Gramma's house in the morning and help her with the chores she couldn't do alone. Then, when we were done, we'd take iced tea out to the rose garden and look for one perfect rose. We never found one. There'd always be a petal that was bruised, or maybe a bee had spread pollen over a petal and turned it yellow. Some were too big, some were too small. Some weren't white enough or red enough. Never a perfect one. But it didn't matter. They were all wonderful, every single rose. Gramma used to say the roses tried harder for us because they knew we were going to look at them every day.''

"My grandmother loved these roses, too.''

"I know she did. I can feel it.'' She stood and wiped her hands on her skirt. "The roses just want a chance to grow, Jase. That's all. They don't want to be fussed with or interfered with. They just want a chance.''

Just like Becca. He was not oblivious to the parallel. Becca wanted a chance. That was all. No fuss, no interference. A chance to grow and flower, and maybe someday to produce one perfect rose.

"How could I dig them out?'' he asked. She was standing within touching range, and it seemed the most natural thing in the world to touch her. He picked a boxwood sprig from her hair, and his hand lingered there when the sprig was gone. Finally it dropped to his side. Her gaze had never left his face. She seemed to be holding her breath, waiting for something to happen. He knew the feeling.

"Then they can stay?'' she asked.

"I wouldn't want it any other way. Will you teach me what I have to know to take care of them?''

"Just visit them every day. That's all. They'll do the rest if you let them.''

"I don't think…that will be hard.''

"Thank you.'' She reached for his hand and squeezed it, then dropped it immediately. "I'd hoped you'd understand.''

"I think I understand too well.''

She didn't ask him what he meant. She just smiled again. He felt the impact for the rest of the day, even when he was miles away.

Chapter Six

Jase visited the roses as frequently as he could. They grew inches every day, sturdy and thriving. Becca didn't grow inches, but she thrived, too. Sometimes he and Becca were so surrounded by workmen that they hardly had a chance to speak; sometimes he caught her alone and got a private tour of the work on the house or grounds. Inside, the work was progressing faster than he had planned, but outside it was moving slower. Reclaiming the gardens and the lawn was a lengthier process than digging up and replanting would have been, but since his intention was to keep Becca on the payroll as long as possible, both her stubbornness and perfectionism suited him.

On the Saturday of Memorial Day weekend, Jase spent the morning having brunch at Pamela's house in Vermillion, along with his parents. His mother had agreed to organize the party to raise funds for converting the abandoned factory into apartments, and talk of the gala evening dominated the conversation. For once she and Pamela were not at odds, and the morning passed pleasantly enough.

Jase drove almost all the way home before he realized he had no other plans for the day. Cara had invited him to take the ferry to Put-in-Bay on Sunday to visit friends who were opening their island home for the summer, but the rest of this day was his. No one was working, and although there was always paper to push, a holiday weekend seemed no time to push it.

Briefly he considered going home to begin the process of deciding what he would take when he moved and what he would sell or give away. He had a collection of contemporary art chosen almost entirely by a former woman friend who had owned a small gallery, and he couldn't imagine it hanging on the walls of the house in Shaker Heights. He had never loved any of it—although for a while he had thought he loved the woman—and he imagined that Marnie would be glad to sell it again and make them both a profit.

The late spring sunshine heated his car, and with his windows down to catch a breeze, he could hear the shouts of children and the screeching of crows. He couldn't imagine cooping himself up inside his penthouse. The sun was too bright and the air too magnificent. He wondered what Becca was doing on this nearly perfect spring day. He could almost imagine her in the side garden near the roses, drinking lemonade and watching the world go by.

The picture appealed to him. After changing lanes, he chose the exit that would take him to his grandmother's house. He supposed that soon he was going to have to start calling the house and the exit his.

When he reached the house he parked in the driveway. There was a truck at the far end, but Becca's car was nowhere in sight. She had fussed about the car repairs, just as he'd known she would, and demanded that he take fifteen dollars a week out of her salary to cover the cost. But she had opened the trunk immediately to be sure her few possessions were still there. Nothing had been removed, and the look of pleasure on her face had been all the gratitude he'd needed.

He went to the cottage first to find that the door was locked. Inside the house he encountered the owner of the truck, a plumber who was obviously using the quiet Saturday to finish some work. Jack Ferris looked as out of sorts as a man could look.

"Even I don't expect people to work on a holiday weekend," Jase said.

"Every time I turned off the water to fix this, somebody complained. I got sick and tired of hearing them—" He looked around, as if he expected to see his mother standing in the doorway, hands on her hips.

"Complain?" Jase suggested.

"Yeah. So I came in today. Nobody around here to... complain today."

"Becca's not here?"

"Nah. She left yesterday, after everybody but me was gone for the day."

"Did she say when she was coming back?"

"Nah. Just that she wouldn't be here today, so she gave me a key."

Jase went back to his condominium to begin sorting his possessions and settled for a lonely whiskey and water instead of lemonade with Becca.

For the next twenty-four hours he wondered where she might have gone. He sat with Cara on the deck of their friends' island home and considered that Becca might have run away. If so, from what? He knew little about her, not nearly enough to put clues together, but obviously something had driven her to Cleveland. Could the same force, benign or malignant, have driven her away?

He smiled and chatted with his friends. He strolled around downtown Put-in-Bay, a tiny town preparing itself for an onslaught of summer visitors, and helped Cara choose a birthday gift for the mother she rarely saw. But Becca was in the back of his mind the entire day. By the time he dropped Cara off at her apartment and pleaded another early morning appointment as an excuse not to linger, the sun had gone down.

He wasn't far from the house in Shaker Heights. Ten minutes and he could be there. He weighed the peace of knowing Becca was all right against the guilt of knowing he was checking up on her. She owed him no explanations. She was doing a wonderful job of watching over the renovations and landscaping the yard. No one could, or should, work constantly without a break. If she had gone somewhere, she had the perfect right. There was no reason why she should have consulted him.

Ten minutes later he was at the cottage.

Becca wasn't there; the absence of her car in the driveway was the only proof he needed. Still, he parked and unlocked the cottage door. Inside, the three rooms were as neat as a museum. Not a piece of furniture was out of place. The first roses of the season in a vase on the table were still fresh; the faint scent of fresh-baked bread lingered in the air.

He went from room to room looking for proof that she would be returning. Some of her clothes were in the closet, but not the peach sweater and turquoise skirt, and not the spring green outfit she had worn the day she had told him about the roses. She hadn't taken the book beside her bed, a four-inch-thick encyclopedia of gardening, or the notebook with diagrams of the house and yard.

But why would she have taken them if she never intended to come back?

He wondered why he hadn't pushed harder to learn more about her past. As it was, he knew nothing about her except her name and the state where she had been raised. Was Hanks a married name or the name she had been born with? He might be able to trace her if Hanks was her maiden name, but even then he didn't know if Becca was short for Rebecca or if it was a name indigenous to the area of Kentucky that she came from.

A more important question was why he cared so much.

He settled himself in a comfortable armchair and put his feet up on a matching hassock. Becca wasn't there, but the same imagination that conjured visions of skyscrapers where vacant lots stood brought her to life for him. He remembered the first time he had seen her. She was hardly the same woman now. Along with gradually blooming health and beauty, her spirit had bloomed, as well. The same qualities that had ensured her survival made her a woman worth knowing. She had maintained her independence in the face of all odds. She was intelligent, lively, not afraid to speak out for what was important to her. She was not afraid of him.

And why should she be? Who had he become? He wasn't sure, but he knew who he wasn't. He wasn't Jason Millington, hard-nosed developer with a bad case of tunnel vision and a worse case of self-righteousness. Somehow, somewhere, his view of the world had changed. It no longer consisted entirely of skyscrapers and million dollar deals. Now it included people and causes and a house he had never expected to live in. It included Becca.

From the table his grandmother's roses were sweetly fragrant. The scent brought back memories of the lazy summer afternoons of his childhood, and he shut his eyes to enjoy it.

Becca pulled her car into the driveway beside a dark sedan. Late at night, distinguishing features were at a premium. The car looked like Jase's, but she couldn't be sure. What reason would Jase or anyone have to be here at this time of night? Jase certainly had a right to be at the house anytime, but she doubted he had used the weekend to move in. The repairs weren't completed, and he wasn't given to impulsive actions, When he moved, it would be according to a well thought out timetable.

She got out of the car reluctantly. She doubted anyone who meant her harm would park in the driveway, but the night was dark, and she was too exhausted to think sensibly. At best she suspected a confrontation ahead, and all she really wanted was sleep.

She checked the house first, although she refused to climb the stairs and check the bedrooms. She called Jase's name, but when there was no answer, she locked the doors behind her and went to the cottage.

In the living room she empathized with the shock of the three bears who had found Goldilocks asleep in Baby Bear's bed. No porridge had been touched here, but there was obviously a stranger asleep in her house. Except, of course, that this particular cottage belonged to the stranger, who wasn't really a stranger at all.

Jase didn't wake when she approached him. He was dressed casually, as if he had spent the day somewhere other than his office. From the knees down, his legs were bare, and she admired the tanned, muscled length of them before she turned her eyes to his face.

His hair fell over his forehead boyishly, but there was nothing else boyish about Jase Millington the Whatever. Even asleep he looked exactly like what he was, a one-step-from-ruthless businessman, the modern version of a riverboat gambler whose luck with the cards was legendary.

She moved closer. "Jase?"

He stirred, but he still didn't wake up. She touched his shoulder. "Jase?"

His hand covered hers, and his eyes opened. He smiled, and the slow, sleepy grin was like a caress. "Becca?"

"Well, who else did you expect to find here?" She knew she should remove her hand, but it didn't seem to want to drop back to her side. Before she could give it an order, Jase stretched his other hand toward her. She felt it slide along her waist and press against the small of her back.

"You're here."

"That seems obvious."

He pulled her closer. "Not obvious enough."

She resisted, but only long enough to make a decision. Then she was in his lap and in his arms. She had never dared imagine what it might feel like to have Jase hold her again. Even before he had come back into her life, she had buried her memories of the man who had protected her from the cold, memories of his arms around her, the warmth of his body against hers.

Jase's hand slid up her back, and she knew that the memories had never been buried at all. He felt familiar, but familiar was oh-so-different from ordinary. He felt like a thousand promises and a million dreams. Her body resonated in ways she had forgotten it could. Every place he touched absorbed his heat, until it felt as if he were touching her all over.

He lowered his mouth to hers, and she lifted hers to meet him. His lips were as warm as his hands, and as tempting. Her lips parted. His parted, too, and the kiss became a slow dance, a prelude to something yet to come.

Only when his hand spread welcome heat to her breast did she pull away. In the dim lamplight his eyes were the green of a tumultuous sea. She gazed at the man who had given her so much and knew she could not take another thing from him.

She slid off his lap, and he didn't try to stop her. But when she tried to walk away, he stood and took her arm. "It's time, don't you think?"

"Time?" She played for more of it.

"You don't owe me any explanations about where you went. I'm not buying explanations when I pay your salary. But I was worried about you."

"You shouldn't have been."

"But I was." He touched her chin, hoping to make her look at him. "I care about you. I guess I just made that known."

"You were half asleep. Maybe you thought I was somebody else."

"Maybe I didn't."

"I think you'd better go home."

"Why did you pull away?"

She still hadn't looked at him. "Things were getting out of control."

He touched her chin again. This time she complied. "No, they weren't. I could show you what out of control means, Becca."

Her eyes widened, and he knew she was seeing the same visions that he was. "Things can't get out of control," she said at last. "You don't know me, Jase. You only think you do."

"I can only know you if you let me."

She stared up at him and realized she had no choice. Jase had cared for and about her in a way that no man ever had. She owed him the truth about herself, even if it meant that he would see her differently afterward.

She turned away. "I'll make coffee."

"It's the middle of the night."

"I'll make tea." She started toward the kitchen. He followed close behind.

"I'm going to tell you a story," she said, refusing to look at him again. "It's not very pretty, and it's not easy to tell. But you should hear it."

"It never occurred to me that your story might be pretty. Pretty stories don't have chapters like yours did."

"No. I guess not." She heard the slide of a chair and knew he was sitting at the table. She ran water into the tea kettle and set it on the burner. She prepared the teapot before she spoke.

"I come from a place called Blackwater. Ever heard of it?"

"No."

"'Course not. Nobody's heard of Blackwater. I don't know why I asked."

"Maybe to make the story easier."

"Maybe. Anyway, I was born and raised there. My mother died early on, and my father raised me and my brothers. He worked in a coal mine, and he died from it, choking and coughing until there wasn't any room for air in his lungs. I was seventeen. My brothers were gone by then, and one of them was already dead. So I went to live with a cousin of my mother's who lived on the other side of town. I'd always wanted to go to college. Our school wasn't good, but I was a good student, made straight A's except in gym. I never could serve a volleyball."

He heard pride when she reported her grades, and he was touched by it. "I'm sure you were the kind of student any teacher wishes she had."

"Matty, my cousin, was good to me. Don't think she wasn't. She had three kids of her own that needed watching, but she never once took advantage of my being there. She and her husband didn't have much, and I strained what little they did have. Matty wouldn't touch the money I got from the mining company after Daddy died. She wanted me to save it all for college and be somebody. I'd wanted that, too, only after Daddy was gone, I didn't seem to want it as much. I was sad, and I stopped working so hard in school."

"But it was natural to be sad, Becca. Your whole life had changed."

"Well, I went and changed it again. I stopped wanting to leave

Blackwater. It seemed like the only place for me. After Daddy died, everything was different, but Blackwater was still the same. There was a man, Dewey Hanks, who wanted me to stay, too. Dewey was the son of Bill Hanks, the man who owned the Hanks Hardware Store, and he was about five years older than me. The Hanks were good people, church-going and upstanding, but Dewey was wild. When you're seventeen you want somebody wild, because you think you can tame him.''

"And did you?"

She busied herself with the tea. The kettle had boiled, and she took her time pouring water over the tea bags. She only spoke when the lid was back on the pot.

"Nobody could have tamed Dewey, only I was too sure I was 'somebody' to realize that. I thought I had something special, some kind of magic that would make him quit drinking and running around with his buddies. Dewey told me I did. We ran off and got married, and I quit school at the beginning of my senior year. Matty cried for two days, and Bill and Alice, Dewey's parents, like to have had a fit. But they got used to the idea after a couple of weeks and let us move in with them. Dewey said it was only going to be temporary. He was going to find us a place of our own just as soon as he got a better job than the one he had at his father's store.''

Jase watched her fill a plate with gingersnaps. He had no intention of eating even one, but he knew she needed something to do with her hands. "So far nothing you've said is much of a shock, Becca. Girls…women make mistakes like you did all the time. That's what divorce is about.''

"I didn't divorce Dewey." She set the gingersnaps in front of him. "He tried to be a good husband at first. We worked together in his father's store. Bill had had a heart attack a year before Dewey and me got married, and he never recovered the way he was supposed to. He let Dewey take over the store a little at a time, until finally there was hardly a day in the week when Bill was there for more than an hour or two. But as soon as Dewey realized everyone was counting on him, he just kind of went crazy. It was like the pressure was too much. He started staying out nights. Sometimes I didn't see him for days at a time. I worked at the store, trying to hold things together and making excuses for Dewey, but his parents knew something was wrong."

"You were still living with them?"

"We had a little apartment on the side, in the old carport. They'd come visiting, and they'd ask where Dewey was. I'd tell them he was out running errands or fixing something at the store. They got so they didn't believe me, of course, but at first they did. They wanted to so bad, that at first they believed anything I said. By the time they stopped believing, things were really awful. When Dewey was at the store, he made mistakes. He could never figure how to use a cash register, and when he'd come in after a drunk, he'd push more wrong buttons than right. It got so coming to Hanks Hardware was better than going to the bank.

"And that was just one thing. He'd forget to order things. Then, if I wanted to keep customers satisfied, I'd have to drive over to the next town and buy whatever they wanted retail, come back and sell it for the same price. Sometimes he'd just take whatever was in the register and leave. We weren't making money, and Dewey was as good as giving away or stealing what we had. Some days he'd be so charming customers would stay and gab with him for hours. Some days he'd be so rude, they'd swear they were never coming back."

Jase was getting a clear picture of the man Becca had married, but one thing was still unclear. "You said you didn't divorce him. Are you still married?"

She shook her head. "After we'd been married almost a year, two of the mines in the area shut down. People started moving away to find new jobs. By that time Bill knew what had been going on. He figured if he didn't go back to work, between Dewey and the mines closing, his store was going to close, too. He was shocked when he saw what a state things were in, and he blamed it on me. He and Alice always blamed Dewey's problems on me."

He was surprised there was no self-pity in her voice. "Why?"

"I guess they couldn't face what Dewey was. They'd done the best they knew how when he was growing up, but Dewey wasn't the son he should have been. They couldn't accept any of the responsibility, and they couldn't give any of it to Dewey. So they blamed me. Bill was blaming me at the top of his lungs one day when he had another heart attack."

She poured tea that he wanted as little as he wanted the gingersnaps. He touched her hand. "It wasn't your fault."

"I know. Dewey knew, too. When he found out about his daddy, he cried. He said everything was going to change. While Bill was in the hospital, Dewey came back to work, but I think he saw it was too late. There wasn't anything anybody could do by then to save the store. But Dewey never took no for an answer, so he came up with a plan."

She sat down across the table from him. For the first time she looked at him. "A couple of nights later Dewey asked me to take a ride. It was the first time in a long time that he'd asked me to do anything with him. It was like we hadn't really been married for a long time. When Dewey was drinking, he would get mean. Sometimes he'd hit me or call me names. After his daddy's heart attack he seemed to sober up. I was happy, real happy, he wanted me with him that night. I had something to tell him, and the time just hadn't been right."

"What happened?" He reached for her hand. She let him take it.

"Dewey asked me to drive. I should have figured that was strange, but I was just so happy he was being nice to me. When we were out on the highway he told me to drive over to Baldwin, the next town. He wanted to get a six-pack of beer to take down to the river. I didn't want to do it, but Dewey said it would be like old times. It was a chilly night, so when we got to the convenience store, Dewey told me to keep the engine running so the heat would stay on. Then he got out and went inside. I wasn't paying much attention. I was thinking about what I had to tell Dewey. But when I looked inside, I saw a man with a ski mask and a gun robbing the store. That man was Dewey."

"Becca." He turned her hand palm up, lifted it to his mouth and kissed it.

"Before I really understood what was happening, Dewey came running out and pushed me into the other seat. I was so scared that all I could think about was getting out of there. I let him take off for Blackwater, but I screamed and screamed at Dewey that I was leaving him that night. I screamed so loud that I didn't hear the siren until the highway patrol was almost on top of us. There were two cars, coming at us from both directions. Dewey pulled over and jumped out before the car had even stopped completely. He fired his gun at one of the police cars, then he took off running. One of the police fired back. I don't think he meant to hit Dewey, but he did. He died right away."

Jase couldn't imagine what purpose would have been served if Dewey Hanks had lived, but his thoughts were colored by the agony in Becca's eyes. "He made a choice and he paid the price," he said.

"No. I paid the price." She pulled her hand from Jase's. "They charged me as an accomplice to the robbery, and to the attempt on the policeman's life. By the time I came up for trial, I was six months pregnant. That was the secret I hadn't had time to tell Dewey. He died not knowing. I didn't have money for a lawyer. I'd put all the money I'd got when Daddy died into Hanks Hardware, paying back money Dewey took or gave other people by mistake. Matty didn't have any money to help me, either, so the court appointed a public defender. He had a lot of people to take care of, and he wasn't very interested or very good.

"There'd been a lot of robberies—always are when times get tough and folks get desperate. They decided to make an example out of me. I was sentenced to three years, and the defender thought that was pretty light, considering. After all, I sure had the motive to help Dewey rob the store. I was pregnant, married to a good-for-nothing, and scared to death I wouldn't be able to take care of my baby.

"They let me stay in Blackwater to have the baby. It turned out to be more than one. I had twin girls, Amanda and Faith, and I got to spend four weeks with them. Then they gave custody to Bill and Alice and put me in jail. I served a year before they let me off on parole.''

"You were railroaded!"

Becca was gratified at the fury in Jase's eyes. She had been so frightened she would see pity or distaste. She had even slipped her hand away so he wouldn't have to hold it. Now she covered his. "No. I wasn't."

"You had nothing to do with it, and if you'd had a decent lawyer, you would have gotten off scot-free!''

"I didn't know anything about Dewey's plans beforehand. I really didn't. But when Dewey came out of that store, I knew what he'd done. I should have gotten out of the car then, but I panicked. I let Dewey take the wheel. I was terrified, and I wasn't thinking straight. But those seconds cost me my babies, a year of my life and what little self-respect Dewey left me.''

"The way you acted was understandable. You didn't have time to make a decision!''

She stood to fuss with the teapot again, although neither of them had taken a sip. She just couldn't sit still. "I made a decision. Just not the right one. And until I make something of my life and get my girls back, I won't be able to forgive myself.''

"Were you in Blackwater this weekend?''

"I went to see my babies.''

"How old are they now, Becca?''

"Three. They're beautiful." She swallowed. Hard. "Sometimes I miss them so much I could die.''

He was up, and his arms were around her in seconds. "Becca.''

She wanted to resist. But she found herself slipping her arms around his waist. "The Hanks love them, but the girls are a strain. Bill's totally disabled now, and Alice has to take care of him, too. They don't have much money, just what they get from social security. Alice feeds the girls too many sweets, and Bill gets mad when they do something wrong. I have to get my babies out of there.''

He held her tighter. "Will they give you custody?''

"I think so, even though they hate me. They know I didn't have anything to do with the robbery, but they still think Dewey went wrong because of me. If I hadn't married him and forced him to take on a role he wasn't ready for, then Dewey would never have robbed the store. If I'd been a better wife, I would have known what he was planning and talked him out of it." She gave a bitter laugh. "As if I could have. But they think I should have settled him down and made a good husband out of him. They think if I'd told him he was going to be a father, that would have made a difference."

"What do you think?"

"I think it would have made him more desperate."

"I think so, too."

She pushed him away because he felt too good and it was too tempting to lean on him. He resisted for a moment, then let her go. She turned away from him, because it was easier. "By the time I got out of prison, Blackwater was almost a ghost town, and there weren't any jobs. I knew better than to look for anything in the next town, where the robbery took place. My parole officer got me a job in a laundry a hundred miles from Blackwater. But the laundry closed down after a few months. I started traveling, looking for work. I could have gotten in trouble for going out of state, but my parole officer looked the other way. He knew how badly I needed money. I took anything I could find and sent as much as I could of what I earned back to the Hanks for the girls. I lived wherever I could. I never had the money to rent a real place of my own because I had to send money back. I knew if I didn't, the girls would suffer, and nobody would believe I really wanted them. Things just got worse and worse."

He could imagine the rest. Unskilled and undereducated, only rarely did someone like Becca make more than minimum wage. Even with overtime, there wouldn't have been enough money to support herself and the girls. So she had stopped supporting herself. Eventually she had succumbed to illness and exhaustion. And she had almost died.

"I have pictures." She faced him and smiled tentatively. "The

Hanks have an instant camera, and they let me use it this morning. I took two. Would you like to see them?"

"Of course."

Her smile broadened a little, but he saw it tremble. "Prepare yourself for the prettiest babies in the world."

He expected her to find her purse, but she lifted the photographs out of the pocket of her blouse. He realized she had kept them next to her heart. She held them out to him. "You have to hold these by the edges."

"I promise." He took the first photograph. A blond-haired urchin with jelly on one cheek grinned at him. The resemblance to Becca was there. Something grabbed at him. The girls were real. Becca's story was real. She had lived through hell, and these children were on this earth to show for it. "Which one is this?"

"That's Amanda." She traded photographs.

An identical urchin with jelly on her chin was sticking her tongue out at him. "Faith?"

"I should have come up with something a little livelier. Like Scarlett."

"They are beautiful." He watched her put the pictures back in the same pocket. He realized it must have broken her heart to leave her children this morning. His own heart felt suspiciously weakened after the horror story she had just told him.

He had imagined a better history, and he had imagined worse. But at no time had he imagined anything with the pathos of this tale. Becca had been abandoned after her father's death, abused and neglected by her husband, vilified by his parents and dragged into a robbery resulting in the death of her husband and her own prison sentence. Then, when life could hardly have looked blacker, her new twin daughters had been taken from her and given to the very people who had refused to acknowledge the kind of son they had raised.

And through it all, somehow, she had remained determined to make the best of what she had been handed. She had struggled through her marriage, lived through her prison sentence, and worked her hardest to support the children she was not allowed to keep. Worked so hard, in fact, that she had almost worked herself into the grave.

"How long did you live in your car?" he asked. "You said you could never afford to rent a place. How long were you living in that car?"

"On and off."

He gripped her arms and made her look at him. "How long?"

"A lifetime."

He dropped his hands. "You could have died."

"Sometimes I wanted to. I would have gladly, if I hadn't had my babies to think about."

He wanted to grab her again, to hold her against him, but he knew she would reject him now. He didn't know what he was feeling other than anger at a justice system that could imprison this woman and anger at all the people who had watched Dewey Hanks ruin her life. Unless he sorted out all his feelings, Becca would believe that whatever he offered her sprang from pity.

He ran his hand through his hair. "Why didn't you tell me this earlier?"

"I'm sorry. I should have."

"You're damned right you should have."

"I'll pack my things and be gone by morning."

He stared at her. "What?"

"I'm a convicted felon. I had no right to drag you into my life. I should have told you the truth right away." She tried to smile, but she couldn't. "It's just that..."

"What?"

She flinched a little at his tone. "I wanted to start over. I wanted a chance. And I took one. At your expense."

"Are you done yet?"

She nodded.

"No, you're not. Before you pack and leave, why don't you tell me what I've done to make you think I'd turn you away! What was it I said, Becca, that convinced you I wouldn't want you to stay? Aren't I paying you enough? Haven't I shown you enough concern? Was it the scene in the living room a little while ago?"

"No, I—"

"My turn! You've said enough. You're not leaving. Is that clear? You're staying. I'm going to raise your salary, and we're going to buy children's furniture for the other bedroom so your daughters can come here to live. I'll hire a lawyer for you to get custody. You can finish high school and get some job training. I'll pay whatever tuition costs there are."

His words fell into empty space. She stared at him, absorbing what he'd said. "You would do that for me?"

"I'm going to do it for you. You can stay here forever, as far as I'm concerned. I don't need this space."

"No."

"No what?"

"Thank you, but no." She waved her hand to stop him when he started to argue. "I finished high school in prison. I even got a college credit. I'm going to straighten out my life the same way, with my own hard work, not with anyone else's. Do you think I lived all those months with Dewey and didn't learn anything? Every day was a lesson, Jase! I tried to change Dewey. His parents tried to change him. We bribed him. We threatened. We cried. Dewey didn't change because Dewey didn't want to. And even if he had, he didn't know how to work for anything. If change had come easily, maybe he would have tried it. But change comes one tiny little step at a time. I know. God, how I know."

"I'm not trying to change you, Becca, I'm trying to help you!"

"You're trying to do the work I have to do. If I'm ever going to have any self-respect, I have to change myself and my life. Can't you understand that?"

"You almost died trying to change your life. When are you going to realize that you're not the problem? Life's handed you nothing but bad breaks. Now I'm trying to hand you a good one!"

"I made choices. I quit school and married Dewey. I stayed with him. I sank my money into Hanks Hardware to save Dewey and his parents. I didn't get out of the car when I should have!

I made those choices. And I'm making another one. I can't take what you're offering. I thank you for it, from the bottom of my heart. But I can't take any more help from you."

He was speechless. He could think of nothing to say to refute her. He didn't agree, but there was no point in telling her that. She believed every word she'd uttered, and her decision was carved in stone.

"Then you're leaving?" he asked at last, when the silence had stretched forever.

"Not if you don't want me to. I'll stay and finish the landscaping. I'm earning my way here."

Relief filled him. "More than earning it."

"But I won't let you send me to school. And I won't let you pay me a higher salary. And I won't let you help me get custody of my girls. I'll find a way to get them back, and soon, but it will have to be by my own hard work."

He had never been faced with a situation he couldn't change. He had never been faced with a person he couldn't sway. The world had always been putty in his hands. Becca was granite.

"How could you ever have believed I would want you to leave?" he asked.

"I don't think much of myself, I guess. Prison does that to you."

Once again he was filled with the urge to pull her against him and keep her there. She needed protection and hope, and he needed...

He didn't know what he needed, except that he needed Becca. He didn't know how, and he didn't know why. But he had learned tonight that she was much more than a cause, much more than someone who was just wandering across the edges of his life.

"You can think what you want, but I hope you'll hear this." He put his hands on her shoulders, but gently, carefully. He didn't push or pull, and he didn't grasp. "I think enough of you for both of us."

"I can't think about anyone but myself and the girls, Jase."

"Is that a warning?"

"I'm pleading," she said softly. "I don't need any more hurting. I'm still trying to get over the first time."

"Not all relationships bring hurt."

"Maybe I'll have to learn that, too. But not now. I'm not ready."

He wanted to kiss her again. She badly needed kissing and holding and reassurance. But he knew better than to try. She would be stubborn about that, too.

Jason Millington the Fourth had learned to bide his time when ambushes or stampedes didn't work. He could bide his time now. His hands fell to his sides, but his fingers were clenched. "Will you tell me before you go trotting off to Blackwater next time? I was worried about you."

"It's nice to have someone worried."

"Will you tell me? Just so I'll know?"

"I will."

He bent forward and touched her cheek with his lips. Gently, carefully. Then he straightened. "I'll be moving in soon."

"Already?"

He thought of all that still needed to be done in the house. "It's the right time of year to sell my condo. I'm putting it on the market tomorrow. I'll probably move out in the next few weeks."

"You don't have to be here to check on me."

"That never entered my mind." He turned away, but not before she had seen his smile.

"It *is* because of me."

"I heard every word you said, Becca. And I'm willing to comply."

She heard the "for now," even though it was unspoken. She watched him leave. She was still in the same spot, staring at the doorway, when she heard him start his engine and back out of the drive.

Chapter Seven

"Relax. There's not a thing in the penthouse that wouldn't benefit from the mover dropping it to give it some character."

Jase shot Pamela one of the looks he was renowned for, but she only smiled and continued. "I can take care of everything here, Jase. I really can. I'll be sure everything's safely loaded on the truck before I go home. You go on over to the house and make sure everything's ready for the arrival."

He watched the movers exit his building with a couch that he planned to put in the study of the house. They were using extreme care. Someone—himself, he supposed—had scared them to death. "All right. I'll see you over there later. Thanks for helping."

"I'm so glad to see you moving into Kathryn's house, I'd carry your furniture by myself if I had to."

On the drive to Shaker Heights he considered his decision to move. The house wasn't finished, but enough living space had been cleared to make him comfortable. The decorator had clucked and chortled, but he had managed to finish Jase's bedroom so that at least at night he could pretend there wasn't going to be a troop of workmen going through the house for the next three months.

He liked the bedroom. In fact, he more than liked it. He had
grown used to wide open spaces and sleek, contemporary lines,
but now he found the smaller, cozier spaces in the Tudor house
appealing. He had made some structural changes. His bedroom
had once been two smaller rooms. Downstairs, a tiny breakfast
room and pantry had become extensions of the kitchen. He had
degrees in both engineering and architecture, and by nature he
was unsuited to leave anything exactly the way he found it. But
much of the house was still as it had been when Kathryn had
lived in it. The wallpaper and paint, the drapes and some of the
furniture, were different, but Kathryn would recognize and be
comfortable in the house if she came back from the grave to
visit. And knowing Kathryn, she might just try.

Becca had wielded a surprising amount of influence on the
decorator. The first decorator, highly recommended by Jase's
mother, had wanted to paint the walnut and mahogany paneling
in the den and dining room blue and white, like Wedgwood.
Becca had told her that she didn't know what kind of trees
Wedgwood came from, but it sure wasn't walnut and mahogany
trees, so kindly keep her paintbrushes to herself. The next decorator and Becca had been able to compromise. Jase had been
consulted frequently at first, but less frequently as it became clear
he was perfectly happy to let the two of them make decisions.

What Becca didn't know about Tudor homes and architecture
she had learned from reading every book available. When she
wasn't working, she read constantly. He had discovered that her
knowledge of antiques had been gleaned from books she'd read
in prison and a class she had taken there on furniture refinishing.
She was like an empty sponge, soaking up every bit of knowledge that came her way. She asked his work crew questions,
then got them to demonstrate. She was picking up knowledge
about electricity and plumbing, and she could already rewire a
socket and unclog a drainpipe like a pro.

He had never met anyone so eager to learn, so determined to
make something of herself. He couldn't tell her that she was
already something. She wouldn't believe it. Since the night
nearly two weeks ago when she had told him the circumstances

that had brought her to Cleveland, he had understood her better. But he still couldn't comprehend why she wouldn't let him help her. She was so bright, so filled with potential, but she had tied his hands. She could be in college, studying physics or Greek, yet she dug weeds and learned to nail shingles on roofs instead, because that was available to her and she could do it on her own.

Her refusal to accept his help both infuriated and intrigued him. She was the only woman he had ever met who not only had no interest in his money but would probably appreciate him more if he didn't have it.

At the house, he went inside to inspect the areas where his furniture was to be stored until all the rooms were ready. He ended up on the sunporch. Everything was prepared, but he had known it would be, because Becca had been in charge.

"What do you think?"

He turned and found her in the doorway. "I think I'm moving."

"Looks that way."

He admired her. Her legs were long and tanned, and her shorts fit almost as well as his hands would in the same place. Her bright gold T-shirt proclaimed Fun and Sun in Miami, straight across her breasts. He wished he could take her there.

"I guess you'll be unpacking most of the night and won't have time to make yourself dinner."

He wasn't going to admit that he never made himself dinner, unless warmed-over coffee with bologna sandwiches qualified. "Probably not. But there are plenty of good restaurants nearby." And he was on first-name basis with the hosts and hostesses at every one, he frequented them so often.

"I'd like to make you dinner, if you'll let me."

He heard her struggle to sound casual. He would almost bet that she wanted very much to cook for him but was trying not to sound too eager, in case he refused. She still couldn't, didn't, believe that he wanted her company. Visions of Becca in his lap, being soundly kissed, filled his mind. He wondered what other proof she needed.

"I'd love that," he said, "if it's not too much trouble."

"Are you picky?"

"Not a bit."

"I'll make something that can sit on the stove until you're ready to eat it." She left, and he admired the back of her shorts until she was out of sight.

Becca was sure she could make a mean spaghetti sauce. There had been cooking classes in prison, and she had taken every one of them. In fact, she had taken every class she had been allowed to. She wanted to know things, everything, but that had only been half the reason. The other half had been to keep herself from going crazy.

She tried not to think about prison, about what it had been like to wake up every morning knowing that someone else was holding her babies, someone else was feeding them, watching them sit up for the first time. But sometimes the memories invaded anyway. Barren, sterile rooms lined with beds and windows so high that what light they let in faded before it reached the floor.

She supposed she had been lucky. She had been assigned to a minimum security prison. No one had seriously believed she was a threat to society. She had been sentenced by a hanging judge, to show the world he meant business. And she couldn't blame him, not really. There were a lot of people out there like Dewey, people who thought they were owed something for nothing. Of course, not everybody in prison was like that. Some of them, a surprising amount, really, had been more like her. Dragged into committing crimes because they didn't think hard enough. People who had made mistakes, then let the mistakes build on each other, over and over, until society shoved them out of sight for a while to think.

She'd had plenty of time to think, more time than she could handle. So she had taken classes, gone to rehab groups, started with A in the prison library and read clear through to H. Somewhere in the midst of all that she had seen what she had to do to change her life. She had to take responsibility for herself in a way she never had before. She had given responsibility to

Dewey when he was alive, and she had allowed him to manipulate and abuse her. She would never give responsibility to anyone else again.

She added canned tomatoes and fresh herbs to the ground meat and chunks of hot sausage that she had browned with onions and bits of green pepper. The man who would eat the spaghetti sauce tonight wanted to take responsibility for her life. He was nothing like Dewey. Jase would hold her life carefully in his hands, mold it with skill, and probably leave her a better person for the experience. But any success she achieved would belong to him. She couldn't, wouldn't, let that happen.

The sun was going down by the time she brushed fresh Italian bread with melted butter, garlic and cheese. The movers had arrived an hour ago, and through the cottage kitchen window she had watched them carry Jase's possessions into the house. Now, as she looked on, they slammed the back doors of the truck and drove away. She turned up the heat under the water simmering in wait for the spaghetti.

Jase arrived ten minutes later looking disgruntled. She plopped the spaghetti in before she greeted him. "All done?"

"Whose idea was this?"

"What, the move or dinner?"

"The move." He collapsed into a chair to watch her bustle around the room. "I can face citizens' committees and city government hearings and angry contractors without blinking an eye. But I'm never going to move again."

"You'd better not. I'm not doing all this work in the yard so some bull goose loony can move in and chop it all down."

"Your work is safe." He propped his feet up on another chair. "Is everything in?"

"Everything I'm moving. The rest goes other places."

She stole a glance at him as she went to the refrigerator to get the salad. He looked tired, disgusted and thoroughly masculine. He was wearing jeans, well-faded jeans that would have suited the Jase she'd met on a cold March night. His polo shirt was an eye-catching jade that stretched across a chest and shoulders that would have suited the men who had done his moving. All of it suited Jase Millington the Whatever.

"Would you like a drink? I have club soda, and I bought some beer in case you wanted it."

He was pleased she had thought so far ahead. He took a beer and let her bring him a glass. "Dinner smells wonderful."

"I hope you like it." She stirred the sauce, keeping a close eye on the spaghetti.

"Your grandmother's recipe?"

"No. Yours. I found it when I was cleaning out the house. I copied it and saved the original for you."

"I can't believe it was Kathryn's. She never cooked. She'd eat everything raw rather than bother with a stove. She had a woman who cooked for her sometimes. I don't know her first name, but we always called her McDaniels. McDaniels probably forced the recipe on Kathryn."

"You called your grandmother by her first name and the hired help by her last?"

"McDaniels was never thought of as hired help. She was more of a companion to Kathryn, a friend. She spoiled Pamela and me rotten. And now that you mention it, I remember her spaghetti, and it smelled just like yours."

"What was growing up like for you?"

He was so used to denying that his childhood had lacked anything that for a moment he almost did it again. But Becca's story had made him confront some of his own past. Maybe honesty about who you were and where you had come from was part of what Becca called taking control of your life.

He tried to be honest, now. "Good in some ways, not so good in others. My parents don't show their feelings. Pamela and I were close to compensate. We escaped to Kathryn's every chance we got."

"That's what it's supposed to be like to grow up rich. That's one of those stories the rich spread around so that poor folks will feel happy they're poor."

He laughed, and she granted him one of her extraordinary smiles. "I had mountains of friends, as rich as I was," he said, "and about half of them came from intact, loving families, and the other half didn't. Was everybody you knew happy and loved?"

"Not hardly. Most of them were so busy trying to make it from day to day, they didn't know how to be happy. A lot of them were sick and dying from working in the mines."

"But the government has programs to help black lung victims."

"Sorry, rich man, but the government gives money to less than ten percent of the people who need it. You've got to be half dead to get it, and then it doesn't mean much."

"I didn't know."

"Most people don't. Who's going to speak for a bunch of Appalachian nobodies?"

"You're not an Appalachian nobody."

"I told myself that every day when I was living in my car. It helped, but not a whole lot." She turned and leaned against the stove, crossing her arms. "You know what I want to do?"

"What?"

"I want to be somebody important enough to speak out. I want to be somebody who people listen to. I want to tell people what it's like to be poor and hopeless, not so everybody can throw money, then forget the people they throwed—threw—it at, but just so people will know, and knowing will change them."

He couldn't think of a word to say. She had exposed her heart.

"I guess that's silly."

"No."

"Well, that's what I want to do." She turned back to the stove. "And I will, but whether it will change anybody or not depends on them, doesn't it?"

"Do you believe people are good?"

"I think we all have a chance to be, but some have a better shot at it than others."

He watched her drain the spaghetti and put the finishing touches on the rest of the meal. He tried to imagine anyone he knew—with the exception of Pamela or Shareen—making such an impassioned statement. Passion, at least this particular kind, was out of favor these days. The people he knew gave money to causes—or threw money at them—but rarely gave more than a passing thought to the people the money would help. Becca gave more than a thought. She had been one of those people, and could be again if no plan was made for her life after the summer.

Becca set the meal on the table and took a seat across from Jase. As he took his first bites, she tried not to watch his reaction, but finally she had to admit his opinion mattered to her. Jase mattered to her. She didn't want him to. Her life was far too complicated, and Jase's ideas for simplifying it didn't agree with her own. But no matter how many times she told herself not to think of him, she still did.

"This is terrific. McDaniels would be proud."

She nodded, trying not to let him see how pleased she was. "Good."

"Is there anything you don't do well?"

"Dewey would have named a few things."

"From what you've told me, Dewey wasn't much of a judge."

"He thought he was. I thought so, too."

The statement was provocative. Jase imagined that since she didn't elaborate, she was talking about something highly personal. He guessed she meant her performance in bed.

He tried to imagine a man not being satisfied with Becca. From everything she had said, he knew she had been young and inexperienced when she'd married. But she was warm and passionate and sensual. No woman who cupped the earth in her hands and kneaded it as she did could be cold. No woman who surrounded herself with flowers and herbs and sunlight could be an unresponsive lover.

"Do you still love Dewey?" he asked. "Or can you let go of him and what he thought about you?"

"I don't think I ever loved him. Not the way a woman loves a man she really believes in. And it's what I think of myself that matters, isn't it?"

"If that's what you really believe."

"I've thought myself right into a new job, Jase."

He put his fork down—which wasn't easy, since the spaghetti was every bit as good as he had said. "What?"

"A new job. At Constantine's. Now, don't look at me like that. I'm not leaving here. But my nights are free, and I don't work more than half a day on Sunday in the yard. I realized I could be waitressing then. I won't be taking even a minute away from the time I'd be working here."

"You know that's not what's worrying me."

"Nothing should be worrying you. Now eat your spaghetti before it turns into slimy little worms."

"I don't want you doing this."

"You've said what's in your heart, and I've listened."

"Not well enough."

She set her fork down, too. "Better than well."

"Look, Becca. You're not recovered, not completely. You still need a couple of pounds and a lot of rest. You bustle around here like someone putting out fires, but at least in the evening and weekends you can take it easy. You need to take care of yourself. You need to watch TV, listen to music, read something for fun."

"And you do those things?"

"That's different."

"How? Don't shake your head at me, Jase Millington the Whatever."

"The Fourth, but don't ever, ever, call me that."

"Jase Millington the Whatever, then. I like that better, anyway. You don't know whatever you are. One minute you think you're my father, the next minute my lord and savior, the next minute you're kissing me!"

"You need kissing!" He was on his feet and around the table before she could respond. She jumped to her feet to confront him. "You need kissing and shaking, mountain girl. You can't take the world on your shoulders. It's not a very nice world. You should have learned that by now. One person can't butt it in the head and make it change. Everybody needs help, only you won't let anybody help you. That's as crazy as anything, crazier than not getting out of the car the night Dewey robbed the store, crazier than marrying him in the first place!''

"Who do you think you are, telling me what's crazy. Let me tell you what crazy looks like. It looks like a man pretending he's a bum just to see how the other half of the world lives. It looks like a man who thinks he's so perfect he knows everything about everything and everybody. It looks like Jase Millington the Whatever!''

"You're going to tell me you feel great? That you feel like you can lick the world? That working two jobs isn't going to run you right back into the ground again?''

She opened her mouth to tell him just that, then snapped her lips together.

He was triumphant. "See?''

"I'm going to tell you to go sit back down and eat your spaghetti before I take your plate away!''

He stroked her hair. He hadn't intended to. One minute he was angry enough at her stupidity to shake it out of her, the next he was caressing her hair. He supposed it was his own well-bred version of shaking. God knows it was shaking him up, touching her that way. "I care about you.''

"Don't.''

"It's too late.''

"You feel sorry for me!''

"Ridiculous. Maybe I did once, but who can feel sorry for a feisty Kentucky hellcat who does whatever she wants, whenever she wants to?''

"You shouldn't be touching me that way.''

"Why not?''

"Because it's just another way to get me to do what you want.''

"I'm touching you because I can't seem to help myself.''

"Let's both sit back down and pretend this never happened.''

"As long as we're pretending." The hand that had been stroking hauled her toward him. Her eyes were defiant, but she didn't resist. His mouth came down on hers like a hawk swooping for its prey, his lips as heated as his words had been. She knew she should be angry, but all she could feel was desire. It swept through her in a wave, dark and flowing, until she was nothing but desire and need.

If their last kiss had been sweet, this one was anything but. This was what the books claimed a woman *could* feel, if she was really a woman. This was what she hadn't even known how to dream. She fell into the kiss as if she were free-falling into clouds. Her arms circled his waist, and her body ground against his. She could feel his arousal, feel exactly how much he wanted her. That knowledge sent her soaring almost as high as the kiss. Jase wanted her. Badly. And everything he did to prove it made her want him just as much.

Finally he pushed her away. "Now you can start pretending!" He stalked back around the table and took his seat. His fork was clenched in his hand as tightly as a sword, but he began to eat.

"I can save some money this way," she said when both of them had choked down most of the rest of their meal. "I can send money home and put some away for the deposit on an apartment. By the end of the summer I'm going to have a place to live and a permanent job. I want my babies with me!"

He kept eating.

"You don't understand," she said when he didn't answer.

"I understand what you're up against, and I understand how you could make it better. How can you save enough if you don't let anybody help you? The tips at Constantine's aren't going to be much. You'll need a thousand dollars to get into a decent apartment, and after the girls are with you, you'll have to hire child care for two. The court is going to look at that when you go for custody."

"I can do it."

"If anybody can, you can."

"What?"

"You heard me right." He looked up and saw one of the smiles he had learned to hope for. "Do you think I want to help you because I don't trust you to do it on your own? I have more faith in you than in almost anybody I know. I just know how hard it's going to be. And I don't want it to be hard."

She couldn't swallow. She stood and took what was left of her dinner to the sink. She hadn't been there for more than seconds when she felt Jase's arms around her.

"I don't know what to think about you," she said.

"Do you think about me?"

"More than I should."

"Likewise."

"I made raspberry cobbler."

He stood there and held her in his arms. She didn't lean against him, and she didn't turn. Had she done either, he didn't know what would have happened.

"I'm going to Blackwater tomorrow," she said after he finally forced himself to step back. Even to herself, she sounded breathless. "I won't be able to go very often once I start working weekends."

"Do the girls know?"

"I write them every day. I think the Hanks read them my letters. They don't like me, but they love Amanda and Faith. They wouldn't hurt the girls to get even."

"When are you leaving?"

"Late afternoon. After your crew's gone home."

"Go in the morning. I'll be here all day tomorrow getting unpacked. I can give orders for a change. They'll find it refreshing."

"No, I have things to do in the yard before I go."

"Go." He turned her to face him. "Give the yard a rest. Let it grow a few new weeds. Go to Blackwater. You've earned a day of vacation by now, don't you think?"

"You're sure?"

No one would ever have to tell him what hope looked like. "I'm sure."

"Thank you."

"It's a little thing."

"Not to me." She touched his cheek, just a whisper-soft brush of her fingers. "Nothing you've done is a little thing. You've given me a chance. Don't think you have to give me more."

He pulled her to rest against him, but he didn't kiss her again. There was so much more he wanted to give her. He just hoped that someday she would accept it all.

Chapter Eight

Jase awakened to the sounds of hammering. As the sole resident of the house, he wanted to wrench the hammer from the hands of whoever was using it and toss it out a window. As the man paying whoever was using it for putting in a full, productive day, he wanted to applaud. Instead of either, he showered and went down to the kitchen to make coffee.

It was the kind of day that Clevelanders dreamed about through every long, gray winter. Outside the kitchen window he could see artfully trimmed evergreens and borders of annuals, gold and pink and white flowers of various sizes and shapes, none of which he could identify. By summer's end they would be wide drifts of color. The sun was shining brightly, though the air was still cool. The day was perfect for Becca's trip to Blackwater. He wondered if she had already left.

He took his coffee outside to get away from the noise. The woman wielding the hammer was relentless, one of the best carpenters he had come across in his search for top-notch work crews. She was the only person he would have trusted to repair and replace the ornate woodwork in what would be his study, but right now he wished she was a little less conscientious.

At Becca's insistence, a brick patio had been laid across from the rose gardens. It was a herringbone design masterpiece, and he had to admit it was going to be a welcome addition. Becca and John, the decorator, had purchased graceful iron furniture— next he expected a perfectly level croquet lawn—and now Jase decided to try it out.

He had settled down with his coffee before he realized he was not alone. He sat forward and peered into the roses. "Becca?"

She stood, dusting grass clippings off the knees of her jeans. "Hi."

"What are you doing here?"

"This and that."

He took his coffee and started toward her. "You're supposed to be on your way by now. It's a long drive to Kentucky."

"I know." She held up a book. "I got this at the library yesterday."

He saw it was a book on old roses, but he couldn't imagine what it had to do with her trip to Blackwater. "Becca—"

"I'm trying to identify these, now that some of them have bloomed. I'm making a list for you."

He wanted to know why she wasn't in her car on the highway, not the names of his rosebushes, but he recognized her reluctance to talk about the trip. He bided his time. "So you've had some luck?"

"More than I thought. I've narrowed down several of them and definitely identified two." She was talking fast, as if she didn't want him to interrupt. "I'll show you."

He followed her into the midst of the rosebushes, trying to figure out how to turn the conversation back to a more relevant subject. "Show away."

"Old-fashioned roses are divided into classes. The first class is—"

"Spare me a horticultural lecture."

"You're not being very nice. I wanted to show off. Anyway, this mess in the corner against the fence is a wild rose."

"That's a class?"

"Technically it's a species rose. Variations grow all over the world. Most people weed them out of gardens. Your grandmother kept this one to fill this corner. Take a deep breath.''

The rose was huge and sprawling, despite the pruning Becca had given it early in the season. Covered with hundreds of small white blossoms, it had a light, sweet fragrance.

"A lot of the climbing roses started from this old honey. Over here's a different kind. It's a damask rose. It's called Gloire de Guilan, or I think it is, anyway."

He had never heard French spoken with quite that accent. He stepped closer to hide his smile and buried his nose in a light pink blossom. The flower was intensely fragrant, and the bush was covered with more just like it.

"This one was discovered in Persia in this century, but damask roses have been around since the Roman Empire. Imagine, Jase."

"Have you found one perfect rose this season?"

"I'm still working on it. This one comes close. Isn't it pretty?"

"Beautiful."

"It comes from China, if it's what I think. Old Blush—at least, I hope it is. They were growing in Europe before this country was founded."

He saw a back door into the subject he really wanted to talk about. "What ever happened to your grandmother's roses, Becca?"

"They're still blooming away at the home place. Matty lives there now. Someday when I'm settled, I'll take slips, so I'll have them with me, too. There was one bush, Gramma called it a pillow rose. It's in this book, only it's really called American Pillar. I want to have it growing against a fence of my own someday."

"Why don't you see if you can get a cutting while you're in Blackwater this weekend and start one here? There's room."

She scrubbed her foot against the wood chip mulch covering the rose bed. "I'm not going."

"Why not?"

"I can't."

He debated whether he had the right to push her. He decided he didn't, then pushed anyway. "Why can't you? You have the day off and the desire to go. You have the transportation." She looked up, and he saw that he'd discovered the problem. "Your car?"

She sighed, and it was answer enough.

"Why didn't you say so? Let's take a look at it."

"Mary Lou already did. She says it won't be going anywhere for a long time."

Jase knew enough to trust Mary Lou, the carpenter who had awakened him so early. The day Mary Lou decided to retire her hammer, she could get a job in any auto shop in the city. "I'm sorry. My mechanic did what he could. We'd hoped it would be the end of the year before the engine needed to be rebuilt."

"I guess I was just lucky I wasn't out on the highway."

She didn't look as if she thought she was lucky. She looked ready to burst into tears. He had only seen her this defeated once before, and he couldn't bear it. He put his arms around her, although she tried to push him away.

"Don't you ever cry?"

"What good does it do?"

"For one thing, it washes away that lump in your throat."

"I wouldn't know what to do...without it." She relaxed and let him hold her. It was a mistake. The moment she gave in that much, the dam shattered, and tears began to course down her cheeks. She had forgotten what it was like to cry, what a devastating assault on her will tears could be. Jase held her tighter as she soaked the front of his shirt.

When the tears were finally cried away, he reached inside his pocket for a handkerchief and came up empty. Becca moved away. He stripped off his T-shirt and gave it to her. "Here."

"I couldn't."

"Why not? You already have."

She glared at him, then she took the shirt and wiped her eyes and cheeks. But not before she'd gotten a good look at his bare chest. She was in no shape to think about bare chests or Jase, but the image of tanned skin stretched across broad, square muscles was imprinted in her mind to think about later. "Thanks."

"You can take my car."

"No."

"My parents have a car I can borrow for the weekend. It won't be any trouble."

She realized she was holding his shirt to her cheek with the affection of a child for his favorite blanket. She thrust it toward him. "I'm not driving your car to Blackwater."

He refused to take the shirt. "Good, because I have a better solution. I'll drive it."

She stared at him. It was exactly like Jase to fix everything for her.

"Before you say no," he continued, "listen. I haven't taken a break in over a year. I didn't even take off Memorial Day weekend. I sorted and packed. Now, I've just made a move, and maybe it's not the best time to leave town, and maybe it is. But I've always wanted to see Kentucky."

"Sure you have."

"Almost more than the Orient or Tahiti."

She sighed, then smiled a little. He smiled back, and her heart sped an extra twelve beats to the minute. "You know I can't let you do this."

"No, I don't. You're not letting me do anything. I want to do it. I want to see Blackwater. I want to see Amanda and Faith. If they're anything like their mommy, they're little girls worth knowing."

"They're wonderful."

"Let me judge for myself. I'm an expert at quality assessment."

"You're just doing this because..."

"Yes?"

She couldn't accuse him of trying to change her life. The trip wouldn't change her life; it would only make the next months bearable. She supposed she would work harder and be more pleasant if she let him do this. In the long run it would benefit him. "Who am I trying to fool?" she asked at last. "I want to go, Jase. I've never wanted anything more. You can't tell me this is something you're dying to do, but I can't tell myself to say no. I'd be proud to have you take me to Blackwater."

"Give me an hour to pack a few things. And I've got phone calls to make before we leave."

"I'll be waiting. Whenever you're ready."

"Bring what you need to make those cuttings, too. The house won't be a showplace until I have a pillow rose in my garden."

She told herself not to get used to being treated this way by a man. Not to get used to one caring enough about her to put his busy life on hold. She told herself not to fall in love with Jase Millington the Whatever. But as he walked away she realized she was fast learning what the Whatever stood for, and the variety of adjectives that came to mind made Jase Millington unforgettable.

Blackwater was a hole. By moonlight it was nothing more than a moonlit hole. Nothing was softened; nothing was improved. The houses had been hastily constructed, and now they were slowly dilapidating. Vines covered one house on the main street, and Jase was sure they held the place together.

Farther away, after the road dipped and shuffled a bit, there were several sturdier homes. Becca pointed to one. "That's the Hanks' house."

Even in the darkness Jase could see that by Blackwater standards, the Hanks were rich. The house was a neat brick ranch, with trimmed evergreens and an enclosed carport. There were two little plastic tricycles parked on the porch under the outside light. He imagined the sight of them broke Becca's heart.

Becca turned her face away, as if she couldn't bear to look. "What you see now is all that's left. Blackwater was never much, but at least it used to be alive. Now half the houses are boarded up. You'll see that tomorrow. The other half have been let go. Nobody's going to paint a house if they have to worry about what they're going to eat tomorrow."

"Two mines closed?"

"Nothing's open around here anymore. Men have to drive so

far to work, they just up and move. There's a woodworking plant over in Baldwin. Some people work there, though it doesn't pay too good. But some people have lived here forever. It's home, and they don't want to move on, even if they don't make much money.''

Jase found that hard to understand, although he wasn't going to tell her so. ''You're sure you want to stay at Matty's tonight? I'm sure there's a room for you in Baldwin, too.''

''No, I'd like to stay at the home place. Matty'd make room for you, too. I know she would.''

''How many kids does she have now?''

''Six.''

''And you think there'd be room?''

''There's always Jimbo's bed. But he's not potty trained exactly.''

''A motel sounds good.''

''You know, you don't have to go with me to see the girls tomorrow. You could just enjoy Baldwin.''

''I'll tour scenic Baldwin another time. What time should I pick you up?''

''Come for breakfast. About seven.''

''Seven?''

''Rich tycoons aren't the only folks who work hard. Matty's husband Syl drives fifty miles to his weekend job. That's mountain miles.''

He dropped her off out in the country a bit—although distinguishing between town and country was all a matter of judgment—at a sprawling white house with a wide front porch and a junk car in the side yard. The house had its own kind of tin-roofed charm. He refused to go in, since it was so late, but he waited until she was safely inside before he followed the road to Baldwin and the twelve-room motel that was the finest Baldwin had to offer.

He was up earlier than he needed to be the next morning. The motel walls were thin, and the couple in the next room had to be honeymooners. He had listened to their groans of pleasure most of the night, and he had thought of Becca.

He wasn't oblivious to the differences between Becca and himself. There couldn't be more, and driving through Blackwater had rubbed it in. Neither was he oblivious to the troubled roots of their relationship. When they'd met she had been beaten down and desperately ill, and he had been neither. He had wanted to help her. Even Prince Charming had first seen Cinderella as a beautiful princess, not a cinder-covered scullery maid. Love had preceded compassion.

But even if the fairy tale was reversed, hadn't he still seen the princess under the rat-brown coat and dangerous cough? Right away he had felt more for her than pity. He had felt admiration, a large helping of it, and the more he knew her, the more admiration he felt. Slowly, over the months, admiration had magnified to something brighter and surer until he wanted to be with her, groaning and sighing like the honeymooners next door. He wanted to feel the sweetness of her kisses all over his body. He wanted to caress her new lusher curves and rosier skin.

He was a man with a woman on his mind. A very special woman, who made staying in the room another minute unbearable. Silently he bid farewell to his amorous neighbors, showered and took an early morning tour of Baldwin before he started back up the road to Matty's house.

In the sunshine, the home place had even more charm than he'd given it credit for. Morning glories twined around the porch pillars, and roses—*the* roses, he supposed—bloomed profusely in a neat garden far to one side. By the light of morning he saw that the junk car wasn't. It was an old station wagon, but it was parked, not abandoned. Someone kept it free of the dust of narrow mountain roads.

Matty was dark-haired and pale-skinned. Poverty and too many children too close together had heaped eighty pounds on a frame as fine-boned as Becca's. He understood the reasons for the extra pounds as soon as she ushered him to the family table. The meal was heavy on biscuits and white bread ladled with sausage gravy. Some of the children were barely a year apart. They were clean, bright and certainly not hungry, but the oldest boy needed to see a dentist, and all the girls shared their mother's appetite for sugar and fat.

He listened to the banter and heard the love as clearly. Syl said little, but when he did, everybody jumped. Jase sensed not fear but a profound respect in the family's response. And who wouldn't respect a man who worked seven days a week to provide for his brood? He was thin to Matty's thick, gnarled and grizzled and old before his time. But he was a man with a funny little smile and the occasional wry comment, and by the end of the meal, Jase wished Syl lived in Ohio and worked for him.

He and Becca left after each of the children had showed him the gifts Becca had brought them. They were little things, Cleveland Indians keychains for the boys and magic slates for the girls, but the children were thrilled to have them.

In the car driving toward the Hanks' house, Becca watched Jase for a reaction. He had seemed perfectly at ease, but she had been aware of all the things that had probably been new to him. The chipped dime-store crockery, the jelly glasses filled with powdered fruit drink instead of orange juice, the faint odor of wet mattresses and mildew. She was ashamed of none of it. Not of the sofa with springs that protruded, not of Matty's poor grammar—the same grammar Becca still worked so hard to chase from her own speech. Matty and Syl had always stood by her, and the children were almost as dear to her as her own. She wasn't ashamed, but she wondered if Jase now saw more clearly how different they were.

If he saw it, he gave no sign. He caught her watching him, and the intimacy of his smile bounced her heart rate up another notch.

"Bill and Alice know we're coming," she said as she turned away. "Usually they leave after I arrive, and I have the girls all to myself."

"That's nice of them."

"I don't think they do it to be nice."

He waited for her to elaborate. But he didn't have time to question her when she didn't. He rounded a corner, and the Hanks' house was right there. He pulled up in front, and Becca got out of the car before he'd turned off the engine. He followed her up the path.

The door opened before Becca got to the porch. Two pigtailed whirlwinds came barreling toward her. She knelt and scooped them to her, one in each arm. He hovered a good distance behind, reluctant to interrupt the reunion.

Finally one of the little girls noticed him. She stuck two fingers in her mouth and peered over Becca's shoulder. "Who zat?"

Becca swung around and beamed a teary smile in his direction. "Come here, Jase, and meet my babies."

He started forward. Only then did he notice the woman standing in the doorway. She had a permanent frown etched into her forehead under steel gray, tightly permed hair. Her arms were crossed, and she watched every move that Becca made.

He stooped beside Becca. He didn't know much about kids, but he'd visited The Greenhouse often enough to learn that his height scared some of them. He didn't touch, and he didn't talk loudly. He'd learned that, too. "Okay, who's who?"

"This is Faith."

"Good morning, Faith."

She giggled.

He turned his attention to the other. "Good morning, Amanda." He studied her for a moment, then turned back to Faith. "Now I can tell."

"Can he?" Amanda asked her mother.

"Probably not. Shut your eyes, Jase, and I'll mix them up."

He obeyed, to a chorus of twin giggles.

"Okay, open your eyes."

He did. He squinted at the girls. "Amanda here and Faith here." He pointed as he spoke.

"How'd he know?" Faith asked.

"How did you know?" Becca asked. "It takes most people weeks to tell."

"Magic."

Becca stood the girls side by side and looked at them. "Amanda has blue barrettes, and Faith has pink."

"And I thought I could fool you."

Becca stood, balancing Faith on one hip. Amanda held tightly to her other hand. "Jase, come meet Alice Hanks."

He noticed that she didn't add "My mother-in-law." He guessed that Becca had stopped thinking of this stern-faced woman as any kind of mother a long time ago.

Becca introduced them at the doorway. Alice held out her hand with little.enthusiasm. "Didn't know you were bringing anyone," she said to Becca.

"Jase offered to drive me. My car didn't want to make the trip."

"Dewey always took good care of that car."

"The car is four years older now," Becca said.

"Well, you both might as well come on in. Bill and me were fixing to go out."

"I won't be staying," Jase assured her. "Becca needs time alone with the girls."

Becca shot him a grateful smile.

"Come on in for a minute anyhow and meet Bill."

Jase followed them into the living room. Inside, the house was much the same as it was out, neat and uninspired. There was a large, paint-by-numbers portrait of a matador over a fireplace that looked as if it had never been used. The furniture was the gold and avocado green of the sixties, and the carpet had seen considerable wear.

When they walked in, Bill Hanks got slowly to his feet. Jase watched him struggle to straighten, and any animosity he had felt for the man lessened. Dewey's father had paid his own price for the life his son had led.

Bill's hand wasn't steady when he held it out. Jase grasped it firmly and murmured the appropriate greetings. "The girls've had their breakfast," Bill told Becca. "Don't let 'em fool you into giving 'em any more of that chocolate cereal."

"I won't," Becca promised.

"And they need a nap at two, or we'll pay for it tonight when you're gone."

"I know, Bill. I always give them a nap when I'm here."

"Well, you're not here much, are you?"

There was a moment of total silence. "I'm not here much because I'm working eight hours away," Becca said evenly. "And that's only because there are no jobs here."

"Cincinnati's a hell of a lot closer."

"We've been over this. I had a job in Cincinnati, and the laundry closed down. They said they could hire me in their branch in Cleveland. So I went there."

She didn't add that the Cleveland branch hadn't been interested in her, or that once she was there she didn't have the money to move back to southern Ohio or Kentucky. Those were stories she kept from the Hanks so that when the time came to ask for custody of her daughters, no one could throw homelessness up at her as a reason to say no.

"Seems to me you'd find your way back more often," Bill said.

Jase watched Becca closely. Her expression didn't change. It hadn't since the conversation began. "I find my way back every chance I get. Maybe soon I won't need to."

"What's that mean?"

"It means that I'm going to court to seek custody of the girls just as soon as I've got all the resources to support them. Then you'll have to find your way north to visit." She paused just long enough to make the next statement significant. "You would always be welcome in my house."

"I wouldn't count on anything, missy."

"I've already learned that, Bill. From Dewey."

Alice made a sound deep in her throat. Jase couldn't fathom what it meant, but he did know he wanted to add something. He struggled to sound calm. "Becca's had more bad breaks than anyone is entitled to, Mr. Hanks. She has friends now who are going to make sure she gets good breaks from now on."

"*I'm* going to make sure I get good breaks," Becca said. "And I'm going to support my daughters and raise them. Don't think I'm not grateful that you and Alice were there for them when I couldn't be. But I need my babies now, and both of you need time alone, and rest."

Bill might appear frail, but Jase could see an iron will, with no touch of goodwill to soften it, in the man's eyes. When the time came for a custody battle, Bill Hanks would pull out all the stops. He wondered if Becca knew.

The Hanks left. Becca didn't seem particularly flustered by the confrontation with them. Jase waited until the girls were settled at coloring books Becca had brought them before he spoke.

"Are the Hanks always like that?"

"No. They're—Bill is usually much worse. Bill was on his best behavior because you're bigger and younger than he is, and because you look like somebody important."

"He's a cheap-trick bully."

"He taught his son well. But most of the time he's good with the girls. He has a soft spot for them that he doesn't have for me. I remind him of all his failures. The girls give him hope."

"You're generous."

"I'm resigned. I change what I can and accept what I can't."

"There's more to the prayer that's from. Do you have the wisdom to tell the difference?"

"I think so. Do you think I do?"

"Not always."

"That's something we'll always disagree about."

He thought about the "always" as he headed toward Blackwater to look around. He liked the sound of that "always" more and more.

Chapter Nine

Blackwater proper was little more than two gas stations, a grocery store with a post office in one corner and a pharmacy in the other, plus a community center with a library, a rec hall and a medical clinic that was open twice a week. If a Blackwater resident was sick on Tuesday or Friday, he was lucky. If he was sick on any other day and couldn't wait, he drove to Baldwin, or beyond, if the illness required a specialist or sophisticated technology.

The community center was a converted church, staffed and run by volunteers. The rec hall was open on Wednesday nights for adults and Saturdays for children and teenagers. There were two Ping-Pong tables and a billiard table that had seen more games than a professional hustler. There was a television set and a video recorder with a small collection of donated tapes. With the dearth of commercial entertainment in Blackwater, Jase imagined every citizen had seen the tapes a dozen times.

He had never felt more like a stranger. He was dressed casually, and there was nothing flashy about his car. But he had not grown up here; he had not been married in one of the two tiny churches bordering the road a quarter of a mile from town or buried his parents in the cemetery behind the community center. He was a stranger. He walked like he owned the world, because in fact he owned a pretty damned big piece of it. He had never known defeat or hunger, or what it was like to be sick on a schedule.

He wasn't sure how the people he passed on the sidewalk knew that about him. No one smiled or nodded. His face might as well have been on wanted posters plastered all over the post office for the suspicious looks that were thrown his way.

He started his tour at the grocery store. Small, with a small selection, the store smelled like ripe bananas and bug spray. There was a line at the post office window and another at the pharmacy. He bought an apple and took it to the cashier, a pretty young woman whose hair was already streaked with gray. She checked him out without a word.

His luck was no better at the community center. Children ran from end to end of the rec hall in sync to a video tape of *The Jungle Book*. The apes in the cartoon had more self-control than the children and were friendlier than the man and woman watching them run. He visited the library and asked if the librarian could recommend any good books on the area, but her response was limited to "nothing we have."

His tour had taken him an hour, largely because he had strolled the equivalent of several city blocks to see if there was anything he had missed and because he had visited the cemetery. The cemetery had been the most enlightening stop. Back in the eastern corner he had located Dewey's grave. According to the headstone, Dewey had been the beloved son of Alice and William Hanks. No stranger reading it would ever know he had also been the husband of a woman named Becca or the father of two beautiful little girls.

With nothing else to see and no one who would talk to him, he got back in his car and decided to take some of the side roads to see where they led. Two hours later he was back on the main road heading toward a ramshackle café between Blackwater and Baldwin.

As he drove, his mind was reeling with possibilities. As he and Becca had driven into town last night, he had been oblivious to the scenery. The mountains had been an obstacle and nothing more. This morning he had been so intent on taking the pulse of Blackwater that he had missed the obvious. The pulse wasn't a few buildings set along the road. The pulse was the mountains, the exquisite scenery that had finally shaken him out of his complacency, the Blackwater River that wound its way through upland and hollow and carved out a path that even ruthless mining companies had never quite managed to destroy. There was potential here. There had to be.

He parked in the dirt lot of Better'n Home, next to six pickups and two cars that reminded him of Becca's. Inside he was met with the same suspicious stares that had greeted him everywhere. Most of the tables were taken by groups of men. There were only three women in the room, and one of them was the waitress. Smoke swirled to the beat of a window fan, the only ventilation in the room.

He sat in a booth, a neatly patched vinyl seat with a sparkling clean table. The menu was simple; the day's special was ham with red-eye gravy. He waited to be served.

The waitress, an aging blonde with too much eye makeup, found every excuse not to visit his table. Finally, when no more excuses seemed to be left, she ambled over, but she didn't seem pleased to see him. He ordered the special and watched her amble away. Like the woman at the grocery store, she had managed it all without a word.

He had heard of the reticence of people living in the Appalachians. Kentucky, after all, was the state where the Hatfields and McCoys had carried out their feud. A man either belonged or he didn't. And quite obviously, since no one had ever seen Jase before, he didn't belong. He was surprised, though, that everyone seemed suspicious of him. He wondered what the whole town was worried about.

The waitress returned with ice water and a salad. He decided to take his chances with her before she left. "Miss?"

She waited.

"I'm visiting for the day, and I'm trying to see as much of

the area as I can. Is there anything I should do, anywhere I should go?''

"I don't know."

He was encouraged to find she could speak. "Well, if you'd never been here before, what do you think you'd most want to see?''

"I've always been here." She turned and was gone. He watched her stop by a table at the edge of the room where three burly men smoked and shouted at each other. All three men turned to look at him as the waitress walked away from their table.

He was halfway through his salad before one of the men came to stand beside his table.

"Hear you're looking for places to go."

He eyed the man and saw trouble. "Not hell, if that's what you're about to tell me."

"We don't need no smart-mouthed strangers here."

Jase gestured to the bench across from him. "Look, friend, why don't you have a seat and tell me what's going on? I'm not in town to cause anyone any trouble."

The man didn't move. "S'pose you tell me why you're in town, then?''

Jase weighed that possibility and decided he liked it. What better way could there be to find out how much support Blackwater might offer Becca if a custody battle was to take place? He pushed his salad bowl away. "I'm a friend of Becca Hanks'," he said, watching the man's face. "A very good friend. I came with her to see her daughters for the weekend. I wanted to see the kind of place where they've been raised."

The man's expression didn't change. "Becca Hanks?"

"That's right. Do you know her?"

"Everybody knows Becca. Where is she now?"

"With her girls."

"Cute little rascals."

Jase realized he had been ready to leap to his feet and throw the first punch. He relaxed, gratefully, since he wasn't sure this man wouldn't have flattened him to the ground. "Cutest I've ever seen. Matty and Syl's kids are cute, too. I was there for breakfast.''

"You a friend of theirs, too?"

Jase had the feeling he was passing the test, and, more important, so was Becca. "I hope I am now."

"Damn." The man turned and motioned to his friends. In a moment all three were hovering over the table. Jase slid over, and in a moment they were all seated in the booth.

"I want to know what happened to Becca here," Jase said. "And I want to know how it happened."

If he had wondered if anyone in Blackwater knew how to practice the fine art of conversation, he stopped wondering immediately.

Becca had been everybody's friend; Dewey, on the other hand, had been an arrogant, spoiled good-for-nothing who used everybody he came in contact with. Not a soul in Blackwater believed that Becca had had anything to do with the robbery. Her only fault had been blind loyalty to a man who hadn't deserved it.

The parole board had been flooded with letters and calls from Blackwater citizens, so flooded that Becca had made parole on her first try. There wasn't anyone in town who wouldn't have given Becca a job, if there had been a job to give her. And wasn't it a crying shame that the Hanks were raising her kids? There wasn't anyone in town who wouldn't go to court to have their say about her character.

By the time Jase had finished his lunch he knew more than he'd ever expected to learn. He heard about Becca's brothers and the time she had locked them in a basement until they said they were sorry for taking her bicycle apart. He heard how well liked her father had been, and how he had led the local union in a confrontation over better benefits. He heard how many Blackwater boys had been in love with her and how many of them she had kissed.

He also got an earful of what it was like to live in a town where there were no jobs and no hope of jobs, only mountains, a narrow, winding river and roots that went back generations.

After lunch one of the men took him on a tour, a wild joyride around mountains and through hollows he hadn't found himself. The man's love for the mountains, for this land claimed by his ancestors, was tangible to Jase. When he finally said goodbye, he had been given a view of Becca's life. Blackwater was a place out of time, and although he would never fully understand its draw for her, he understood a little more of it.

As arranged, he arrived at the Hanks' house about dinnertime. Becca had just finished giving the girls their meal when he walked in. Faith was dancing from foot to foot as Becca washed her face. Amanda had obviously already received the same wash-cloth treatment.

"Good day?" he asked when Becca looked up.

"Wonderful." She tried to think of a better word. Perfect? Not quite. It would be perfect when she and her babies had their own home, and naps, meals and face-washing were just daily occurrences.

He sat down, and Amanda skirted his chair, as if trying to get up enough nerve to approach him. He was sure there was a way to encourage her without scaring her to death, but he didn't know what it was. When he sat forward, she backed up three paces.

"Bill and Alice should be home any minute." Becca got to her feet. "I called the motel in Baldwin and got myself a room too. Syl's family's coming in tonight, and the house will be bustin' its seams. I don't want to put them out." She smiled. "Besides, I might have to sleep with Jimbo."

He wondered if she was giving the real reason for not going to Matty's house, or if the thought of facing that exuberant family when her own children were just a mile away under someone else's care was too much for her tonight. He had little time to wonder. Bill and Alice arrived, and there was a flurry of good-byes. Both little girls cried when Becca left, even though she promised she and Jase would be back the next morning to take them out for the day.

"Is it always like that?" he asked when they were halfway to Baldwin.

"Sometimes it's worse."

He didn't know how to console her. He had tallied up what she would have to earn to support them. Even if she saved enough money to get into a shabby apartment and took all the aid a working woman was eligible for, she would still need more money than someone with an equivalency degree could probably earn.

"I saw a restaurant in Baldwin that looks decent," he said.

"I'm not very hungry."

Jase knew Becca well enough to suspect she had barely touched any food at the Hanks'. She would not want to be beholden to them for anything, and Bill Hanks was just the kind of person who would remind her of anything she took, even a sandwich.

He didn't mention the restaurant again. When they arrived in Baldwin he scanned the main street until he found it. Then he pulled into the parking lot. "You might not be hungry," he said, "but I'm starving."

She got out without a word. Inside she picked at broiled fish and cole slaw, shredding more than she ate. She tried to make conversation, but more often than not she stopped in midsentence.

At the motel she was given the room next to Jase's—he hoped the springs on the bed hadn't been damaged by the last occupants. The door closed behind her, and he was left with an evening of television or paperwork he had brought with him. He alternated between the two until ten-thirty, when he finally called it a night.

Without the honeymooners next door, the motel was quiet. He lay awake, hands behind his head, and stared at the ceiling. Everything he had ever touched had turned to gold, yet now, when he wanted to touch Becca's life, she wouldn't allow it.

He pictured the way she had looked with the twins. He saw the graceful swirl of her hair against her cheek, and her huge, earnest brown eyes fixed on Faith and Amanda. Now she was lovely, but never more so than when she had held one of her daughters at the window this afternoon, sunlight streaming around them both like an Appalachian Madonna and child.

As if he had conjured the woman from the vision, he heard her moving around her room. He waited for her to settle down, but there was no reassuring squeak of the bedsprings. He heard footsteps, something that sounded like a shoe hitting the floor, then the rattle of a chain and the scraping of a door. He was out of bed in a second, pulling on shorts.

When he opened his door she was beside the wall between their rooms. "Go back to sleep," she ordered. "I didn't mean to wake you."

"I wasn't asleep." He noted that she was fully, if casually, dressed. She was not going down the covered walkway for ice. "Did you decide you were hungry after all?"

Her gaze swept him. Bare chest, bare feet, denim shorts riding low on his hips and a ten dollar bet there was nothing underneath them. "No."

He lounged in the doorway. "Looking for a nightlife?"

"The nightlife in these parts isn't safe for single women."

He didn't like guessing games. He waited.

"I was going for a walk," she admitted. "I couldn't sleep."

"Are walks safe for single women?"

"Probably. There's a road over that way that leads down to the river. It's not even half a mile. I thought I'd go down there."

"Would you like some company?"

"The first time we met you didn't think I should be out walking by myself, either."

"I was right."

"You usually are, aren't you?"

"May I come?"

"You should be asleep. You don't have to worry about me."

"Okay. I'm not worried. May I come?"

He expected resistance, but the smile she flashed was grateful. "All right."

"I'll be right back."

She was sorry to see him leave. She had liked the view, more than she knew she should. She stood outside his room and thought about the hours she had lain awake considering her life. She had been acutely aware of Jase's presence in the next room.

He was a recent addition to her years of memories, yet when she had tried to think of Dewey and what had gone wrong between them, it was Jase she had thought of. Dewey had taken; Jase gave. Dewey had made her feel smaller than a pinprick; Jase made her believe in herself. Dewey had told her repeatedly that she was not much of a woman; Jase told her with every admiring look, every passionate kiss, that he thought she was all woman.

She felt all woman when she was with him. Tonight she had longed for his arms around her. She didn't want comfort. It was never easy to leave her babies with the Hanks, but she could do it because she knew that soon, somehow, she would have them with her permanently. She had been through much worse and survived it without comforting. Tonight what she had yearned for was affirmation. Was she the person, the woman, she wanted to be? Was she a woman Jase Millington could fall in love with? Because somewhere along the way she had begun to fall in love with him.

He came back out, his chest and legs no longer bare. "You'll have to lead the way."

She wondered if he had been reading her thoughts. Then she realized he meant to the river. She held out her hand. "I don't want to lose you in the dark."

He squeezed it in his own. He had been afraid to touch her, not because he was afraid she would crumble, but because he was afraid she was too caught up in her children to think of him. Her hand was a gardener's, not baby soft like Cara's or the other women of his acquaintance. Firm and slightly callused, the hand was as substantial, as capable, as the woman.

She led him to the river. A full yellow moon lit their path, and they were guided by the sound of water rushing over rocks. It was obvious she had visited this spot before. She tugged him into the center of a clump of evergreens, and he realized they were in a cove, protected by tree branches. She pulled him down beside her on a flat grassy area that curved against the water. The dark ribbon of river reflected moonlight in shimmering, mystical patterns. He could understand why she had wanted to come.

"Sometimes when things would get too bad with Dewey, I'd come here," she said. "I'd borrow Alice's car if she was in a good mood, and I'd drive down here, away from Blackwater. It was like leaving all my problems behind. I'd pretend I never got married, that I'd graduated from high school and was on my way to college. I'd picture myself on a boat on the river, drifting off to a new life." For a moment she couldn't continue. "That was silly, I guess."

"It sounds like something any of us might do if we were desperate."

"Did you have a place like this?"

"Kathryn's house. I didn't have to be perfect there. I could get dirty and eat candy and climb trees. Pamela and I used to have a system. Right before we snuck off to Kathryn's, Pamela would inspect me, and I'd inspect her. We'd notice everything. Then, when we were ready to go home, we'd inspect each other again. If something was dirty or wrinkled, we'd fix it the best we could so our parents wouldn't know where we'd been or what we'd been doing."

"When I was little I was always dirty. And I practically lived in trees. I only got candy for special occasions, though. My daddy said he'd save money on candy and dentists at the same time." She leaned back until she was lying flat, looking up at the moon. Jase reclined beside her. "I wouldn't trade with you, Jase. It was good growing up here. I had people who loved me. I had the mountains and the river. I had friends who believed I could be somebody. Where did I go wrong?"

He touched her cheek, trailing his fingers slowly down the side of it. "You didn't."

"Didn't I? Then how come somebody else got my kids and I ended up living in a beat-up Chevrolet? No, don't say it. I'll tell you what happened. I went wrong when I thought I needed a man to run my life. I was little when my mama died, but I still remember how she'd wait for Daddy at the end of the day. Whatever she couldn't take care of while he'd been gone, they'd take care of it together when he got home. I grew up thinking that when I got married, I'd be more than I could ever be by myself.''

"I grew up thinking that when I got married I'd become half of something.''

"Like you'd shrink?''

"I suppose.''

She turned on her side so she could see him better. "Is that why you never got married?''

He had never thought about it, but he supposed that was the reason. His parents had always seemed half of something instead of individuals. He had never wanted that. He liked his power, his control. He had never wanted to share who he was or alter the balance in his life. He had never wanted to become less than he had always been.

Until that moment he had never realized how his view of his parents' marriage had colored his life, just as Becca's had colored hers. "What did you find out from being married?'' he asked.

"I had a lot of time to think about it in prison. I figured out that marriage can make you half of what you were or three times as powerful and happy, just depending on who you pick. If you pick somebody like Dewey, it's the same as taking one of those shrinking pills, like in *Alice in Wonderland*. If you marry somebody like my daddy, then you just grow and grow until you're just about too big for the White Rabbit's hole.''

Their faces were only inches apart. He saw wariness in her eyes, and right along with it a determination not to let it control her life. "Then you'd risk it again?''

"I didn't say that.''

"Would you?''

"How about you? Are you going to be Cleveland's oldest living eligible bachelor?''

He smiled and moved a little closer. "No woman has ever questioned me about marriage and lived to tell the tale.''

"Would you swallow a woman up, Jase?''.

"I'd probably try.''

"And if she wouldn't let you?''

"I'd probably be glad."

"Probably."

"I'm new at this, Becca. I don't know."

"What are you new at?"

"I'm new at you." He leaned forward and kissed her. Her lips were soft and yielding, and the first taste of her made him realize just how much he wanted her. He made a sound low in his throat and kissed her again.

She lay back and slid her arms around his neck. Thoughts of that, of him, had intruded all day. She had thought of Jase as she fed her daughters lunch, thought of him as she read them a fairy tale before their nap. She hadn't wanted to, but she had found that thoughts of Jase were one thing she couldn't control. She worried about it, just as she worried about the way her body was melting into his, but she didn't worry enough to stop him from kissing her.

His lips trailed to her ear. She could feel the warmth of his breath against her earlobe, and something inside her struggled for freedom. She let her hands drift down his back, kneading his taut muscles until they flowed under her fingers. He gave a groan of pleasure as she touched him. Something similar escaped her lips as he kissed the side of her neck, the hollow of her throat. He was in no hurry to give her pleasure or to take his own. He seemed to want to know every inch of skin, to test it for its pleasure potential and gauge how his touch there affected her.

Her eyelids fluttered shut as he kissed her ear. He stroked her hair and whispered encouragement, flattery, words of affection that were as devastating as his touch.

When he lifted her shirt, her heart sped faster. She had never been kissed or touched this way. His lovemaking was a gift, not something he was taking from her. His hands and lips lulled her, like the hypnotic rhythm of the river; they excited, like the cool mountain air against her skin.

She had dreamed on this piece of ground, but nothing she had ever dreamed had been this impossible. It was impossible that Jase wanted her, impossible that she wanted him. After everything that had happened to her, she still wanted him. After everything he'd had, he wanted her. Her. "I'm dreaming again," she whispered.

"It's not a dream. Not a—" He cut short his own reply by kissing her again. Her skin was so warm, so smooth. He found her bra clasp, and his hand closed over her breast, warmer and smoother still. He savored her soft moan and the rush of heat between his legs. Sensation seemed to pool each place she touched and each hidden place she didn't. His body was taut with yearning. He undressed her slowly, not because he wanted this to last forever, but because his hands were suddenly uncoordinated. He was no longer the man who controlled his world. This piece of it was beyond his control. Becca wasn't his for the taking. She was giving herself, and he was the blessed recipient.

He stripped off his own shirt so that he could feel her breasts against his bare chest. She was slender—he doubted that would ever change—but she was all woman, with breasts that swelled against his hand and hips that curved gracefully from a tiny waist. He kissed her eyelids and watched her smile. He cupped her breast and watched her eyelids part.

"Better than a dream." She threaded her fingers through his hair and pulled him back down to her. "Much...much..."

The Kentucky night air rolled over them, and spray from the river dampened the grass. Nothing could cool the warmth surging through Becca. She was coming alive after months, years, of suffocating her feelings, imprisoning her heart. She didn't know if she was ready for this, but Jase had forced her rebirth. In this one thing he had given her no choice. Fear warred with joy, but joy won easily. No promises had been made except that he wanted her. And she wanted him. More than she had known a woman could want a man.

His hands were magic. He touched her breasts as if he knew just how and where he could give her the most pleasure. He stroked and molded her flesh as if it were his to mold. His lips were magic, too. He kissed her breast, just over her thundering heart. She lifted herself to him as he took more of her in his mouth, then more.

She moaned her pleasure as he unlocked all the secret places inside her where yearning and need had been hidden. She moved against him as if unlocking his secret desires, too. Her legs twined with his; her arms held him; her lips explored what they could. His lips left her breast. He kissed her as if he knew exactly what would excite her now. Her lips parted easily beneath the thrust of his tongue; her legs parted and wrapped around him as naturally as if they had always been lovers.

Somewhere beside the river a bobolink called to his mate. She called to hers by pushing away the final scraps of cloth between them. With her naked flesh against his, she felt fully alive. Heat magnified heat. Flesh called to flesh. He was hard against her, hard and probing and much desired. Still, he didn't enter her. His hands slid to her hips, then one hand to the place where all sensation focused. She held her breath and forgot she was anything but a woman being loved, forgot she was anything but a woman falling in love.

His arms circled her at last, and he held her tightly against him, as if savoring this last, precious moment before everything changed. When he finally made them one, she gave herself up to his passion. She knew that he was a man who had forgotten everything except love.

Chapter Ten

Becca woke up the next morning wrapped tightly in Jase's arms. For a moment she thought they were still on the riverbank. Then she remembered that they had gone back to the motel and fallen asleep together in Jase's room. But not before they had made love again.

She wondered how she had dared to allow this to happen. Loving Jase could change the entire focus of her life. But what room was there for a man like Jase in a life such as hers?

"You're awake?"

She couldn't pretend. "Just."

"And you're lying there having regrets?"

"Not exactly."

"Then what, exactly?"

"I'm lying here thinking how hungry I am. And wishing that I'd eaten that fish last night. I guess that counts as regrets."

He knew that wasn't true, but he didn't want to push. He wanted to remember last night and the woman who had twined herself around every part of him, the woman he had fallen in love with. The woman who would put up every roadblock to love that her pigheaded, shortsighted, thank-you-very-much-but-I'll-do-it-myself brain could come up with.

"There's a room service menu. We can eat here."

She wondered about the pure indulgence of eating in bed, of punching out a number or two so someone could come running with hot coffee and omelets. Jase took room service for granted while she thought a fast-food breakfast was an unbelievable extravagance. It was a reflection of the differences between them.

When she didn't respond, he guessed what she was thinking. "Let me explain something about the financial system in this country," he said, pulling her closer. "Those who have money have to spend it, otherwise those who don't will never get any. Now, that may not be fair, and it may not be pretty, but it's realistic. If I don't pick up that phone, some employee, maybe somebody from Blackwater even, maybe somebody with kids—lots of kids—won't have anything to do this morning. And if he doesn't have anything to do, then pretty soon he'll be let go. And if he's let go, he won't have any money to spend, and pretty soon the man at his grocery store and maybe his gas station will be let go, too."

"So if you don't call for room service, pretty soon the whole town, maybe the whole region, has to move away to find a job?"

"And they move to Cleveland, where the whole cycle continues until I'm out of work, and then you're out of work, too."

"And pretty soon everybody's out of work."

"Now you've as good as got a degree in economics."

She wanted to lecture him for joking about something so serious, but she found herself laughing instead. In a way he was right. Jase had money to spend, and when he spent it, someone benefitted. In this case, she benefitted most of all, since she wouldn't have to get out of bed and get dressed quite yet. She pushed all her doubts about their differences aside for the moment. She was in bed with the man who had taught her what pleasure could mean. She was in bed with the man whose green eyes were sparking warmth in places he had already thoroughly explored. She was in bed with a man who was teaching her that she could love again.

"I've never had room service," she admitted.

"Then it'll be a treat."

"Will they wait and bring it when you ask them to?"

"They will."

She ran her fingers down his chest. "That would be a treat, too."

He made the call, then he gave his attention to more important matters.

As if Alice and Bill wanted to avoid having Becca come into the house, the girls were waiting on the porch when Jase and Becca arrived to pick them up. Today Jase couldn't immediately tell them apart, since their barrettes were the same color, but he was beginning to see differences between them. Faith was quicker to smile and quicker to pout. Amanda was more serene. Their personalities were often reflected in their expressions and in the way they moved. He suspected that by the end of the morning they would not be able to fool him.

Becca had suggested a picnic, and before leaving Baldwin he had bought a bucket of the chicken Kentucky was known for. Now Becca guided him up into the same hills that he had toured yesterday at breakneck speed with one of her many admirers.

"Do you like waterfalls?" she asked.

He wasn't going to admit that when he saw waterfalls he thought of raw power just waiting to be developed and channeled. Pamela had been telling him that he was myopic for years. He was only just beginning to see what she meant.

"Doesn't everybody like waterfalls?" he countered.

"I'm taking you to a bitty one. It's nothing fancy, but hardly anybody knows about it, so we'll probably be alone. First you've got to swear you won't tell where it is."

"Who would I tell?"

"I don't know. You might decide to build a hotel there someday. No restaurant. Nothing but room service."

She flashed him one of her uncommon smiles. He reminded himself that he was a well satisfied man with enough self-control to get through the next hours without making love to her again. Then he reminded himself once more.

They parked and walked to the waterfall, with everybody toting something. He brought the chicken and a blanket; Becca brought the bag with soft drinks, salads and napkins, and each of the girls brought a canvas bag brimming with toys. The fall was a sparkling spray of water cascading over a cliff into a shallow pool. The girls could run carefully beneath the fall to cool off and did so half a dozen times while he and Becca set up the picnic.

"Hasn't anybody told them it's still early?" he asked.

"*They* didn't stay up most of the night playing patty cake."

"Is that what we did?"

"Close enough." She smoothed out the blanket. "You don't know much about kids, do you?"

"Not much."

"Don't you want some?"

He had given it little thought. "I don't think I'm father material."

"Maybe not."

He looked up from unpacking the chicken. "Nobody says you have to agree."

"Well, if you don't think you'd be a good father, you probably wouldn't be. Fathers have to have confidence. They have to enjoy taking charge and making things right. We both know how you hate that."

He smiled at her, although she was bending over and couldn't see him. "I get the point."

"You know what I think? I think you've been so busy moving Cleveland around to make it prettier and grander that you just pushed the idea of kids somewhere far away."

"Maybe."

"It's too bad, too, because you could be a happy man if you'd just let yourself."

"How do you know I'm not a happy man?"

"I didn't mean you weren't happy. I just think you could be happier. You could have something more than a view out the window."

He wondered how she had managed to put his life and everything he had ever strived for into five little words. "A view out the window.'' It fit. He'd spent his life changing that view, but only rarely had he reached for anything he saw.

Dripping wet, the girls came back to flop down on the blanket. Jase had no idea what three-year-olds ate, but after he'd watched these particular three-year-olds make a mid-morning snack of drumstick after drumstick, he guessed anything that had ever been alive was on the list. He watched Becca dole out potato salad and coleslaw as if it were candy, until each girl was begging for more. He watched her make a game of wiping hands and faces and cleaning up.

They were back scampering under the waterfall before he commented, ''How often do they eat?''

''About as often as they can.''

''You're wonderful with them.''

''Do you think so?'' She stopped cleaning up and met his eyes. ''Do you think when I'm gone they remember the things I've said to them? Do they remember I love them?''

''From the way they greet you, I'd say they do.''

''I've got to bring them to live with me soon. Before they start to doubt it.''

He wasn't going to repeat his offer. The time wasn't right, and he was a master of timing. He was going to offer again, though, and soon. The more he saw Becca with her daughters, the more convinced he was that she had to let him help her.

She stood and fumbled through one of the canvas bags the girls had brought with them. ''Here, look at this.'' She came to sit beside him. He noticed the way her leg stretched along the length of his, the way her breast brushed up against his side. The intimacy went along with the sound of children's laughter and falling water, with summer sunshine and clear Kentucky mountain air. Something almost like a shudder passed through him. He wanted to stop time and keep that feeling passing through him forever.

He forced himself to stretch out his hand. Unbelievably, the spell wasn't broken. ''What's this?''

''It's a kin doll. Don't rack your brain. You've never seen one before.''

"Isn't Kin Barbie's boyfriend?"

She poked him. The poke went along with the moment. He grabbed her fingers and brought them to his mouth for a kiss.

"That's Ken. This is a kin doll. Far as I know, they're just made in Blackwater. It's a tradition. Started a long time ago, I guess, because I have a whole set that were mine when I was little. Matty's keeping them for me."

He examined the doll, a fanciful ten-inch rag doll that was beautifully crafted and realistic. "Definitely not Raggedy Anne."

"How old do you think she is? I mean, how old a person is she supposed to be?"

The plump, smiling doll was clad in a plain blue dress with a white apron and sturdy-looking shoes. Her hair was gray, pulled back in a tidy bun.

"She has glasses somewhere, only Amanda always loses them," Becca said.

"I'd say she's supposed to be a woman in her sixties."

"That's right. It took the Ladies Guild a while to get the wrinkles right on this one. Alice and her friends at the Baptist Church make them. Women there have been making them for years for the Christmas bazaar."

"What does 'kin doll' mean?"

"She's kin to a whole family of dolls. She's a grandmother. Alice always lets one of the girls take her when they're going away for the day. That way, if they miss Alice, they can pull out the doll. There's a mama doll, too, only there's no reason to have it here today, since I'm with them."

He imagined the girls with their mama doll when Becca was away. "And they keep it with them when you're gone?"

"There's a whole family. Fathers, grandfathers, aunts and uncles, cousins, babies. Every year the guild makes somebody new. About ten years ago the men got into it and made little books with leather covers that said Family Bible. When you open them, there's room to put the name of every kin in that family and their birthdays. The men make furniture for them, too, rocking chairs and beds and trunks for their clothes. They make more than they can sell.''

She busied herself putting the doll back in the bag. ''When I leave the girls I tell them that I'm giving their mama doll all my love to keep there with them. Any time they miss me they're supposed to find their doll and give her a hug, and then some of my love will be touching them. I don't know what people do who don't have kin dolls.''

He didn't want to think about Becca parting from her children. He felt a rush of anger at her stubbornness, and the magic spell disappeared. ''Not everybody has to worry.''

''Not everybody has to leave kids behind. I know that. But a lot of people do, Jase. Daddies who are divorced and don't have custody, mamas who have to put their kids in day care for most of the day, grandpas and grammas who live far away and only see their grandbabies on holidays. Seems to me a lot of people could use kin dolls.''

He didn't want to talk about dolls. The idea was cute and, to his knowledge, highly original. But it wasn't important. What mattered was Becca bringing her children to live with her so that they no longer needed dolls to remind them of their mother.

He would have told her so, too, timing be damned, except that the twins tired of the waterfall again and came back to see what else there was to do. Becca suggested a walk. They followed a path so old it might once have been used by the Native Americans who had roamed the land. Wildflowers grew deep in woods that loggers had never touched, and Becca taught the girls their names.

They walked farther than they had intended, caught up in the cool beauty of the path. The girls, hungry again, began to whine. Amanda found a rock she liked and refused to walk any farther. Becca picked her up to carry her, and immediately Faith wanted the same.

Jase held out his arms as Becca stooped to put Faith on her other hip. ''Let me carry her,'' he said. ''They're too heavy for you to manage.''

''No, they're not. I—''

He felt another flash of anger. "Let me do something to help."

This time she heard the anger. Startled, she stared at him, but he was already scooping Faith into his arms. Faith went without protest, as if she thought the idea of having this strong, handsome man carry her was a good one.

"I just didn't want you to feel you had to do it," Becca said.

He bit back his reply because he didn't want to argue in front of the girls. Faith settled against him as if he had been carrying her since birth. She put her chubby arms around his neck and leaned her head against his shoulder. He wondered why he had never thought about having children.

It was midnight by the time they got back to Cleveland. They had stopped for dinner along the way, but neither of them had eaten much. He had listened to music on the drive, and Becca had slept. Jase didn't know which had tired her more, the pleasures of their night together or the trauma of leaving her children again.

In the conversational void he had been given lots of time to think, more than he needed. But even with all that time, he knew he still wasn't thinking clearly. His motto had always been Watch and Wait. He almost always got what he wanted because he knew how to bide his time. Emotion had never come into it. He had never wanted anything so badly that he felt any impact if he didn't get it. That objectivity had always served him well, because it meant he could not be manipulated. He had a reputation as a man of ice in business dealings.

He was not a man of ice where Becca was concerned. Something vital inside him had been shredded to pieces over the weekend. If he didn't know which had tired Becca, their lovemaking or parting from her daughters, he also didn't know which had affected him more. He was a man who'd had his share of women, though he had never been indiscriminate. Singles bars weren't his style, and even as a young man fresh out of college he hadn't kept a black book of his conquests. But he hadn't been celibate, either. At no time, in all the years he was fighting his way up the ladder of success, had anyone like Becca come into his life.

It wasn't her vulnerability. God knows, the word must have been invented with Becca in mind. She was vulnerable to life in a way that no one else of his acquaintance had ever been. The simplest things had been denied her, yet still she fought for those things, things everyone unquestionably deserved. Simple things like a home and the right to care for her own children.

Her vulnerability had touched him, but it was her strength, her determination, that had grabbed him and never let go. And now there was so much more. There was the way her dark eyes sparked with life when he touched her, the way her skin flushed, the way she moved when his body was close to hers. Nothing in his life had been so sweet, so powerful, as making love to her. They had not had sex. He'd had sex before, and now he knew the difference. They had made love.

And even if they had not made children together, he had felt some of Becca's pain when she had been forced to leave her girls crying in the Hanks' doorway. Hell, he had felt his own pain. Children grew fast. He knew that much. What would they look like when he saw them again? What new mischief would they have invented? And wasn't there always the chance that he might never see them again, that Becca might not? Becca had to consider that every time she left Blackwater. She could not be there to protect her daughters, and even though the Hanks obviously cared greatly, wasn't it always in the back of Becca's mind that something might happen while she was gone?

He had turned those thoughts over and over as he'd driven the miles between Blackwater and Shaker Heights. In between cycles he had reached for his famous objectivity, but there had been no trace of it.

Now, parked in the driveway of Kathryn's—no, *his*—house he had told himself to let go of it all, to wake up Becca and escort her to the cottage—or into his bed—without telling her about his turmoil. They could talk later, when the time was right. He knew better than to talk now. He knew better.

"Becca?"

She stirred but didn't wake up.

He touched her shoulder, and without conscious permission his hand slid to the back of her neck, warm, soft skin, druggingly sweet. "Becca, wake up. We're home."

Her eyes opened slowly. She turned and smiled. Not fully awake, she touched his cheek. "Where are we?"

"Back in Shaker. Home."

"That's right. I was dreaming about the girls. But we left them, didn't we?"

His hand tightened on her neck. Then he pulled it away. "We did."

"Amanda cried." She rested her head on the back of the seat and stared straight ahead. "Faith is learning not to."

"Let's go inside." He got out of the car before she could answer and came around to open her door.

She was out by the time he got there. "You must be exhausted. I didn't help with the driving at all."

"I didn't mind."

"But I should have helped."

"No, you shouldn't have." His tone was sharper than he had meant it to be.

"What's wrong?"

"Don't you think you're carrying independence to extremes?"

"Sounds to me like we're not talking about who drove and who didn't."

He jammed his hands into his pockets in frustration. "We can get our suitcases tomorrow. It's late now. Let's just go to bed."

"Whose bed? Is that what's bothering you?" Becca realized she was wide awake now. "Are you afraid I'll expect more from you than you want to give me? You didn't make any promises, Jase. I'm not expecting—"

"You don't expect a damn thing, do you?"

She leaned against the car and stared at him.

"Do you?" he repeated. "You don't expect anything. Not room service, not a ride to Blackwater, not help with your kids, not even an explanation of what I'm thinking. What is it, Becca? You talk about my view out the window, but I'm not the only person around here who settles for a view when they could have so much more.''

"A view is more than I've had at times."

"So?"

"You wouldn't understand. You haven't understood before when I've tried to tell you how I feel about being helped."

"You want to know what I understand? I understand that I could make a difference in your life, only you're not going to let me! And you know why? Because you're afraid you're going to be let down again. It's not pride, it's fear that keeps you from taking my help."

"I don't need anybody's help. I'm going to make it on my own. And if you can't understand that, then you can't understand me."

"Maybe I don't. But I understand your little girls. They need their mother. I can give them their mother. Do you know what a drop in the bucket it is for me to help you? Do you have any idea what I'm worth? I can't find enough ways to spend my money, Becca. And here's something good, something that can really make a difference, and I'm not allowed to help. Do you know how that makes me feel?"

She stared at him for a moment before she spoke. "I can't imagine."

"It makes me feel more frustration than I knew I had in me."

"It's good for you."

"What?"

"I said it's good for you. Most of the world feels frustration every day. So maybe, just maybe, Jason Millington the Whatever ought to feel a little now and then, too. Maybe there ought to be some little corner of the world, some little speck in Jase's view out the window, that he can't change! Maybe it'll build his character!"

This time he stared. "So it's my character under discussion? Not the fact that your children are eight hours away in another state when they could be here with you?"

"They will be! The minute I can make it happen. Are you questioning how much I love them? I love them enough to give them a mother who can take care of them! Not the two-bit mistress of a rich man!''

His hands shot out of his pockets, and he took a step toward her. ''What's that supposed to mean?''

''It means that last night has nothing, *nothing,* to do with what I'll take from you and what I won't. I won't let you keep me, Jase, no matter how good you think your reasons are. I slept with you last night, but it was a one-night stand. One night. That's it. I won't do it again, not if you think it gives you rights to my life! I don't need any man poking around in my heart trying to figure out what I need and for what reasons! And I won't have any man telling me I'm not a good mother because I don't want his charity!''

''Charity? You call it charity?''

''Char-i-ty. When one person rescues another. Only I don't need rescuing. I might have once, and thank you very much for everything. But I don't need it again!''

He leaned closer to her, propping one hand beside her head. ''Let's try another word. How about love? Maybe I want to help you because I'm falling in love with you.''

''You don't know what that means.'' Her eyes were only inches from his, but she didn't flinch. ''Love doesn't mean taking over somebody else's life. That's what Dewey tried to do, and I let him. I let him because I believed it was love. But now I know what real love is. Love means trusting another person to do what's right for them, and what's right for you. And I'll tell you, Jase, letting you bail me out of my troubles isn't right for either of us. You'll go on thinking forever that that's the way things should always be between us. Making things right. Making more things right. Never believing that I could make them right without you. Never letting me make anything right for you.''

''That's not true!''

''No? You don't trust me. You don't believe I can make a life for myself without your help. You don't believe I can get the girls without your money or your fancy lawyers. You've been thinking about hiring a lawyer ever since you met Alice and Bill, haven't you?''

"So?"

"So it won't come to that. They'll let me have the girls when I'm ready. I know them. The girls are more important to them than getting back at me. But you don't trust me to know that, do you?'' She slid out from under his arm and went to the back seat to get her suitcase.

In the seconds it took, he realized what he had done. He had not bided his time; he had not waited for the right moment to approach Becca. His timing had been off by a century. He watched her carry her suitcase toward the cottage. All his anger knotted inside him. "I just want to help you," he said loudly enough for her to hear.

"Then forget about this weekend. It was a mistake!'' She hefted the suitcase a little higher, determined not to let him see her drag it.

"If love is trust, then where's your trust in me?"

She turned. "I never said I loved you.''

"No, you never did.''

"I don't have room in my life for love. And neither do you.'' She started back up the sidewalk.

He watched her lift the suitcase higher, as if trying to prove she could manage it alone. But he didn't go after her to help. Before she reached the cottage he was inside the house, and the door was locked behind him.

Chapter Eleven

The door slammed against the wall of Jase's office, and he didn't even bother to look up. "So you think there's some merit in the idea?" he said into the receiver. "A resort seems feasible to you?"

The ear not glued to the telephone picked up the rustle of a skirt. His eyes flickered to Pamela, who was settling herself across the desk from him. "I'm sorry, I missed that," he said.

He listened attentively, nodding at the words of the man on the other end of the line. "Okay. I'll expect all the facts and figures by the end of the week. Sounds like you've done the homework we need." He cradled the receiver and made a few notes before he gave Pamela his attention.

"Resorts, Jase? Heady stuff."

"Just an idea I'm working on."

"Tell me about it."

He picked up his pen, the same one Pamela had said was worth more than half the furniture in The Greenhouse, and tapped out an impatient rhythm. "Since when have you been interested in my business?"

"I'm always interested in everything about you."

"In changing everything about me."

"Not everything. You have a nice smile. I wish I could see it more often these days. What is it? The weather? July's hot as—"

"I know how hot July is. Everybody in town knows it."

"Is it the move? Isn't the house coming along fast enough?"

He pictured the house. *House Beautiful* wanted to picture it in an article on America's Tudor architecture. The grounds alone were a picturebook masterpiece, thanks to Becca. At least, he assumed it was thanks to Becca. He hadn't gotten more than a glimpse of her in three long weeks, but he hadn't sought her out, either. He was a businessman who knew how to cut his losses.

Only it had never hurt before.

"The house is fine. Great, in fact. Everything will be finished by mid-August. I couldn't be happier."

"Oh, I think you probably could," she said dryly. "I mean, if this is happy, you'll have to do unhappy for me sometime, so I can see the subtle differences."

"What's the point of this?"

"So tell me about the resort?"

Jase had grown up with Pamela. He knew mercurial shifts of subject came naturally to her. "Don't mention this to Becca."

"Uh-oh."

"No uh-oh. I just don't want to tell her until I'm sure I want to go through with it. You know she comes from a place called Blackwater in Kentucky."

"She's told me a little."

"It's a hole, only it's a hole surrounded by some of God's finest scenery. There's nothing else there, but the scenery grabs and shakes you." He stood restlessly and went to the window.

A view from the window.

He turned away quickly. "Anyway, when I was there, I started thinking how much they needed some industry to move in and give people jobs. There's nothing now, even the mines are closed. No one's had much training, so it would have to be something that unskilled people could do. The only assets they have are scenery and cheap, cheap land, a lot of which is for sale."

"I think I can see what's coming."

"There's nothing quite like what I'm planning in the area. There are plenty of parks, and there are resorts not too far away. But nothing really exclusive. I want to build a private club and capitalize on the scenery and the isolation. Something better than first class, something only the richest could afford. Lots of acreage between houses, lots of prestige. We could draw from cities all around, Lexington, Louisville, Cincinnati, even as far as Pittsburgh and Cleveland.

"How is this going to benefit anyone in Blackwater?"

He examined her face to see if she was joking. "How could it not benefit them? There would be service jobs galore. There would be a market for any crafts they wanted to sell. There would be patrons for the few stores that are already there and a wide open field for anyone who wanted to build more. Anyone who wanted to raise a garden could sell vegetables. Anyone who wanted to keep a few hives of bees could sell honey. The potential is limitless."

"*You* think so."

"Anyone will think so. It's only a risk to me. I'll have to sink a lot of money into the project." He smiled cynically as he remembered something he had said to Becca. "But I'm always looking for ways to spend money."

She frowned. "What do you mean?"

"I won't come out of this with much, but I won't take a loss, either. It's something I want to do for Blackwater."

"You want to do it for them."

"That's right."

"What happens if they don't want you to?"

The question seemed so absurd that he couldn't even think of an answer.

"You haven't thought about that, have you?"

"Of course they'll want me to. Their standard of living will skyrocket."

Pamela sighed. "You still don't understand people, do you? Not everyone has your enthusiasm for change."

"You're trying to tell me the poor want to stay that way?"

"I'm trying to tell you the poor have a right to decide how they're going to live their lives."

"I know what I'm doing."

She unfolded her legs and stood, coming around the desk to kiss him on the cheek. "That's your fatal flaw. You always know what you're doing."

"I didn't hear this lecture when I came to you with my idea for turning the factory into apartments."

"That's because you weren't taking anything away from anybody. And, by the way, that's what I came to talk to you about." She stared past him at the window. "You know, I don't know how you stand this view day in and day out. I feel like a fish in an aquarium. The whole world's out there, and I can't touch it."

"I don't want to talk about the view."

She turned, obviously surprised by the intensity in his voice. "Sorry. Did I hit a nerve?"

"What did you want to talk about?"

"I just thought you'd want to hear that everything's going better than we expected for Friday night. We finally got the band to donate their time and talent in exchange for the publicity they'll get. And two more restaurants have kicked in donations. One's even going to send a chef to make crepes to order. That was Mother's idea. You should see her manipulate people, Jase. It gives me chills, but it's effective."

"So Mother has her assets?"

"The first time we sat down to plan, she told the board in no uncertain terms that they were a bunch of cowards. She demanded they shoot for three times the goal they'd set or she wasn't going to lift a finger to help."

"Our mother?"

"Ours. The one whose fingers look like they've never been lifted in her life. Then she proceeded to tear into everybody, ripping them open to see what they could do best. By the time she was finished, people were agreeing to do things they'd never thought about before. It was amazing."

"Will you meet the goal?"

"Truly?" She shrugged. "I don't know. Instead of pricey

tickets, Mother insisted we solicit contributions at the party, so who knows? We made up the guest list backward. Mother publicized it in the *right* places. Then people had to call us and ask to come before they got an invitation. A lot of people have invited themselves.''

''Well, that's unique.''

''Everything's unique. Having the party at the factory is unique. There's not even any air-conditioning.''

''It fits the theme.''

'''A Night in the Tropics' isn't exactly my idea of a good time in July. I'd be more inclined to attend 'A Night in the Arctic.'''

''Why are you here, Pamela?''

She perched on the edge of his desk. ''That's pretty good, Jase. We talked for what, a minute, two, before you asked me to get to the point? You're slipping.''

''I have ten hours of work to cram into three.''

''That sounds like an improvement, too. Anyway, I want you to invite Becca to the party. I already have, and she's refusing to come. She's worked as hard or harder than anyone else to make it happen. She's—''

''She's what?''

''She's working two jobs, but she still finds time to make telephone calls, assemble packets of information, anything she can do from the cottage, since her car isn't running anymore.''

''She had the car towed away before I could do anything about it.'' He wasn't oblivious to the symbolism of that act. The day after they had gotten back from Blackwater, he'd come home from the office to find that Becca's car was gone. One of the electricians had told him that a wrecker had taken it away for scrap. And that afternoon, Becca, as she had every Monday, left fifteen dollars for the first round of car repairs in his mailbox.

''She deserves to come to the party,'' Pamela said, ''but she says she has too much to do. We need her there. She's the best example I know why the apartments are so important.''

''You want to show her off like a trained monkey!''

Her eyes widened. ''I beg your pardon?''

He jammed his hands into his pockets. "She's a lot more than a good example of a homeless woman. She's a person. With feelings. Maybe she doesn't want to share her life story with a bunch of people who can't tell that party from the one they attended last week for the symphony or the zoo or the art museum!"

"Boy, you've got it bad, don't you? Excuse me while I pull my jaw off the floor."

"Time to leave, Pamela."

"I'm about to. But let me clue you in on something first. Becca has some other reason for not coming. It's not me. I have never, never, embarrassed the women I work with. I have nothing but respect for them. And I more than respect Becca. What you don't see is that she respects herself. She's not ashamed of anything about her life." She got up to search for her purse. "Maybe you can't say the same."

As she walked out the door he wondered who was left for him to alienate. "Pamela?"

She turned. "I'm ready and waiting."

"I'm sorry. I really am. I know better."

"That's right. You do. So will you invite her or not?"

He was trapped. If he said no, he had to explain. "I'll talk to her."

"Good. I'm counting on you."

He wanted to tell her that this time he had no assurance the famous Millington determination was going to get results. But that was much too hard to admit. Especially after an apology. "I'll do my best," he said.

"We'll both be at the factory this evening working on decorations."

"I'll be there."

The worst job in preparation for the party had been to shovel truckload after truckload of trash and debris out of the factory building. One of Jase's work crews had seen to that, along with ridding the building of all four-, six- and eight-legged occupants and tacking wire mesh over all the windows that weren't boarded over. The theme might be "A Night in the Tropics," but nobody wanted to carry it to extremes.

Once the building was clean, volunteers had swarmed in. Mrs. Millington had insisted the decorations be concentrated in certain areas so that the rest of the building would be uncluttered for guests to examine.

There was to be a display near the entrance showing the plans for the building's renovation and a model of a proposed apartment. There would be information about The Greenhouse and the increasing problem of homelessness and abuse of women. More frivolous areas would be set up throughout the first floor. One entire corner was supposed to evoke a rain forest, another a tropical island with a volcano. Tables with food donated by some of Cleveland's finest restaurants were to be scattered throughout, and liquor was to flow freely. A reggae band was scheduled for the night, and Mrs. Millington had insisted on a limbo contest.

The frivolity was incidental to the real theme, and no one would leave without realizing it. A dozen guides had been trained to lead tours through the building and answer questions about the renovations and the reasons for them. Pledge cards would be given out at the end of the tour, and anyone who pledged five thousand dollars or more would have their name on an ornamental plaque commissioned to be hung in the entryway when the renovations were completed.

When Jase arrived, the rain forest was under construction. Two hundred square feet were slowly being turned into the Amazon basin. The trees and plants, supplied by local nurseries and florists, would arrive on Friday, but in the meantime, the rest of the area was being readied. He found Pamela cutting thin strips of iridescent plastic to hang from the high ceiling. He had vetoed the use of an industrial humidifier spewing mist into the air because of possible damage to the floors. The plastic—much to his mother's chagrin—was going to have to simulate rain.

"Remind you of your high school prom?" he asked.

Pamela looked up, a waif incarnate with her hair plastered to her head from the heat and old jeans cut off at the tops of her thighs. "The Eleanor Rexford Academy was too snooty to have a prom. We had a spring formal, and it was held at a country club. Decorations were considered tacky."

"Maybe that's why these fund-raisers have appeal. Everybody who attends was deprived of the public school experience."

"You're welcome to help me make rain."

"Thanks, but I'm here to see Becca."

"She's over in the forest. Probably on a ladder. She's the only volunteer who's not afraid of heights."

"She's spent a fair amount of time on my roof learning to patch slate."

"Go get her, tiger."

"I don't do miracles."

"No? Have you admitted that before?"

Becca was easy to spot. Jase skirted the men setting up a stage for the band and a crew of half a dozen women covering chicken wire with papier-mâché to resemble a volcano. Becca stood out, since she was the only person balancing on one leg twelve feet above everybody else attaching strips of artificial rain.

He didn't like the looks of her ladder. And he particularly didn't like the way she was ignoring the principles of physics.

"Becca." He didn't shout, but doubtlessly his voice carried to the rafters beyond.

She didn't answer.

"Becca? Would you come down for a minute?"

"When I've finished what I'm doing."

He winced as she leaned farther out. "If you come down, I can move the ladder so that will be easier."

"Don't you think I know how to move a ladder?"

He noticed that the papier-mâché crew had stopped their chatter to listen. "Nobody moves one better. I just needed something to do."

"Why? Isn't there anybody here you can boss around? We should all do what we do best."

He ignored a gasp from the direction of the volcano. "Shall I come up there?"

"Suit yourself."

He eyed the ladder and decided there was no assurance it would hold them both. "Where did this thing come from, anyway?"

"I believe it belongs to Jason Millington the Whatever. So don't worry, it must be perfect."

He was on rung three before he realized she had goaded him into this. "You're being unreasonable."

"Now that's not how we'd say it in the hills of Kentucky. We'd say something like—"

"Never mind how you'd say it." He climbed to rung six. His face was level with her heels. He climbed until it was level with her backside. One part of him admired the curves three inches from his nose. The other part wanted to turn those curves over his knee. "Are you happy now? I've humiliated myself and put us both in danger just to give you what you wanted."

"I never said I wanted you up here."

His face was level with her shoulders now. Becca could feel the warmth of his breath against the bare skin of her back. "Don't you?" he asked.

"Go away."

"Not until you've talked to me."

"You picked a funny time to have a talk. I live one hundred yards from your house, but you haven't been inclined to talk to me there in weeks."

"I haven't seen you!"

"You don't see if you don't look."

"Why would I look for you? You as much as told me to get out of your life."

"Well, apparently you didn't listen too well."

"Will you get off this damn thing and come outside with me for a little while?" His lips were inches from the sweetest curve of silk smooth skin along her spine. "If you don't, I'm going to kiss every vertebrae in reach and give these virtuous ladies something to talk about for the next twenty years."

"It's your reputation, not mine. I have no reputation."

"Becca."

She could fight everything except the warmth mushrooming

inside her at the way he said her name, the warmth and the tiny, betraying shudders that had started as soon as he was close enough to touch her. "Back on down. I need a break, anyway. But just for a little while."

"Have you eaten?"

"You're taking care of me again."

"No, I'm taking care of myself. I'm starving."

"Fine. We can grab something cheap, and you can talk with your mouth full."

"Kathryn always said that was a good idea. She was highly in favor of doing two things at once, as long as both things were fun."

"Don't expect this to be fun."

He started down. "I don't know why not. Some of the most pleasurable moments of my life have been spent with you."

"Don't start that, Jase, or I'm not going anywhere."

He waited for her at the bottom of the ladder. She took her time backing down. He glanced in the direction of the volcano. "Ladies, your papier-mâché is drying out."

The volcano crew returned to work with renewed and guilty vigor.

Becca joined him on the floor. "I meant what I said about cheap. I'm dressed to work."

"I know a place you'll like. We can walk. It's on the edge of the Flats."

He waited until Becca had washed her face and hands, then walked with her down the street. The Flats was rich with Cleveland history. There on the banks of the Cuyahoga River, in 1796, Moses Cleaveland had first set foot on the land that would someday bear his name—or a reasonable facsimile thereof. Shipping and industry had made their mark over the centuries, leaving behind imposing bridges and impressive old buildings. In recent years the Flats had become a fashionable playground, and bars and restaurants cluttered the winding streets.

Jase and Becca walked under bridges and across parking lots. "So how's Constantine's?" he asked when Becca still hadn't said a word.

"You ate there the day before yesterday. You should know."

"How do you know I ate there?"

"Mama told me."

He had specifically asked Mama not to mention him. Now he knew where Mama's loyalties lay. "What else did she say?"

"She said you were asking about me."

"Did she phone you while I was there, or did she at least wait until I'd left?"

"I don't like you checking up on me."

He had been so glad to see Becca again that he had swallowed all irritation at her sarcasm in the factory. Now irritation rose in his throat. "Look, I wasn't checking up on you. Not the way you mean. I care about you. I wanted to be sure things were going all right. You vanished from my life like a magician's assistant. How am I supposed to get my information if I don't see you? If you won't talk to me? I needed reassurance."

They walked another half a block before she answered. "I guess I can see that."

"So how is Constantine's going?"

"Fine."

"Great."

She heard the angry way he clipped his "t." As long as she hadn't come face-to-face with him in the last weeks, she had managed to convince herself that she had every right to be upset at Jase's interference. He had no rights over her just because they had made love. He'd had no right to tell her what she should do with her future or how to do it. And he'd had no right to suggest, even in a roundabout way, that she was doing less for her children than she could.

Now she realized that she had never once let herself consider Jase's feelings. She had been afraid to consider him. She was afraid, period, and she wasn't even sure of what. All she knew was that she was afraid, and walking beside him magnified that fear. Knowing she had hurt him enough to make him angry made it even worse.

"I don't make a lot at Constantine's," she said, "but it's

better than minimum wage. And the more the regular customers get to know me, the better they'll tip.''

He relaxed a little. "Is the work hard?''

''My feet are tired by the end of a shift, but I'm holding up well. I know you don't believe this, but I'm strong. I can handle a lot now that I'm well again.''

"You look good.''

She resisted the urge to pat her hair. "That should increase my tips.''

''You look great. You look like somebody I've been wanting to see for three weeks.''

''Then why haven't you?''

''Because you told me to get out of your life.''

She didn't know what to say to that. And in a second she didn't have a chance, anyway. They walked up an incline toward a sign advertising Shorty's, an unprepossessing building set off from the rest of the bars and restaurants.

Once they were inside they were back in the fifties. The decor was glass block and shiny silver sheet metal. The booths were vision-shattering turquoise, and each featured a coin-operated jukebox. Jerry Lee Lewis was just finishing ''Great Balls of Fire.''

Despite her stated preference, she had expected Jase to take her someplace deathly quiet with hovering waiters. The waitresses here, dressed in white uniforms, black aprons and saddle shoes, didn't hover. They ran, and as she watched, one dropped into a booth to chat and calculate the bill with her customers.

''Bring back memories?'' Jase asked.

''I wasn't alive in the fifties. I can see I should have been.'' She smiled at him.

The smile was a brilliant stab in the gut. He realized he was addicted to her smile. And three weeks without one had left him shaken.

They were early enough that there was no line to get in, although that wasn't often the case. They were led to a booth and sat across from each other as Jan and Dean crooned ''Little Old Lady from Pasadena.''

The menu was diner food. Becca ordered an egg salad sandwich, and Jase got the Blue Plate Special, a patty melt and fries.

"So, why did you come looking for me this evening?" she asked when the waitress had gone. "If you thought I'd told you to get out of my life."

"Didn't you?"

"I told you that you had to learn to trust me."

"There's nobody I trust more."

"Are you listening to yourself? That's not the same as saying you trust me completely. So maybe I'm tops on the list, right along with Pamela and whoever else you've let yourself be close to—if there is anybody else. But the only person you really trust is yourself. You think you're the only one in the world who can make the right decision, whether it's for you or for somebody else."

"If I didn't trust myself completely, I wouldn't have gotten where I am today."

"And if you don't start trusting somebody else, you're going to stay exactly where you are today and never move another inch."

He was staring into eyes so dark they should have been impenetrable. But they weren't. He saw pain, right along with courage. "How'd you get so wise?" he asked at last.

"The Commonwealth of Kentucky gave me a lot of time to think."

"I'm going to back off. Your life is your life. I'm sorry."

She could only guess how hard it was for Jase to apologize. And her guess was that this was one of the few he had ever uttered. She reached for his hand, and a rush of gratitude filled her. She had missed him more than she could ever have told him. Now he had paved the way for their being together again.

She threaded her fingers through his, and the image of their bodies entwined danced before her eyes. She looked up at him and saw that the images lived for him, too. "Thank you for understanding," she said.

"I'm trying."

She brought his hand to her cheek. "Is that what you wanted to tell me?"

"No. I wanted to interfere in your life again."

"There's a sign on the wall over there that you should read."

He turned and his eyes followed her pointing finger. The sign read We Do Not Serve Bullies.

"I'm not going to bully you. Pamela asked me to talk to you about going to the fund-raiser. She wants you there. I want you there, as my date. But if you don't want to come, don't."

"Good for you."

"I really would like you to come with me."

"I'd be pleased to come, Jase. I just couldn't imagine being there when you and I were still angry at each other. I didn't want to…"

He squeezed her hand. "Didn't want to what?"

"I didn't want to watch you with another woman."

He realized they had never talked about that aspect of his life. She had told him about Dewey, but she had never asked him for reassurance that she wasn't just one of many women he hopped in and out of bed with. She had trusted him.

"I wouldn't have been with another woman. There is no other woman, hasn't really been one since I met you." He thought of Cara and the new man she was dating. He hadn't done it consciously, but since he'd found Becca, he had cut everyone else out of his life. He had made a commitment without knowing it.

"Why?"

He smiled. "Now who needs reassurance?"

"We're so different, Jase. How can anything come of this?"

"Do you remember the story you told me about your grandmother and her search every summer morning for one perfect rose?"

"Sure."

"Well, I guess I've been searching, too. But I discovered something your grandmother never did. Wild roses with lots of blooms and thorns, the kind that scramble to survive in the worst soil, are as close to perfect as roses ever get. I guess I'll take a wild rose over a pampered hybrid any day."

She smiled at him. "Just don't try to train this wild rose to any trellis. She has to grow in her own place and her own way."

"I'll try to remember."

"I've missed you."

"We wouldn't have a chance if you hadn't."

"A lot."

They only dropped hands when the waitress brought their dinner.

Chapter Twelve

"So what in heaven's name are tropical play clothes?" Becca looked at a copy of the invitation to the fund-raiser that Pamela had brought with her to the cottage. "Play clothes are what I buy my girls, and I don't think I'd feel too playful in corduroy overalls."

"Play clothes are my mother's idea of communicating what her rich and oh-so-cutesy friends should wear. Nothing formal enough to be ruined by the heat or doing the limbo, but nothing as low class as casual."

"As my great, great, great, great-uncle Daniel Boone must have said and often, I'm still lost."

"I'm going to dress like I'm going on safari. Shorts with enough pockets to store food for a week's camping trip and a jungle-print shirt. Some people will come in serviceable rhinestones."

"I'm fresh out of both."

"Why don't you go Hawaiian?"

"I don't—"

"I do. Stand up." Becca complied. Pamela looked her over with a practiced eye. "I know just the thing. I have a bikini top—now don't get excited, it's a very conservative bikini—and there's a short wrap skirt to go with it. It doesn't fit me anymore, but it will be perfect for you. It's a bright tropical print.''

''You're talking about a bare stomach.''

''Exactly. You'll appreciate it in the heat. You could wear silk flowers around your neck. Much classier than rhinestones.''

''Real flowers.''

''Even better. And sandals. Do you have any? They're on sale everywhere this month, or we can look at The Greenhouse.''

Becca liked the way Pamela just took her financial status for granted. She didn't make outrageously generous offers, and she didn't pretend Becca could afford anything expensive. She accepted Becca's lack of money just as she accepted her brown eyes and Kentucky accent.

''You don't think I'll look silly?''

''Silly?'' Pamela stepped back a little. ''Becca, you're really lovely. Don't you know that? There will be women there who spend four hours a day on their faces and bodies, and every one of them will wish she looked just like you.''

Becca could feel her cheeks heat. ''I don't want to embarrass your brother.''

Pamela's face grew serious. ''Look, this is none of my business, but is there something going on that you want to talk about?''

''Would you like some iced tea?''

''Please.''

Pamela followed Becca into the kitchen. She had made her offer to listen, now she waited.

Becca got the ice out of the freezer. She didn't look at Pamela. ''Your brother and I are as different as two people can be. I know what I am, Pamela. I'm a nobody from the Kentucky hills. Worse than a nobody. I've spent time in jail. I'm not ashamed of that, but I know it puts me on the other side of the world from Jase.''

''And Jase has told you that? He's made a point of it?''

''No.''

''I don't think I understand.''

''He's never made a point of it. But I have eyes. Jase likes to fix things. He can't stop himself. I have a life that needs fixing, so he steps in and tries to do it himself. I don't know if I'm real to him. If I didn't have so many problems, would he even look twice at me?''

Pamela watched her put ice in two glasses, add mint leaves and sun tea from a jug on the windowsill. ''Let me be sure I've got this. You're afraid my brother is falling in love with you simply because he thought somebody needed to fall in love with you to improve your life?''

''I didn't say anything about love.''

''Well, I did.'' Pamela held out her hand for the tea and took a sip. It was just strong enough, just sweet enough. ''I've been watching you two fall in love, and I've got to say, it's been hard to see. I've never seen two such bullheaded people in my life. You're both trying so hard to make sure everything's perfect. I don't know which of you is the worst perfectionist.''

Becca took the time she needed to let that sink in. ''How can I be a perfectionist? Look at my life.''

''You're a fixer. Look at this yard and the garden at The Greenhouse. Look at Jase's house. Look at this tea! And from what you've told me about your past, you worked so hard to fix things for your husband and his family that you ended up in jail because you didn't know when to stop.''

''Because I tried to fix things?'' Becca had never thought about herself quite that way.

Pamela nodded. ''Just like my brother. But let's be clear about one thing here. I don't know if Jase has ever risked himself to fix anyone's life before—no one's but mine, anyway. He grew up trying to make life bearable for me, stepping between me and my parents so I wouldn't get hurt, sending me funny cards and letters when I was away at school, sneaking me in and out of the house so I could do things normal kids did. He got used to fixing things early, and he went on to fixing his part of the world as soon as he could. But along the way he never let himself get too close to anyone but me. Not until you came along.''

''But maybe that's because no one else needed him as much as he thinks I do.''

"Or maybe it's because he never needed anyone as much as he needs you."

"Tell me why. Why would Jase need mc?"

"Because he can't fix things twenty-four hours a day, Becca. He's got to have a refuge. You look at yourself and see a life that's still a mess. He looks at you, I look at you, and we see a woman who'll never be beaten. That's what he needs, and somewhere deep inside he knows it. He needs someone with the same strengths that he has. Someone strong enough for him to lean on from time to time."

Becca finished her tea before she spoke. "I'm in love with him, Pamela. I was only in love once before, and that time was a terrible mistake."

"This time won't be."

"I hope you're right." She stood to clear away the glasses. "When can I borrow the bikini?"

Pamela stood, too. "I'll bring it over tonight. Roll up your T-shirt and work on a tan while you're pulling weeds."

"Thanks. Thanks a lot."

Pamela touched her shoulder. "No. Thank you. You're the best thing in Jase's life. And he's always going to be one of the best things in mine."

On Friday a late afternoon rain cooled the air and raised the humidity. Becca picked roses and marigolds, zinnias and daisies, before the storm, preserving them in the refrigerator along with the ferns and vines she planned to use on her Ohio leis. She had found a book at the library with instructions, and she left herself part of the afternoon to make two, one for herself and one for Jase. They were his flowers, after all.

By seven the leis were finished, and she was nearly ready. If the bikini top was conservative, she was a terrible prude. It covered the essentials, but only just. She had made her lei extra thick and long to compensate—she wasn't sure it did anything except draw attention to all the bare skin above and below it. The skirt was shorter than some of the shorts she owned, and when she moved, it bared one leg outrageously.

She was tucking roses into her hair when she heard Jase's knock. She stepped back from the mirror for one more look. She was tanned from all her hours in the sun, and that same sun had lightened her hair until it was unmistakably blond. The turquoise and lavender print at the top and skirt set off the warm glow of her skin. She liked what she saw. She just hoped that Jase did, too.

He did. Unmistakably. He stared at her as if she were a vision from another place and time. "I guess I did okay," she said.

"A masterful piece of understatement."

"I made you a lei, too." He was wearing an aloha shirt—she imagined he'd had more than one occasion to buy one on Wai-kiki. "It will look perfect."

He slipped off her lei and set it on a table by the door. Then he hauled her close and kissed her. She shut her eyes and tasted the full range of flavors and emotions his kisses always inspired. His hands stroked her bare back as he kissed her. Thoughts of the party disappeared.

He was the first to pull away. "Enough of that, or we'll never get there."

"Wouldn't that be a shame?"

"Don't tempt me."

"Then maybe I'd better go put on something else to wear."

"No, you can tempt me a little. More than a little." He picked up the lei and slipped it back over her head. It was laced with wild roses, and the light sweet fragrance went right to his gut. He kissed her again. Lightly. "Part of the tradition."

She crossed the room to get his, then returned the favor.

They were almost to the factory when she brought up something that had been bothering her. "You know, I haven't met your mother yet. I was never decorating while she was there."

He heard all her unspoken questions. What was his mother going to think of her? Was he going to introduce them? Was he going to tell his mother the truth about Becca's life?

He tried to put her mind at rest. "I'm not close to my parents. I've never told them about you because we don't discuss anything important. But I want you to meet them. I love them, even if I don't understand anything about them.''

"What are they going to think about me?"

"Honestly? I don't have any idea. I don't think I know them well enough to guess.''

"Go ahead and try.''

"They'll think you're not good enough for me, just the way they think nobody is good enough for any Millington. They see themselves as aristocracy, even though the first Millingtons on this continent came over from England straight out of debtors' prison.''

"You're just saying that.''

"The next generation wasn't much better. One deserted during the Revolution and had to leave the colonies to escape being hanged. The rest of the family kept moving west to get away from their problems, and finally my great-great-grandfather hit it big in Ohio, although there's plenty of evidence that he stole and gambled his way to prosperity. I heard all the stories from Kathryn, who thrived on family history. My parents refuse to discuss it.''

She laughed. Out loud, from somewhere deep inside her. "Thank you.''

"I thought maybe a little perspective wouldn't hurt.''

"It didn't hurt a bit.''

They left Jase's car with a valet at the factory's front door. Becca lifted her chin and steeled herself to get through the rest of the evening.

On the first floor, lighting, a forest of plants and weeks' worth of decorating had transformed the old factory into a tropical paradise. She had been there that morning to help oversee the arrival of the forest, but she had not been able to visualize the finished project. "It's perfect,'' she said, taking Jase's arm. "Perfect!''

"It's hard to believe.'' He put his hand over hers when she started to pull it away. "Come on, let me introduce you to some people.''

"I thought I'd just go see if anyone I knew—''

"You're staying with me. For a while." He looked down at her and smiled. "Please?"

"Because you asked."

Immediately he was the center of attention. The idea was his, the factory was his, and the lovely young stranger with the figure his mother's ladies-who-lunch crowd would kill for appeared to be his, too. He introduced her to couple after couple. He had no way of telling her who they were, what giant corporations they represented or what portion of Cleveland they owned, and he was just as glad. He introduced her as Becca. The guests exchanged five or six words with her and wanted to know if she was acquainted with the Reynolds or Jacksons or Hennesseys of Louisville. Lovely state, Kentucky. Such beautiful horses and acres of bluegrass, such fine mint juleps and Southern hospitality.

She smiled and chatted as if she were perfectly at ease. Jase listened to her and relaxed. He had worried that she would be too uncomfortable to enjoy the party. He realized he should have known better.

"Jason, I don't think I've had the pleasure of meeting your friend."

Jase turned and found his mother at his elbow. "I'll introduce you in a minute, as soon as Becca gets a break." He kissed his mother's cheek. She was dressed in a khaki silk jumpsuit that had probably cost more than some of the donations they would receive tonight. "You've done wonders, Mother. The party's already a success."

"Do you think so?" She asked the question as if there could be no doubt.

"You've never done anything more worthwhile. This will make a difference to a lot of people."

"You're beginning to sound like Pamela."

"Worse things could happen."

"The two of you always did gang up on me."

"You needed ganging up on."

He wondered why he had never told his mother what he really thought about anything. He had detached himself so early from his parents that in a way he had never given them a chance.

"This cause is Pamela's heart, Mother. And it's becoming mine, too. You've endeared yourself to both of us by working so hard for something we believe in. Relax and be proud, and when Pamela thanks you, give her a hug, not a lecture, and tell her she's welcome."

Surprisingly tears sprang to her eyes. "I don't know what you mean."

"Jase, you haven't introduced me yet."

He turned and found Becca at his side, obviously concerned that something was wrong. He made the introduction.

Becca extended her hand. "Mrs. Millington, this is a wonderful party. You can't have any idea how much it will mean."

Jase's mother took her hand. She had quickly gotten herself under control. "So I've been told."

"I've never seen anyone who could have organized something like this and made it work. Now I know where Jase gets his talents."

"You're not saying they come from me?"

"Sure I am. That's exactly what I'm saying." Becca smiled warmly. "It's a very big compliment."

"The party wasn't so difficult."

"Oh, I've been watching it happen. I know how much work it was. I'm one of the people who took orders for the last weeks."

"You've been helping?" Dorothea cocked her head. "How did you get involved? Through my son?"

"I used to live at The Greenhouse."

"Oh, you're on staff."

"No, I was a resident. I was homeless and sick and badly in need of help. I got it there, and then your son gave me a job overseeing the landscaping and renovations on his house."

Dorothea looked stunned. "You lived at The Greenhouse?"

"I sure did." Becca refused to look penitent. "And if I hadn't lived there, I might not be alive to be having this conversation. So, you see, I know what you've done firsthand. And I know what this place will mean to women just like me when it's finished."

Dorothea stared at her. Jase was just about to step into the humiliating gap in the conversation when she exploded. "How on earth could something like this have happened?"

"Mother..." he warned.

She pushed away the hand meant to restrain her. "How could somebody like *you* be without a home?" she asked Becca. "What kind of world is this, anyway?"

"A middling unfair one."

"Will you tell me how this came about? I don't want to pry, but I want to understand."

"I'd be happy to."

Jase watched his mother spirit Becca off into an undecorated corner. He was still standing there staring after them when Pamela found him. "Where's Becca?"

"She's off being quizzed by our mother."

"And you let that happen?" Pamela asked angrily. "Mother has no right!"

"She knows that. She as much as told Becca the same thing." He gripped Pamela's arm when she started off to find them. "Don't you dare butt in."

"Somebody's got to—"

"Get off the white horse, Pamela. Mother's about to need a mount herself."

"What on earth do you mean?"

"I mean that all those years we were so sure we didn't have anything in common with her, the seeds of who we are were there in Mother all along."

"You're not making any sense."

"That's because you're listening through twenty-eight years of hurt. Dorothea Millington didn't know how to be a mother, and sometimes she wasn't even sure how to be much of a person. But there's been a decent woman hidden in there all along. And right now she's fighting like hell to come out. With Becca's help you and I are going to sit back and watch her emerge."

Becca stood on the sidelines with Jase's arm around her waist as speeches were made. The evening had been a remarkable success. The pledges had begun to come in, and there was excitement in the air that the goal would be reached. She and Dorothea had discussed the final push that would be needed to make it happen. She hadn't discussed it with the man beside her.

She wasn't sure she exactly liked Jase's mother. Becca looked at Dorothea Millington and she thought about the day she had seen somebody drowning in Blackwater River. The swimmer, a young man, had been so sure of himself, so certain he was strong enough to get across. Halfway out, he had begun to flounder. She still remembered the horror of watching him go under once, then again. She had been a child, hardly old enough to dog paddle, but she had wanted more than anything to save him.

She remembered his hand, waving, waving, as he sank for the third time. Then another hand had grabbed his, and somebody had pulled him to shore. His rescuer hadn't been nearly as big as him, and hadn't seemed nearly as strong. But he had rescued him anyway.

And somehow, for some silly reason, when she looked at Mrs. Millington, she thought of the young man who had been so sure he could make it and almost hadn't.

She didn't know why.

Now she watched Mrs. Millington come back into the center of the circle of party-goers. Shareen had just spoken. She looked like an African goddess tonight, and her speech had been just about that powerful. Becca saw the dawning of understanding on the faces of some of those gathered to listen.

"There's someone else who I've asked to speak tonight," Mrs. Millington said. "Someone who has opened my eyes a little as to why we're really having this party. There's probably no way that anybody who's here just to have a good time and give a little money can really understand what it's like to be alone, without resources and hope. I guess I don't understand it myself and never will. But Becca Hanks does, and she's going to say a few words about that. I listened a little while ago. I hope you'll listen now." She smiled at Becca. "Ready?"

Becca felt Jase's reaction. He stiffened, and his arm tightened around her. She drew away from him before it tightened enough to keep her from moving. Then she was in the center of the circle. She could see people whispering to each other, and for a moment she wished she hadn't agreed to this.

She threw her head back, and she caught a woman's gaze and held it. "I look like you, don't I?" she asked. "I look like I belong here, and I don't know how many times tonight I've been asked if I come from Louisville, or if my folks have had a horse in the Derby. Well, when I was growing up, I didn't know what the Derby was, because we didn't have a television set, and the only horse I'd ever seen pulled a plow on a rocky acre of land down the holler a ways."

She took a deep breath. "I come from coal mining country. Only there're no mines there anymore, no jobs to speak of at all. There's a lot of poverty, though. More than you can imagine. Just about as much as you've got here in Cleveland, though not nearly as many rich folks to go with it. When I was seventeen and my parents were both gone, I thought maybe I'd settle for that, and I married a man who didn't know what it meant to work or dream. I ended up in prison because of a crime he committed, and I lost custody of my twin daughters."

She could see the shock on the faces surrounding her, but she had their attention. There wasn't a sound in the room. "When I got out, I knew I had to change my life. Only there wasn't a way to do it where I came from. So I worked everywhere I could, and I followed a trail of jobs to Cleveland. I sent most of my money home to my children, and there wasn't enough for a place to stay. So I stayed in my car. I'd tell you to try that sometime, but don't really want you to, because it's hell. And I wouldn't wish hell on anybody else.

"You can't find a job or keep a job if you don't have an address. Pretty soon you can't find an address because you don't have a job. You start going hungry, and in the winter you're not sure you're going to make it through the next cold night. You still want to work, to make a life for yourself, only you can't, because you're sinking too fast. That happened to me. Then one day I woke up in a place I didn't know. I saw a woman in white bending over me, and I thought I'd finally died and gone to heaven. But it was a hospital. Those ladies in white just barely saved my life.''

She smiled a little, because she was trying not to cry. "There wasn't much left to save, but there were some folks who didn't let that stop them. The Greenhouse took me in, and they took care of me when I was able to leave the hospital.''

She swallowed and looked around the room. The guests seemed transfixed, as if she were someone from another planet giving a lecture. "Jase Millington gave me a job I could do and be good at. The Greenhouse, Jase, they gave me respect for myself again. Now I'm working two jobs and saving money so my little girls can come to Cleveland and live with me. But that wouldn't have happened if somebody hadn't reached out a hand. I didn't want a hand, folks. I wanted to do it alone. But that's the thing I had to learn. Sometimes everybody has to have help. All of us need help sometimes. And a little help can make the difference between a life wasted and a life saved.''

She looked straight at Jase. "I'm not telling you this because I like to talk about what I went through. I'm not telling you this so you'll feel sorry for me. There's no reason to feel sorry for me now. I'm on my way. But there are a lot of women like me who aren't. Not yet. But they will be if you dig deep inside your pockets tonight and give what you can.

"This may look like a big old factory to you, but when Jase and The Greenhouse board are through with it, it's going to look like home to a lot of people. And there's nothing that looks better. I can tell you. There is nothing that looks any better than home.''

She nodded. "Thanks for listening." Then she started toward Pamela, who was wiping her eyes. In a moment she was being hugged hard by both Pamela and Shareen. She could hear Mrs. Millington in the circle behind her.

"Now you know what this is really about," Mrs. Millington said. "Think about that when you write your checks. I thought about it when I wrote mine. I'll be thinking about it for quite some time." She signaled to the band, and they began to play.

Becca felt her knees grow weak and tears well in her eyes.

She didn't like either sensation, but when she felt strong arms circle her and turn her against a broad, masculine shoulder, she gave in to both. She sobbed, and she shook, and she let Jase hold her.

"Becca." He smoothed her hair. "You were wonderful." He put his lips against her ear. "So brave. Too brave."

"Somebody had to tell them."

"It didn't have to be you."

"I'm glad it was." His arms tightened. "But now everybody knows about me, Jase."

"So? What do they know? They know you're full of spit and courage."

"You don't have to hold me."

"Yes, I do. Try and stop me."

She pushed him away a little and gazed into his eyes. "You're holding an ex-con. And now everybody knows it."

"I'm holding the woman I love."

She didn't even have time to react. She felt a hand on her shoulder, and she turned. A man she hadn't met was standing there. He was elderly and rotund, with half a ring of feathery white hair, almost like a halo, just above his ears. "That was quite a speech, young lady."

She managed a smile. "Thank you."

"My name is Juno McIntire." He thrust his hand into his coat pocket. He was the only man in the room wearing a suit and tie. "Here's my card. I want you to come and see me tomorrow. At one?"

She frowned. "About a donation?"

"In a manner of speaking."

"All right."

"I'll send a car for you."

"I can take the transit."

"No, a car will be faster. Just give me your address."

She looked at Jase. He nodded slightly. She borrowed his pen and scribbled the address of the cottage on the back of Juno's card.

"She's quite something," Juno told Jase. "You have better taste than some of your projects downtown have indicated."

"It's good to see you here, Juno. I didn't expect you."

"I like to go where I'm least expected."

Becca handed back his card. "I'll see you at one."

"I'll look forward to it." He made his way toward the door.

"Odd," Jase said.

"Did you say I was the woman you loved?" Becca asked, Juno forgotten.

He smiled down at her. His eyes gleamed suspiciously. "That was a long time ago."

"Did you?"

"I'll tell you when we get home."

"I'd like to leave now."

"Pamela's getting my car for us."

"I want to fly."

He thought about what awaited them. At home, in his bed. Together. "I'm planning on it."

"I love you, Jase."

He held her close and smothered her words against him to keep them warm and safe. "Tell me that in an hour. Over and over again."

"I promise."

As always, her word was good.

Chapter Thirteen

Jase had one leg between Becca's, an arm thrown over her back and his cheek snuggled against her neck. She awoke to the sensation that her life had changed. Thoroughly. No longer was she alone. She could protest. She could demand her independence—and would—but Jase was in her life to stay. Now she knew what love for a man really was. And she knew what it meant to be loved.

She felt his hand glide over her naked back. She wasn't surprised that they had awakened together. Jase was sensitive to every movement, every sound, she made. He had been sensitive to changes in her from the moment they had met.

"Can't sleep?" he asked against her shoulder.

"It's late. Do you know how late?"

"I don't care."

"Don't you have places to go and people to see?"

"You're the people I want to see. This is the place I want to go."

"It's almost eleven."

"What?" His head came up. "You're kidding."

"About something as serious as wasting time?"

His eyes were heavy-lidded, his smile slow and worth waiting for. "Did we waste time?"

"Sleeping's always a waste of time."

"What about the rest of the time?"

"I can't seem to remember anything else."

"You might need a refresher course."

She stretched, moving against him as she did. "Do you think so?"

He grasped her hand and moved it to the place where their bodies entwined. "Part of me thinks so."

She pretended surprise. "My memory's slow coming back."

His hand slid up her side and rested against her breast. "Is anything clearer now?"

"You might want to try that again."

His thumb began a slow rotation. "I'll try something better."

"Umm…" Her leg curved over his in possession. "I remember two people on a bed. Together. Just like we are now."

"Are they sleeping?"

"Definitely not."

"You're doing fine." His lips sought the curve of her neck, the line of her collarbone, the luscious swell of her breast.

"Oh, Jase." Her arms tightened around him.

"Do you remember someone saying that last night?"

"Definitely."

"Was it you?"

"Definitely."

"Are you repeating yourself?"

"Definitely."

He lifted his head to see her expression for the next question. "Shall we stop now that your memory's returned?"

"Definitely not."

Juno McIntire's office was on the top floor of a downtown skyscraper. Becca tried not to be impressed, or rather, she tried not to let how impressed she was show. She was still in shock from the limo ride. She hadn't realized what Mr. McIntire had meant when he'd said he would send a car. Now she wondered how she could have been so silly. Had she thought he was going to operate a two-door compact by remote from downtown? Had she really expected the car to show up without a driver?

The truth was that she hadn't thought at all. Limos and skyscrapers were so far out of her experience that they were objects from fairy tales. Six months ago she had entered this same building hoping to get a job cleaning. The maintenance manager hadn't even looked twice at her when he'd found she was an ex-con. She hadn't been good enough to scrub the sinks and toilets, yet here she was on an elevator heading straight for the penthouse.

She tried to remember what Jase had told her about Mr. McIntire. Eccentric millionaire, he'd said. One of Cleveland's richest men. Other things Jase had said this morning were much more memorable. She had been too enchanted with them to ask many questions about Juno McIntire.

Eccentric and rich and respected. She knew about the respected part because when the lobby guard had learned her destination he had practically bowed and scraped. She didn't understand why people got so fired up about other people with money. Money was important only because it could buy the things a person needed to survive. After a certain point, it didn't matter anymore. Jase—who should know firsthand—had said he had so much money he didn't know how to spend it all. There was something wrong with that.

Since it was Saturday, the building was largely deserted. The limo driver was accompanying her to the top floor, though she wasn't sure why. What were they all afraid of? Did they think she could get lost in an elevator? When the elevator stopped, the driver stepped in front of the doors to keep them from closing on her. She wanted to tell him she had never been squashed between elevator doors before, but she suspected he knew her acquaintance with elevators was limited. The only elevators in Blackwater had led straight down into the center of the earth.

"Mr. McIntire told me to take you right to his office," the man said.

"I suppose you're not going to just point me in the right direction?"

The man smiled for the first time. "I'm going to personally escort you there."

She walked beside him. She'd already learned that if she tried something as simple as following him, he stopped, as if that was the height of bad manners.

He stopped at the end of the hall and knocked on a shiny wood door with a brass nameplate. "What kind of name is Juno?" she asked.

"One that makes men in corporate boardrooms shiver with fear."

"I didn't see anything to shiver about last night."

"May it always be so."

He opened the door at a barked order from the other side. "Good luck."

She shook her head, perplexed that he thought she would need luck. "Thanks."

Inside she saw Mr. McIntire far across the room. His office reminded her of a storybook she often read her daughters about a sultan and genies and magic carpets. The Oriental carpets on Mr. McIntire's floor weren't magic, but no one who could afford them would need magic, anyway. The wood lining the walls was unfamiliar but exquisite, exotic grain matching exotic grain.

"Well, what a pretty place to work," she said, approaching his desk.

He stood. "You like it?"

"It's big enough for a family."

"How do you like my view?"

She walked past him to the windows and looked down. "Can't grow things in the air. It's pretty, but I think I'd rather be able to walk outside and see something I'd planted."

"You've got your feet firmly on the ground."

"I guess." She turned back to him and smiled. "Do you work every day, Mr. McIntire? You're the only one in the building besides me, your driver and the guard."

"No. I'm just here because of you."

She was intrigued. "I could have come on Monday."

"I wanted this settled. I never wait. That's how I came to have an office like this one."

"Well, if I ever aspire to an office like this, I'll remember that."

"I've been doing some checking on you."

"Have you?"

He came around his desk and gestured to a cluster of chairs and a table in the corner. "Let's make ourselves comfortable."

She crossed the room and seated herself, sinking deeply into plush blue upholstery. He joined her. "Damn silly world," he said, "when a man can find out anything he wants in a few hours. There's a trail of paper following each one of us around everywhere we go. You've got one, too."

She wasn't surprised. Some of it would have the official seal of the Commonwealth of Kentucky on it. "And what does my paper say?"

"That you're a good woman who got caught in a bad situation. Did you learn anything from it?"

For some reason she wasn't offended. She liked Juno McIntire, although for the life of her she wasn't sure why. "I did. I learned that I have to do what I know is right, no matter what anybody else thinks. And I learned that I have to take care of myself, no matter what anyone else wants to do. And I guess I learned that sometimes that means accepting a little help now and then. But only if you're willing to pay it back."

"And you've found ways to pay back The Greenhouse. I know that."

"Little ways. Nothing could really pay them back. They gave me my life."

"If you had a lot of money, Becca, and you were going to give it away, would you give it to The Greenhouse?"

She smiled. She had hoped this was the reason for his invitation today. He was considering a large donation. She just hoped she could convince him. "I sure would. See, there're things you look for when you're giving money away. Not that I've ever had any to give. But still, I think I know a few things about it."

"Let's hear them."

"First, you have to be sure the organization you're giving money to has the right idea. It's not right just to throw money at people. The right thing to do is help people learn to take care of themselves. I mean, some people can't, and that's a fact. But most people want a chance to try. They want jobs or training so they can find a job. They can't work or go to school, though, if they're sick or hungry or homeless. So people's needs have to be put in order. You know what I mean? You've got to handle the basics first, but always with the idea of moving people away from needing help, not getting them hooked on it."

She paused for breath. "I didn't say that very well."

"You did fine."

"What if there was a flood somewhere? The first thing you'd have to do is find new places for people to live, right? Make sure they had food and medicine, too. But later, when the waters went down, you wouldn't want to keep giving them food and medicine and shelter. You'd want to build dams or levees, so there was never another flood. Then they wouldn't need help again. That's what The Greenhouse tries to do in its own way."

"I see that."

She smiled. "Do you? I'm glad."

"And I see that you've got some excellent ideas. I thought maybe you might have."

"It's nice you think so, but—"

"In fact, your ideas are exactly mine."

"Are they?"

"So exactly mine that I have a job for you right here working with me."

"A job?" For a moment she didn't understand. Then she was touched that he wanted to help her. "Oh, you must have thought I was talking about myself when I talked about people needing jobs. But I wasn't. I've got two jobs right now. You don't have to make up one for me."

"Oh, I'm not making up a job, Becca. I've had an opening for six months, but no one I've interviewed has fit the slot. You fit it perfectly." He held up his hand to stop her response. "I know you'll be done with the landscaping at Jase Millington's soon. And I'm willing to wait until you are. But hear me out now. Because I think you'll like what I'm going to say. And I know I'll like having you work for me.''

Jase lounged in the doorway of Constantine's and watched Becca bustle around the room taking care of the last of the evening's customers. She poured coffee and cleared tables as if they were the most important jobs in the world. Constantine and Mama had made a good decision when they'd hired Becca. She was worth two of almost anyone else.

She bustled by with someone's check and saw Jase standing in the doorway. She flashed him her knock 'em dead smile. ''What are you doing here?''

''Waiting for you.''

''You didn't have to do that. I take the bus.''

''I know. I wanted you home faster.''

This time her smile was different. It almost sizzled. *He* sizzled just witnessing it. ''Let me get you some coffee while you're waiting,'' she said.

''Don't bother.''

He chatted with Constantine, who sang Becca's praises until she was finally finished for the night.

Outside in the fresh air she took his arm. ''It's been such a day!''

He knew it had been such a morning, such a perfect morning waking up with her in his arms and keeping her there an hour longer. He didn't know anything about the rest of her day, but his had felt strangely empty, even though he had been busy. He had wanted her with him to share what he'd learned about the possibilities of a Blackwater resort. He had wanted to see her surprise, then her pleasure, when he told her that he was going to help make profound changes in the way people lived in the town of her birth.

''How did your appointment with Juno go?'' he asked.

''I'll tell you when we get home. I want to see your face.''

He unlocked her door, but he pulled her close before she could get in and reminded himself of the pleasures of kissing her. He couldn't remember ever feeling as if he didn't want to let go of a woman, but he didn't want to let go of Becca. He was beginning to believe he was never going to let her go.

They were home before either of them spoke again. "My place or yours?" Jase asked.

"They're both yours. You choose."

He led her toward the cottage. The house reminded him of work that still needed to be done, and he was in no mood for that. At the point where the path forked, she pulled him right. "There's a full moon. Let's look at the roses."

He let her take him there. Moonlight silvered the garden, but it was the roses that gleamed and preened themselves under its caressing rays. Becca had wrought a miracle here. He thought how pleased Kathryn would have been.

He put his arm around her waist. The night was perfumed with the roses' fragrance. "I'm almost through here," she said. "There isn't much more I can do. Everything's been cleared and trimmed and given a chance to grow again. I've done what I could to make it easy for a yard service to come in and weed and mulch and fertilize a couple of times every year. By the end of the week I'll be finished."

"I'll still need somebody here to supervise the renovations."

"I'll stay till the end of the summer. I can keep up with the yard, too, but I won't take any more money. My rent will be enough for what I'll be doing."

"Don't be crazy. What are you going to live on? You don't get paid enough at Constantine's to support yourself and send money back to Blackwater, too."

"I'm not being crazy."

"You'll earn every cent I pay you."

"No cents."

"No sense."

"Jase, let's not fight. Besides, you don't know everything yet." She slipped her arm through his. "There's more to tell."

He felt something unfamiliar creep through him. A moment passed before he realized it was fear. He could almost feel her slipping away from him. He had just found her, and now she was slipping away. "Go ahead and tell me," he said.

"Let's go inside."

Inside the cottage she busied herself flicking on the lights. The little house had become so much hers that Jase knew he would never enter it again without seeing her here. Now it was warm with the glow of lamplight and polished wood. Vases with summer flowers were tucked into corners. Mementoes of Kathryn's that he hadn't wanted had found their way here. Watercolors hung on the walls; old straw hats decorated with faded silk ribbons hung from the arms of a wooden coatrack.

"I'll make coffee."

"It's late." He held up his hand. "I know, you'll make tea."

"Mint tea. From the garden. I'll have to show you where everything grows, Jase. So you can pick it for yourself when I'm gone."

"You don't have to go."

"I think I do."

She busied herself with the tea and teapot. He thought of the night she had told him about her past, thought of perfectly brewed tea neither of them had wanted and a plate of gingersnaps that had remained untouched. Tonight was different. She fluttered, but not from fear or shame. She was bursting with excitement. He admired the self-control it took not to share it, even as he battled his own growing apprehension.

She didn't speak until the pot was on the table between them. Black-eyed Susans sat in a vase beside it, mixed with tall blue ageratum. The tablecloth was beautifully mended linen and lace. He had the strangest feeling that in this nearly perfect setting, she was going to tell him that she wanted him out of her life.

"I told you I'd tell you what happened at Juno's."

He noted that she was calling his old adversary by his first name. He had the utmost respect for Juno McIntire, although they had never agreed on anything and never been on the same side of any dispute. Juno had his ideas about the direction Cleveland should go in, and Jase had his. And right now Jase had his first taste of real dislike for the older man. "I'm assuming he gave money for the renovation of the factory."

"I think he will. But that's not what we talked about."

He heard alarm bells that weren't really ringing. "What did you talk about?"

"Me."

"By far a more interesting subject."

"He must have thought so." She sat forward so that she could see his face. "He offered me a job."

"Did he?"

"A wonderful job. He's the chairman of a charitable foundation, funded mostly with his money, I guess. Anyway, he fired his director at the beginning of the year. He said she didn't have any horse sense. She had an education, and that was all. She kept trying to fund projects to research ways to help people, instead of just helping them. So Juno's been looking for someone to take her place. He wants somebody who knows what it's really like to be poor, Jase. He wants somebody like me. He wants me!"

Her enthusiasm and pride were almost blinding. "What did you tell him?"

"Well, I listened first. I had to be sure he wasn't just making this up. But he showed me volumes of records about what the McIntire Foundation has done in the past. He's not inventing anything. He has a job, and he needs me to do it. He even showed me payroll records so I'd see what the last director was paid. He wants to pay me the same. He says I'll be doing the same work, only doing it right, so I should get the same money. It's more than I ever dreamed I could make! Enough to rent an apartment, pay child care expenses, take care of the girls and even save some so I can go on to college. There's a company car that goes with it, too. And I can set my own hours. If one of the girls is sick, I can stay home and work, or just make up the time later. It's a job made in heaven!"

He couldn't think of better news. Yet if that were true, why did he feel as if someone had just punched him in the gut? "Juno's not an easy man to get along with."

"I like him. I don't know why anybody's scared of him. He's really a pussycat."

"Pussycat? Juno McIntire?"

"Well, if I'm not scared of you, why should I be scared of him?"

"So you're leaving here. Just like that."

She cocked her head and watched him. There was something going on that she didn't understand. "Not just like that. I told you, I'll finish what needs to be done in the yard. And I'll stay on to watch over the renovations. That way I can save enough for a deposit on an apartment. Juno says I can ease into the job there whenever it's not a problem for me to be gone here. I'll have to quit work at Constantine's, but not right away. I'll give them time to find and train somebody else."

He didn't care about the renovations or the yard. She could leave tomorrow and he would still have gotten a bargain. She was going to let Juno McIntire solve problems she wouldn't let Jase solve.

She frowned. "Aren't you happy for me, Jase?"

"Of course I am. It's wonderful."

The frown eased a little. "I could hardly wait to tell you."

He knew he should let her bask in her good fortune a little longer, but he felt isolated, as if it had nothing to do with him. He wanted to be part of the excitement on her face, the sparkle in her eyes. "I have something to tell you, too."

"Good news? I don't know if I can stand any more good news, but I'm sure willing to try."

"I think it's good news. Great news. I've been doing some research. It's an idea I had when I went down to Blackwater with you."

"Blackwater?"

"It's about Blackwater and something that could make a big difference there. It's probably hard for anybody who's lived there to see, but Blackwater's got enormous potential. Maybe not under the earth anymore, but above it. It's got some of the prettiest scenery I've ever come across. And there're always people looking for scenery. I want to build a resort. There's plenty of cheap land to do it on, and there's land by the river for sale right now, near the waterfall where we took the girls.''

Her frown had returned. ''A resort?''

''A big, expensive resort. Summer homes for people in nearby cities. People who want mountain air and views. People who want clear lakes for sailing—''

''There aren't any lakes in that area.''

''But there could be with a little manipulation of the river and some of the creeks. It would be a gold mine for Blackwater. There would be jobs for anyone who wanted them, markets for things people wanted to sell—''

''Dam up the river? That river's been running through those mountains for centuries. And houses mean cutting down trees, bulldozing roads through the mountains, tearing up more of the land.''

''Nobody's going to destroy anything that doesn't need it. We're not a bunch of strip-miners. The whole area would look better than it does now. It would have to. Blackwater would get a face-lift.''

She stared at him, horrified. ''It wouldn't be Blackwater anymore. It would be some fancy resort town with shops full of designer clothes and cute little ice cream parlors.''

''And those shops would be run by people from Blackwater.''

''No, they wouldn't. Maybe Blackwater folks would get to work in them sometimes, and maybe they wouldn't. You have to have money to build or lease a shop like that. Who has it? Strangers, that's who. And who'd want a bunch of hillbillies selling designer clothes? The only jobs the local folks would get would be the dirty ones. And maybe they wouldn't even want those. Blackwater wouldn't be their town anymore. Why would they want to stay there?''

''Are you listening to yourself?'' Jase slammed his fist on the table. ''Don't you see that's what's wrong with places like Blackwater, Becca? Nobody there has any vision of what needs to change.''

''Maybe they're too busy trying to survive to have visions. Maybe visions are a rich man's luxury!''

"Well, I've taken the luxury of having visions for them, then. I thought you'd be excited. I thought you'd be glad that somebody cared enough to want things to change for those people."

"Nothing would change! Don't you see that? You'd be as bad as the mining companies. You'd come in and tear up the land, give folks little, piddling jobs that don't amount to nothing. Somebody'd benefit, all right, but it wouldn't be the folks who live there!"

"They could help make decisions."

"What kinds of decisions? Whether they want this creek or that creek dammed up? Whether this house or that house gets torn down to the ground? Whether this mountain or that one gets blasted away so some rich folks can have a nice flat place to put their million dollar summer cottages?"

"You're not thinking straight."

"My thinking is as straight as the line between this cottage and your house!" She leaped to her feet. "And I'd like you to walk that line right now!"

He stood and grabbed her arm. "What's wrong? Do you hate it so much when I try to make a difference in your life? I was doing this for you!"

"No. You were doing it because you can't leave anything alone! I'm nothing but a project to you! Something you can change, just like you have to change everything to suit yourself. I thought maybe you loved me, that maybe it was really me, *me,* you loved. But it's not, is it? You look at me and you still see something that needs changing. You've tried to change me often enough. Now you're trying to change a whole town, a whole way of life you don't even understand. Why, Jase? Can't you just accept me and love me the way I am? Can't you be proud and happy for me when I make changes myself?"

"I am proud. I am happy!"

"No you're not. You don't want me to take this job of Juno's because you didn't think of it first! I knew something was wrong, but I couldn't see what. Now I do. You want to be my Prince Charming. You want to be the one to change my life, stick the old glass slipper on my foot and make me live happily ever after.

You can't stand the thought that I've found my own way. You can't love me for that. So you go off and try to change where I come from!''

His hand dropped to his side. "I've had enough of this." He turned to leave.

"Oh, no, you haven't. Not yet. You've got to hear one more thing. I love you. And I want you to love me, not love what you can do for me. You're not comfortable unless you're meddling. You've got to learn to be comfortable before I'll have you back, Jase. I don't want to be something you do. I want to be what I am. A woman who can take care of herself. A woman who can take care of you when you need her. A woman whose roots are what they are! A woman who's just plain all right like she is!''

He didn't turn. "I'm going back to Blackwater! And I'm going to see what the people there think of my idea.''

"You mean you haven't talked to them already? Didn't it occur to you before this that they might want to have their say?''

"They'll have their chance.''

"Are we going to have ours?''

He heard something like a sob in her voice, but he still didn't turn. "Apparently not. You want me to take you just the way you are, but you don't want me the way I am. This is me, Becca. I don't sit still. I move. I change things, and I'm not sorry I do.''

"You can change *things*. You can't change people. You can't change me. I'll do that myself. All I need you to do is watch and be proud.''

"If you just need an audience, you're looking for it in the wrong place. I thought you needed a lover, somebody who cared enough about you to want to make things better if they needed to be better. I guess I was wrong.''

She didn't answer, and he didn't wait. He left the cottage, and with each step he took, he knew he was leaving her life.

He could not make himself turn around.

Chapter Fourteen

Blackwater was dingier, sadder, than Jase had even remembered. There were no historic or interesting buildings to renovate or restore. Becca had been right about one thing. Most of what was here would have to be torn down or changed so completely that it would no longer be a shadow of itself.

He saw nothing wrong with that.

Anger had carried him the necessary miles to Blackwater. He hadn't wasted his time driving. On Sunday, the day after his fight with Becca, he had flown to Lexington and rented a car. Charlie Dodd, the man who had done his initial research and feasibility groundwork, had met him at the airport.

Charlie was all business, a middle-aged, climb-the-ladder-of-success kind of guy who had little appreciation for the scenic beauty around him. He had talked dollars and cents all the way to Blackwater.

They drove to the site and walked every inch together. Charlie waved his arms and paced off sections. He pulled figures out of the air as if they were dangling there for his convenience.

"You aren't going to make a bundle," he said as they drove back to Baldwin, where they both had rooms for the night. "No one else is going to do this if you don't. Hardly anybody could afford to invest so much money to get so little. I still don't understand why you want to do it.''

''Because it needs to be done.''

Charlie made a noise to indicate that Jase's logic was beyond him. ''These people don't want anything to change. They're happy being poor.''

Jase answered that in one compound word that his work crew wouldn't have dared to use around Becca.

''Why are they poor, then?'' Charlie demanded. ''This is a free country. Nobody has to be poor.''

''They're poor because they haven't had a chance to be rich.''

''And you're going to give them one? This deal isn't like you at all, Millington. Don't fool yourself. This project's not going to make anybody rich, not even you.''

Jase dropped Charlie at the motel but turned down his invitation to dine there. He'd had enough of Charlie and conversation about the resort. He had hoped Charlie and his facts and figures would help him keep his mind off of Becca. Instead he'd heard her voice loud and clear over Charlies' incessant chatter. He couldn't turn it off, just as he couldn't block out his visions of her. He didn't know how he was going to sleep in the same motel where they'd made love so passionately.

He wondered what Blackwater's residents did for fun on an evening like this one. At least once the resort was built there would be more entertainment available. The fancy ice cream parlors that Becca had taunted him about were just one improvement that would follow in the resort's wake. Stores and movies and fine restaurants would open. Blackwater's residents would have choices of things to do.

He pictured Matty and Syl and their kids mixing with Louisville and Cincinnati's well-to-do. The picture was incongruous. Not because Matty and Syl weren't good enough for anybody, but because they wouldn't have the cash for that kind of entertainment. Not even if Matty got a job—and what kind of job would Matty get?—and Syl was able to work in town instead of fifty mountain miles away.

He realized where his thoughts and his car were leading him.

He was halfway back to Blackwater before he pulled off the road at Better'n Home. There were roughly the same number of cars and trucks in the dirt lot that had been there before. He hoped his joyriding buddy was available for a little heart to heart.

Inside, the blond-haired waitress greeted him as if he was an old friend. He felt like an imposter, since his ticket to friendship, his relationship with one Becca Hanks, had been summarily canceled. But he wasn't going to announce that to the world. He imagined Better'n Home, with its huge contingent of Becca's admirers, would never be an appropriate place for that announcement.

He sat in the same booth where he had eaten ham and red-eye gravy. He remembered that the biscuits at Better'n Home had melted in his mouth, and he wondered if the cook would take a job at the resort or struggle to keep this place going instead. He couldn't imagine Lexington's finest eating regularly at Better'n Home.

The night's special was chicken and dumplings, enough for two men his size. He was on the second man's portion when three members of Becca's fan club walked in and came over to his table, including the joyrider who had taken him on the wild trip through the mountains.

He greeted them and gestured to the empty seats. They sat and ordered pie.

Jase waited until everybody was happily occupied with chocolate meringue or coconut cream before he mentioned the resort. He eased his way into it.

"What would you think if somebody wanted to open a resort just outside of town, a place where city people would buy houses and come, mostly in the summertime?"

"What kind of resort and where?" The joyrider seemed to have been informally appointed spokesman. He was a large man, bearded and pot-bellied.

Jase explained. He wanted honesty, so he was honest about his intentions. Becca had been right about more than how much of Blackwater would have to be torn down. She had been right when she questioned why he hadn't consulted anyone living there. He never wanted her to make the same accusation again.

There was silence for a while after he'd finished. The men seemed to be digesting his words along with their pie.

"Smells bad," one of the men said at last. "Smells real bad."

Jase was genuinely surprised. "What does?"

"Comin' in here. Changin' things."

"Don't things need to be changed? How many of you are working? Don't you need jobs?"

"Doin' what? Carryin' some rich man's golf clubs? Diggin' his swimming pool where I used to go swimmin' in the creek? I work west of Baldwin. I'll drive the distance and come back here, but not if it's changed."

Jase wondered if he was the only sane person left in two states. "I guess I don't understand."

"Blackwater needs changes," the joyrider said. "Don't think we don't know it. But not changes from outside. Not from somebody who doesn't know who we are."

Jase didn't flinch. After all, he'd heard the same line, or something close to it, before. "Who the hell are you, then?" he asked wearily. "I guess I really *don't* know."

"We're like these mountains. We can take a lot of swipes, even take it when our guts are ripped open to make money for somebody that's already got it. But we stand tall, and we're still here when those folks are gone. Things change in Blackwater, though maybe not so's a stranger could tell. But nobody gave us a medical clinic. We got that for ourselves 'cause we got sick and tired of watching our friends die. And we got ourselves a library 'cause we got sick and tired of our kids not learnin' to read good enough. We've got a rec center because we made it happen. Every year that goes by, we do something good for Blackwater. The best thing you can do is leave us alone."

Jase wondered how many times he had to hear a message these days to finally listen. "There's got to be something I can do. There's always something."

"Not if it means you want us to change. We'll change when we're ready, and then maybe not the way you think we should.

But this is our piece of God's earth, and we'll keep it the way we found it. You try a resort, we'll fight you every step of the way.''

Jase looked at the three stern faces and knew he'd been bested. They weren't three lone men. They were part of something he still didn't completely understand. But he was understanding it better. He *was* understanding it better.

He was still working on a cup of coffee when the men left. Their parting words had been friendly, but the threat was implicit now. No one was going to thank him if he tried to make Blackwater into what he thought it should be. And if he thought city government was a pain in the neck to work around, he really ought to give a bunch of ex-coal miners a try.

He was on his way back to Baldwin when a familiar curve in the road caught his attention. He slowed and pulled to a stop in front of Syl and Matty's house. The kids were in the front yard chasing each other in circles, and Matty was sitting out on the porch watching them run. He guessed that Syl wasn't home from work.

He got out of his car and walked up the rise to see Matty. He ruffled the oldest boy's hair and called greetings to the others before he got to the porch. His arrival barely called a halt to the frantic game of tag.

Matty stood and waited for him. She looked tired, the way anyone looked after a long, satisfying day. He wondered what Matty had to be satisfied about.

"You didn't bring Becca," she said.

"She's back in Cleveland." He wasn't about to tell her that he would probably never bring Becca anywhere again.

"Sit a spell," she said. "It's so pretty this time of evenin'."

He sat because it was better than lying in a motel room wishing he was anywhere else.

"You want to tell me about it?" she asked.

"I'm that transparent?"

"Just about."

"I don't understand your cousin."

"And you thought maybe I could help?"

He hadn't realized it, but that was why he was sitting here. He was sitting here waiting for somebody to help him, because for once he couldn't help himself.

"There's nuthin' much to understand about Becca. She wants somebody to love her, somebody who sees what she has to give. She hasn't had much luck that way. First man she loved used her like a doormat. Second one kept trying to convince her she wasn't good enough for him."

"Second one?"

"You."

He stopped rocking. He hadn't even realized he'd started. "Good enough for me? Of course she's good enough for me."

"Just the same way Blackwater's good enough for you? With a change here, a change there. Changes you think it needs."

"How do you know all this?"

"Think we don't have phones here? It's Blackwater, not Backwater. We've got phones and TV, and some of our men and women've even been to college."

In the yard, fireflies flickered as the children laughed and shouted. The mountain air smelled of roses and honeysuckle. Laughter and fireflies and roses. Simple pleasures he had never taken time to enjoy. Right beside simple truths he had never taken time to know.

"The two of you are from different places," Matty said. "Can't get much more different, and that's a fact. But the way you can get along is to respect those differences. You can't change each other. Nuthin' you can ever do will make Becca just like you, not even if you burn Blackwater down and build Disneyworld where it used to be. Blackwater's Blackwater. You're you. Becca's Becca. There's room for everything and everybody."

He thought about the woman he knew so well now. Did he really want to turn Becca into Cara or a woman like his mother? Hadn't it been Becca's uniqueness, her pride, her damned stubborn pride, that had charmed him in the first place?

"I wanted to make her life easier," he said.

"Ain't nobody's right to make life easy. It's not supposed to be easy. Dewey wanted life easy, and look where it got him and her. Seems to me you just want to make your own life harder. You just keep pushin' and pushin' when you don't have to."

"What do I do now?"

"You look at yourself, and you see if you've got what it takes to love a woman like Becca. Then you let her lead the way."

Even the idea made him uneasy. But the truth was that Becca had been leading him from the first day he'd met her. While he'd been trying to change her, she had been changing him. If she hadn't, he wouldn't be sitting on Matty's porch having this conversation.

"I'll call off the resort," he said. "It was a bad idea."

"Terrible. But leastwise you see it now."

"I love her," he said, and he knew it was really true. He loved Becca enough to want her to be who she was. And what greater gift could she ever give him?

"Are you going to go back and tell her?"

He thought about all the ways he could do that and wondered if she would believe any of them. Over and over again he had shown her that he didn't trust her to make it on her own. What reason would she have to believe an apology?

He rocked and considered. "Matty," he said at last, "I need help."

"Be glad to."

"Good. Because you're the only one who can."

He described what he needed, and she nodded. "Easy enough. Come back early in the morning."

Jase knew she was right when she said this would be the easy part. The hard part was yet to come. But he'd always liked challenges. He just hoped that this time his good luck held out, because he was going to need every bit of it.

It took three transfers to get from Shaker Heights to The Greenhouse. What would have taken twenty minutes by car took Becca more than two hours by bus. Usually when she took the bus she brought a book to read. Today she stared out the window. Soon she wouldn't be riding the bus at all, but the joy of that, the thrill of having her life on the right track, hardly touched her.

Jase had left early that morning, for Blackwater, she supposed. He hadn't said goodbye, of course, but she had heard his tires screech as he backed out of the driveway. She imagined he was there now, plotting and scheming to make Blackwater his next success story.

She could hardly bear the thought that he'd left so angry. She'd been too angry at first to feel anything else. Then, little by little, other feelings had crept in. Hurt, then love, a rush of it, swifter than the river after a flood.

He'd been wrong to think he could just walk in and make Blackwater over to suit himself, but he had done it because he loved her. In his own bullheaded, ornery way he had been asking over and over again to be part of her life. She had shut him out, shut him out and slammed the door. Sure, she'd had her reasons, most of them good ones. But she hadn't once thought about him or what he needed.

For too long she'd had to think only about herself and the girls. She hadn't left room in her life for Jase or any man. He'd tried to make room, and all she had done was get angry at him.

She got off the bus three blocks from The Greenhouse and took her time getting there. The block was looking better. One change spurred another. Little by little the neighborhood was coming back from a long, slow decline. That was how it had been for her, too.

She stopped in front of The Greenhouse and saw the changes that had been made here. The fence was perfect now. No pickets were missing, and it glistened with fresh paint. Someone had continued her work in the flower beds. Striped petunias and bronze marigolds stretched toward the sunlight. The gingerbread trim on the house itself was no longer flapping in the breeze. New trim had been integrated with the old. She imagined Jase was responsible. He had never mentioned it to her, but that was like him. He never asked for credit for what he did. He liked to make a difference. Usually that was reward enough—unless it was her he was trying to help.

She saw a flash of skirts in the side yard at the swing set. There were new children at the house, girls the age of her own. She felt such gratitude that now she would finally be able to bring her babies to live with her. They would be the family they had never been able to be before. But they would be a family without Jase as her partner, without Jase as their father. Her eyes widened. She realized where her thoughts had led her, where they had probably been leading for weeks.

"You look shocked about something."

Becca looked up to see Pamela in the doorway. "I—I guess I was just admiring the new trim."

"Nice, isn't it?"

Becca started up the sidewalk to the house. "Real nice."

"What brings you here?"

"I came to talk to Shareen. I didn't know you'd be here."

"Dorey's having a birthday party, so I'm filling in for Shareen this morning. Will I do?"

Becca didn't think Pamela would do at all. She was too close to Jase to be objective about Becca's decision. But there was a two-hour bus ride, two hours each way, that made it impractical to come back tomorrow when Shareen would be in. If she wanted to settle things, she had to do it now with Pamela.

"Come on into the parlor and I'll get us some tea," Pamela said. "Did you take the bus?" She watched Becca nod. "I'm leaving in half an hour. I'll drop you at home if you're ready to leave. I've got some errands to do in that direction."

"Thank you. I have to go to work this afternoon." Becca followed Pamela inside and went to the parlor to wait. When she had lived at The Greenhouse she had loved this room. Now it reminded her of Jase's house. For a long time to come, everything was going to remind of her Jase.

She was rearranging a basket of dried flowers when Pamela came in with two glasses of iced tea.

"You can't sit still for a minute, can you?" Pamela asked. "Just like my brother." She thrust out a glass. "It's too strong and probably not sweet enough. I should have let you make it."

"I want to come back here." Becca took the glass but didn't

even raise it to her lips. She set it on an end table, and she spoke fast. "Not for long. Just for a little while, until I can get an apartment. I've saved most everything I've earned, except what I've sent back to Blackwater for the girls. And I'm starting a new job next week where I'll be making good money, so I can save faster."

"There's room for you."

Becca sighed, and all her defenses drained away. She sat. "Is there?"

Pamela flopped into a chair. "Did you want me to say there wasn't?"

"No. I've made up my mind."

"And I know what that means."

"I'll work while I'm here. There's more gardening I can—"

"Cut it out, would you?" Pamela stretched her feet in front of her and wiggled her sandaled toes. "You're welcome. Isn't that good enough?"

Becca felt tears fill her eyes. "Welcome?"

"Welcome. And if you need to stay longer than our limit, you can come to my place. You'll always be welcome there."

Becca had expected a lecture, or at least a discussion. She hadn't expected to be so readily embraced. Pamela trusted her feelings in a way Jase did not. "I don't know what to say."

"Don't say anything, then."

"Don't you care why? I mean, it doesn't matter to you?"

"I assume you and Jase had a fight. But it's not my business, is it? The two of you have to work out your own relationship. And if you can't do it by talking about your differences, if you have to do it by running away, then maybe that's what you have to do."

"I'm not running away."

"Did Jase ask you to leave?"

"Of course not!"

Pamela cocked one brow. "You didn't run away, and he didn't ask you to leave. Maybe the cottage burned down."

"I made an awful scene. Well, helped make it, but a lot of it was me."

"Did you ever fight with Dewey, Becca?"

For a moment Becca was confused by what seemed like a change of subject. "Sometimes I'd try to reason with him. He hit me pretty often, hard enough to knock me to the ground one time."

"And I guess that was a good reason not to fight with him if you could help it. Would Jase hit you?"

"No!"

"So what's the worst thing that can happen if you fight?"

Becca put her head in her hands and rubbed her forehead. Pamela was clever. Kind and clever. With just a few sympathetic questions she had gotten right to the heart of the matter. "I could hurt him."

"I'm sure you could."

"I did hurt him, Pamela. No matter how hard I try, I keep hurting the people I love." She thought of Matty, of Dewey and the twins, even of the Hanks. And all the people in Blackwater she had let down when she'd gone to jail. All the people who had believed in her.

"Well, you're no different than anyone else. We all end up hurting the people we love," Pamela said.

"I try so hard to make everything right, but it never really is! I keep making mistakes. I don't want to make any more. I don't want to hurt Jase anymore!" Tears fought their way free. In a moment Becca was sobbing.

Pamela sat across the room from her and let her cry. She was afraid to offer comfort, because she knew how badly Becca needed to cry this out. When it looked as if the flood was abating, she crossed the room for a box of tissues. She brought them to Becca and knelt in front of her. Becca took a handful.

"You're always going to make mistakes," Pamela said. "And sometimes you're going to hurt people. But most people are just about as tough as you. They can survive your mistakes. Jase certainly can. The two of you have just got to stop trying to make everything perfect. Nothing's ever going to be perfect."

Becca wiped her eyes. "I told myself on the way over that I wouldn't let myself get talked out of moving."

"You're still welcome here."

"But I was just being bullheaded. I make up my mind and that's that. I don't really want to leave the cottage."

"I know."

"I love Jase. I think I've just been afraid that if I loved him too much, it would be like it was with Dewey. I guess there's still a part of me that thinks I'm to blame for what Dewey was."

"And there's a much bigger part that knows better."

"There is." Becca gave her a watery smile. "But when I'm scared, the other part comes creeping out."

"And Jase scares you."

"What I feel for him scares me." She blinked away the rest of her tears. "Outside I was thinking that now he would never be a father to my girls. I'm thinking about marriage! That scares me to death."

"Lord, it would scare me, too."

"We haven't even talked about it."

"That doesn't surprise me. You've both been too busy trying to change each other."

"I don't know how to say I'm sorry. I said it so many times to Dewey that I promised myself in prison I'd never say it to another man again."

"You know the line that goes, 'Love is never having to say you're sorry'? It's baloney. If you're sorry, you're sorry. What you promised yourself in prison is that you'd never say it unless you really meant it."

"He's going to be sorry, too. I know him."

"Then you can apologize together."

Becca managed a smile. "We must look like a couple of crazy people to you."

"Crazy in love."

"You're right about us trying too hard, and about me being scared to death to make mistakes."

"Actually, you're the one who pointed that out. You just needed to tell somebody and try it on for size."

"I paid for my mistakes."

"No. You paid for everybody else's. For Dewey's. For a society that doesn't care enough about vulnerable people. Heck, you've earned so much credit paying for other people's mistakes you can afford to make as many as you want."

Becca hugged her. Then she stood. "I'm going to go check on the garden, see if the carrots are ready to pull."

"You do that."

"I'll be ready to go when you are."

"And you won't be coming back?"

"I won't be coming back. I guess I knew that all along."

"Good. Because we can always use the bed for somebody who needs us. You don't need us anymore."

Becca gazed at her for a moment. "I guess I needed a friend."

"You've got one. For life."

"Someday maybe I can do something for you."

"Maybe so. It seems to me with all this love in the air, I might just fall victim myself someday."

Becca smiled. This time it felt real. "I can hardly wait to watch."

Chapter Fifteen

Jase pulled up in front of the Hanks' house and parked his rental car. "I'll be back in a few minutes," he told Charlie. "We'll get to Lexington in plenty of time for both our flights out."

Charlie made a noise that could have been interpreted any way. Last night, while Jase had been at the Better'n Home café and Matty's house, Charlie had gone out to survey the local Baldwin nightlife. Charlie was five drinks and four hundred dollars in the hole this morning, and his opinion about the intelligence and cunning of mountain people, particularly crapshooting, poker-playing mountain people, had risen to a new high. His opinion of himself was at an all-time low.

"I'll just die here," he mumbled. "Slowly."

Jase didn't tell Charlie that that couldn't happen soon enough to suit him. He just slammed the car door after he got out. As hard as he could.

He took two little packages out of his suitcoat pocket on his way up the walk. He didn't know what had possessed him to buy Amanda and Faith presents. He had almost missed his plane because the line in the airport gift shop had been so long. But now he was glad he had made the effort. He wanted to see the girls, not only to report on them to Becca—she would have to let him talk to her if he was talking about her children—but just for his own satisfaction. He knew Becca was right in believing the girls were well cared for here. But he didn't like either Bill or Alice Hanks, and he wanted to reassure himself that they weren't passing on their sour view of life to Becca's children.

Alice answered the door, and surprise wiped away her perpetual frown. "Didn't know you were coming."

"I'm on my way out of town. But I brought the girls presents. Could I see them for a few minutes?"

"Becca's not with you?"

"She's working this weekend."

"Seems to me she'd take off and come see her babies."

"Seems to me she's killing herself so she can *get* her babies. And it seems to me you'd understand how hard she has to work to send you money and take care of herself, too. When she remembers to take care of herself!" He thrust the packages toward her. "Never mind. Please give these to the girls and tell them I was here." He turned without another word and started down the walk.

"You can see them if you like."

He counted to three before he turned. "Good."

She stood aside and let him pass through the doorway, but her frown was firmly fixed in place again. She led him through the house, into the backyard where the twins, in green and blue rompers, were digging in a sandbox. There was no sign of her husband.

He immediately knew which girl was which. And he knew more. The two little girls looked like the woman he loved. He hadn't brought them gifts because he wanted to check on them. He had brought them gifts because he wanted to see them. They made him feel close to Becca. They always would.

He went to the sandbox and sat on the edge. Both little girls looked up at him, then back down at the sand.

"I have a sister," he said. "When she was little, she always wanted to play in the sand with my cars. Do you have cars?"

Faith looked up again and favored him with her mother's smile. "No."

He held out the package. The clerk at the gift shop had wrapped it in tissue paper and stuck on a bow. Faith made short work of it. "Cars!"

He didn't know what had gotten into him. He wondered if the Hanks would approve of such whimsical presents for little girls. Faith approved. Wholeheartedly. She squealed, and in a moment the five tiny metal cars were in a heap in her pile of sand.

"Me, too?" Amanda asked.

He handed her the other package. Her squeal was more lady-like, but just as delighted.

Faith got up to plop her little sandy bottom in his lap. She put her arms around his neck and laid her blond head against his shoulder. "Where's Mommy?"

He prided himself on honesty and integrity, but now he thought seriously about kidnapping the children and taking them back to Ohio. Seriously enough to be quiet for most of a minute. Then he realized that he couldn't. All he could do was wait for Becca to settle her life. To trust her to settle it. Her own way. And with Juno's help, it wasn't going to take long. He said a silent prayer of thanks to old Juno, something he would never have guessed he would do.

"She's back in Ohio," he said. "Thinking about you both. She sends all her love."

"Her's coming soon?"

"Soon as she can."

Faith snuggled against him, and he held her tight. But Amanda got up and went over to a tree where a heap of toys lay. She searched through the pile, as if she was looking for something special. Then she came back, clutching something to her chest.

"What have you got, Amanda?" He held out his hand.

She shoved a doll toward him. It was blond, like her, a young child with pigtails. From the beautiful craftsmanship he recognized it as one of the kin dolls that Becca had told him about at the waterfall.

He took the doll and examined her. The doll looked remarkably like both girls. He suspected that wasn't a coincidence.

"Did your grandmother make this?" he asked. "At her church?"

Amanda put one finger in her mouth, but she nodded.

"She looks like you."

"Give her to Mommy."

For a moment he didn't understand. Then something inside him broke in two. "You want me to take it with me and give it to your mommy?"

Amanda nodded again. Faith reached for the doll and kissed and hugged it; then she handed it back to Amanda, who did the same. Solemnly Amanda held it out to him again.

She frowned when he didn't take it right away. She moved a little closer and stared up at him. "You're crying?" she asked.

He held out his free arm, and she went to him to give him comfort.

Jase followed Mrs. Hanks to the front door, the kin doll tucked against his chest. He had left the girls out back, making roads and tunnels in the sand for their new cars. Just from watching he was already certain that Faith was going to follow in his footsteps at M.I.T.

"I appreciate you letting me see them," Jase said.

"I been thinking about what you said."

That surprised him, although he doubted her thoughts had been productive ones. "I don't want to see Becca hurt any more. She's been hurt enough by this family to last her a good long while," he said.

"We're taking care of her children. That's not good enough for you and her?"

"You're taking care of your son's children. If they were just Becca's children, they'd be out in the streets." He exhaled slowly. "But I don't have any rights here. And you're doing a good job with Amanda and Faith. I can thank you for that much."

"What are you to Becca?"

"I'm the man who's going to marry her. As soon as she's willing."

"The girls need a father."

His expression didn't change. "And a mother."

"Don't you think I know that?"

"You want the truth? No, I don't. I think you're going to make it hell for her to get them back. She doesn't think so, but I do."

"She's right. You're not."

He waited.

She turned toward the door. "My son was everything to me. When he died, I wanted to kill somebody myself. You know what that's like?"

"No."

"I hope you never do. I couldn't kill nobody, couldn't do it if somebody'd put a loaded gun in my hands and pointed it for me. But I could hate. I found out what it was like to hate. I been hating for a good long time now, turning most of it toward Becca. But the way Dewey turned out wasn't Becca's fault. He was all Bill and me had, and we spoiled him till he thought he could do anything he wanted. I liked hating better'n knowing that. But now I know it, and I can't hate Becca anymore. We could have helped her stay out of jail, wrote letters about her, mortgaged the house so's she could have a real lawyer, but we didn't. So we got to give her something back. When she's ready to take care of the girls, we won't fight her."

Jase didn't really know Alice Hanks, but he guessed that was probably the longest and most emotional speech she had ever made. Once again Becca had been right, and he had been dead wrong. He wanted to comfort Alice, but he knew there was no comfort to offer.

"What about your husband?" he asked. "Will he fight it?"

"No. Bill's too sick to take a fight. Truth be told, I think he wants the girls out of here so he can get more rest. Just as long as we can see them from time to time. Watch them grow up."

"They'll always be your grandchildren."

"You'll tell Becca what I said? I won't tell her myself."

"Maybe you'll be able to someday."

She shook her head, and he knew she meant it. She had come as far as she was going to.

"I'll tell her, then. She'll want to have the girls soon."

"I'll have them ready when she does."

Charlie was asleep in the car when Jase got in. He slept all the way to Lexington, and Jase had plenty of time to think. He had time to think in the airport and on the late flight back, too. He didn't know if a man could change much in a couple of days, but he wasn't the same person he had been when he'd left Cleveland for Blackwater. He was humbled—probably as much as he would ever be—and for once he was unsure of his future.

Nothing had ever been hard for him. Now the hardest moments of his life lay ahead. Somehow he had to convince Becca that he loved her the way she deserved to be loved. As a whole person, a person he trusted completely, a person who could run her life her own way. He wasn't sure where compromise came in anymore, or when he had a right to state his opinion. Giving up control, giving up power, was so new to him that it was uncharted territory. But he knew he could get through it with Becca at his side.

If she was willing to stay by his side.

He had a special package, a cardboard box wrapped in plastic bags, that he'd carried on the plane, along with the kin doll the girls had given him to bring back to Becca. When he finally got to Cleveland he carried both to his car, along with his garment bag, and stored them carefully in the back seat. Then he started for home.

Becca couldn't sleep, even though she was exhausted from a busy afternoon and evening at the restaurant. She'd had no reason to expect Jase to come back tonight, but somehow she had. She didn't want another moment to pass with anger between them, but it looked as if at least another day was going to go by. The problems between them were crazy ones. They were too much alike in some ways and a million miles apart in others. But the problems could be solved if they both wanted them to be.

She didn't know if that was what Jase wanted or not.

By midnight she gave up pretending she was even going to shut her eyes. The moon was still almost full, although the night was cloudy. She remembered the evening just a few nights before when she had stood beside the moonlit rose garden and told Jase that soon she would be able to leave him. She had been so full of herself, so proud of her new independence. But in her rush to show him that she could make something of herself, she hadn't shown him or told him that she still wanted to be part of his life. She had wanted to prove she could make it alone before they made it together. Only she had forgotten to add the last part.

How could she have forgotten?

She slipped on a summer dress and the sandals she had bought to wear to the fund-raiser. She couldn't stay inside another moment. She wanted to visit the roses again, inhale their sweet fragrance and think about how to talk to Jase when he came back home. The old roses seemed a tie to both her past and her present. She needed their comfort.

Outside she breathed the sweetly scented night air. The smell of rain was in the air, too, a sharp clean smell that blended with the fragrance of flowers.

The yard was as lush, as perfectly cultivated, as a city park. She felt a thrill of pride that she had done this herself. As the yard had changed and thrived again, so had she. She could make things grow, make things blossom and bear fruit. She wandered toward the roses, caressing leaves and picking flowers. She would teach her daughters to garden so that someday they would know the same triumph.

She had almost reached the roses when she saw a shadow moving among them. She stepped behind a tree and watched, her heart beating in her throat. There was crime in Shaker, just as there was anywhere, but she had always felt safe in Jase's yard, even at night.

The shadow stood, and she saw it was a man. The shadow moved with purpose and economy, and she saw it was Jase.

She almost called out to him, but she stopped herself and

watched instead. He walked to the side of the garden and bent low, then lifted something from the ground and carried it back to the row where he had been working. He knelt there, as prayerfully as she had often knelt in the same place.

"Jase?" She stepped out from behind the tree. "What on earth are you doing?"

He turned his head and gazed through the darkness. "Becca?"

She moved toward him. Slowly, half afraid she was dreaming this. "What are you doing? I thought you were a burglar, though I guess a burglar wouldn't be too interested in the roses."

"Stop. Be careful where you step."

She looked down and saw that just ahead of her, laid out in a neat row, were half a dozen small clumps wrapped carefully in newspaper and tied with twine. "Mercy. What on earth?"

"Roses."

She bent and examined them. "Roses?"

"From your home place. Matty helped me dig them up. She said the old roses send out shoots all the time to make new plants. We tried to get one of every kind for you. They might not all make it, but if they don't, Matty says there're more where they came from. There's a good-sized pillow rose. We forgot to get it when we were there before."

She touched one of the clumps in wonder. "You saw Matty?"

"Yesterday, and early this morning. We dug them together, before I left Blackwater, so they wouldn't dry out. But I was afraid they might not last the night, so I'm heeling them in until you decide where each one should go. We might have to enlarge the bed."

"Who taught you about heeling them in?"

"Matty did. Matty taught me a lot." He stood and started toward her.

"Roses, Jase? For me?"

He reached her, but he didn't touch her. He wiped his hands on his pants. "A piece of your life here, Becca, with a piece of mine. Pieces of both our hearts."

She stood. "They'll thrive here. But you're right. We'll need to dig a bigger bed."

"I'll help."

They stared at each other, and then they were in each other's arms. She wrapped herself around him so tightly that she wasn't sure anything would be able to part them. "I thought I'd lost you," she said. "I'm so sorry. So, so sorry."

"For what? For being strong enough to survive without me? That's what I love about you, but I couldn't see it before."

"No, for not telling you that I want you to be part of my life. I was just so busy being proud of myself."

"You had every right to be proud!"

"And I am, but not so proud that I don't want to be with you. I just needed to know I could make it, Jase. But I never wanted to make it so far you wouldn't be there with me."

He kissed her forehead, her nose, her cheeks, her lips. He held her so tightly that he wasn't sure she could breathe. But he couldn't seem to let her go.

Slowly they sank to the thick, dewed grass bordering the roses. They were surrounded by roses, sheltered from prying eyes. Even the moon seemed to look away, its silver glow dimmed by gathering clouds. Becca wasn't sure who undressed whom, who fumbled with buttons and zippers and belt buckles, but in moments they were undressed and exploring each other as if to be certain nothing had changed—although everything had.

His skin was sleek and warm, the shape and angles of his body familiar. She buried her face against his chest, seeking, knowing with her lips, all the places she had kissed before.

His hands found her breasts, her hips, the secret, most vulnerable part of her, and she gasped with pleasure. Their legs tangled; their arms embraced; their bodies caressed, until there was nothing, no part of either of them, that was hidden from sensation.

She lifted herself to Jase as he sank into her. There was nothing tender or gentle about their reunion. She demanded and he possessed. He demanded and she took everything from him. She gave, then took more, until there was nothing else to take except pleasure so shattering she wasn't sure either of them could survive it.

They did. She lay in his arms for a long time afterward, breathing in the scent of roses and their lovemaking.

"I can't believe we did that," she said at last. "Here, in front of the roses."

"They approved." He helped her up and found her dress. The clouds had thickened, and he felt the first drop of rain. "Put this on, then help me get the roses into the ground. The rain will take care of the rest."

She giggled, a carefree, joyous sound he had never heard from her before. In the immediate aftermath of their lovemaking he had wondered if they would ever reach such heights again. Now her laughter stirred more than his heart. He wanted her again, and soon.

"You, a gardener," she said as he pulled on his clothes.

"And what's wrong with that?" He swung her around, over and over because he couldn't let her go, and kissed her once more. Then, as the rain began to fall, they set the rest of the roses in the trench he had dug and buried their roots in the rich loam of the garden.

They were soaked by the time they raced for the house, chosen instead of the cottage because it was closer. Inside he saw that she'd been busy while he had been in Blackwater. Vases of flowers filled the rooms.

Becca saw that he had noticed. "It was all I could think of to do," she said. "I wanted you to know you were on my mind while you were gone."

There were flowers in his bathroom, too. Bouquets on the sink and the wide ledge of the whirlpool bath. He ran the water, then undressed her again so that they could enjoy the tub and the flowers together.

It was only afterward, when they were cuddled together under his sheets, that he found the concentration and the courage to talk to her. She lay half sprawled across him, a position as perfect as any he could think of. But he slipped out from under her caressing leg and left the room for a moment.

Becca watched him go. She knew that they still had things to talk about, but she didn't know if she was ready to say anything more. Everything was so perfect. For just a little longer she wanted to hold on to the feeling of being loved without reservation.

Jase came back into the room. She savored the breadth of his chest, the muscled length of his legs. She couldn't imagine ever looking at his gloriously naked body without her breath catching a little.

"I brought you a present." He sat beside her and held out the kin doll.

She took it and without a thought clasped it to her chest. "Where did it come from?"

"Amanda gave it to me to bring for you."

Tears filled her eyes. She blinked them back. "I won't need one before long."

"No, you won't." He touched her leg. "When you're ready, Alice and Bill will give you the girls. Alice told me so today."

"She did?" She looked at him from under wet lashes. "You didn't..."

"Pressure her? Threaten her? No, I didn't. Not that I didn't want to. But I wouldn't have, even if she'd told me she was going to fight for custody. What you do, and the way you do it, is up to you. I realize that now."

She covered his hand. "What did she say?"

"In her own way she said she was sorry. She knows that the trouble in your marriage was Dewey's fault, not yours, and she knows she owes you something. She says she and Bill will give up the girls without a fight as long as they can still see them."

She rested her cheek against the doll's yellow pigtails and said a silent prayer of thanksgiving.

He watched her holding the doll and knew that soon it would be one daughter or both in her arms. "Alice will never be able to tell you that herself."

"It doesn't matter."

"There's something I have to tell you, too, but there's nobody to carry my message. So I guess I'll have to do this myself." He felt her hand tighten on his, and he smiled at her. "I don't feel very courageous."

"You don't know what it means to be afraid."

"I do now. I was afraid I'd lost you."

"I was afraid you wouldn't want me anymore."

He bent forward so that he could look into her eyes. "I was wrong about Blackwater, Becca. I wanted to change it because you wouldn't let me change anything else in your life. I wanted to help, even if nobody else wanted me to. I'm too used to changing things and taking charge."

"You wouldn't have felt that way if I'd let you into my life. But I didn't know how to, not without giving up my pride." She touched his hair. "But I want you in my life, Jase Millington the Whatever. I want whatever you have to give me."

"Nobody I talked to in Blackwater wants a resort. You were right. It would destroy what's there, but it took a lot of pounding for me to see that. Change has to come from the people who live there, the kinds of changes they need and want."

"So you're giving up?"

He smiled a little. "I tried to. I really did."

"And?"

"I have an idea. But I won't do a thing about it if you don't like it. It's up to you and the people of Blackwater to decide if it's a good idea or not."

She realized she wasn't even nervous about what he had come up with this time. She believed him when he said he wouldn't push. They had both learned a lot. Jase would never change completely. He would always be full of ideas, most of them superb. But she knew he was going to struggle not to force others to accept what they knew wasn't good for them. Just as she was going to learn to accept what she needed and not let her stubborn pride shut him out of her life.

"Let's hear it."

He took the kin doll. "This is Blackwater's wealth. Family. Roots. Tradition. You said it yourself by the waterfall. I didn't pay much attention, because I was too busy bulldozing mountains in my mind. But the kin dolls could go a long way toward solving some of the town's immediate problems."

She was fascinated. "How?"

"By making and marketing them out of Kentucky. You were right. Families live all over now. Children grow up without roots and ties. There are a lot of people who need kin dolls and what they represent. I have a friend who's marketing manager of an upscale catalogue. I know she'll be interested. Handmade dolls would sell for a lot. Eventually they might even be mass produced. The people who make them can form a cooperative. I can help them get started, or someone more informed about it could help. The point is that the people can decide how they want to go about setting up a business. All I'd have to do is give a little nudge."

"Nudge?" She smiled. Gloriously. "Nudge, Jase?"

"Just a little one."

She threw her arms around his neck. "It's a wonderful idea! Perfect. This comes from them, not you. It's just that you're the only one who's seen the potential!"

He relaxed and held her. He had really been afraid she would be angry. "Help me tell the difference from now on, okay?"

"Always."

"Always?"

She released him. "We've never talked about always, have we?"

"I think always is another wonderful idea. Let me know if I'm wrong."

"I come with a family."

"I want the girls. I want you, too, if you'll have me. When you're ready."

She knew she was going to be ready sooner than he suspected. But she was too busy kissing him to discuss a timetable.

There would be plenty of time to make plans. All the time in two lifetimes.

*   *   *   *   *

DREAM MENDER

Sherryl Woods

For Karon Gorham,
with thanks for her insights and technical expertise,
and for sensitive burn-unit experts everywhere

Chapter One

Frank Chambers prowled the narrow hospital room, feeling like a foul-tempered bear awakening from hibernation with a thorn in its paw. He stared at his own bandaged hands and muttered an oath that would have curled his mother's hair and earned him a sharp rap across his already-injured knuckles. He wanted to smash something, but settled for violently kicking a chair halfway across the hospital room. It skidded into the pale blue wall with a satisfying crash, but did nothing to improve his overall mood. His mother, a wise woman with little sympathy for self-pity, would have said it would have served him right if he'd broken his toe.

The door opened a cautious crack and yet another nurse peered in, an expression of alarm on her face. "You okay?"

"Just dandy," he growled.

When he didn't throw anything, she visibly gathered her courage and stepped inside, marching over to his bed and folding her arms across her chest, assuming a stern posture clearly meant to intimidate. Considering her tiny size, it wouldn't have been an effective stance even if he hadn't been feeling surly.

"You ought to be in bed," she announced. She pulled back

the sheet and gestured in the right direction just to make her point.

He glared at her and ignored the invitation. "I ought to be at home. I'm not sick."

"That's not what your chart says."

"I don't give a—"

She never even took a breath at the interruption. She just kept on going, talking over his swearing. "Less than twenty-four hours ago you were in a serious fire. When they brought you in, you were suffering from smoke inhalation. Your blood gases still don't look all that good. You have second-degree burns on both hands. You need rest and therapy."

It was not the first time he had heard the same detailed recitation of his medical condition. "I need to go home," he repeated stubbornly. He tried another fierce scowl to emphasize the point. Grown men had cowered at that scowl. He was certain of its effectiveness.

Clearly unintimidated, the nurse rolled her eyes and left. He doubted she'd gone to get his release papers. None of the others had, either. Hell, his own mother hadn't sided with him when he'd insisted he didn't need to be admitted in the first place. He'd been whisked up to his room and hooked up to oxygen so fast it had left his head spinning. He'd tried bribing each of his brothers to spring him, but they'd ignored his pleas. Not even his softhearted baby sister had taken pity on him. She'd patted his arm and suggested to the afternoon-shift nurse that they tie him down if they had to.

"*Et tu, Brute,*" he'd muttered as Karyn had winked at him over her shoulder. Then she'd linked arms with her new husband and sashayed off to dinner.

The attitude of the whole Chambers clan rankled. That good-natured defiance was the thanks he got for all those years when he'd put his own life on hold to help his mother raise his five brothers and his sister. When his father had died, he'd reluctantly stepped into the role of parenting and discovered that it fit, even at seventeen. Maturity and responsibility had been thrust on him, but he'd somehow liked being needed, liked being the backbone of a large and loving family. In a curious sort of way he'd even suffered through the empty-nest trauma, watching as his siblings had matured and struck off on their own.

Karyn's recent marriage to race-car driver Brad Willis might have been the first wedding in the tight-knit family, but it was hardly the first sign he'd had that it was time to get on with his own life. He'd been told to butt out so often in recent years he'd had no choice but to start focusing on himself instead of his siblings. He'd been doing just that—most of the time, anyway— until yesterday afternoon. Now, suddenly, at forty he was discovering what it was like to have the tables turned on him, to have to depend on others for his most basic needs. And, he didn't like it, not one bit. What man would? No wonder his brothers chafed at all his well-intended meddling. Now they were giving it back to him in spades.

Left alone with his unpleasant thoughts through the long night, Frank tried to face facts. He told himself he could live with the pain the doctors were warning him to expect as the nerves in his hands healed. Hell, he could even live with the long-term scars. He'd seen burn scars, and while they weren't pretty, his big, work-roughened hands hadn't been much to write home about anyway. What *was* killing him, though, what was creating this gut-wrenching fury, was the absolute, utter helplessness of it all.

He couldn't do the simplest things for himself with these layers of gauze wrapped around his fingers, turning them into fat, clumsy, useless appendages. Forget holding a fork. Forget turning on the shower or washing himself. Forget pushing a button on the damned TV remote or holding a book. He couldn't even go to the bathroom on his own. Nothing, ever, had left him feeling quite so humiliated. They might as well have lopped the damned things off at the wrist.

And all because of a stupid accident. One careless instant, a still-smoldering cigarette butt tossed into a trash barrel by one of his unthinking co-workers, and the next thing he'd known the entire woodworking shop had been in flames. He'd grabbed for a fire extinguisher, but the metal had already been a blistering red-hot temperature. He'd done the best he could, but with all

the flammable material around, it had been like battling a towering inferno with a garden hose. He'd managed to get a few
things out of the workroom before the blaze and smoke had
gotten out of control, eventually destroying everything. He'd
gone back in one last time to rescue one of his co-workers who'd
panicked and found himself trapped in a workroom with no exit
except through the fire. Only when he was outside, gulping oxygen and coughing his head off had he noticed the blistered, raw
layers of skin on his hands. The adrenaline high had given way
to shocked horror as paramedics rushed him to the hospital. His
co-worker had been treated for smoke inhalation at the scene.

The injuries could have been worse, they'd told Frank in the
emergency room. Third-degree burns, with the possibility of
damaging tendons and bone, could have been devastating for a
man who worked with his hands. His career, most likely, would
have been over. He would have lost the woodworking skills that
had turned his imaginative, finely crafted cabinetry into an art
that was making its way into some of the finest homes in San
Francisco. With second-degree injuries, he had a chance.

The recovery, though, would be slow, tedious and painful.
Frank had never been out sick a day in his life. Now it appeared
he was headed for a long vacation, courtesy of workmen's comp.
The concept didn't sit well. Worse was the faint, terrifying possibility that he might never again be able to do the delicate,
intricate carving that made his work unique and gave him such
a sense of accomplishment.

By morning, after hours of focusing on the "what ifs," panic
had bubbled up deep inside him. He dragged air into his injured
lungs. Each breath hurt and did nothing to calm him, nothing to
wipe away the bleak images of a future without the work that
he loved.

Determined to get out of the hospital, even if he had to escape
on his own, he used his foot to lever open the closet door. The
task was easier than he'd expected, and his confidence soared.
Hope crashed just as quickly with the realization that the only
clothing hanging in the closet was his robe. His sooty shirt and
jeans were no doubt ditched in some trash receptacle. He'd never

get past the nurses' station, much less out of this place, wearing just an indecent hospital gown and a robe that still had a price tag hanging from the sleeve.

On the nightstand beside the bed the phone rang. Grateful for the interruption, Frank lunged for it, knocking it to the floor with his inept hands. Another stream of profanity turned the air blue. How the hell was he supposed to answer a phone with fingers that stuck straight out like prongs on a damned pitchfork?

"Nurse!" he bellowed, rather than bothering with the call button. "Nurse!"

He glared at the door, waiting for it to open, fuming because he couldn't even manage that simple task. This time, however, rather than inching open bit by cautious bit, the door was suddenly flung wide. Instead of a nurse, therapist Jennifer Michaels stepped into the room with all the confidence of a woman who's head hadn't yet been bitten off by the fuming, foul-tempered patient in Room 407.

Frank recognized her at once. He had still been dopey from medication when she'd poked her head into the room the previous afternoon, but he hadn't forgotten that perky, wide smile and that mop of shining Little Orphan Annie curls. Nor had he forgotten the cheerful promise that she would be back in the morning to begin his therapy.

"What do you want?" he asked, regarding her suspiciously.

Ignoring his challenging tone, she stepped briskly into the room, took in the situation at a glance and, with one graceful move, retrieved the phone from under the bed. "I was at the nurses' station when we heard your dulcet tones echoing down the hall," she told him.

"And you drew the short straw?"

"And I was on my way to see you anyway. How'd the phone land under the bed?" she inquired, as if it weren't obvious.

He stared at her incredulously, then glanced pointedly at his bandaged hands.

If he'd expected pity or understanding, he didn't get either. She shrugged and hung up the receiver. "I suppose some people would consider that an excuse."

Frank glared at her just as the phone started to ring again. He stared at it, cursing it for the helplessness it stirred in him again. He took all of his frustration out on the therapist. "Get out!"

As skinny as she was, he was surprised his bellow alone hadn't blown her from the room. She didn't budge, every puny inch of her radiating mule-headed stubbornness. A tiny little bit of respect found its way into his perception of Ms. Jenny Michaels.

"I thought you wanted someone to answer the phone," she said, all sweet innocence over a core of what was clearly solid steel.

"I'll manage."

"How?" she said, voicing his own disgruntled thought.

"What the hell difference does it make to you?"

"I'll consider it the first step in your therapy."

She waited. He glowered, his muscles tensing with each damnable ring of the phone. Finally, thankfully, it stopped.

"It's probably just as well," she said. "It is time for your therapy. I usually like to start with something less complicated."

"Push-ups perhaps," he suggested sarcastically.

"Maybe tomorrow," she said without missing a beat. "In the meantime, why don't I just show you how to start exercising those fingers? You can repeat the exercises every hour, about ten minutes at a time."

"I'm not interested in therapy. I just want to be left alone."

Ignoring that, she ordered, "Sit," and waved him toward the bed.

"Forget it," he said, bracing himself for a fight. He'd been itching for one all morning. Everyone else had sensed that and run for their lives. Jennifer Michaels wasn't scaring so easily.

"Okay, stand," she replied, not batting an eye at his surliness. "Hold out your hand. I'll show you what I want you to do."

He backed up until he was out of reach. "What about me? What about what I want?" he thundered. "Don't you get it, lady? I'm not doing any 'exercises.'"

"You'd prefer to have your hands heal the way they are now?"

Her voice never even wavered. Frank decided in that instant that his initial impression had been right on target: Jennifer Michaels was one tough little cookie. He took another look and saw the spark of determination in her eyes. He tried again to get through that thick, do-gooder skull of hers.

"Listen, sweetheart," he said with deliberate condescension. "I know you have a job to do. I know you probably think you can accomplish miracles, but I'm not interested. The only thing I want out of life right this second is to be left alone, followed in very short order by my discharge papers."

She winced once during the tirade, but recovered quickly. After that her expression remained absolutely calm. Not stoic. Not smug. *Calm.* It infuriated him. The only people he'd ever seen that serene before had been drugged out or chanting. Around San Francisco it was possible to see plenty of both.

"I could leave you here to stew," she said as if honestly considering the possibility. "Of course, it would make me a lousy therapist if I let you get away with your bullying tactics."

"I'll write you an excuse you can put in your personnel file. The patient was uncooperative and unresponsive. That ought to cover it, don't you think?"

She nodded agreeably. "It's certainly accurate enough. Unfortunately you won't be able to hold the pen unless you do the exercises."

"Dammit, don't you ever give up?" he said, advancing until he was towering over her. She swallowed hard, but stood her ground as he continued to rant. "I'll type it. I ought to be able to hunt and peck, even with my fingers like this." He waved them under her nose for emphasis.

She leveled her green eyes at him and tried to stare him down. When he didn't back off she shrugged. "Suit yourself."

She headed for the door and suddenly, perversely, Frank felt uncertain. At least she was company. And as long as they were hurling insults, he wouldn't be alone with his own lousy thoughts. "You're leaving?"

"That is what you said you wanted. I have patients who are interested in getting better. I don't have time to waste on one who's feeling sorry for himself. Think about it and we'll talk again.''

She pinned him with an unflinching green-eyed gaze until he couldn't stand it anymore. He turned away. A sigh shuddered through him as he heard the door shut softly behind her.

Well, Chambers, you definitely made a horse's ass out of yourself that time, he told himself. Not that Jennifer Michaels couldn't take it. There had been that unmistakable glint of steely determination in her eyes and an absolute lack of sympathy in her voice. At almost any other moment in his life that combination might have impressed him. He admired spunk and dedication. He was not in the habit of dishing out garbage the way he had just now, but on the occasions when his temper got the best of him, he appreciated knowing that the target had the audacity to throw it right back in his face. Jennifer Michaels had audacity to spare.

In her case, the unexpectedness of that tart, unyielding response had caught him off guard. He doubted she'd learned that particular bedside technique in therapist school. But he had to admit it was mildly effective. He felt guilty for a full five minutes before reminding himself that, like it or not, he was the patient here. Nobody was exactly coddling him.

Not that he wanted them to, he amended quickly. The papers might be calling him a hero for rescuing his co-worker, and his family might think he was behaving like a pain in the butt, but either label irked. He didn't feel particularly heroic. Nor was he ready to don a hair shirt just because his attitude sucked. He figured he had a right. With his hands burned and his livelihood in jeopardy, it was little wonder that his stomach was knotted in fear. If he wanted to sulk, then, by God, he was going to sulk, and no pint-size therapist with freckles, saucer eyes and bright red curls was going to cheer him up or lay a guilt trip on him.

But to his amazement, the memory of her sunny disposition and sweet smile began to taunt him. It couldn't be easy dealing with angry patients, some of them injured a whole lot worse than he was. How did she do it day after day? How much of the abuse did she take before lashing back? How much would she withstand before truly giving up? Somewhere deep inside he knew that she hadn't given up on him after this one brief skirmish. She'd only staged a tactical retreat, leaving him with a whole lot to think about.

Frank spent the rest of the day intermittently pacing, staring at the door, waiting. Every time it opened, his muscles tensed and his breathing seemed to go still. Each time, when it was just a nurse or a doctor, disappointment warred with relief.

Finally, exhausted and aware that, like it or not, he wasn't going anywhere today, he crawled back into bed. He was stretched out on his back, counting the tiny pinpoint holes in the water-stained ceiling tiles, when the door opened yet again. This time he didn't even bother turning his head.

"Hey, big brother," Tim said from the foot of the bed. "How come you're not out chasing nurses up and down the corridors? There are some fine-looking women around here."

"I hadn't noticed."

His youngest brother stepped closer, a worried expression on his face. He placed a hand against Frank's forehead. "Nope. You're not dead. Must be the smoke. It's addled you senses."

"My senses are just fine." He paused. "Except maybe for touch."

Tim chuckled. "That's better. A little humor is good for healing. I'll go tell Ma it's safe to come in now."

"She's here?"

"They all are. They're just waiting for me to wave the white flag."

Frank groaned. "All of them?"

"Everyone. You're the one who taught us to travel in packs in times of crisis. We're here to cheer you up. Feed you your dinner. Help with a shower. Of course, if it were me, I'd invite one of those gorgeous nurses to give me a sponge bath."

Frank's lips twitched with a rueful smile. "I'm sure you would."

"I know you're much too saintly to think in such terms. I'm a mere mortal, however, and I don't believe in wasting opportunities that come my way. If life hands you lemons, make—"

"I know. Make lemonade. If you ask me, too damned many opportunities have come your way," Frank grumbled, treading on familiar, comfortable turf. "You're like a bee in a field of wildflowers. It's a wonder you don't collapse from overexertion."

"Do you realize how many women get on a bus every single day?" his brother countered. "You want me to make an informed choice, don't you?"

"I knew I should have insisted that you work your way through law school by cutting lawns for little old ladies instead of driving a MUNI bus."

Tim stared at him thoughtfully. "I wonder if I could get them to bandage your mouth shut for a couple of weeks."

Frank sighed. "You and most of the staff around here."

"Yeah, that's what your therapist said."

Immediately interested, he searched Tim's face for some indication of his reaction to the conversation. "You talked to Jennifer Michaels?" he prodded.

"Listened is more like it. That woman can talk a mile a minute. She had plenty to say, too. I'd say you got under her skin, Brother. What did you do? Try to steal a kiss? Ma's out there trying to calm her down and convince her that at heart you're a good-natured beast worthy of saving."

"She's just frustrated because I won't do her damned exercises."

"I wouldn't mind doing a little exercising with her. She's a fox."

The observation, coming from an admitted connoisseur of the fair sex, irritated the daylights out of Frank for some reason. "Stay away from her, Timmy."

A slow, crooked grin spread across his brother's face. "I knew it. You're not dead after all. Just choosy. Actually, I think you've made an excellent choice."

"I didn't make any damned choice."

Tim went on as if he'd never uttered the denial. "Redheads are passionate. Did you know that? Fiery tempers and all that."

Frank thought about the therapist's absolute calm. "I think

our Ms. Michaels may be the exception that proves the rule. She's unflappable.''

"Are we talking about the same woman? Not five minutes ago she told Ma if you didn't get your butt out of this bed and down to therapy in the morning, she was going to haul you down there herself. I think she has plans for you.''

The first faint stirrings of excitement sent Frank's blood rushing. "I'd like to see her try to drag me out of here," he said, a hint of menace in his tone. The truth of the matter, he suddenly realized, was that he really would like to see her do just that. If nothing else, going another round with Ms. Miracle Worker would relieve the boredom. Maybe if he tried her patience long enough, he'd witness a sampling of that fiery temper Tim claimed to have seen.

Before he could spend too much time analyzing just why that prospect appealed to him, the rest of the family crowded into the room and filled it with cheerful, good-natured teasing and boisterous arguments. Once he'd finished the tedious task of eating tasteless chicken and cold mashed potatoes with the help of his nagging sister, Frank leaned back against the pillow and let the welcome, familiar sounds lull him to sleep.

Tonight, instead of the horrible, frightening roar of a raging fire, he dreamed of a fiery redhead turning passionate in his embrace.

Jennifer Michaels could feel the tension spreading across the back of her neck and shoulders as Frank Chambers's chart came up for review at interdisciplinary rounds. The doctors and nurses on the burn unit had their say. Then it was her turn. It was a short report. In a perfectly bland voice she recited his status and his refusal to accept therapy. At least she thought she was keeping her tone neutral. Apparently she was more transparent than she'd realized.

"You sound as if that's something new," Carolanne said when rounds had ended and the others had left the therapy room. "Almost every patient balks at first, either because of the pain, because they're depressed or because they refuse to accept the seriousness of the injuries and the importance of the therapy.''

Jenny sighed. She'd delivered the same lecture herself dozens of times. "I know. My brain tells me it's not my responsibility if the patient won't begin treatment, but inside it never feels right. It feels like failure.''

"Must be that Catholic boarding school upbringing again. You haven't developed a full-fledged case of guilt in months now. You were overdue.''

"Maybe.''

The other therapist watched her closely. "Or maybe something specific about Frank Chambers gets to you.''

Jenny thought of the anger in his voice, the strength in his shoulders, the coiled intensity she had sensed just beneath the surface. Then she thought of his eyes and the wounded, bemused look in them that he fought so hard to hide. He was getting to her all right. Like no patient—or no man—had in a very long time.

"I'm right, aren't I?'' Carolanne persisted. "Want me to see him tomorrow? I can take over the case.''

Jenny hesitated. That would be the smart thing to do, run while she had the chance. Then she thought of the lost, sorrowful expression in those compelling blue eyes.

Because she understood that sadness and fear far better than he or even Carolanne could imagine, she slowly shook her head. "No,'' she said finally. "Thanks, but I'll see him.''

How could she possibly abandon a man who so clearly needed her—even if he couldn't admit it yet?

Chapter Two

"When am I getting out?" Frank demanded as his doctor bent over his bandages first thing in the morning. Nathan Wilding was one of the top burn specialists in the nation. In his fifties, he was compulsively dedicated, returning to the hospital at a moment's notice at the slightest sign of change in any of his patients. Occasionally gruff, and always demanding, he insisted on excellence from his staff. Because he accepted no less from himself, his staff respected him, and his patients elevated him to godlike stature. He'd been featured in almost as many San Francisco newspaper stories as 49ers quarterback Joe Montana and treated with much the same reverence. Frank considered himself lucky to be the patient of a true expert, but that didn't mean he wanted to hang around this place any longer than necessary.

"When I say so," Wilding mumbled distractedly as he carefully snipped away another layer of gauze. When the nasty wounds were fully exposed, he nodded approvingly. Personally Frank thought they looked like hell. He stared with a sort of repulsed fascination.

"Am I going to be able to work again?" he asked, furious because his voice sounded choked with fear.

"Too soon to say," Wilding replied. "Have you been doing your therapy?"

Frank evaded the doctor's penetrating gaze. He sensed the doctor already knew the answer. "Not exactly."

"I see," he said slowly, allowing the silence to go on and on until Frank met his eyes. Then he added, "I thought you wanted to get full use of your hands back."

"I do."

"Then stop giving Ms. Michaels so much grief and get to work. She's one of the best. She can help you, but only if you'll work with her."

"And if I don't?"

"Then I can't promise you'll have any significant recovery of dexterity." He pulled up a chair and sat down. "Let me spell it out for you, Mr. Chambers. Your injuries are severe, but not irreversible. Maybe even without therapy, given time, you'd be able to hold a glass again or grasp a fork, if the handle is wide enough."

He waited for that to sink in. Certain that he had Frank's full attention, he went on, "It is my understanding, however, that you are a craftsman. In fact, my wife bought one of your cabinets for our den. The workmanship is extraordinary in this day of fake wood and assembly-line furniture production. The detail is exquisite. If you ever hope to do that sort of delicate carving again, there's not a minute to waste. You'll do Ms. Michaels's exercises and follow her instructions without argument. She's a damned fine therapist. Cares about her patients. She doesn't deserve any more of your abuse."

Frank could feel an embarrassed flush creep up his neck. "She complained that I behaved like a jerk, right?"

"She didn't tell me a thing."

"Then she wrote it in the chart."

"The chart mentioned that you were uncooperative and unresponsive." Amusement suddenly danced in the doctor's eyes, chasing away the stern demeanor. "It also mentioned that you told her to write that."

As the doctor rewrapped each finger in solution-soaked gauze, he said, "Listen, I know you're frustrated and angry. It's understandable. I'd hate like hell being in your position. A doctor's not much use without his hands, either. But the fact of the matter is that you're the only thing standing in the way of your own recovery. If you think it's bad now, just wait a couple more days until the pain starts full force. You're going to hate the bunch of us, when that happens. There's not one of us you won't think is trying to torture you. You're going to be downright nasty. You'd better hope you've made a few friends around here by then. We can walk you through it. We can remind you that the pain will pass. And Ms. Michaels can see to it that you don't let the pain make you give up and decide to find a new career that doesn't demand so much of your hands."

"In other words, it's time to stop feeling sorry for myself and get to work."

"That's about it."

The last time Frank had had a straight, no-nonsense lecture like that he'd been a teenager similarly hell-bent on self-destruction. Angry over his father's death, terrified of the sudden, overwhelming responsibilities, he'd gone a little wild. He'd been creeping into the house after three in the morning, staggering drunk, when his mother had stepped out of the shadows and smacked him square on the jaw. For a little woman, she had packed a hell of a wallop.

Having convinced him just who was in charge, she had marched him into the kitchen and poured enough coffee to float a cruise ship. While he'd longed for the oblivion of sleep, she'd told him in no uncertain terms that it was time to shape up and act like a man. He'd sat at that table, miserable, unable to meet her eyes, filled with regret for the additional pain he'd inflicted on her.

And then she had hugged him and reminded him that the only things that counted in life were family and love and support in times of trouble. She'd taught him by example just what that meant. She was the most giving soul he'd ever met. Some instinct told him that deep down Jennifer Michaels might be just like her.

If he'd learned the meaning of love and responsibility from his mother, Frank had learned the meaning of strength and character from his father. Until the day he'd died of cancer, his body racked with pain, the old man had been a fighter. Reflecting on his own behavior of the past couple of days, Frank felt a faint stirring of shame. He resolved to change his tune, to cooperate with that pesky little therapist when she finally showed up again.

"She'll have no more problems with me," Frank assured the doctor. "I'll be a model patient."

Unfortunately that spirit of cooperation died the minute she walked into the room pushing a wheelchair, her expression grimly determined. He didn't even have time to reflect on how pretty she looked in the bright emerald green dress that matched her eyes. He was too busy girding himself for another totally unexpected battle.

"What's that for?" He waved his hand at the offensive contraption.

"Time for therapy," she announced cheerfully, edging the chair to the side of the bed. "Hop in, Mr. Chambers. We're going for a ride."

"Are you nuts? I'm not riding in that with some puny little wisp of a thing pushing me through the halls. My legs are just fine."

She backed the chair up a foot or so to give him room. "Let's see you move it, then. The therapy room is down the hall. I'll give you five minutes to get there." She spun on her heel and headed for the door, taking the wheelchair with her.

"Something tells me I'm not the one with the attitude problem today," he observed, still not budging from the bed, arms folded across his chest.

Jenny abandoned the wheelchair, moving so fast her rubber-soled shoes made little squeaking sounds on the linoleum. Hands on hips, she loomed over him, sparks dancing in her eyes. The soft moss shade of yesterday was suddenly all emerald fire.

"Buster, this attitude is no problem at all. If I have to bust your butt to convince you to do what you should, then that's the road I'll take. Personally I prefer to spend my time being pleasant and helpful, but I'm not above a little street fighting if that's what it takes to accomplish the job. Got it?''

Frank found himself grinning at her idea of playing down and dirty. In any sort of real street fighting, she'd be out of her league in twenty seconds. He gave her high marks for trying, though. And after what he'd put her through the previous day, he decided he owed her a round. He'd let her emerge from this particular battle unscathed.

"I'll go peacefully," he said compliantly.

She blinked in surprise, and then something that might have been relief replaced the fight in her eyes.

"Good," she said, a wonderful smile spreading across her face. That smile alone was worth the surrender. It warmed him deep inside, where he hadn't even realized he'd been feeling cold and alone.

"I had no idea how I was going to haul you into that chair if you didn't cooperate," she confided.

"Sweetheart, you should never admit a thing like that," he warned while awkwardly pulling on his robe. "Tomorrow I just might get it into my head to stand you up for this therapy date, and now I know I can get away with it."

"Who are you kidding?" she sassed right back. "You knew that anyway. You're nearly a foot taller than I am and seventy pounds heavier."

"So you admit to being all bluster."

"Not exactly." She gestured toward the door. "I have a very tall, very strong orderly waiting just outside in case my technique failed. He lifts twice your weight just for kicks."

"Which confirms that you weren't quite as sure of yourself as you wanted me to believe."

"Let's just say that I'm aware of the importance of both first impressions and contingency plans," she said as she escorted him to the door.

Outside the room she turned the wheelchair over to the orderly, who was indeed more than equal to persuading a man of Frank's size to do as he was told. "Thanks, Otis. We won't be needing this after all."

The huge black man grinned. "Never thought you would, Ms. Michaels. You're batting fifty-eight for sixty by my count. It's not even sporting fun to bet against you anymore."

"Nice record," Frank observed wryly as they walked down the hall. "I had no idea therapists kept scorecards. I'd have put up less of a fight if I'd known I was about to ruin your reputation."

"Otis is a born gambler. I'm trying to persuade him that the track is not the best place to squander his paycheck."

"So now he takes bets against you?"

"I'm hoping eventually he'll get bored enough to quit that, too. I think he's getting close." She peered up at Frank, her expression hopeful. "What do you think?"

What Frank thought, as he lost himself in those huge green eyes, was that he was facing trouble a whole lot more dangerous than the condition of his hands. His voice gentled to a near whisper. "Ms. Michaels, I think a man would be a fool to ever bet against you."

Her gaze locked with his until finally, swallowing hard, she blinked and looked away. "Jenny," she said, just as softly. "You can call me Jenny."

Frank nodded, aware that they were suddenly communicating in ways that went beyond mere words. "Jenny," he repeated for no reason other than the chance to hear her name roll off his tongue. The name was simple and uncomplicated, not at all like the woman it belonged to. He had a hunch he'd done a whole lot of miscalculating in the past couple of days. It might be fascinating to discover just how far off the mark he had been. "And I'm Frank."

"Frank."

They'd stopped outside a closed door marked Therapy and might have stood right where they were, awareness suddenly throbbing between them, if Otis hadn't strolled past, whistling, giving Jenny a conspiratorial wink. Suddenly she was all business again, opening the door, pointing to a chair. "Have a seat. I'll be right with you."

Frank stepped into a room filled with ordinary, everyday items from jars to toothbrushes, from scissors to jumbo-size crayons. He wasn't sure what he'd expected, but it certainly wasn't this dime-store collection of household paraphernalia. He hooked his foot under the rung of an ordinary straight-back chair and pulled it away from a Formica-topped table so he could sit. He eyed the assortment of equipment skeptically. He suspected his insurance was going to pay big bucks for this therapy, and for what? So he could play with a toothbrush? His spirit of cooperation took another nosedive.

"What's all this?" he asked derisively the minute Jenny joined him.

"Advanced therapy," she retorted. "If you're lucky and work hard, you'll get to it in a week or two."

He regarded her incredulously. "It's going to take two weeks before I can brush my teeth? I thought you were supposed to be good."

"I am good. You're the patient," she reminded him. "Two weeks. Could be longer. The bandages won't even be off for three weeks. Think you can handle it sooner?"

There was no mistaking the challenge. "Give me the brush," he said.

"Get it yourself."

He reached across the table and tried to pick it up. He managed it with both hands, by sliding it to the edge of the table and clamping it between his hands as it fell off. At least his quick, ball-playing reflexes hadn't suffered any.

"Now what?" Jenny said, all bright-eyed curiosity. The woman was just waiting for a failure. Frank was equally determined not to fail. He was going to set a few recovery records of his own.

He pressed harder to keep the brush from slipping and tried to maneuver it toward his mouth. "Do you have to watch every move I make?" he grumbled, sweat forming across his brow with the taxing effort.

"Yep."

Irritated by his inability to manipulate the brush and by her fascinated observation of the failure, he threw it down. "Forget it."

"Maybe we ought to work up to that," Jenny suggested mildly. There wasn't the slightest hint of gloating in her tone.

He scowled back at her, but her gaze remained unwaveringly calm. "Okay, fine," he bit out finally. "You call the shots. Where do we start?"

She sat down next to him, inching her chair so close he could smell the sweet spring scent of her perfume. "We'll start with flexing your fingers. I'll do the work this first time, okay? It's called passive motion."

Momentarily resigned, he shrugged. "Whatever you say."

With surprising gentleness, she took his hand in hers. At once Frank cursed his fate all over again. He couldn't even feel the unexpected caress. His imagination went wild though. He wondered if her skin was as soft as it looked, if the texture felt like rose petals. He was so fascinated with his fantasizing, in fact, that he barely noticed what she was doing, until she said, "Now you try it."

"Mmm?" he murmured.

She regarded him indignantly. "Frank, weren't you paying a bit of attention?"

"My mind wandered."

If she was aware of exactly where his wayward thoughts had strayed, she showed no evidence of it, not even the faintest blush of embarrassment. She picked up his other hand.

"Try to pay attention this time," she said as she slowly flexed each finger back and forth. The range of movement was minuscule. Frank couldn't believe how little she expected or how inept he was at accomplishing it. He *needed* her to move his fingers for him—and he hated that weakness.

"That's it?" he scoffed when she stopped. "That's your idea of therapy? You dragged me all the way down here for that?"

"You could have done it in your room, but we tried that routine yesterday and you didn't seem to like it. It occurred to me you might take it more seriously if I brought you down here.

Just remember there's an old saying that you have to walk before you can run.''

"It usually applies just to babies.''

Jenny rested her hand on his forearm and regarded him intently. Compassion and understanding filled her eyes. "In this instance it might be wise if you think of your hands as being every bit as untutored as a newborn's,'' she told him. "The instincts are there, but the control is shaky. Right now we're just trying to assure that the joints don't stiffen up as you heal and that the skin maintains some elasticity.''

Frank wasn't interested in baby steps. He wanted desperately to make strides. "All I need is to get these bandages off and I'll be just fine.''

"You will be if you do the exercises religiously, ten minutes an hour. Got it?''

"I've got it.''

"Want me to walk you back to your room or send for Otis?''

"Hardly. My legs aren't the problem.''

"I'll be in later to check on you.''

Her tone was all business and her gaze was directed at his chart as she scribbled in a notation. Frank found it thoroughly irritating that he'd apparently been summarily dismissed now that she'd gotten her way. He was just about to tell her in grumpy detail what she could do with her ridiculous therapy, when the door opened and another patient was wheeled in by the formidable Otis.

The young girl was swathed in bandages over fifty percent of her body. Only one side of her face peeked through the gauze and only one arm remained unbandaged. Even so, she struggled for a smile at the sight of Jenny. Frank felt his heart wrench at the pitiful effort.

"Hey, Pam, how's it going?'' Jenny asked, her own smile warm, her gaze unflinching.

"Pretty good. I just beat Otis at poker. He has to go out and bring me a hamburger and fries for lunch.''

Otis leaned down, his expression chagrined. "I thought that was going to be our little secret.''

Jenny chuckled. ''That will teach you, big guy. There are no secrets between therapist and patient. As long as you're buying, you can bring me a hamburger, too.''

''Women! The two of you are going to put me in the poor-house,'' the orderly grumbled, but he was grinning as he left.

Frank watched the byplay between Jenny and the teenager for a few more minutes, irritated by their camaraderie, the easy laughter. He could feel the pull of the warmth between them and envied it. Feeling lonelier than he ever had in his life, he finally slipped out the door and went back to his room.

Late into the night, long after he probably should have been asleep, he struggled to move his fingers just a fraction of an inch. He wasn't sure whether he was trying to prove something to himself...or to Jenny.

Chapter Three

Jenny had met some tough, self-defeating patients in her time, and Frank Chambers ranked right up there with the worst of them. Right now he was suffering more from wounded pride than he was from his physical injuries. A man like Frank, used to doing for others, according to his family, would hate being dependent, even temporarily. And she could tell that he was going to fight with her every step of the way, try to hide his unfamiliar weakness. She had to make him see that it took real strength to admit the need for help.

She'd once heard a burn therapist from Miami say that a patient who was a winner in life before his injury would be a winner afterward. Despite his initial surliness, she could tell that Frank Chambers was a winner. She just had to remind him of that. She had to get him past his anger and fears and on to more practical things that could speed his recovery. Sooner or later his intelligence would kick in, and he'd realize that his attitude was only hurting.

Fortunately Jenny was by nature a fighter. She'd fought her own personal demons in this very hospital, and she'd learned from the humbling experience. Sometimes that enabled her to reach patients other therapists wanted to abandon as lost causes.

Knowing how easy it was to slip into despair strengthened both her compassion and her determination to keep that self-defeating slide from happening.

Yesterday, by threatening to force Frank into a wheelchair, by hinting he was worse off than he was and allowing him the victory of proving her wrong, she had won the first round. Yet it was a shaky, inconclusive victory. Today was likely to be more difficult. He was going to be expecting miracles, and if he hadn't improved overnight, he'd consider the therapy a failure and her an unwelcome intruder.

She considered sending the massive, intimidating Otis after him, but decided it would be the cowardly way out. She did take along the wheelchair though, just in case Frank needed a little extra persuasion.

Jenny breezed into the room just in time to see his breakfast tray hit the floor. She grabbed an unopened carton of milk in midair and guessed the rest. He'd gotten frustrated over his inability to cope with the milk and the utensils.

"Hey, I've heard hospital food is lousy, but that's no reason to dump it onto the floor," she said, keeping her expression neutral as he made his way from the bed to the window.

"I wouldn't know," he muttered, his rigid back to her as he stared outside. His black hair was becomingly tousled from sleep and his inability to tame it with a comb. She was touched by the sexy disarray and poked her hands in her pockets to avoid the temptation to brush an errant strand from his forehead. The shadow of dark stubble on his cheeks was equally tempting, adding to a masculine appeal she was finding it increasingly difficult to ignore.

"You could have asked for help," she said mildly.

"Dammit, woman, I am not a baby. I don't need to be fed."

"You may not be a baby, but at the moment you're acting like one. You've been burned, not incapacitated for life. There's nothing wrong with accepting a little help until you can manage on your own."

He whirled on her. "And when in hell will that be? I've been doing your damned exercises."

"Since yesterday," she reminded him.

He ignored her reasonable response, clearly determined to sulk. "Nothing's changed. I still can't even open a damned carton of milk."

She regarded him with undisguised curiosity. "Do you actually like lukewarm milk?"

"No," he admitted. "I hate the stuff."

"Then what's the big deal?"

He scowled, but she could see a faint flicker of amusement in his eyes before he carefully banked it and returned to his study of the foggy day outside. "It's the principle."

"Pretty stupid principle, if you ask me."

"Who asked you?"

"Call me generous. I like to share my opinions."

"Share them somewhere else where they're appreciated. I'm sure there are a dozen places on this corridor alone where Saint Jennifer's views would be welcomed."

The barb struck home. It wasn't the first time she'd been accused of being a Pollyanna, of nagging where she wasn't wanted. It came with the job. Even so, she had to swallow the urge to lash back. Forcing a breezy note into her voice, she said, "You probably wouldn't be nearly this cranky if you'd had your breakfast. Come on. If you don't squeal on me, I'll treat you to a couple of doughnuts and a cup of coffee in the therapy room. I guarantee there won't be anything you have to open. And the doughnuts are fresh. I stopped at the bakery on the way in."

He turned finally and regarded her warily. "Are you trying to bribe me into coming back to therapy?"

"I'm trying to improve your temper for the benefit of the entire staff on this floor. Now come along."

Blue eyes, which had been bleak with exhaustion and defeat, sparked briefly with sheer devilment. "Do I have a choice?" he inquired, his voice suddenly filled with a lazy challenge.

"You do, but just so you know, the wheelchair's right outside."

"And Otis?"

"He's within shouting distance, but I didn't think I'd need

him today." Her gaze held a challenge of its own. She could practically see the emotions warring inside him as he considered his options. She pressed a little harder. "So, are you coming or not? I have jelly doughnuts. Or chocolate. There's even one that's apple-filled."

Temptation won out over stubbornness. She could see it in the suddenly resigned set of his shoulders. Apparently she'd hit on a weakness with those doughnuts.

"You are a bully," he accused, but he followed her from the room.

"Takes one to know one. What's it going to be jelly, chocolate or apple?"

"Jelly, of course. You could probably see my mouth watering the minute you mentioned them."

"I did sense I had your attention."

"Why do you do this?" he asked as they walked down the hall.

"Buy doughnuts?"

The evasion earned a look of disgust. "You know what I meant."

"They pay me to do it."

"So you've said. I'm more interested in why someone would choose a profession that requires them to put up with nasty-tempered patients like me."

"Maybe I'm a masochist."

"I don't think so. What's the truth, Jenny Michaels?"

There was a genuine curiosity in his eyes that demanded an honest response. "Sometimes," she said softly, "sometimes I can make a difference."

He nodded at once with obvious understanding. "Quite a high, huh?"

She grinned at the way he mirrored her thoughts. "Quite a high."

He glanced sideways at her. "I'd guess the lows are pretty bad, though."

Jenny sobered at once, thinking of the patients who struggled and lost against insurmountable odds. "Bad enough."

Inside the sunshine-bright therapy room, she put two jelly doughnuts on a plate and poured a cup of coffee for Frank as he nudged a chair up to the table with some deft footwork. She sat beside him and encouraged him to talk about himself. As he did, almost without him realizing, she broke off bits of the doughnuts and fed them to him. More than once her fingers skimmed his lips, sending a jolt of electricity clear through her. He seemed entirely unaware of it, thank goodness.

"So you worked odd jobs from the time you were a kid and helped your mother raise all of those handsome characters I've met," she said.

"You think they're handsome?" he asked, watching her suspiciously. "All of them?"

She nodded, playing on the surprising hint of vulnerability she detected. "One of them is a real charmer, too. What's his name? Tim?"

"He's a little young for you, isn't he?" he inquired, his gaze narrowed, his expression sour.

Jenny chuckled at his obviously suspicious response to her teasing. "Who are you looking out for? Him or me?" She decided not to mention the third alternative, Frank himself.

"You. Tim learned to take care of his own social life long ago. It's very active."

"And yours?"

He suddenly looked uncomfortable. "Not so active, at least not lately."

"Why not? You're the best-looking one in the bunch," she said. She wasn't above using flattery to get her way, but in his case it wasn't necessary. Frank Chambers had a quiet strength and serenity about him when he wasn't raging at the universe. He seemed like the kind of man a woman could depend on. And everything she'd heard about him from his adoring family confirmed that. Plus, his slightly crooked nose, the firm, stubborn line of his jaw and the astonishingly blue eyes gave his face a rugged appeal. She'd always preferred that type to the polished professionals in their designer shirts, designer watches and phony smiles. In Frank's case the internal strength and diamond-in-the-rough exterior added up to a potent and very masculine combination.

"I'm astonished no woman has snapped you up," she said with honesty, wondering as she did so why she felt so glad that he was free and unencumbered. She never got involved with her patients. Lately, in fact, she never got involved with any man. Keeping her tone light and bantering, she added, "You're obviously domesticated. You probably even do dishes."

He shook his head adamantly. "Oh, no. Not if I can help it. That's probably the single greatest advantage I can think of having so many younger brothers and a baby sister. When I was younger, my turn to do dishes only came about once a week. If I was really on my toes, I'd land a job mowing lawns whenever it was my turn, or bribe one of the others to take it. Karyn earned more doing dishes for me than she ever did baby-sitting."

Suddenly his gaze fell on the empty plate and coffee cup. His expression became perplexed. "How'd you do that?"

She grinned at him. "It's all a matter of technique."

"That kind of sleight of hand belongs on stage."

"Hey, for all you know, I ate it all myself."

"Not a chance."

"How come?"

Before she realized what he intended, he scooted his chair closer, reached over and brushed the tip of one bandaged finger across her lips. The gauze tickled, but there was nothing humorous about the emotional impact. Jenny felt the sizzle of that touch somewhere deep inside. "No jelly," he said softly. "No powdered sugar." He looked suddenly regretful. "I almost wish there were."

"Why?" she said in a voice that trembled as she lost herself to the intensity of his gaze.

"So I could see if it tastes even sweeter on you."

Jenny's pulse skittered wildly. She swallowed hard and dragged her gaze away. Countering the rush of unexpected feelings, she was suddenly all business.

"Talk about distractions," she murmured, partly to herself. The sizzling tension shattered like fragile glass as she injected an energetic note into her voice. "All this talk has kept you from your therapy. Let's get to work. Do something a little more challenging. Try squeezing this washcloth."

She handed him a cloth that had been folded into a thick rectangular wad. With infinite patience, she closed his hand around it. It would be days before he could complete the closure, days before the tips of his fingers could comfortably touch his own palm.

Frank, obviously, didn't understand the difficulty. He shot her a look of pure disgust. "Any two-year-old can do that," he said, obviously ignoring the difficulty of yesterday's even less taxing assignment.

"Then it should be a breeze for you."

She deliberately turned her back on him, sat at her desk and attacked her paperwork. When his cursing turned the air blue, she smiled, but she didn't give an inch.

"You're doing this just to break my spirit," he muttered finally.

Jenny glanced up and saw the furrows in his brow as he struggled with the simple task. "Mr. Chambers..."

"Frank, dammit!"

"Frank," she said quietly, countering irritation with determined calm. "A rodeo bronc rider couldn't break your spirit. What I'm going for here is a little spirit of cooperation."

"Right," he muttered between gritted teeth. But when the time came for him to return to his room, she had almost as much trouble getting him to leave as she'd had getting him there in the first place.

Something astonishing had happened to Frank in that therapy room, while doing those ridiculous yet nearly impossible exercises. He'd decided to fight. Not in some half-baked way, either, but with everything in him. Maybe it was because the prospect of doing anything else didn't sit well with a man used to being firmly in control of his own life. Maybe the smoke had finally cleared from his brain so he could see things straight again.

Or maybe it was just that one flash of insight he'd had, when he'd realized that he'd do almost anything to earn Jenny's approval, to win one of her warm and tender smiles. He'd searched a long time to find a woman who was part hellion and part angel. And something told him he'd finally found her.

He was back in his room, still squeezing the devil out of that washcloth, when his mother turned up. He smiled at her entrance. She was sixty-two now and her once-raven hair had turned gray, but nothing had daunted her spirit. She came in with all the bustle of the briskest nurse on the floor.

"You've eaten your lunch?" she said, fussing around him.

"Hours ago," he said, resigned to the straightening of the sheets, the rearrangement of the flowers crowded on top of the room's small dresser, the quick check of the trash can to assure that the housekeeping staff was on its toes.

"Brushed your teeth?" She straightened up the things on his nightstand. Flicking away some invisible speck of lint.

He endured the bustling activity as long as he could, then said, "Ma, settle down."

Not used to being still, she spent about ten seconds in the chair by the bed before she was up again, fiddling with the blinds until they let in the pale light of the sun as it burned off the last of the day's fog. "You still giving that therapist trouble?"

"No."

She nodded. "Good." She shot him a pointed look. "She seems like a nice girl."

"She is."

"Pretty, too."

The description was far too bland to describe Jenny, but he nodded anyway. "Yes. What's your point?"

Shrewd blue eyes danced with amusement. "If you can't figure that one out, boy, there's no hope for you."

Frank nearly groaned aloud. If his mother got it into her head to play matchmaker, neither he nor Jenny would have another moment's peace. "Stay out of it, Ma."

The remark was met with startled innocence. "Out of what? I was just making an observation."

"Your *observation* is duly noted."

"Is she married?"

"Ma!"

"Okay, okay, you do what you want. You're not like your brothers. They're always looking. Saturday night doesn't pass, they're not out with this one or that one. There are times I think I did you a terrible disservice by giving you so much responsibility. Maybe you think you've already finished raising your family. I just thought maybe you needed reminding that Karyn and your brothers aren't the same as having a wife and kids of your own."

"Believe me, I'm aware of that."

"Are you really? You didn't exactly rush into marrying Megan. Kept her dangling long enough."

At the mention of his ex-fiancée's name, Frank felt a familiar tightness in his chest. "I don't want to talk about Megan."

"That's the trouble. You never did. You kept it all bottled up inside. Five years you dated that woman and then, poof, it was over. You never did say what happened, not even which one of you broke it off."

"And I don't intend to say so now. Megan is history."

"Then let's get back to the present. When are you seeing this Jenny again?"

"Ma!" The muttered warning gave way to a chuckle. "You're incorrigible."

She bent over and planted a kiss on his cheek. "There, then, that's much better. It's good to see you laughing again, Son. I've been worried about you. You've been entirely too glum these past few days."

"I'll survive."

"I know that. Even when you were a little boy, you were a survivor. Of all my kids, you were the one who never shed a tear. Your father used to say you'd been born with a stiff upper lip."

"Not so stiff," he countered. "Half the time, it was split from losing control of my bike on the hills and slamming into some wall or car."

They were laughing at the memories when Jenny came by. Frank saw her hesitate in the doorway. "You can come in."

"I'm so used to hearing shouts from this room, I wasn't quite sure what to make of this new cheerful sound. Thought for sure I had to be in the wrong place."

Frank caught the beaming smile of welcome on his mother's face, the speculative gleam in her eyes.

"Come on in, child. We were just talking over old times," his mother said.

"I could come back later," Jenny offered.

"No, indeed," his mother said. "You sit right over here." She shoved the room's only chair even closer to the side of the bed. "I think maybe I'll go get myself a cup of coffee."

Jenny backed away a step. "Really, it's not necessary. Maybe if you stick around, he won't grumble quite so much about the therapy."

"Don't you believe it. He enjoys shocking me with his language. He knows he's gotten too big for me to wash his mouth out with soap."

"Ma, you never once washed my mouth out with soap," Frank protested, enjoying the expression of amusement on Jenny's face.

"Only because you didn't use any of those foul words until you knew you outweighed me."

Frank turned to Jenny. "Don't believe her 'poor, pitiful me' act. She wouldn't hesitate to take on any one of us no matter our size or our age."

"That's the truth," Kevin said coming through the door just then. "She may be tiny, but she has us all cowed."

"Says you," Tim scoffed, entering right on his brother's heels. "I'm not scared of Ma."

Mrs. Chambers drew herself up to her full height, which was about as intimidating as a sparrow's. "Well, you ought to be, young man," she said sternly. "Where were you last night?"

Tim immediately blushed furiously. Avoiding Jenny's laughter-filled eyes, he said meekly, "I had a date."

"What kind of date lasts until three a.m.?"

"Whoa," Frank said, enjoying seeing Tim squirm. "Now you're going to catch it, baby brother. You know what Ma's like when she doesn't get her beauty rest."

Tim gave a dramatic shrug. He slid his arm around Jenny's waist. "Since I'm already in hot water, what are you doing tonight?"

"She's going home," Frank said, suddenly no longer amused.

Jenny's gaze shot to him, and her lips formed a mutinous frown. "Oh, really? Who made you the keeper of my social calendar?"

Frank's eyes narrowed. His voice dropped. "Do you want to go out with him?"

"Oh, for heaven's sake," she said with a shake of her head that set her curls bounding indignantly. "Whether I do or I don't is not something I intend to discuss in front of a roomful of people."

"We could go outside," Tim said at once, his eyes bright with mischief.

"You do and I'll be right behind you," Frank countered.

His gaze locked with his brother's. In that instant of masculine challenge, a clear message was sent and received. Tim draped an arm around his mother's shoulders. "Come on, Ma, I guess it's you and me, after all. Kevin, you, too."

"But we just got here," Kevin grumbled.

"Now," Tim said with the kind of firm diplomacy that would have made him the perfect State Department emissary. Of course, the family liked to tease him that by the time he finished law school, he'd probably be too old to board a plane, anyway.

Blessed silence descended the minute they were gone. Jenny began inching backward toward the door.

"Sometimes, they're a little overwhelming," Frank said. "But they mean well."

"I can see that."

"Did you come by for a reason?"

"I just wanted to check and see how things were going with your therapy before I took off for the night. They should be in soon with your dinner tray."

"Do you follow all your patients this closely?"

There was no mistaking the hint of pink that tinted her cheeks. "As a matter of fact, I do."

"Then why does it bother you that I asked the question?"

"Who says it bothers me? Look, if you're okay, I'll be on my way."

"I'd be a lot better if you'd stick around."

"And do what?"

"Talk to me."

"Your family could do that. Why'd you chase them out?"

"I didn't chase. They left. Besides, they talk to me all the time. I've heard all their stories. I'd like to hear yours."

Jenny sighed, but she stopped inching toward the door. "My stories aren't all that fascinating."

"They would be to me."

She stared at him, her brow knit by a puzzled frown. "Why?"

"Does there have to be a specific reason?"

"There usually is," she said with a distinct trace of cynicism.

"I'm not exactly likely to put any moves on you," he said, holding up his bandaged hands.

The remark earned him a genuine chuckle. "True."

"Then there's nothing to be afraid of, is there?" Frank wasn't sure why he was pushing or why she was so afraid. He only knew it was important to his soul in some elemental way to keep her from leaving. When she finally sat, even though she kept the chair a careful distance away, he breathed a sigh of relief.

"So, Jenny Michaels, exactly what makes you tick?"

Chapter Four

Frank scowled at the ringing phone. How the devil was any man with five interfering brothers and one doting sister supposed to get to know a woman? he wondered as the phone rang for the third time in the hour since he'd encouraged Jenny to tell him all about herself. It was not the first time in his adult life that he'd been faced with the dilemma. Which was probably why it had taken him five years to figure out that Megan was the wrong woman for him and another two months to let her down gently. She'd fit in so well with the entire family, he hadn't noticed until too late that she didn't suit him. He had no intention of making the same mistake again.

"Karyn," he told his sister after listening to five minutes of household-repair questions, "I love you dearly, but why are you asking me how to fix the sink, when you have a perfectly good husband? Is Brad out?"

He glanced over and caught Jenny's amused expression. Rather than seeming frustrated by the nonstop interruptions, she appeared relieved. In fact, she seemed to enjoy them. She tucked the receiver between his chin and his shoulder each time and eavesdropped blatantly.

"No, but my husband races sports cars and sells ritzy sedans,"

Karyn retorted. "What makes you think he knows anything about sinks? Talk about sexist remarks."

"Any man who can tear a carburetor apart and put it back together again in five minutes flat ought to be able to open a trap under the sink and clean out whatever's stopping up the drain. For that matter, you ought to be able to do it yourself."

Karyn sighed heavily. "With six brothers in the house, who needed to learn?"

"Now who's being sexist?"

"Never mind. I'll call the plumber."

"Are you sure the sink's actually clogged?" he inquired suspiciously.

"Well, of course it is. Why else would I call?"

"Maybe you just don't want me to feel useless while I'm lying here in my hospital bed."

"Frank Chambers, I am standing here in an inch of water and you're accusing me of lying?"

"It wouldn't be the first time, Toots. I love you for trying, though. See you tomorrow."

He heard her indignant huff as he signaled to Jenny to put the phone back in its cradle. "I swear to you I didn't ask you to stay just so you could answer the phone."

"It's okay. I love seeing you with your family. How many are there again? When they're all here, it seems like dozens."

"Five brothers. One sister. One brother-in-law. All trouble."

She studied him thoughtfully, her green eyes intent. "Something tells me you don't really mind," she said after a thorough examination that nearly left him breathless, despite its innocence. Never before had he been with a woman who had the uncanny ability to see inside his soul.

"Am I that transparent?"

Apparently she detected the nervousness in his voice, because she laughed and reassured him. "No, it's actually something you said the other day. You understood what I meant about making a difference, about being needed."

"You get the same fix from your patients."

"Absolutely."

"No brothers or sisters?"

"Nope. I'm an only child. My parents live back East. I don't see them that often."

Frank couldn't imagine what it was like for her being separated from the only family she had. For all his grumbling, he rarely went more than a day without dropping in to see his mother or one of the other members of the tight-knit Chambers clan. They all checked in daily by phone, just to touch base, exchange news or seek advice. To his occasional regret, the latter was growing increasingly rare.

"Don't you miss your parents?" he asked Jenny.

"Yes, but we were never as close as your family is. We love each other, and they're great people, but they raised me to be independent. When the time came, they nudged me out of the nest just like a mother bird does. None of us has ever looked back. Holidays generally give us enough time to catch up."

The phone rang again. Frank glowered at it. "Tell 'em I've gone to Tahiti," he suggested.

"You wish," Jenny countered, answering it and then putting the receiver next to his ear.

"Well, well," Jared said. "Look who's answering your phone at seven o'clock at night. Does she get overtime for that?"

Frank scanned Jenny's face to see if she'd overheard the teasing comment with its sly innuendo. She seemed awfully intent suddenly on settling just so in the chair by his bed. She smoothed her dress over her knees, crossed her legs, smoothed her dress again.

"She's not a nurse, and cut the jokes," he muttered to his irreverent brother. "Did you call for a reason?"

"I take it I'm interrupting something," he said with delight. "Did you share a cozy dinner of Jell-O? Maybe some fruit cocktail?"

"You always were the perceptive one. Why aren't you hanging up?"

"You've got me mixed up with Tim." Jared went blithely on, refusing to take the hint. "Want to talk about what color you'd like me to paint your house? I thought I'd take a couple of days off work and work on it. We've been talking about it for a while now. I was thinking something cheery, maybe bright yellow.''

The thought horrified Frank sufficiently to draw his attention away from the fascinating way Jenny's dress clung to her curves. He knew that Jared was perfectly capable of slapping on the most outrageous shade of paint he could find. The walls in his own apartment were the color of tangerines. The year before his bedroom had been neon green until his girlfriend rebelled. Frank did not want Jared near his house with a paintbrush unless he was on hand to watch every move and to inspect the bucket of paint.

''You paint my house yellow and it will seriously impair any plans you might have for a future family life,'' he warned as emphatically and discreetly as he could. Jenny's eyes danced with merriment.

''Okay, no yellow,'' Jared said agreeably. ''How about mauve? Maybe with green trim.''

Frank groaned. ''And have the place look like a damned bouquet of violets? You've got to be kidding. Do we have to discuss this now?''

''Absolutely not. We don't have to discuss it at all. I can choose.''

''Good God, no! How about white? Simple, straightforward, normal.''

''Boring,'' Jared retorted succinctly.

Frank glanced at Jenny. ''What's your favorite color?''

''Blue,'' she said without hesitation. ''Why?''

''The lady says blue. Bring the paint chips by tomorrow and we'll decide on the shade. Now go away.''

Jared chuckled. ''Your seduction technique has taken a fascinating turn, big brother. I wonder how Ma'd feel if she knew you were painting your house to impress a woman. She'd probably start ordering wedding invitations. Should I pass on this startling development?''

''Go to hell.''

''Night, pal.''

This time Jenny was slow to hang up the phone. Her expression was a mix of curiosity and astonishment. "You're going to paint your house blue on a whim?"

"Actually Jared's going to paint it."

"You know what I mean."

"It needs to be painted. Blue's as good a color as any," he said, determinedly making light of his decision to pick a color that might please her. He wasn't entirely sure himself why he'd done it. "With white trim. What do you think?"

"I think you're nuts."

"Don't say that to Dr. Wilding. He'll find some shrink and send him in for a consult."

The night nurse poked her head in just then. "You want anything to help you sleep tonight?"

Frank shook his head. "Nope," he said, glancing straight at Jenny. "Something tells me I'm going to have very pleasant dreams."

He held her gaze until he could see the slow rise of heat that turned her cheeks a becoming shade of pink. For some reason he enjoyed the thought that he could fluster the usually unflappable therapist.

"Maybe I'd better get out of here and let you rest," she said, clearly nervous at the intimate turn the conversation had taken.

Instinctively he reached for her hand, then realized he couldn't grasp it in his gauze-covered mitts. He drew his hand back, but held her in place with the sheer force of his will. "Don't go, please. It gets too damned lonely around here."

She shook her head. "I can't stay."

"You have plans?"

"No, not exactly."

She looked so miserable, he finally relented. "I'm sorry. It was selfish of me to ask. You probably can't wait to shake this place at the end of the day."

"It's not that. It's just that this…"

"This?"

"Being here with you, it's not such a good idea. I should never have stayed."

"Will it make the other patients jealous?" he teased.

Suddenly she looked angry. "Don't act as if you don't know what I mean," she said, marching toward the door. He could read the conflicting emotions warring on her face as she cast one last helpless look at him and left.

"Sweet dreams," he murmured.

Frank's dreams, however, were anything but sweet. He awoke in the early hours of the morning to the slow return of sensation in his hands. At first there were just tiny pinpricks of feeling. In no time, though, his hands felt as if someone had stripped off the skin and dipped them in acid. The excruciating pain blocked out everything else.

In agony he fumbled for the call bell and tried to press it. The effort cost him all his reserves of energy, and he wasn't even sure he'd succeeded in rousing anyone at the nurses' station. As he waited, he sank back against the pillow and tried to fix a picture of Jenny in his mind. Her image brought him some small measure of comfort as he fought to hypnotize himself against the pain.

He couldn't say that Dr. Wilding hadn't warned him. He'd always held the mistaken notion that healing meant an end to pain. In the case of burns, however, he was just discovering that the healing of the nerve endings brought with it a nearly unbearable torture.

The door opened and one of the night nurses peeked in. "You okay?"

"I've had better nights," he said, his teeth gritted together.

Her relaxed, middle-of-the-night composure was instantly transformed into alert briskness. "Pain," she said at once. "I'll be right back. There's an order in your chart."

The five minutes it took her to get the medication and bring it back were the longest of Frank's life. Even the shot, with its promise of relief, brought no immediate change. Nor did the nurse's soothing words. He tried to remember all those spills from his bike that he'd survived so stoically, but none had affected him like this. Nothing had ever hurt like this.

The door whispered open, but with his eyes clamped shut he couldn't tell if someone had come in, or if the nurse had simply

left. Suddenly the scent of spring flowers seemed to fill the room.
Jenny!

He opened his eyes. "What are you doing here at this hour?
It must be three or four in the morning." He winced as his hands
throbbed.

Still wearing the same bright silk dress she'd had on earlier,
she came closer. With cool, soothing fingers, she caressed his
brow. "It won't be long now before the shot kicks in. Think
about something quiet and peaceful."

Her voice was low, hypnotic, but he fought the effect. He had
to tell her…something. His aching hands kept interfering. He
fought the pain as he tried to capture the elusive thought.

"You knew, didn't you?" he said finally.

"Knew what?"

"That the pain might start tonight. That's why you stayed."

She didn't bother denying it, just pressed a finger to his lips.
"Quiet. Close your eyes."

Frank didn't want to close his eyes. He wanted to keep staring
at the woman who cared so much that she'd spent the night at
the hospital on the off chance she might be needed. Despite his
efforts, though, the medication began to take hold and he found
himself fading out. He fought for one last glimpse of Jenny,
who'd drawn the chair close beside him and was gently rubbing
his arm. Maybe his own weary eyes were playing tricks on him,
but it seemed for just an instant that he could see tears shimmering on her lashes.

He reached out to her, found her hand and touched her gently.
"Thank you."

At last he was able to relax into the pain, rather than fight it.
Finally, thankfully, the pain dimmed and he fell asleep. This time
his dreams were sweet indeed.

Every therapy session over the next couple of days was torture
for the both of them. It made the fire and those first days of
exercise seem like child's play. Though Frank was in agony, he
was stubborn. His therapy sessions were scheduled right after
the dressing changes when the medication was in full force, and

he was determined not to miss one. Jenny was equally unrelenting. She pushed, and pushed some more. He had to admire her spunk, even as he sometimes cursed her dedication and his own weakness.

He couldn't have pinpointed the precise moment when his feelings for Jenny began to change into something more than respect, when her magnificent, gentle spirit invaded his soul and made him whole again. Maybe it was when she was giving him hell. Maybe it was when she touched his bandaged hands with a gentleness that took his breath away. Maybe it was when he caught the glitter of tears in her eyes, when his pain was just this side of unbearable and neither of them backed away from it. Maybe it was simply when she sat by his bed and talked him through the endless nights. He didn't know quite what to make of the new feelings, but they were there and growing hour by hour.

"Go home," he said after the third night, when she'd stayed with him yet again. "You look lousy."

"Flattery will win me over every time." Her tone was light, but there was no mistaking the exhaustion in her eyes, the pallor of her skin. Even her bouncy red curls seemed limp.

"I'm not interested in flattering you. I'm interested in seeing you get some sleep. You can't stay awake with me and then turn around and work all day."

"I'm okay. I get home for an hour or so in the morning to take a shower and change. Then I sneak in naps in the staff lounge."

"Well, that certainly eases my mind," he said dryly. "Jenny, go home. If you don't, I'll skip therapy, my hands will heal like this and you'll be to blame."

"Oh, no, you don't," she countered. "I'm not falling into that trap. I didn't burn you and I'm not responsible for your recovery. My only obligation is to show you the way to get your strength and dexterity back. What you do with that information is up to you."

"Tell me, does this treatment you're obliged to provide include being mean and nasty?"

"When it's called for."

He grinned. "You think you're pretty tough, don't you?"

"Tough enough."

"Oh, Jenny, I hope you never figure out what a marshmallow you really are."

"A marshmallow?" she said indignantly. "You're not in here wallowing in self-pity anymore, are you?"

"No."

"And who badgered you out of it?"

"You did," he said dutifully. "But, lady, you don't know the meaning of badgering until you've seen what I'm capable of. Go home."

Her chin rose a stubborn notch. "And if I don't?"

"I have the name and number of the director of physical therapy right here." He patted the pocket of the pajamas he'd had Jared bring him when he could stand the flapping, indecent hospital gown no longer.

Those impudent, saucer eyes of hers widened. "You wouldn't dare," she said.

He folded his arms across his chest and grinned. "Just try me."

"That's blackmail."

"I prefer to think of it as tough love."

At the mention of love, Jenny went absolutely still. Her previous serene eyes were filled with a riot of emotions. "You're breaking that vow."

"What vow? I don't remember any vow. You must be hallucinating. Due to lack of sleep, no doubt."

"In this very room. Two nights ago. You were muttering in your sleep."

"Ahh," he said knowingly. "So, now I'm the one who was asleep. You can't hold me accountable for what I said then."

She glared at him. "You woke up and said...something."

"And what did you say to this incredible declaration of... something?"

"I told you that all patients feel that way."

His gaze narrowed. *"All patients?* I am not just any old patient, Jennifer Michaels."

She sighed heavily. "I didn't mean it that way. Why are you doing this? You swore you'd drop this crazy idea that you..." She hesitated, stumbling over the obvious word. "That you like me."

Frank did not recall a single word of the conversation she was describing, but that didn't mean it hadn't happened. The words seemed to reflect all too clearly the thoughts that had been on his mind a lot the past few days.

"Like?" he repeated. "Now there's a word without much oomph. No, Jenny Michaels, I can't say I *like* you." His low, suggestive tone left no doubt as to an alternative word choice.

"I'm leaving," she said at once.

His grin broadened. "Now I know the trick," he said smugly. "Mention love and you run like a scared rabbit."

"Nobody in this room mentioned love," she retorted. "And no one will, if they have a bit of sense."

"Yes, ma'am," Frank said as she stalked from the room.

But it was pretty damned hard not to fall in love with a woman with that much sheer audacity. He'd just have to keep his feelings to himself until it suited him—and her—to make them perfectly clear. While he was still in the hospital was not the time, but soon, though. *Very soon.*

Chapter Five

"Hey, Otis! You got a break coming up?" Frank called out as the orderly passed his room pushing Pam to her therapy session. Otis paused, and the teenager gave Frank one of those wobbly smiles that came close to breaking his heart. He winked at her.

"In thirty minutes, why?" Otis said.

"I've got a deck of cards. Care to try a little five-card stud?"

Otis's eyes lighted up. "Stakes?"

"Matchsticks. Aspirin. Nickle-dime. Whatever."

A little of the gambling enthusiasm waned. "Better than nothing, I guess. Where'd you get the cards?"

"My sister. I told her I wanted to play gin rummy."

"Ah, a devious man after my own heart."

Frank shook his head. "No, a man who is bored to tears. Do you know how outrageous daytime television is? I'm not sure I could watch one more talk show deal with men who like to wear ladies' panties or women who've been tortured by drug-addicted kids. It's giving me a very peculiar and very depressing view of society. I will even stoop to luring you into a poker game to escape watching another one of those illuminating discussions.

God will no doubt punish me for my sins and for my shortsight-
edness about society's ills.''

"I don't know about God, man, but Jenny's gonna have your
hide.'' Otis chuckled. ''Mine, too. I'll be back in a flash.''

"Wait a sec,'' Pam said, a glint of mischief in her eyes. ''I
want to play, too.''

Frank and Otis exchanged a look. ''I don't know,'' Frank said.
''Leading Otis down the road to perdition is one thing, but
you're just a kid.''

"A kid on her way to therapy,'' she reminded them pointedly,
her dark brown eyes very serious.

"Meaning what?'' Frank countered, trying to contain a grin
at her blatant blackmail tactics.

"Meaning she'll blab her head off if we don't say yes,'' Otis
grumbled. ''She and Jenny are thick as thieves.'' He peered
down at her. ''You know, Pam-e-la, I just might decide to park
you in a linen closet and forget where I've left you.''

"You wouldn't dare,'' she said knowingly. ''If Doc Wilding
found out, he'd make you pay him back that ten you borrowed
to bet on the Giants' opening-day game. A game they lost, in
case you've forgotten.''

"For a skinny kid who's confined to a bed, you sure know a
lot,'' Otis grumbled.

"Enough,'' she said proudly. ''This place has more gossip
than *General Hospital*.''

"Okay, say we let you play,'' Frank said, studying the teenager. ''You any good?''

"I can hold my own,'' she said with what was probably sheer
bravado. Even wrapped in gauze bandages, she managed a jaunty
demeanor.

"You know a straight from a full house?''

"I know the full house wins. Four of a kind and straight flush
beat that.''

Frank grinned and relented, which he'd known he was going
to do from the moment she'd asked. Nobody could refuse a kid
like Pam, who was trying so hard to be brave and upbeat. ''Be
in my room in thirty minutes.''

Pam beamed. "You bet. Otis, don't you dare forget to pick me up in the therapy room."

The orderly shook his head. "No, ma'am. Wouldn't dream of it." He looked at Frank. "Something tells me the kid here is gonna mop the floor with the two of us."

"I'm not worried," Frank said. Not about Pam, anyway. However, he was just the teensiest bit concerned about what Jenny was going to have to say if she ever found out about the card game.

There was approximately ten dollars in change piled in front of Pam when he found out exactly how Jenny would react. His own neat stacks of nickels and dimes had been dwindling almost as rapidly as Otis's. It didn't matter since Jenny sent the entire supply of change flying with one sweep of her arm. The coins rained down like sleet, tinkling on the linoleum and rolling every which way.

"You two should be ashamed of yourselves," she said, glaring from Frank to Otis and back again, her hands on her hips.

"What about her?" Otis grumbled, turning an indignant look on Pam.

"I was winning!" the teenager protested accusingly to Jenny. "Why'd you do that? I almost had enough to buy two new magazines and a box of candy from the gray ladies this afternoon."

Jenny looked defeated and miserable. She sank down on the side of the bed. "I don't believe this. You've corrupted her."

"Corrupted her?" Frank said. "I'd like to know how. The girl has the instincts of a Las Vegas house dealer. She's a shark."

Pam looked pleased. Jenny didn't.

"And that makes it right?" Jenny snapped. "Couldn't you have played just for fun?"

"This was fun," Frank countered reasonably.

"But you lost how much?"

"A couple of bucks, less than I would have spent to go to a movie, and I can't even get to a movie."

"What about you?" she said to Otis.

"About the same."

"And added to what you've lost this week, how much does that make it?"

Frank interrupted before Otis could respond. "Look, it's my fault, okay? I was bored. I suggested the game. A little cash made it more interesting. That doesn't mean we're all candidates for Gambler's Anonymous."

"Maybe not you and Pam," she said pointedly.

Otis rose slowly to his feet. He glowered down at her. With his size, it would have made Frank think twice about arguing with him. It didn't daunt Jenny in the slightest.

"Don't you try to intimidate me, Otis Johnson," she said. "I thought you wanted to buy a new car, find a nicer apartment. How do you expect to do that if you keep losing your shirt on these crazy bets. Dammit, Otis, you promised."

It seemed a lot of people were making promises to Jenny that they weren't keeping. Frank almost felt sorry for her, but he wasn't sure what all the fuss was about. Making a few bets was no big deal.

"Ain't nothing crazy about betting on a flush, king-high," Otis grumbled.

"Did you win?"

"The kid had a full house. What can I say?"

Jenny sighed. "I don't get it. Where's the fun in throwing away your money like that?"

"Stick around and I'll show you," Frank offered.

"I'm not betting one dime in a card game."

"You won't have to," he promised. He exchanged a look with Otis who apparently guessed his intentions. The orderly suddenly glanced at his watch.

"Break's over," the orderly said hurriedly. "Come on, Pam, I'll give you a push back to your room. Leave those coins on the floor. I'll pick 'em up later."

"And bring me my share," Pam warned.

"Don't worry, kid. You'll get what's coming to you," he promised.

When they'd gone, Frank waved Jenny toward a chair. "Take

a seat.'' He nodded toward the cards. "You'll have to shuffle and deal. Just sit the cards in this contraption Otis rigged up.''

She scowled at him. "This is ridiculous.''

"You wanted to see why we think poker's so much fun. I'm going to show you. Deal. Five cards.''

He watched the way Jenny handled the cards and suddenly the temperature in the room seemed to soar about ten steamy degrees. He imagined those strong, supple hands working their magic on him. The effect on his body was immediate and downright uncomfortable. If Jenny had any idea of what the stakes were now, she'd have run for her life. Instead she shuffled intently.

"You might consider locking the door,'' he said blithely.

She shot him a startled look. "Why?''

"The game I had in mind isn't meant for observers.''

Her gaze narrowed suspiciously. "I thought we were playing poker.''

"We are. Strip poker.''

The cards hit the table with a smack. Her eyes flashed dangerously. "Oh no you don't, Frank Chambers. Are you out of your mind?''

"What's the matter?'' he inquired innocently. "Chicken? You have to admit it would be a whole lot more fascinating than nickles and dimes.''

"In your dreams.''

He nodded cheerfully. "That's as good a place as any to start.''

She bundled up the deck of cards and stalked to the door. "If I catch you trying to lead Otis and Pam astray again, I'll…'' She seemed suddenly at a loss for words.

"What?'' he taunted, grinning.

"I don't know, but you won't like it.''

His smile widened. "Bet I will.''

"You are impossible.''

"You wouldn't want to bet on that, would you?''

Jenny groaned. "I think maybe I liked you better when you were surly and unresponsive.''

"That's just because you don't trust yourself around me now."

"Oh, no," she said. "That's where you're wrong. In fact, that's one bet I'd take you up on."

"Liar," he taunted, but he said it to her back just before the door slammed behind her.

Okay, so she lied. Jenny wasn't quite sure what to make of this mellower Frank Chambers or her own response to him. Though his initial anger had impeded his progress at times, at least it was an emotion she understood. Now, suddenly, his personality had undergone a complete turnaround. He was joking with the staff, playing cards with Otis, no longer badgering the doctors for his release. He was hardly meek, but he was cooperative. She should have been grateful. Instead she was scared to death. He spent so much time in the therapy room these days, he could have taken over with the other patients. Whenever he was there, she had trouble concentrating. Her gaze kept shifting to him, and each time it did, her pulse raced.

As a patient in trouble, Frank had been someone in need of caring, in need of her help. Now she could no longer ignore the warm-as-honey, deep-inside response she felt to the sexy, generous man. The transition endangered her objectivity. Far worse, in the long run she feared it endangered her heart.

She was sitting in the therapy room stirring cream into her coffee when Carolanne came in and sank down in the chair across from her.

"What a day," the other therapist declared wearily. "It's days like this that make me wish I sold little cones of frozen yogurt for a living. No stress. No life-or-death crisis. No temper tantrums."

"Obviously you've never been around a three-year-old whose cone just upended on the ground."

"It couldn't possibly be any worse than this," she said fervently, then turned her full attention on Jenny. "Come to think of it, you don't look so perky yourself. Even your curls have lost their bounce. What's the story, or need I ask? What's the gorgeous Frank Chambers done now?''

''He invited me to play strip poker.''

Carolanne's eyes danced with amusement. ''Well, well, that is progress. Talk about incentives to get those hands working again. You've obviously inspired him. You should be proud.''

''Proud? The man terrifies me.''

''Because you're responding to him, right? So what's the big deal? It's about time you let yourself fall in love again.''

''Who said anything about falling in love? All I mentioned was a sneaky attempt to get my clothes off.''

''A man like that would not strip you naked in a hospital room unless his intentions were very serious.''

Jenny groaned and put her head down on her arms. ''This isn't happening.''

''What isn't happening?''

''Frank Chambers is not interested in me and I am definitely not interested in him.''

Carolanne nodded slowly. ''Okay. I think I get it. Nothing's happening between the two of you, so there's no reason for you to go crazy, right?''

''Right.''

''Then why have you added cream to a cup of cold water?''

Jenny glanced down and saw the murky white liquid in the coffee cup. ''Oh, dear Lord.''

''*He* might give you an answer,'' Carolanne said. ''But there's someone a lot closer who could really clear things up.''

''Who?''

''Frank Chambers.''

''He can't clear anything up. He's the problem.''

''Why?''

''If I knew that, there wouldn't be a problem.''

Carolanne looked more bewildered than ever. ''One of us in this room is going to be in need of psychiatric counseling very shortly, and something tells me it's going to be me unless you start talking plain English.''

Jenny drew in a deep breath. "All patients tend to form a bond with their therapist, true?"

"Yes."

"So what Frank thinks he feels for me is no more than a passing infatuation, right? Maybe mixed in with some gratitude?"

"That's not the look I saw in his eyes, but I'll go along with you for the sake of this conversation."

Jenny shot her a disgruntled look. "I should be used to that kind of reaction. It's never bothered me before."

Carolanne's expression suddenly brightened with understanding. "But it does this time, because you're falling for him."

"I am not!" Jenny's blurted denial echoed in the therapy room.

Her friend sighed. "If you say so, though why you're fighting it is beyond me. At least half a dozen nurses on the unit are taking bets on which one can win the man's heart, and he hasn't asked any of them to play strip poker. I'm going home to my simple, uncomplicated cat."

Jenny mustered a faint smile. "There is nothing uncomplicated about Minx. She's as neurotic as the rest of us."

"Speak for yourself," Carolanne said, getting her purse from her locker. She paused at the door. "Call if you need me, okay?"

"Sure. Thanks for listening."

When the other therapist had gone, Jenny tried to concentrate on some of the supervisory paperwork entailed in the job, the paperwork she couldn't seem to get done when Frank was in the room. She couldn't work up any enthusiasm for it now, either. An hour later, tired of fighting the inevitable, she headed back down the hall to Room 407.

Outside Frank's door, she could hear the deep rumble of conversation, the frequent bursts of laughter. Opening the door a crack, she peered inside and saw that he was once again surrounded by family. One of the men, a little shorter and stockier than Frank but unmistakably a Chambers, was holding up a handful of paint chips. It had to be Jared, she thought, grinning at the sight of all those shades of blue.

Just as she was about to let the door drift closed, Frank looked up, his gaze locking with hers. That jolt of awareness that came each time their eyes met shot through her. Her knees nearly buckled with the shock of it.

"Hey," he called softly. "Come on in. You're the one who got me into this. You have to choose."

Half a dozen pairs of fascinated eyes immediately turned to her. Jenny tried to ignore the not-so-subtle exchange of glances—from Jared to Frank to Tim to Karyn and yet more of the Chambers brothers she had yet to meet. The family resemblance was obvious, though.

As if they'd sensed her discomfort, every one of the brothers began to talk at once, spurred by Karyn's blatant attempt to distract them with what was clearly a familiar family argument. In the midst of the chaotic babble, Jenny's gaze sought Frank's again. The look in his eyes drew her closer. "Sit here," he said, sliding over on the bed until there was room on the edge.

Seated next to him, hip to hip, her pulse skittered wildly. He held out the dozen or so paint chips. "What do you think?"

The shades ranged from vivid royal blue to palest turquoise, from chalky Wedgewood to deepest azure. The one that drew her, though, was the clear blue tint that matched Frank's eyes.

"This one," she said at once, suddenly oblivious to the crowd of fascinated onlookers. She was surprised when a heated debate erupted over the choice.

"Why that one?" Tim demanded.

"I'll bet I know," Karyn said, meeting Jenny's gaze with a look of instinctive feminine understanding.

Jenny found herself grinning despite the risk of embarrassment. "I'll bet you do, too."

"Why?" came the masculine chorus.

"Never mind," Karyn said briskly, giving Jenny's hand a warm squeeze. "Let's get out of Frank's hair, you guys. I think he's due for another therapy session."

"At this hour?" Jared said, then blinked rapidly at a forceful nudge from his sister. "Oh, yeah. Just like the other night. Let's go, guys."

"Pretty intuitive bunch," Frank said when they'd swarmed out. "Is that what you had in mind, a little therapy?"

Jenny shook her head. "I'm not sure what I had in mind."

"Maybe an apology?"

Her defenses slammed into place. "From me? I haven't done anything to apologize for."

"No, but I have. I guess I didn't realize that you were really worried about Otis's gambling. I've been thinking about your reaction ever since you left here this afternoon. I'm sorry if I did anything to make it worse."

She shook her head, weariness settling in. "I shouldn't blame you. I can't run his life for him. All I can do is encourage him to get help if it gets out of hand. I have a hunch he makes it sound a whole lot worse than it is just to bug me."

"Has he ever borrowed money from you?"

"A few dollars before payday, but he's always paid it back. Other people around here have given him loans, too." She stood up and began to pace. "He's not a deadbeat, though. I don't think he's really in debt to anybody. If it were just a form of entertainment like going to the movies, I wouldn't worry so, but he seems a little compulsive about it."

"And I took advantage of that just to keep from being bored. It won't happen again."

"Thanks."

His gaze fastened on her. "So if you didn't stop by to drag an apology out of me, why did you come?"

"Must be your charming company." She tossed the words out casually, but she sensed that her nervous pacing of the room betrayed her. Frank seemed to see right through her.

"Want to tell me what's really on your mind?" he said quietly. He moved to where she stood by the window.

She wondered what he'd do if she simply blurted out that he was affecting her deeply in a way that made her long for things she'd nearly forgotten: love, family, companionship, romance. Not that she was likely to make that kind of an admission and damage their professional rapport.

"Maybe this?" he suggested, leaning close to brush his lips across hers.

The kiss was no more than the whisper of butterfly wings, but it rocked her. When his arms clumsily drew her closer, she stiffened, then relaxed into the wonderful sensation. His lips covered hers again and this time there was nothing sweet or innocent about the touch. It was all heat and hunger and claiming. If the first had been a gentle spring rain, this was all lightning and thunder. Just when she felt as if the world might be spinning off its axis, buffeted by the powerful force of that kiss, he pulled back.

"Of course, I could be wrong," he said in a voice that was meant to be light, but seemed somehow choked. The blue of his eyes was shades darker than the color she'd matched only moments before.

Jenny couldn't seem to catch her breath or to form a single sensible thought. She was still caught up in the taste and feel of that potent kiss.

"We could always play poker," he teased, when she remained silent.

She finally found her voice and even managed a little feigned indignation. "Forget it. I hid the cards."

"If you really want to stick around, we could watch TV."

That struck her as innocuous enough. "Okay."

Frank moved back to the bed and hit the remote control to turn it on. "There's room next to me, if you'd care to snuggle up."

That kiss made her cautious. She grinned and pulled up the chair. "Don't press your luck."

"Too bad there's no popcorn. What's a movie date without popcorn?"

The cozy image was too appealing to ignore. "I could go get some from the vending machine and put it in the microwave."

"Do you want some, too?"

She thought about it and nodded. "Yes, as a matter of fact. I'm starved."

It wasn't until she'd come back with the popcorn and the sodas that she realized exactly how devious Frank's suggestion really was. The only way he could eat the buttery kernels was if she sat next to him on the bed and fed them to him.

"You're a sneak," she accused as she perched uneasily by his side. "And don't turn that innocent look on me. You're about as innocent as Don Juan."

"You didn't have to share the popcorn," he argued.

"Sure. I could have stayed in the chair, munched away and watched you pout."

"You wouldn't have done that."

"You think you know me pretty well, don't you?"

"Well enough."

"And?"

"I think you've finally decided to stop fighting me."

Jenny sighed and gave herself up to the unfamiliar feeling of contentment that was stealing over her, to the memory of that intense kiss. "Just for tonight."

For once, Frank didn't argue with her. "That's a start, sweetheart. That's a start."

Chapter Six

Frank felt as if he'd been sucker-punched. After days of progress, after days of focusing more intently on Jenny then on his own situation, he suddenly slammed into reality. The bandages were off for good, the skin healed over sufficiently to avoid the danger of infection. He stared at his badly scarred hands as if they belonged to someone else.

Sure, he'd glimpsed them during other dressing changes, but somehow he'd been expecting an improvement, some miracle that would cause the scars to vanish overnight. Now Dr. Wilding was telling him matter-of-factly that wouldn't happen, that the redness would fade eventually, but the scarring was permanent. He tried to imagine spending the rest of his life with this kind of disfigurement. He'd thought it wouldn't bother him. Now his stomach churned at the prospect.

"Not bad," the doctor murmured in satisfaction. "You can think about plastic surgery, skin grafting, if you like, but I don't think you'll see much improvement over this or I would have recommended it sooner. You're lucky, young man. It could have been worse."

Lucky? What was lucky about having hands that ought to be covered with gloves around the clock? He tried to remind himself of the way they'd looked before, of the nicks and cuts, the calluses that had made his work-roughened hands anything but picture perfect. Even that had been a hell of an improvement on this.

Frank finally tore his gaze away from the fresh scars and dared to meet Jenny's eyes. His whole body tensed as he waited for some faint sign of repulsion.

She was frowning, her lower lip caught between her teeth, but he'd come to realize over the past few days that she did that often, whenever she was worried or deep in thought. Slowly her lips curved into a familiar reassuring smile. It reached all the way to her incredible eyes, but Frank wasn't convinced. Doubts very nearly overwhelmed him. What woman would ever want hands like this touching her? He tried to imagine the tight red skin against the perfect pale silk of Jenny's breasts, the curve of her hip, but his imagination failed him.

The anger of those first awful days, the doubts he'd had before about his professional future, were nothing compared to the agonizing emptiness that now stole into his soul. He would never know the sweetness of an intimate moment like that, never to allow himself to sully her perfect beauty with his ugliness.

There was a bitter irony to discovering a woman he could love, only to realize that a relationship between them could never happen. Gentle, tenderhearted Jenny was filled with compassion, not just for him but for the entire world. He'd seen it in the way she cared for her other patients, in the way she worried about Otis. It was sweet temptation to let himself bask in that warmth, to accept her pity and call it love.

He couldn't do it. Filled with a raging anger at the injustice, he vowed he wouldn't. He steeled himself against all the longings that had been building for the past days. It would take every bit of his strength not to act on the desire that teased his senses whenever she was near. That one deep, drugging kiss they had shared the night before would never be repeated, not if he could help it. The minute those discharge papers were signed, he'd walk out of this hospital and out of her life.

* * *

As the last days of his hospital stay passed, Jenny knew exactly what was going through Frank's mind. She'd seen it all before. She recognized that gut-deep uncertainty that had him shouting at everyone within range again. The reaction might be typical, but in Frank it was magnified a thousand times because of the kind of man he was. Used to creating flawless beauty, he was being forced to come to grips with imperfection. It might be superficial and unimportant in her eyes or anyone else's, but to his artistic view that first this-is-it view of his burn-scarred hands must have seemed devastating.

After that one instant of raw anguish she'd read in his eyes when the bandages had come off for good, he'd shut himself off from her—maybe even from himself. For the past three days he had come into the therapy room on schedule, but he'd barely spoken. Today was more of the same.

He sat now, his back rigid, doing his exercises with ferocious intensity, oblivious to the beads of sweat forming on his brow, ignoring the tension that was evident in the powerful muscles across his shoulders. When she could stand it no longer, she pulled out the chair next to his and sat. Her heart aching for him, with one hand she reached over and stilled his.

"Enough," she said.

The quiet order brought his head up, his combative gaze clashing with hers. She sensed he was about to argue, but then his gaze slid away. He slowly and deliberately withdrew his hands and hid them beneath the table, his emotional and physical retreat complete.

"No," she insisted and held out her hand. "Please don't ever hide from me. Don't hide from anyone."

As she waited, she could hear each tick of the clock as its big hands clicked off the passing minutes. Finally, an eternity later, Frank put his hands back on the table. Jenny took the right one in hers and gently stroked the marred skin. The muscles in his forearm jerked, then stilled. His jaw clenched, but this time he didn't draw away from her. Nor did he look at her.

"Such wonderful, powerful hands," she murmured. "I've

been to see your work, you know. I've never seen anything so beautiful.''

"That's over now," he said, his expression bleak.

"You know better than that," she said impatiently. "You've had a temporary setback because of the fire, that's all. You'll work again. You're improving every day. Can't you see that?''

He shrugged with clearly feigned indifference. "Maybe. Maybe not.''

She studied him, the way he avoided looking at her, the way he glanced at his hands—and hers—then at the floor, his dismay evident. "You're worried about how the scars look, aren't you?" When he started to shake his head in denial, she stopped him. "No. Don't even try to deny that little bit of vanity. It's perfectly natural.''

He regarded her with angry astonishment. "You think this is about something as trivial as my vanity?''

"Isn't it? We're the sum of all our parts, you know, not any one. Yet we have a way of focusing totally on what we perceive as our flaws.''

She watched him closely, trying to gauge his reaction. His eyes were shuttered. "Have you ever noticed that?" she prodded. "We're the first to mention an imperfection in ourselves, to draw attention to it, joke about it, just to let everyone know we're aware of it, just to get in the first critical remark. You've heard women joke about their thighs or men kid about their baldness. They want the world to know it doesn't matter to them, when what they're really proving is that it does matter terribly...to them.''

Frank listened attentively, but his expression remained skeptical. Not even her touch seemed to reassure him. She tried again to coax him out of his self-pity.

"If you let the scars become important to you, then they'll be important to everyone you know. Accept them, Frank. Accept them, just the way you do the color of your eyes and the beat of your heart. They're a part of a man who's very special.''

As she spoke she could feel her throat clog with emotions she rarely allowed herself. Her words had a too familiar ring, dredging up old hurts, old emotions she had thought long buried. A tear clung to her lashes, then spilled down her cheek. When the dampness fell onto Frank's hand, he lifted a startled gaze to meet hers. Whatever he was feeling, though, he covered it, as usual, with anger.

"What the hell do you know about it?" he demanded roughly. "Is this lesson number ten on the road to recovery? It's all so pat. You're good, Jenny. I'll give you that. You almost had me believing you. The tears did it. Did you major in therapy and minor in acting?"

This time she was the one jerking away. This time she was the one who could feel the fury building up like the winds of a hurricane. "Damn you!"

"Someone beat you to it. I've already been damned. I look at these hands and all I see is the ugliness, all I feel is the pain. How can you even bear to touch them?"

"What you feel is self-pity, you arrogant, self-centered jerk!"

For the first time in her career, Jenny allowed her fury to overrule her professional demeanor. It felt wonderful. She couldn't have banked the anger now if her entire career had depended on it. Emotions that had little to do with Frank and much to do with her own tattered pride came pouring out.

"Do you think you're the only person ever to be badly scarred? Do you?" she demanded. "There are a dozen patients in the unit right now who are worse off than you. Some will have hideous facial scars that no amount of surgery will fix. Some will be lucky to survive at all."

He waved a hand dismissively. "I'm not talking about them. I know that compared to them I'm damned fortunate. I look at Pam and it makes me sick to think what she'll go through. Right now, though, I'm talking about you. Where do you get off telling me or any one of the others how to feel, how to live our lives and accept ourselves? I'm sick of the platitudes, sick of the condescension."

She stared at him in astonishment. "Condescension? You think that's what this is all about? Damn you, Frank Chambers hasn't it ever occurred to you that I could know exactly how you feel? *Exactly!* Maybe my scars aren't visible, but they're there.''

He opened his mouth, but she cut him off, her outrage unmistakable. ''You listen to me for once,'' she insisted. She sucked in a deep breath, then said more quietly, ''When they cut off my breast to rid me of cancer, they left me with an ugly gash across my chest. Oh, the surgeon was good enough. He prettied it up with neat stitches, but there's no mistaking that kind of wound. You try telling me, telling any woman that losing a breast doesn't matter. Try telling us we're still whole. We won't believe you. Every swimsuit ad, every television commercial, says otherwise. We know what feminine beauty is all about.''

She was barely aware of Frank's sudden indrawn breath, the tenderness that instantly replaced cold fury in his eyes.

''Don't you get it?'' she asked him. ''We can only learn to live again when we can say it to ourselves, when somewhere deep inside we do believe that we're whole and attractive despite the scars. So, don't you act like some macho jerk because your hands aren't pretty. You'll live, dammit, and in the end that's the only thing that matters.''

''I'm sorry,'' Frank whispered, his voice ragged. He was shaken to the very depths of his being by Jenny's astonishing tirade and even more unexpected revelation. When she turned away, when she would have run, he grabbed her, oblivious to his own pain, tormented by hers and the inadvertent way he'd added to it.

''Don't you know how beautiful you are?'' he said, holding her. He raised his fingers to her cheek, hesitated, then forced himself to caress the silken curve of her jaw, knowing as he did so that from this moment on he would be lost. There would be no turning back now from the love he felt for her, from his need to protect and cherish her. He wouldn't be able to make the noble sacrifice of walking away, not when she was filled with so much pain, so many doubts of her own. ''Don't you know how proud any man would be to be with you?''

A deep sigh shuddered through her, but still she wouldn't look at him. Her gaze was fixed firmly on the floor as if there were something in the pattern of the tiles more fascinating than anything he could possibly say.

"Jenny, I'm sorry. I'm sorry for being such a fool."

She sighed heavily and her arms slid around his waist. She pressed her cheek, damp with tears, against his chest. "You don't get condemned to hell for being a fool," she muttered finally.

"Maybe not by God," he agreed. "How about by you?"

She lifted her head then, very slowly. More tears had welled in her eyes and were spilling down her cheeks. "I've never condemned you for hurting, Frank. I've just wanted to make it stop. I've just wanted you to know that I understood what you're going through. It's not easy picking up the pieces and going on when life slams you with a setback like you've had, but you have to do it. Sooner or later, you have to let go of the anger and do whatever needs to be done."

"And have you done that?" he asked, certain that she hadn't been nearly as good at taking the advice as she was at dishing it out. "Have you let go of the anger?"

"Most of the time. Maybe it's easier for me, because I can hide the scar. I don't have to deal with it, not out loud."

He studied her closely and sensed that there was so much she wasn't saying, so much she might not even be admitting to herself. "But out loud isn't the hard part, is it?"

She gave him a wobbly smile. Like Pam's brave attempts, it shattered his heart.

"No," she admitted. "It's what happens deep inside in the middle of the night. That's when there's no stopping the doubts, no holding back the terror."

As Frank held her, he prayed she could feel the compassion surround her, strengthen her if only she'd let it. For some reason, though, he could tell she was holding back, refusing to take what he was offering.

"Have you been with a man since the surgery?" he asked out of the blue, guessing suddenly at the real reason for her torment. Some fool had fed her doubts, had failed to offer the reassuring touch that she had just offered him. His voice was gentle, but from her instantaneous transformation, he saw that the question ripped through her defenses and opened old wounds. Jenny reacted to the raw pain with instantly renewed fury.

"How dare you ask me that? Have you forgotten what our relationship is? It's professional. I'm a therapist. You're my patient. No more. That doesn't entitle you to pry into my personal life."

"You opened the door. From the first day you walked into my room, we've both known there was something more between us, something we couldn't walk away from if we tried."

"No," she denied too quickly. She raised her hands as if to ward off any further painful intrusions. "You're wrong."

Backing away from him, from the emotions, she said, "I have to go. Dr. Wilding intends to discharge you in the morning. I'll try to come by before you leave."

But she didn't come by. Frank waited, watching the door all morning. When he could stand it no longer, he left his room and walked down the hall to the therapy room. Otis was standing just outside the door.

"Hear you're going home today," the orderly said. "How am I supposed to win any money with you gone?"

"I'm afraid my gambling days are over."

"So she got you, too?" he asked with a chuckle. "That woman thinks she can save the whole wide world. She's got a good heart." Eyes the color of melted chocolate watched Frank's reaction. "You ain't mistaking that for something else, are you?"

Frank shook his head. What he felt for Jenny was no mistake. What she felt for him was just as powerful. He had to convince her of that. He had to apologize, though, for the way he'd intruded so crudely into her personal life last night, asking questions that he hadn't led up to first with flowers and sweet words to prove how much he cared. He had to show her that there was no need for secrets between them. He had to know if some foolish man had shattered her fragile self-esteem with a careless remark, a flicker of revulsion at the sight of her scars. He would spend the rest of his life making that up to her, proving that she was all woman, both inside and out.

"Is she in there now? I need to see her."

"She's with a patient." He didn't move an inch, his body blocking the door.

Frank's gaze narrowed. "Otis, did she say something to you about me?"

The orderly's expression remained perfectly bland, but there was no mistaking the streak of protectiveness in his stance. "Is there something to say?" he countered.

Frank sighed. "No. Nothing. Tell her I'll be in my room another hour or so. Kevin's picking me up on his lunch hour."

Jenny had recognized what was happening with Frank even before last night. Hell, she and Carolanne had even talked about it. She'd had patients think they were in love with her before. She'd blithely ignored their protestations, knowing that as soon as the link of therapy was broken, they would resume their old lives. They had. And once Frank left today, he would be no different.

Except in her heart. Something about the wonderful, foul-tempered beast had gotten to her. He had so much love to give. He was a living monument to the theory that the more love you gave, the more you had to give. She'd never met a man who had more people relying on him and who thrived on it so.

For nearly two weeks now she'd been on the fringes of all that love and loyalty, and she'd felt like a kid with her nose pressed to the window of a toy store. But as much as she'd come to care for Frank, as recklessly as she'd indulged in her fantasies about sharing the warmth of his family, a life for the two of them simply wasn't in the cards. Once he'd coped with his own scars, she wouldn't burden him with hers.

She hadn't planned to tell him as much as she had about the breast cancer. It wasn't something she hid from her friends, but it certainly wasn't relevant to their patient-therapist relationship. At least it never had been with any other patient. If they'd thought her compassion deeper than most of the staff's, they'd never seemed to wonder why. With Frank, though, a lot of things about that professional relationship were shifting like sands at the whim of an angry tide.

She was standing just inside the door of the therapy room when she thought she heard his voice. She could hear Otis's mellow tones countering Frank's. Her heart climbed up to her throat and seemed to lodge there. When it was finally silent again in the hallway, she peeked out.

"He's gone," Otis said dryly, "though why you'd want to be avoiding him is beyond me. I ain't seen a man so far gone over a woman in a long time."

"I think the psychological term is transference."

"Funny, I thought it was lust."

She glowered at him. "You can leave now, Otis."

"I've done my part, so you don't need to listen to what I have to say? I don't think so," he said, backing her into the room, his big hands shooing her toward a chair. "You sit for just a minute, miss, and let me tell you what I see here."

"Otis!" she warned.

"Don't you go all prim and proper on me. You and me, we've always understood each other, from the day I wheeled you down the hall to surgery and back again. You held this hand of mine and spilled your guts, so I guess I've got a pretty good idea what's on your mind now."

"Otis, I really don't want to talk about this," Jenny said.

"That's okay by me. You can just listen. That's a fine man who just left here. Any man who's got the love of a family the way he does has done something special to deserve it. You'd do well to hang on to him. If you don't, that's up to you. The way I've got it figured, though, you owe him."

She opened her mouth to argue, but he kept right on lecturing. "You're the one who single handedly gave him the will to fight. You abandon him now, he just might give up, and we both know he's a long way from being recovered. Now you can send Carolanne or one of the others over there to help him settle in at home, and you can assign one of them to work with him when he comes in as an outpatient, but that's the coward's way out. Maybe I'm wrong, but I don't think you're a coward.''

He waited a beat, his gaze expectant. Jenny could feel her cheeks turn pink. Satisfied with her embarrassed reaction, Otis nodded. ''I guess I've said my piece. You think about it.'' He turned on his heel and walked out, leaving her with more to think about than he could possibly imagine.

''But I *am* a coward,'' she whispered to his retreating back. She wasn't just running from Frank. She wasn't simply afraid of loving.

She was terrified she wouldn't be around long enough to make it last.

In her heart, she knew Otis was right. She couldn't abandon Frank now. If it took every ounce of courage she possessed, she would see this through to the end.

Chapter Seven

Frank stood in the doorway of his private woodworking shop at home, unable to tear his gaze away from two intricately carved, skillfully crafted cabinets in unfinished cherry and oak. He rarely did his cabinetry at home, but these had been special orders and he'd spent his spare time rushing to complete them. His dedication had saved them from the fire. He wondered, though, if they would ever be finished, if the twining flowers along the edges would ever reach as high as he'd intended.

His gaze moved on to the smaller, partially carved blocks of wood that sat amid the fragrant shavings on top of his worktable. Smooth, polished pieces, ready for summer gallery showing, lined a shelf along one wall. Each one was a triumph of his artistic imagination over nature. It wasn't until he'd studied the grain of the wood that he decided what shape it would take. It was as if each square or rectangular block spoke to his mind's eye. Stepping inside, he slowly approached the complete figures, his heart aching at the prospect of never again being able to create such beauty.

He'd heard it said that the first step in any difficult task was always the hardest, and this one had been pure hell. It had taken him days just to work up the courage to come this far. He'd insisted that Kevin shut the door to the back room the day he'd come home from the hospital. He'd skirted the room ever since, not even glancing at the closed door when he could avoid it. He'd spent the days going for walks. Long, exhausting walks. Nights, he'd lain in bed and thought of Jenny and a future that seemed even emptier without her. It was still impossible for him to accept that she hadn't come, that she'd meant it when she'd said there could be nothing between them. And he thought of the painful revelation that, to her way of thinking, might have made it impossible for her to come. He drifted to sleep eventually filled with terrible questions.

When he'd awakened late this morning, he'd known he could no longer put off the inevitable. He had to know just how bleak the future was, just how crippling his injury had been. Once he knew that, maybe he'd know what to do about Jenny as well, whether he dared to pursue her, whether he'd have the strength to help her face her own demons.

Now that he was inside the room with happier memories crowding in, risking it seemed like a lousy idea. Maybe it would be better not to know just how terribly inept his fingers had become. Maybe he should just accept that fate had intervened and set his life on a different course. But what course? What the hell would he do with the rest of his life if not this?

For years, beginning at the age of seventeen, he had taken safe, low-paying, unskilled jobs to help out at home. Only when his extra income was no longer needed had he dared to begin the uncertain career that had beckoned to him from the first time he'd held a stick of wood and been taught whittling by his Tennessee-born father. From the first day of his apprenticeship to a master craftsman, he'd been filled with a soul-deep sense of accomplishment. What if all that was truly over? How would he handle it? Could he go back to those other less challenging, less satisfying jobs?

Finally, when he could bear it no more, he reached for one of the unfinished pieces. Gritting his teeth against the pain, aware of the tautness of his skin as it stretched almost beyond endurance, he closed his hand around the chunky block. With an artist's tender touch, he rubbed his still raw fingertips over the wood, stroking it as if it were alive, caressing the rounded shape of a blue jay's belly as it emerged from the uneven surface.

There were those who said that it was possible to distinguish each fragile feather on figures he'd carved. On this piece he had yet to complete the basic carving, much less start the delicate detail. Fingers trembling, he reached for his knife. Slowly, painfully, he closed his hand around it, defying Jenny's warning not to rush his attempts to hold smaller objects, not to allow his expectations to soar too high. With grim determination, he touched knife to wood, only to have the sharp instrument slide from his feeble grasp.

With a muttered oath, he picked it up and tried again, ignoring the agony, ignoring the sting of perspiration that beaded across his brow and trickled into his eyes, ignoring the sick churning of fear in his belly. Again, the knife clattered to the floor.

With each faulty effort, with each demoralizing defeat, his determination wavered, but he tried again...and again. Sweat ran down his back. His arms and shoulders ached from the effort of trying to master no more than a firm hold on what had once seemed a natural extension of his body.

It was on his tenth try or his thirtieth—he had lost track—when he heard the whisper of sound. He turned to find Jenny standing in the doorway, her face streaked with sympathetic tears. The leaden mass that had formed in his chest grew heavier still at the sight of her brokenhearted expression.

"How'd you get in?" he asked dully, his shoulders slumping.

"I knocked. I guess you didn't hear me. I tried the door and it was open." With her distraught gaze fixed on his hands, she said, "You shouldn't be doing this. It's too soon."

"I had to try. I had to know the worst."

Something that looked like guilt flickered in her eyes. "I should have been here," she said, almost to herself. Her gaze rose, then met his. "You're my patient. I should have come the first day you missed your outpatient appointment."

"Why didn't you?" he asked accusingly.

"It just seemed so complicated. I kept thinking you would

come back to the hospital. Today, when you missed the second appointment, I knew there was no choice. I had to come.''

The weight of her guilt got to him. ''Don't go blaming yourself,'' he said, feeling a twinge of guilt himself. Had he known that staying away would bring her to him? Maybe so. Maybe the real blame was his. He said only, ''I knew the risk I was taking by not continuing the therapy. I figured a few days off couldn't matter all that much.''

''A few days?'' she questioned. ''Or were you really giving up?''

He shook his head. ''Not until today.''

Tears welled again in her eyes, but she blinked them away. ''I won't let you do that, Frank.''

Those tears were going to be his undoing. ''Don't cry,'' he pleaded, his own voice ragged with emotion as he found himself offering comfort to a woman whose slightest smile had come to mean comfort to him. He yearned to take her in his arms, to touch her as he had no right to touch her, to show her what she'd come to mean to him.

She started to speak again, then shook her head.

''What the hell,'' he said with pure bravado, hoping to win a smile, an end to the unbearable tension throbbing between them. ''I can always hold the handle of a saw. Maybe I can build houses.''

''You will carve again,'' she vowed. ''I promise.''

Grateful beyond belief that she had come at last, Frank was still in no mood for promises that might never be kept. In a gesture of pure defiance, he swept his arm across the worktable, sending wood and tools flying. ''No, dammit! Don't lie to me, Jenny. Never lie to me. Let me adjust. Let me get on with my life.''

A familiar mutinous expression settled on her lips, firmed her jaw. She swiped away the tears. ''What kind of a life will it be, if you can't do what you love?'' she demanded. ''You can't stop trying.''

''I can,'' he said, just as stubbornly. ''And I will.''

She sucked in a breath and stood straighter, every inch filled with that magnificent indignation that could have daunted kings or generals. He was no match at all when she declared, "I won't let you."

Frank's laugh was mirthless, just the same. "Jenny, there's not a blessed thing you can do about it," he mocked.

As if he'd thrown down a gauntlet in some medieval challenge, she marched into the room. "Watch me," she said, picking up the first tool she came to and slapping the handle into his hand. "Squeeze it, damn you."

Raw pain seared his flesh, but by instinct his fingers curved around the instrument, the skin stretched taut, the nerve endings on fire.

"Tighter," she demanded, her body pressed against him in a way that had him thinking of things far softer than oak, far more compelling than carving. The force of the desire spiraling through him shook him to the very core of his being.

Their gazes clashed, hers filled with furious determination, his own filled with God knew what revelation. When the knife threatened to slide from his grasp again, she folded her own hand around his, adding enough pressure to secure it. Every muscle in Frank's body tensed at this new and very difficult strain, but he refused to let go, refused to acknowledge the agony of the effort. Jenny was clearly willing to goad him into trying, and he was too stubborn and too proud not to accept the challenge. Nor could he bear the thought of her moving away. God help him, he wouldn't deny himself the sweet, sweet pleasure of her nearness.

"You know the drill," she said finally, her voice oddly breathless. "Ten minutes an hour."

"Who's going to be around to make me?"

"I am."

"Your job as my therapist ended when I walked out of the hospital."

Green eyes sparked with emerald fire. "Like hell. A condition of your discharge was that you continue therapy as an outpatient. If I hadn't come today, Dr. Wilding would have sent me over to find out where the hell you've been."

Despite himself, Frank's lips twitched with amusement. A whisper of relief sighed through him, and he felt himself begin to relax. "Think you're pretty tough, don't you?"

That earned a dimpled smile that faded quickly into a clearly feigned scowl. "You bet," she declared.

"And if I don't cooperate?"

"You don't want to know what kind of tortures I can invent for an uncooperative patient."

He chuckled, fully aware of the kind of tortures she could impose without even trying. His body ached from them. "Is that so?" he taunted. His gaze fastened on the lush curve of her lips.

"Care to test me?" she taunted right back.

"Lady, I intend to give you a run for your money." He winked as he said it, suddenly feeling better, more hopeful, even if hope was folly. "By the way, what do I get if I cooperate?"

"You get to work again."

"I had something a little more intimate in mind."

"I'll just bet you did," she retorted. As if suddenly aware of the way her body had molded itself to him, she backed away, a step only, but it was too far for him. Frank wanted to curse at the sudden deprivation.

"You finish that blue jay and then maybe we'll talk," she said.

"Talking is the last thing on my mind," he said bluntly so there could be no doubts about his intentions.

A blush crept into her cheeks, but her eyes were stormy. Hands on slender hips, she said, "Mister, if your hands heal half as well as your libido, you'll be in great shape in no time."

At the sound of a deep-throated chuckle, they both whirled around to see Tim lurking in the doorway. Amusement danced in his eyes. "Hey, Bro, what's this about a libido? I thought I had the reputation in the family for chasing skirts."

Disgruntled by the untimely interruption, Frank said, "Listen, *Bro,* you're interrupting my therapy."

"Oh, is that what this is? Where can I sign up?" He winked at Jenny, and the brazen little hussy winked back. Frank wanted to throttle them both as the charged atmosphere disintegrated.

Another few seconds of sparring, another half dozen words of challenge and Jenny would have been in his arms, maybe even in his lonely king-size bed just down the hall. A betting man— Otis—could have made book on it.

"If you don't get out of here in the next ten seconds, your broken arm will qualify you," Frank said grumpily.

Jenny shook her head. "Okay, enough, you two. I'm out of here. Play nice."

Tim's eyes widened at the teasing admonition. "You sound just like Ma."

"Is it any wonder, when you sound like a couple of five-year-olds?" She turned her very best, most intimidating therapist-to-patient glare on Frank. "And you, ten minutes every hour. Got it?"

"Have you ever thought of a career in the military?" he inquired.

"Why, when I have guys like you to order around already? Be at the clinic tomorrow. Bring your tools with you. We might as well work with the things that are relevant to you."

"Why not have the sessions here?"

There was no arguing the logic of the suggestion, but Jenny's instantly terrified expression spoke volumes. She wasn't about to spend an hour a day with him in his home, where they both knew that therapy would take second place to mounting desire.

"Policy," she said tightly, her tone daring him to contradict her.

Much as he wanted to, suddenly Frank didn't have the stamina for it. The previous hour had stolen the last of his reserves of energy.

"I'll be there," he said.

When she nodded, secure again in the victory, he added, "But don't think you're one bit safer there, Jenny."

Patches of pink colored her cheeks for the second time in minutes. Avoiding Tim's laughing gaze and Frank's challenge, she scooted to safety.

Only when she had sashayed out of the room, the determined picture of feigned self-confidence, did Frank collapse onto his workbench. He was exhausted with the strain of coming into this room, of confronting his frailty all over again. The swing of his emotions from hope to defeat and back again had taken its toll.

Tim's expression immediately turned worried. "You okay?"

"Just a little tired."

"From the therapy, or from the stress of keeping your hands off the therapist?"

Frank grinned ruefully. "The only interest the therapist has in my hands is their increasing manual dexterity."

"Sounds promising."

"Very funny."

Tim's expression sobered. "What about you? You're really attracted to her, aren't you?

"What's not to like? She's beautiful. She's bright. She's caring. She's gentle. She's sexy. And all she feels for me is pity." He said the last as a diversion, praying it wasn't entirely true, unwilling to admit it might be.

"I don't think so."

"You didn't see the look on her face when she walked in here an hour ago."

"Did it ever occur to you that maybe it was compassion, not pity? Jenny strikes me as a woman who feels things deeply. Maybe what she was feeling was the ache inside you. Anyone who knows you can see what kind of hell you're going through."

Frank prayed that Tim was right, that his own instincts about Jenny's susceptibility to him were equally on target. He regarded his brother curiously. "You know something, little brother? I think maybe I've been selling you short all these years. Under all that flirtatious, chauvinistic attitude beats the heart of a true romantic. I predict that once you truly fall for a woman, it's going to be a crash heard round the entire Bay area."

"God, I hope not. We have enough quakes as it is."

Jenny discovered that just because Frank was on her turf, just because he'd agreed to continue the therapy at the hospital's outpatient clinic, it didn't stop the lingering looks. Every time their fingers brushed, her whole body came alive. It was the most amazing reaction. She would have sworn that his were the damaged nerves, yet she felt as if it were her own that were healing. Contact meant only to guide took on a deeper meaning. She began to long for those casual, innocent touches, needing them for the good they did her, rather than the comfort and guidance they gave him. It had been years since she'd allowed herself to hunger for that kind of physical closeness.

She was careful, though, to make sure that there were always other patients around. When the scheduling failed her, she begged Carolanne to stay in the therapy room to finish paperwork.

"What are you afraid of?" Carolanne demanded. "Frank Chambers is getting too close, isn't he? He's tearing down that wall of reserve, brick by brick."

"That's about it."

"What's so terrible about that?"

"Yeah," an all-too-familiar voice echoed. "What's so terrible about that? I'm a nice guy."

With a fiery blush creeping up her neck, she turned to meet Frank's laughing eyes. Carolanne made a beeline for the door. "Traitor," Jenny muttered as her so-called friend left.

When Carolanne had gone, she bustled around the therapy room, giving orders, avoiding Frank's gaze, ignoring the thudding of her heart, the quick flare of heat deep inside.

"What'd you do last night?" he inquired casually as he dutifully began his exercises.

She blinked up from the paperwork she was pretending to read and stared at him. He didn't usually ask personal questions. "What?"

"I asked what you did last night."

"Why?"

He grinned. "What's the problem? That's a fairly typical question among friends. Fits right in there with 'Hi, how are you?' So, what did you do?"

She had to search her brain to recall what had filled the lonely hours until sleep had claimed her. "I read a paper on the importance of infection control in burn therapy."

"Sounds dull," he said, but he looked smug for some reason that eluded her.

"Actually it was fascinating." She launched into a desperate detailing of every word she could remember. She was only sorry the paper had been so short. More of the medical jargon might have dampened the unmistakable gleam she saw in his eyes.

"Still sounds dull," he said when she'd finished. "How come you didn't have a date?"

"Why the sudden interest in my social life?"

"I've always been interested in your social life. I've just never asked about it before."

"Why now?"

"Just scouting out the competition."

"There is no competition. You're not even in the running." The rapid clip of her pulse called her a liar.

So did the skeptical look in Frank's eyes. A lesser man would have been insulted. He apparently twisted the words to suit himself. "We'll see," he countered mildly.

Flustered, and determined not to let him see it, she moved to stand squarely in front of him and demanded, "Why are you doing this?"

"Doing what?"

"Trying to turn this into something personal. I can't continue working with you, if you insist on doing that. I'll have to turn you over to Carolanne."

"Hmm," he muttered thoughtfully. "That raises an interesting point."

"Which is?"

"If you're no longer my therapist, then you'd be free to go out with me. Am I interpreting this correctly?"

Jenny felt as if she were falling off the top of a very tall building with no net below. The sensation was heady but terrifying. "No. Absolutely not. That is not what I was saying at all," she sputtered with enough indignation to draw an unrepentant grin.

"You know what they say about ladies who protest too much."

Jenny might have slapped that smug expression right off his face, if she hadn't had just enough sense left to realize how he'd interpret that. "That's no protest, buddy," she said quietly. "That's a fact. You and I are patient and therapist or we are nothing. Is that clear enough for you?"

He smiled happily, which was not the reaction she'd been going for at all. "Very clear," he said cheerfully.

Why, if he was being so agreeable, did she have the feeling that she'd just lost a dangerous final round?

Chapter Eight

"I could really use some help from you in the kitchen," Frank mentioned casually to Jenny at the end of his third outpatient therapy session. "If you're not too busy, that is."

Jenny's instantly suspicious gaze shot to his. It was astonishing how deeply she distrusted his motives. Rightfully so, in this instance, he conceded ruefully.

"Meaning?" she said.

"I keep dropping those little microwave containers. Half the time my dinner ends up on the floor."

He made it sound as pitiful as possible, as if he were very likely to starve to death without assistance. The time had come to take drastic measures if he was going to get Jenny to begin trusting him outside the safety of the therapy room. For the time being, he wasn't going to worry about how trust might suffer when she discovered his sneaky, underhanded tactics.

"Couldn't your mother or Karyn help you out?" she suggested, a definite note of desperation in her voice. "Maybe your brothers could take turns."

Actually they had been doing exactly that, but Frank was not about to admit that to her. He didn't need their company. He needed hers. He needed the incredible lightness that his soul experienced when he was surrounded by her tenderness and optimism. He needed to give back to her some of the strength she'd shared with him. Most of all he needed the hot, urgent stirring of his blood that just being in the same room with her brought.

"Ma's been really good about bringing things over for dinner," he admitted. "It's getting them on the stove and then the table that's the problem. I don't want to tell her that, though. She'd just worry more than she already does. As for Karyn, she's left town with Brad while he preps for the Indy 500. She's a lousy cook anyway."

"That still leaves five brothers."

Fortunately Frank had anticipated all of her arguments and prepared. "Tim's working nights and he has his law classes all day. Jared's just started helping a neighbor paint his house. The others do what they can, but I want to be independent. I'm not used to having other people wait on me. If you could help me out a little, maybe fix up some gadgets so I could handle things better, I'd be able to make do on my own. A few more weeks and I should be past the worst of this, right?"

Suspicion darkened her eyes again. He could tell she was torn between that and the very real possibility that he hadn't had a decent dinner in days. "I'll come by tonight," she said finally. "About six?"

"Whatever's good for you. Consider it a treatment. Put it on my bill."

She scowled at him. "Don't be ridiculous."

"No, really. I want this to be strictly professional. I don't want to take advantage of you. I know how you feel about me not stepping over that line."

He sounded so noble, he couldn't imagine her not believing him. Even so, there was a long silence while she obviously continued to weigh his apparent sincerity against her doubts. "You can share the dinner with me. That'll be payment enough," she said finally, though she was clearly unnerved by the prospect of sitting across from him at a dinner table. She was staring at the wall when she made the offer.

"That'd be great," he said with a shade too much enthusiasm.

He quickly banked it, when her gaze shot back to him. "I mean, if you have the time."

"I do," she said curtly. "Shall I pick up the groceries, or do you already have something you'd like me to fix?"

"Surprise me," he said, his gaze locking on hers. He lowered his voice to a seductive pitch. "I really love surprises."

"Frank," she began, her voice filled with renewed doubts.

"Yes?"

She sighed. "Never mind. I'll be there at six with the groceries."

"Reach in my pocket and grab my wallet," he suggested. "There should be enough in there for what you'll need from the store."

She looked every bit as panicky as if he'd blatantly suggested they make love in the linen closet down the hall. "This is my treat," she said hurriedly, taking a quick, revealing step back.

"No. I insist. How can it be your treat, if dinner is supposed to be my way of paying you back for cooking it?" He fixed his most innocent gaze on her. "My wallet's in the back pocket." He helpfully turned his backside to her.

Jenny complied with the enthusiasm of someone told they could have a million bucks as long as they didn't mind a few electrical shocks during the snatching of it. Only a seasoned pickpocket had the knack for removing a man's wallet without intimate contact. But for all her gifted hand gestures in therapy, Jenny was no pickpocket, and the photo-crammed wallet was a snug fit.

His breath caught in his throat as her hand slid nervously into his back pocket. Clumsiness turned the move into a lingering caress. Heat roared through him. Every nerve in his body throbbed in awareness. Even after Jenny had the wallet and was extracting a twenty-dollar bill, Frank trembled. If she was equally shaken, she hid it well, leaving him to wonder just who'd been the victor in this devious war of nerves.

Only when she glanced up and he saw the riot of emotions in her eyes did he declare the victory for himself. She shoved the wallet back in his pocket with so much force, he was surprised the denim didn't rip.

"I'll see you at six," she said and raced from the room.

Laughing, Frank went down the hall in search of Pam. Aware of the monotony of a long hospital stay, he'd been dropping by after his therapy sessions. He found her in her room with the TV on, but her face was turned toward the wall.

"Hey, beautiful, how are you?"

Instead of greeting him with her usual courageous, perky smile, the teenager kept her face averted. Then Frank noticed that the bandages on her head were gone. He swallowed hard against the tears that seemed to clog his throat at the sight of the red, scarred skin stretched taut over her cheekbone.

Drawing in a deep breath, he went around the bed and pulled up a chair. "Where's my smile?" he demanded, looking straight at her. "I thought you'd be glad to see me."

She tried to turn away again, but he touched her shoulder. "Don't," he said.

A tear slid down the unmarred side of her face. "But it's so awful," she whispered, pulling a pillow over her head. Her voice was muffled, but he could make out the rest of her heartbroken words. "I didn't know it was going to be like this. I'd seen the other patients, but I thought I'd be different."

Frank moved to the side of the bed, tugged the pillow gently away and forced her to face him. Then he opened his arms. With a sob, Pam launched herself at him and clung. "I'm never going to have any friends. Never. And I can't blame them. Who'd want to look at this?"

"I would," he said, his heart aching. "You know why? Because nothing that's important about you has changed. Inside, you're the same wonderful, funny, feisty girl you always were. You know what Jenny told me once?"

"What?"

"She said that how we react to our own flaws will determine how others react to them, too. If you're very brave, if you concentrate on how beautiful you are inside, then that's what your friends will see, too."

She sniffed and looked up at him hopefully. "Do you really think so?"

"I know so," he said, praying it would be so for her, praying that she'd chosen friends who wouldn't cruelly abandon her.

"My dad can't even stand to look at me."

"Oh, baby, I'm sure that's not true."

"It is. He was here when Doc Wilding took off the bandages. He walked out and he hasn't been back. That was hours ago."

Frank wanted to curse the man's insensitivity, even though he could understand what a shock it must have been to see his once-gorgeous, vivacious teenager so cruelly scarred.

"I think maybe he's just hurting inside because of what happened to you," he said finally. "He's probably feeling a whole lot of guilt that he didn't do something to prevent it from happening."

"But the fire wasn't his fault," she replied adamantly. "He wasn't even home when it happened. He was away on a business trip."

"That's exactly what I mean. He's probably telling himself if he'd been there, it wouldn't have happened."

"He always told Mom not to smoke in bed. He told her," she said, her voice thick with sobs. She stared helplessly into Frank's eyes, touching his soul. "Oh, God, why did she have to do it anyway? Why didn't she listen?" And then in a low, sad cry, "Why did she have to die? I tried to get to her, but I couldn't, I just couldn't."

Frank felt as though every breath was being squeezed out of him as Pam revealed what had happened at home the night she'd suffered these terrible, disfiguring burns. He'd never known, never realized what torment this poor child was dealing with. It made his own injuries seem insignificant. For the first time since the accident, he realized how truly fortunate he had been. Pam had the additional burden of grief and guilt weighing on her, when recovery alone would have been challenge enough.

He stayed with Pam for what seemed like hours, rocking her in his arms, wishing he had the words or the certainty to swear to her that things would be okay. Finally he noticed a man only slightly older than himself standing in the hallway, his face haggard, his eyes red-rimmed. He motioned to him.

"Pam, honey," he said gently. "You've got company."

Pam slowly faced the door. "Daddy." Her voice quivered with hope and fear. This time her father didn't flinch, didn't look away. He moved to the other side of the bed and sat on the edge. Pam eased away from Frank and held out her hand. Frank held his breath until finally the other man grasped Pam's hand and pressed his lips to the scarred flesh. "I'm sorry I ran out before, baby."

"Oh, Daddy," she whispered.

Frank left them together, praying harder than he ever had in his life that they would be okay, that together they could handle the grief and anger and pain ahead.

He was greatly subdued when Jenny finally arrived at his house just after six. He led her into the kitchen, pointed out where things were, then sat at the table to watch as she immediately set to work. Her motions were efficient, yet he found them subtly provocative. Her quiet calm was soothing. There was comfort in her presence tonight, a comfort almost more important than the fierce longing that usually tormented him the instant she was near.

When the dinner was bubbling on the stove, she poured them each a glass of iced tea and sat down across from him. The look she directed at him was inquisitive.

"You've been awfully quiet ever since I got here. What's going on?"

"I saw Pam today after I left you."

She nodded, her own expression suddenly tired. "I heard you'd been visiting her regularly. She had a pretty rough time of it today. She said your visit helped."

Still troubled by the teen's anguish, he asked, "Will it get any better for her?"

"Not anytime soon. She has a lot of plastic surgery ahead."

Frank sighed wearily. "That poor kid. She could probably use some counseling as well. I had no idea how much she's been struggling to cope with."

"She's already seen the psychologist a few times. She'll make it. She's a fighter. She'll get past the shock of the scars and be ready to move on to the next step."

"That's what I told her. I found myself quoting you."

She grinned. "I'm glad something I said made an impression."

"Everything you said made an impression. I didn't always want to hear it."

"That's pretty much par for the course with burn patients."

He shook his head as he envisioned contending with emotional crises like Pam's day in and day out. "Jenny, why do you do this? How can you take it day after day? I know we talked about this before, but I'm just beginning to realize the toll it must take."

"It's what I do, the same way you're an artist. Can you imagine being anything else?"

"I suppose not, though I have been other things from time to time to help pay the bills."

"You've held other jobs," she corrected. "But only one career really means anything, right? I think maybe what I went through with my own surgery makes me even better able to deal with the fears patients have. I truly understand how scared they are, how damaged they feel."

The reminder of her cancer surgery surprised him. It was the first time she'd mentioned it since the day she first told him about it. He wanted to keep her talking, sensing that there were more things she needed to say, but probably never had. "Who's been there for you when you needed a shoulder to cry on?"

She dumped a spoonful of sugar into her iced tea and stirred it for so long he thought she might not respond. Finally she said with studied nonchalance, "Family, friends. Otis was with me when I went into the operating room. Usually the orderly just wheels you into pre-op, but he stayed right by my side until they put me under. I'll always be grateful to him for that."

Frank didn't even try to hide his dismay. "Your parents weren't here?"

She shook her head. "Actually I didn't tell them until after it was over. There wasn't any point in worrying them. There wasn't a thing they could do until I knew what I was up against.''

Frank regarded her incredulously. ''They could have been here for you. That's what families do. They share the bad times and make them a little easier.''

She gave him a faint smile. ''That's what *your* family does.''

There was just a hint of envy in her voice. Frank wanted to say right then and there that it could become her family, too. The thought slammed into his consciousness like a car going sixty. In an instant of absolute clarity, he knew that was what he wanted more than anything else. He wanted to marry Jenny Michaels and teach her all about love and laughter and family, as she had taught him about fighting back and recovering. Although his physical wounds were not yet healed, thanks to her his emotional wounds were very nearly a thing of the past. He knew that no matter whether he carved again or not, he would be just fine as long as she was with him to make his blood race and his spirits soar. He could cope with whatever the future brought.

He also knew that she would run if he suggested it, if he dared to hint at what he was thinking. He couldn't imagine why she was so terrified of him. He'd never before encountered a woman so skittish. Megan had found being with him and his family totally comfortable. And his one or two other reasonably serious involvements had been with women who'd been quick to accept the idea of a relationship.

Not that he was such a prize, he amended quickly. But most women found him uncomplicated and nonthreatening. He tended to say what was on his mind. The directness and lack of pretense appealed to women who'd encountered too little of either. Jenny was clearly the exception. She regarded him every bit as warily as she might a snake...or a notorious Don Juan. Who had created this distrust in her? Was he the specific target or was it all men? He had to understand her before he could expect to make any progress.

Jenny had moved back to the counter to roll out the biscuit dough she'd prepared earlier.

"Any special man in your life?" he inquired lightly, reopening a topic she'd successfully evaded in the past.

The rolling pin hit the dough with a thud. "I thought we'd discussed this."

"We did. Your answer wasn't very illuminating."

"Why do you want to know?" she said as the pin hit the dough again, sending a puff of flour into the air like late-afternoon fog rising on San Francisco Bay. Her gaze was carefully averted. Biscuit dough had apparently never been so fascinating.

"Curiosity," he admitted candidly.

"Prying is more like it."

"Let's try this from a different direction," he said. "How do you spend your spare time? You can't possibly read medical journals every night."

"Actually I could, but I don't."

"When you're not reading them, what do you do?"

He caught the subtle hesitation before she said, "I go to movies."

"Good. Now we're getting somewhere. I like movies." He listed several. She hadn't seen any of them. "What was the last movie you saw?"

She frowned, then finally named one.

"Sure," he said cheerfully. "I remember that one. It won an Academy Award."

She blinked at him. "It did?"

"Sure did." He paused, then added, "Last year."

"Oh." Her voice was meek. Her fascination with the biscuit dough increased. If she rolled it any flatter there wasn't a baking powder in the world that could make those biscuits rise higher than a silver dollar.

"So far we've accounted for one night in the last year that you didn't read a medical journal. Anything else?"

"Aerobics class," she said in a rush, looking ridiculously pleased with herself. "I take aerobics."

"And?" he prodded.

"And what?"

"There has to be more, I mean for a woman with an active social life such as yourself."

"We go out to dinner after class."

"We?"

"A friend and I."

"Must be a woman friend."

She glared at him. "Why must it be a woman? Men take aerobics."

"But if it had been a man you'd have told me all about him ten minutes ago to get me to shut up and leave you alone."

Ignoring his comment, she cut out half a dozen very flat circles and slapped them onto a cookie sheet, then put the tray into the oven.

"They'll do better if you turn on the heat."

She whirled on him then, flour-covered hands on slim hips. "I don't have to do this, you know."

"I know," he said very seriously. "Why are you doing it? Why did you come?"

"Because you asked me to. You said you needed help."

"I need you," he corrected.

She was shaking her head in denial before the words were out of his mouth.

"It's true," he insisted. "In fact, I think if I don't kiss that smudge of flour on your nose within the next ten seconds I might very well die."

She stared at the floor until he reached out with the tip of his finger and tilted her chin up. Her gaze was defiant.

"Do it, then," she challenged. "Just do it and get it over with."

He grinned at her attempt to stare him down. "You're not going to shame me into backing off, by implying that I'm pushing you into something you don't want."

A reluctant sigh shuddered through her. "Who says I don't want it?" she asked.

Frank was taken aback by the hard-won admission. "Oh,

Jenny,'' he murmured, drawing her slowly into his arms. With a sigh of his own, he settled his lips on hers. After an instant of stunned stillness, her arms circled his neck. Her body melted against his. Her skin was warm and flushed from bending over the stove. Her soft springtime scent drifted around them. She tasted of tea and sugar and a dusting of flour. It he held her in his arms like this for a lifetime, he knew his hunger for her would never be sated.

His fingers traced the line of her brow, the curve of her jaw. With each touch, she trembled. With each touch, his need built. One kiss would never be enough. He wanted to discover everything about her, every curve, every texture, every taste. His hand slid to her hips and tilted them up tighter until neither of them could deny the heat or the urgency. Then, without thinking of anything except the hunger to know every shape, every intimate detail of her body, he touched her breast, the caress as natural and needy as breathing.

With a startled cry, she broke free.

"No," she whispered tearfully, backing away. "No. This can't happen. Not ever."

And then she ran.

Chapter Nine

When the realization of what he had done slammed into him, Frank cursed himself for an insensitive fool. By the time he recovered from the shock of Jenny's anguished reaction to his touch, she had left the house, leaving the door wide open behind her. He raced outside and saw that in her haste to escape, she'd simply run, leaving her car parked halfway down the block. He took off down the hill after her.

He caught up with her at the corner. She was huddled under the street lamp, her arms hugging her middle against the chilly night air that plagued San Francisco even in May. She stood perfectly still, as if she couldn't make up her mind what to do next, where to go. With the silver mercury light filtering down on her through the fog, she looked lost and alone, so terribly alone. He reached out to her, but she seemed to withdraw to some safe and distant place he couldn't reach. As he put his hands in his pockets, Frank felt the painful wrench of her hurt deep inside.

"Jenny, please," he said urgently. "I'm sorry. I didn't mean to upset you. I wasn't thinking. I just knew how much I wanted you, how much I thought you wanted me. Let's talk about what happened, about why you're so scared. We can work this out."

"There's nothing to talk about," she said flatly. "Nothing."

The emptiness in her voice shook him, but the determination was worse. How could he fight that? "At least come back to the house," he urged as a first, crucial step. "It's too cold to be out here without a jacket."

As if to prove his point, she shivered. He pressed her then, afraid that she'd wind up sick if she stubbornly insisted on staying outside much longer. "I promise not to bring up what happened until you're ready," he said with reluctance. "And I won't touch you, if that's the way you want it."

Her eyes reflected her distrust and again he cursed himself. How much damage had he done in that one careless moment? In instinctively seeking to touch her breast, to discover every shape and texture of her, apparently he had reminded her graphically of her own fears of being an incomplete woman, her obviously deep-seated terror that she couldn't satisfy a man. Because she radiated such strength and self-confidence, he had forgotten that she was a special woman with a need for very special care, especially the first time they became intimate. He owed her all of the gentle tenderness that she had shown him when it came to his own scars.

Now he could only wait and pray that the damage of his gesture wasn't irreparable. Eventually a sigh seemed to shudder through her. Without a word, she began to slowly climb the hill. When she didn't stop at her car, Frank released the breath he'd been holding.

When they were finally outside his house, she stopped and looked up. The faint beginnings of a smile tugged at the sad, downturned corners of her mouth. "You did it," she said in a trembly voice. Tears she hadn't shed earlier sparkled in her eyes. "You painted it blue. I didn't notice when I came in."

"Jared finished yesterday. You chose the color, remember?"

She looked from the house to him and back again. "I was right," she said finally.

"About what?"

"It does match your eyes."

He chuckled. "So that's what Karyn's been gloating about. She guessed, didn't she?"

"She never said, but I think so."

"There's a touch of the romantic in you after all, isn't there, Jenny Michaels?"

She immediately shook her head in denial. "I'm a hard-headed realist. Ask anyone."

"You'd like to believe that, because it's safe, but it's not true," he said just as adamantly. "You have the same dreams as any other woman."

"What makes you think you know anything about a woman's private dreams, especially mine?" she said, a trace of anger in her voice, but an expression of undeniable yearning on her face.

"I know because you shared them with me in that kiss. We felt the same things, the same wanting not to be alone, the same need to love."

There was a spark of defiance in her eyes. "Chemistry. Pheromones. Lust. Not dreams."

"Oh, no," he said with certainty. "A woman like you could never separate the two. You would never let some casual lover get that close. You wouldn't take the risk of being rejected." He knew he was taking a risk himself by so bluntly stating the facts as he saw them.

For an instant, Jenny looked as though he'd slapped her. Then, to his relief, she began to laugh. "Giving me a taste of my own medicine, aren't you? No man's ever been that direct with me before."

He stared at her for several heartbeats, then said gently, "Maybe no man has ever cared as much as I do." He held out his hand. "Come inside."

It was ten seconds, thirty, an eternity before she sighed deeply and slid her hand into his.

Inside, Frank was careful to keep his distance, to let Jenny set the tone and the pace. The thawing of icy tension was slow, but eventually they laughed about the hard-as-rocks biscuits and savored the rich beef stew. They talked about old movies—the only ones Jenny really had seen—and about sports. To his astonishment, she was both an avid football fan and an ardent baseball fan. Unfortunately she foolishly preferred the Boston teams to his own 49ers and Giants. She cited flimsy statistics in support of her imprudent loyalty.

"I hope you don't actually bet on your convictions with Otis," he teased, relieved that they were close to recapturing the earlier friendly tone.

"I don't bet anything with Otis," she reminded him. "Though goodness knows, he tried to convince me to wager against him by offering outrageous spreads. What the devil is a point spread anyway?"

"Considering your views on the evils of gambling, you don't want to know. You'd probably confiscate his paycheck and make him live on an allowance."

"I can just see him agreeing to that."

Frank laughed with her, then turned serious. "I doubt you have any idea just how persuasive you are. I think you could get a man to agree to just about anything."

She looked startled, then pleased. She held his gaze for just an instant before looking nervously away and getting to her feet. "Even helping with the dishes?" she said with the kind of rush born of deep-rooted caution. She was not going to make things easy for him. There would be no overnight burst of faith, no quick readjustment of her tendency to hide behind a brusque professionalism.

He wiggled his inept fingers at her. "I don't have enough dishes in the house for me to go tampering with the ones I do have."

"You could manage if you really wanted to," she countered, the mood settling comfortably at last into the light banter with which she obviously felt more at ease. "I seem to recall that you have a particular aversion to doing dishes. I think you're just using your injury as an excuse to get out of helping."

He grinned back at her. "But you'll never know for sure will you?"

"Maybe not," she said as one of his few good plates seemed

to slide from her grasp. With his lightning-quick reflexes, Frank caught it in midair.

"Then, again," she observed, amusement dancing in her eyes, "looks to me like your recovery's a whole lot further along than you've been letting on."

"You little rat," he muttered. "You did that on purpose to test me."

She grinned. "You bet. You wash. I'll dry."

For the first time in his life, Frank actually enjoyed doing dishes. He was tempted to pull out every mismatched plate, every scarred mug and chipped cup in the cabinets just to keep Jenny around a little longer. He knew that the minute they were done, she'd go, fleeing her emotions, chasing the illusion of safety.

In fact, as it turned out, she had her jacket on and her car keys in her hands before he could drain the water from the sink. He didn't waste time arguing with her.

"I'll walk you to your car."

Wishing he could do the gallant thing and open the door for her, he stood by helplessly while she unlocked the car and got in. "Thanks for tonight," he said, when she'd rolled down the window.

Jenny nodded, her face upturned expectantly as if waiting for his kiss. Frank leaned down and brushed his lips across hers, fighting against the urge to linger and savor the velvet warmth. "It's not over, Jenny Michaels. Not by a long shot."

He whistled as he turned and walked back up the hill. It was a very long time before he heard the car start and saw Jenny drive off.

Frank made a resolution as he lay awake later that night. With the finely honed instincts of a man used to caring for others, he had seen through Jenny's veneer of steel to the fragility and insecurities underneath. For the first time he realized that the complexities of his own recovery were nothing compared to hers. She had taught him all about acceptance and fighting back. He was about to teach her all about joyous, unconditional love.

Though his financial future was uncertain, he could offer her that much at least.

He would start his fight to overcome Jenny's shattered self-esteem with tender, potent kisses. He had seen the longing in her eyes, so much longing that it made him tremble. And, no matter what she said, there was no doubting that she had kissed him back. She would again. It would just take some old-fashioned wooing.

He might, he decided reluctantly, have to get a few tips on that from his experienced baby brother.

Tim was delighted to help out with some expert advice over lunch the next day. So, unfortunately, were Kevin, Jared, Peter and Daniel, who turned up en masse. The word that big brother had the hots for the therapist spread through the Chambers clan faster than a wildfire on a windy day. Even Karyn, still in Indianapolis with Brad for the Indy 500 trials, knew by dinnertime. She called just to stick in her two cents.

"I knew it," she gloated. "I knew that she was crazy about you the day she came out of your room all hot and bothered because you wouldn't do your therapy."

Frank groaned, tempted to hang up on her, but unwilling to give her the satisfaction. "Karyn, at that point the woman had spent approximately fifteen minutes with me and I was not especially charming. I don't think she was smitten. I think she was mad."

"Anger. Passion," she said dismissively. "They're both pretty powerful emotions. People get them confused all the time."

"Another five minutes of this and I am going to get passionately angry at you."

"Don't threaten me," she countered cheerfully. "It's payback time. You've been meddling in our lives from day one. Do you recall the night you stormed into Brad's hotel to rescue your precious baby sister from his evil clutches?"

"Only too well."

"I've never been so humiliated in my entire life. I may not rest until I've had a chance to get even."

"The man lied and said you weren't there," he reminded her. He was still none too pleased about that, but he had to admit that Brad was treating Karyn okay. The two of them were obviously crazy in love.

"He lied to protect my honor," she said. "It's about time you forgave him for that. Now let's talk about you. Forget anything Tim or the rest of those chauvinistic brothers of ours told you. Here's how you go about winning Jenny's heart. Trust me..."

Jenny did not sleep well, not that night, not for days. Like an old-fashioned newsreel, the scene in Frank's kitchen played through her head. Her panic was just as real in the middle of the night as it had been at the time.

Only once since the surgery had she allowed a man to touch her as intimately as Frank had. She had thought she loved Larry Amanti, thought he loved her. He had been warned about the scar. He'd told her it didn't matter, had sworn that he loved her just as she was. Then, when he had stripped away her clothes, when she was naked and vulnerable, she had seen the flicker of revulsion in his eyes, had shivered as he tried desperately to overcome his instinctive reaction and touch her anyway. Humiliated beyond belief, she had yanked the sheet around her and ordered him from her bed. He had fled, gratefully if the look in his eyes had been anything to go by.

In the days and months that followed, she'd realized that perhaps she was the one who had overreacted. With her insecurities close to the surface, she had never given him a chance to adjust to the disfigurement for which no amount of advance warning could adequately prepare a man. Even with that new self-awareness, though, she was not prepared to take the risk again. Rejection was always painful, but it would be doubly so if it came from a man like Frank, a man with whom she'd fallen hopelessly in love because of his kindness and sensitivity.

Although she couldn't bring herself to turn Frank's therapy over to Carolanne—it would be an open admission to him that she did fear what was happening between them—she did keep her distance. Not once over the next couple of weeks did she squeeze his shoulder in encouragement or place her hand on his to add pressure to his grip. The slightest contact seemed to stir desires she had no business having. It was better not to feel that flaring of heat, better not to respond to that tug deep within her, better not to experience the racing of her pulse.

To her chagrin, Frank seemed oblivious to the withdrawal of physical contact. If anything, he was even more businesslike than she was. He smiled. He joked. He even winked on occasion, a gleam of pure devilment in those wicked blue eyes of his. But his attention never wandered very far from the exercises. When the sessions were over, he thanked her politely and went off to visit with Pam, leaving Jenny vaguely discontented and out of sorts. He was doing exactly as she wanted, wasn't he? So why did she feel so damned lousy?

One day, feeling thoroughly abandoned, she followed him down the hall, then lingered outside Pam's room as the two laughed uproariously over stories she couldn't quite overhear. She hated to admit, even to herself, how much she missed that easy camaraderie, the teasing banter, the undeniable sexual overtones that made her pulse tremble.

"Eavesdropping?" Otis inquired from behind her.

Jenny backed up so fast she almost stumbled over his big feet. "No, of course not," she said.

Otis shook his head and rocked back on his heels. "You two got to be carrying on the strangest romance I ever did see."

Though her cheeks burned with embarrassment, Jenny retorted quickly and, she hoped, convincingly, "Romance? There's no romance between Frank and me."

Otis rolled his eyes. "You expect me to believe that? I've seen the way you've been mooning around here the last couple of months."

"Yes, I do expect you to believe it, because it's true."

"Oh, Jenny, Jenny. Are you just lying to me or to yourself, too?"

"Go away, Otis."

He grinned at her. "I'm going," he said. "By the way, I'm

betting on a fall wedding. Don't let me down. I've got a bundle riding on it.''

Horrified, Jenny chased after him. When she caught him, she backed him against the wall, fire in her eyes. ''Who would you make a bet like that with?'' she demanded. ''Otis, if you've been spreading gossip all over this hospital, you are history, dead meat...'' She searched for a fate so terrifying it would put the fear of God into him.

''Don't go getting yourself in a dither. The bet's with Pam.''

''Pam?'' she repeated incredulously. Her friend, her pal, was engaging in bets with Otis behind her back? And about her wedding to a man she was barely even speaking to?

''She's betting on May,'' Otis said cheerfully. ''Personally, I don't think either you or Frank is smart enough to make a move that fast. Only a few more days left in the month. Told her that, too, but the kid's a real romantic. She really wants a May wedding. She's probably in there right now working on Frank.''

Jenny clenched her teeth. ''There will be no wedding,'' she said slowly and emphatically. ''Not in May. Not in the fall. Not ever.''

Otis's smile spread across his face. ''You want to make a bet on that, too? I'll give you great odds. Wouldn't even mind losing this one. I like the man. I think he's good for you. Puts a little color in your cheeks. Like now. Pink as can be.''

Jenny groaned and went back to the therapy room, where she threw every piece of foam rubber in the place as hard as she could. When that didn't even dent her frustration, she started on noisier supplies. The door opened just as a jar sailed across the room. Frank ducked as it shattered mere inches from his head.

''Having a bad day?'' he inquired lightly.

''A bad day. A bad week. A bad month.''

''Something happen after I left?''

''No.'' Nothing that she was about to admit to him.

''Been to that aerobics class lately?''

''What aerobics—'' She stopped herself as she recalled that she'd told him about the way she spent her evenings. ''Oh, of course, I told you about those. I forgot.''

"Forgot you told me or forgot to go?"

She was very tempted to tell him to go to hell just to wipe that smug grin from his face. Instead she inquired testily, "Did you come back for a reason?"

"Sure did. I meant to tell you earlier that Tim got tickets for a Giants game tonight. He can't go. Want to come with me?"

Peanuts, popcorn and Cracker Jacks, all the lures of the song about the ballpark tempted her to say yes. "It wouldn't be a date or anything, right?"

He nodded agreeably. "Whatever you say."

How much trouble could she possibly get in with thousands of people around? Frank would be so busy yelling, he wouldn't even have time to notice her. Lately he hadn't seemed to notice her all that much anyway. "Okay," she said finally. "What time?"

"Now," he said at once.

"Now?"

"I didn't want to give you time to think it over and back out. Let's go."

During the first inning, Jenny was thoroughly self-conscious. She kept waiting for Frank's hand to squeeze hers, for his arm to slide around the back of her seat, for one of those bone-melting looks. His eyes never once left the ball field, and his hands were occupied with those peanuts and that popcorn she'd been daydreaming about earlier. She munched her own popcorn in oddly disgruntled silence.

By the third inning, she was just hoping for some small sign that he remembered she was there at all. When a soft-drink vendor passed by on the aisle, Frank actually blinked, glanced in her direction and inquired if she wanted anything. She was absurdly grateful for the attention and took a soft drink she didn't even want.

When the crowd stood for the seventh-inning stretch, Jenny decided there was no longer anything to fear...or hope for. Frank had brought her to a ballgame because he knew she liked baseball. It wasn't part of some grand seduction scheme. Why did

that seem to irk her so when she had no intention of letting their
relationship progress?

She was still pondering that when the game ended with a
winning bases-loaded homer by the Giants center fielder. Suddenly Frank's arms were around her and he was swinging her in
the air. His genuine exuberance was contagious. She was still
laughing with him when the innocent embrace turned serious.

She slid slowly down the length of his body as he lowered
her feet to the ground. She was aware of every inch of contact,
every exciting flare of heat between them. Her breath left her as
her toes touched down. Fortunately Frank showed no intention
of releasing her. If he had, she was certain her knees would have
buckled.

His gaze searched her face, his blue eyes darkening with desire. Her own heart was pounding.

"Oh, damn," she murmured finally as the strength for the
battle with her own emotions ebbed.

Frank gave a low chuckle at her heartfelt sigh. "Yeah, I know
what you mean."

"You did this deliberately, didn't you?"

"Did what?"

"Kept your distance until tonight, until just now?"

"I was advised by an expert that heightened anticipation can
accomplish miracles."

Jenny felt something shift inside her at his hopeful expression.
"Frank, don't," she warned, but without much force.

He grinned at her faint warning. "Don't waste your breath.
This is one argument you will never win. I intend to prove to
you that what we have isn't going to vanish overnight, that it
isn't some quirk of the patient-therapist relationship. I love you,
Jenny Michaels, and one of these days you're just going to have
to accept that."

Jenny wanted to. Dear God, how she wanted to. But fate had
dealt both of them a couple of low blows. She didn't trust it not
to have another one in store.

Chapter Ten

It took Frank three weeks after the baseball game to convince Jenny to once again spend some time with him outside of the hospital. She displayed an inordinate amount of distrust of his motives. No doubt that had something to do with the undeniable arousal he was sure she'd detected when he'd taken her into his arms in the bleachers at the end of the game. It they'd been anywhere but in the middle of a stadium, she might not have escaped so easily. At the very least, he would have kissed her the way he wanted to, slowly and deeply and convincingly.

"Hey, I'm fighting for my life here," he teased, trying to overcome her reluctance with the humor she seemed to prefer to serious declarations. "What's one measly little afternoon? Surely you can trust yourself not to attack me and ravish me in that length of time."

Her brows rose a disapproving fraction. "I'm not the problem," she reminded him pointedly.

"Handcuff me," he suggested.

She chuckled at the outrageous option. "I don't think we need to go that far."

Frank seized the faint hint of surrender. "You're wavering. I can tell. What'll it take? A promise written in blood? A chaperon? I'll even ask Karyn to fly home and take your side. She'd love the chance to give me a little grief. She claims I made her dating life a living hell.''

Jenny immediately appeared fascinated. "How? Too protective?"

"Maybe a little," he admitted ruefully. "She's itching to even the score. I will invite her, though. Just say the word."

"No," she said finally. "I guess I can trust you."

"Your faith is overwhelming."

"Don't pout. Besides, I'm not finished. I'll agree to see you, but only if I get to choose what we do. Something therapeutic."

Frank groaned, but agreed. "Anything you say. What's it going to be?"

"You'll see," she said with an unexpectedly impish little gleam in her eyes. "Sunday afternoon at three. Be ready. I'll pick you up."

Frank was so enthralled by the gleam in her eyes, so caught up in the seductive possibilities, that he forgot all about the Chambers Sunday dinner tradition. When his mother called that night to remind him, as she had every week since he'd moved out of the family home, he braved her wrath and announced, "Can't make it this time, Ma. I've got an important date."

Her startled silence lasted no more than a heartbeat. "Important?" she repeated with obvious fascination. "You'll bring her along. That's no problem."

"It's a problem. She's already made plans."

"What plans?"

"I don't know. It's a surprise."

"Well, you just surprise her and tell her you're coming here. Is it Jenny?"

"Yes."

"Wonderful. She'll fit right in. Four o'clock, same as always."

She hung up before he could argue. Maybe they could do both, he thought reluctantly. Maybe Jenny wouldn't mind at least dropping by for dinner, though the prospect of subjecting her to the fascinated examination of his family on a more concentrated level than the ones she'd been exposed to at their hospital visits was daunting. Tim and the others were not known for their subtlety. The already-skittish Jenny was likely to take off before dessert and never speak to him again.

He hadn't been off the phone five minutes when it rang again. "Frank?"

From the sudden leap of his pulse, he would have known it was Jenny, even if he hadn't recognized that tentative note in her voice. The only time she ever sounded that uncertain was when she was talking to him about their relationship, rather than the progress of his therapy. "Hi. Didn't we just see each other? You aren't calling to cancel our date already, are you?"

"I'm not sure. I just had the oddest call from your mother."

Frank muttered a curse under his breath. He should have guessed she'd leave nothing to chance. "What did she want?" he inquired, though there wasn't a doubt in his mind that she'd taken that Sunday dinner invitation into her own capable hands.

"She said she wanted to personally invite me over on Sunday. She seemed to think you might not relay the message, something about a traditional family dinner."

"An astute woman, my mother."

"Frank, is your family getting the wrong impression about us?" Jenny definitely sounded troubled.

"I doubt it," he said. "It seems to me they've got it pegged."

"What?" She sounded even more alarmed.

"Never mind," he said quickly. "What did you tell Ma?"

"What could I say? I told her I'd be delighted, but Frank, I am not delighted." Each word was said with slow emphasis.

"Then we won't go. I told my mother we had plans."

He heard Jenny's deep sigh. "I tried that, too. She doesn't seem to take no for an answer. That's when I caved in and said yes. That woman should pick a charity and become a fund-raiser. She'd rake in millions."

"Believe me, I know the feeling. Trying to argue with her is like jogging straight into a brick wall. It's up to you, though. We do not have to go, no matter what you told her. I'll take care of it. I don't want you to feel uncomfortable," he said, though, now that he thought of it, the idea of watching Jenny interact as a part of his family held an undeniable appeal.

Now that she knew she had his support, she seemed to hesitate. "Is everyone going to be there?"

"Everyone. I think these Sunday dinners were part of the compromise when we all started to move out. We swore that we would always come back once a week."

"Then you can't very well back out of this one. You go. We'll do something another time."

Frank grabbed desperately at the first response that came to him. "And have my entire family know that you broke our date because you were scared of them?"

"I'm not scared of them," she countered. "Well, not exactly, anyway. I just don't want them to get the idea that there's anything serious between us."

"It might be too late for that," he admitted. "They all know how I feel. If you don't show up Sunday, I guarantee each one of them will probably pay you a visit to tell you what a great guy I am. I don't think any of them will beat you up..."

He allowed the possibility to linger before adding, "They're not usually violent. We all do tend to be pretty protective though."

There was a long pause before Jenny said, "Are you saying I might have to listen to six separate sales pitches on your behalf?"

"Seven. Ma's a real tigress. Come to think of it, *she* might beat you up."

Jenny finally started chuckling. "You're teasing me, aren't you?"

"Oh, no, sweetheart. This is gospel."

"It might almost be worth it to stay home and see who turns up to list your attributes."

"You already know my attributes. Well, most of them, anyway. I'd be glad to share the rest anytime you're ready."

"I'll just bet you would. Okay, forget my surprise. We'll go to dinner with your family. But I swear to you, if the words wedding or marriage even creep into the conversation in a whisper, I'll turn you over to Otis.''

''That's no threat,'' he scoffed. ''He's on my side.''

''I was hoping you didn't know that.''

''I'm sure you were. See you Sunday.''

Frank found himself looking forward to the prospect with a very odd mixture of buoyant optimism and gut-deep dread. The combined forces of all the Chambers would either win Jenny over, or scare her away for good.

Jenny stood outside the Chambers's small, unpretentious home, Frank beside her, and battled the flutter of a thousand butterflies in her stomach. A fresh coat of paint in sedate white lost its innocent air in the red trim. The combination reminded her of the family, old-fashioned with an intriguing hint of quirky daring. Frank epitomized those qualities, though she doubted he saw himself that way.

There was no mistaking the fact that he'd been courting her for all these weeks now, setting a pace that was just shy and patient enough to relax her guard. At the edge of all that caution, though, was the sly promise of dangerous desires about to be unleashed. Jenny was captivated, despite her best intentions to maintain a careful distance between herself and the man who was so trustingly offering her his heart.

She'd been lured here today by curiosity and longing. It seemed like forever since she'd felt part of a family. Never had she even imagined belonging to a clan as boisterous and tight-knit as this one. She'd been unable to resist the chance to spend one brief afternoon in an environment filled with warmth and acceptance and love. It might be the only chance she ever had to experience what it could have been like had she dared to believe in Frank's love, had she dared to make a forever commitment. Though she would never have admitted it to him, she was indulging herself in a dream, a dream that was both alluring and forbidden.

''You're shaking,'' he observed, snapping her out of her lovely daydream. ''Scared?''

"Of course not."

"Then you're a braver soul than I am," he said fervently, making her laugh and forget her fears.

"They're your family," she reminded him.

"Then my reaction ought to tell you something. Are you sure you wouldn't rather go skydiving?"

"Absolutely not. I can't wait to see why they have a grown man like you quaking in your boots."

He grinned and held out his hand. "Then let's get it over with."

Before they'd made it up the front walk, the door was thrown open. Mrs. Chambers, wearing a simple navy dress with a prim, lacy, white collar under her apron, waited for them with a beaming smile. She wiped both hands on the apron, then held them out to Jenny. "Welcome, Jenny. Come in. We've been waiting for you. Everyone's here."

As they walked toward the living room, Frank leaned down and whispered, "I warned you. They've never been on time before. Today they couldn't wait."

His mother hushed him. "Maybe they just knew I was making pot roast."

"Ma, you always make pot roast on Sunday."

"I do not. Just last week we had chicken."

"Tasted like pot roast to me," Frank said.

"Me, too," Tim concurred, popping into the hallway. "Looked like it, too. Must have been all those carrots and baby onions you used to hide the meat."

Mrs. Chambers glared indignantly at the pair of them. "Keep it up and there will be no apple cobbler for the two of you."

"Cobbler again?" Peter chimed in with an exaggerated groan as he joined them.

His mother waggled a finger in his direction. "Just for that, you can set the table. Now. Jenny, you go on in the living room and sit down. Daniel, Kevin and Jared are in there. Don't let them gang up on you. If they start giving you a rough time, you can come hide out with me in the kitchen."

Jenny laughed. "I think maybe that's my first choice anyway. Can I come now? I'd like to help."

Frank's eyes widened in dismay. "Bad idea," he warned. "The woman will try to pry information out of you. No secret will be safe. She's going to want to know what your intentions are."

Mrs. Chambers patted Jenny on the shoulder. "Don't listen to a word he says. You come right along. The rest of you, play nice," she added in an echo of Jenny's own advice to Tim and Frank weeks earlier. Jenny understood now why Tim had teased her so over the comment.

Jenny had thought she'd feel safe in the kitchen, out of the reach of all those prying eyes, away from Frank's hopes and everyone else's expectations. And at first she did feel safe. At first it was comforting to be surrounded by the heavenly smell of the roast, the cinnamon-scented cobbler, the yeasty aroma of rising rolls.

"What can I do?" she offered.

"You can sit right over there and talk to me," Mrs. Chambers said, waving Jenny toward a curved breakfast area. She gave Peter a handful of silverware and shooed him toward the dining room. She brought over a bag of beans and began snapping them as she sat across from Jenny. "You've been seeing Frank for a while now, isn't that right?"

"At the hospital," Jenny replied cautiously, trying to decide if the question was innocuous or the start of an inquisition. She grabbed a handful of beans herself and clumsily tried to imitate Mrs. Chambers's quick, decisive motions.

Mrs. Chambers shot her a perceptive look. "Just another patient, right?"

"No, of course not. I mean...oh, dear," she murmured, falling neatly into the maternal trap set by Mrs. Chambers.

"Frank's a fine man," his mother reported.

"I know that."

"Took on a lot of responsibility at an early age."

"I know."

"Just look at this kitchen. He fixed it up for me, put in new cabinets, that fancy tile."

"It's beautiful," Jenny said honestly. The white, glass-fronted cabinets gave the room an open, airy feeling. The white tile floor and single row of red accent tiles amid the white on the walls added to the cheerful ambience. The built-in breakfast nook was a similar combination of white Formica and red seat covers. "Did Frank build this breakfast area, too?"

Mrs. Chambers beamed with pride. "Isn't it something? Used to be a pantry here. He knocked out the wall and the next thing you know the kitchen was nearly twice as big as it used to be. How many men would have thought to do that?"

Jenny admired all the extra touches that she was certain were Mrs. Chambers's, the framed prints on the walls, the bright dish towels, but Frank's mother wasn't interested in her own contribution. She was pushing her son's. In case Jenny hadn't gotten the message, she added, "He'd make a wonderful husband."

"Mrs. Chambers, really, Frank and I are just friends."

"Good way to start."

"Start?" Jenny said weakly.

"Of course. My husband and I started out as friends, too. Makes a lot more sense than the way kids do things these days. They fall into bed, get married and then discover they don't have a thing in common. Do things slow and you do them right. You two take your time, if that's what you need."

Suddenly the large room seemed to be closing in on Jenny. "But..." The protest was barely begun before it was interrupted.

"Of course," Mrs. Chambers said cheerily, "I always did think a fall wedding was mighty nice. The church could be decorated with bright yellow mums. Karyn would look real good in that coppery shade that you see in all the fancy fashion magazines."

"Karyn?"

"Of course, I don't mean to be pushy. I know you have your own friends, but I always think it's nice if someone from the groom's family stands up with the bride, too, don't you?"

"In theory," Jenny said, wondering desperately if there was

any polite way she could escape to the living room or find a pit of vipers to throw herself into. If she stayed here much longer, she was liable to end up married before anyone heard her protests. She crumbled the beans in her hands into little, bitty pieces before she realized what she was doing.

The kitchen door swung open. "How's it going in here?" Frank inquired. "You two getting acquainted?"

"Oh, my, yes," his mother replied. "We were just discussing the wedding."

Frank's startled gaze shot to Jenny. His eyebrows rose a quizzical half inch. "Wedding?" he repeated. "Whose?"

"Why yours, of course," Mrs. Chambers said, back at the stove and still oblivious to Jenny's panic.

"Ma!"

She turned and waved a spoon at him. "It never hurts to give a girl a nudge, let her know she'll be welcome in the family."

A twinkle of amusement appeared in Frank's eyes as he scanned Jenny's face. She was sure she must be pale as a ghost. "You feeling welcome?" he asked.

"Very," she said, injecting the single word with ominous implications.

"Maybe you'd like to come back in the living room with me," Frank suggested hurriedly.

"I'd love to."

Mrs. Chambers gave them an approving smile. "You two go right along. I'm sure Jenny and I will have a chance to talk more later."

Jenny nearly moaned as she left the kitchen.

"I tried to warn you," Frank said, his arm circling her shoulder.

She twisted away from the embrace. "You're enjoying this, aren't you? You're letting your mother do your dirty work."

"What dirty work is that?"

"The woman practically proposed on your behalf."

His expression brightened. "Really? What did you say?"

"Say? She didn't want an answer. She took the answer for granted." Jenny knew her voice was climbing, knew that her attempts to cover her earlier irritation with humor were starting to fail her now. This was exactly what she had feared would happen. The whole Chambers family was going to sit around all through dinner staring at her, waiting for an announcement that was not going to come. And she was going to have to put up with it.

Why? she thought suddenly. Why shouldn't she just lay things on the line? Frank might be a little embarrassed at first, but wasn't that better than allowing this whole misunderstanding to get entirely out of hand? Or was the real problem that a tiny part of her wanted the charade to be perpetuated? If she were to be perfectly honest, hadn't she enjoyed sitting in that kitchen and playing prospective daughter-in-law?

Okay, yes, dammit! Was that so terrible? It wasn't going to happen, but couldn't she indulge herself for a few minutes or even a few hours in the fantasy of becoming Mrs. Frank Chambers?

She looked up at Frank then and caught the speculative spark in his eyes. It was as if he could read her mind, as if he knew that she was waging an internal war and laying odds on the outcome.

Before she could come to a final decision on whether to go or stay, the choice was taken out of her hands. Mrs. Chambers started putting food on the table and the next thing Jenny knew, she was seated beside Frank's mother and they were all holding hands to say grace. When Mrs. Chambers gave thanks that her oldest son had found such a pretty, kind woman, Frank squeezed Jenny's hand reassuringly. She caught herself blinking back the surprising sting of salty tears and trying desperately to hold back the flood of hope.

As they drove home, Frank marveled at the transformation that had come over Jenny during the afternoon and evening. From a shy, unwilling date, she had slowly fallen into the role of fiancée. Though he'd been ready to strangle his mother when he'd first walked into that kitchen, he had to admit now that he should be grateful. After a few token protests, Jenny had apparently taken to the idea. By the time they'd left she'd been teasing his brothers, beating them all at Monopoly and agreeing to return the following Sunday. He still wasn't sure exactly what had come over her, but he'd be damned if he'd complain about it.

"Did you have a good time?" he inquired as she sat beside him, her eyes closed, a pleased smile tilting the corners of her mouth.

"The best," she murmured.

"Did it have anything to do with me?"

She blinked and stared at him sleepily. "Of course, why?"

"Because a few hours ago, you were adamant about defining the parameters of our relationship in very businesslike terms. By the time we left my mother's, if I'm not mistaken, at least seven people were of the opinion that we're engaged. I'm one of them."

She sighed. "I never really said that, did I?"

"No, but you knew that was the impression and you didn't correct it. Why?"

Her lower lip was caught between her teeth as she obviously struggled with an answer. "I guess I just got caught up in a fantasy," she said slowly. "I'm sorry."

His heart thudding, Frank said, "It doesn't have to be just a fantasy. I love you, Jenny. You know that. I want to marry you." He pulled the car to the side of the road and touched her cheek, which was damp with unexpected tears. "I do love you, sweetheart."

Her fingers traced his jaw, then his lips as his breath lodged in his throat. "Oh, Frank, if only..."

"There are no 'if onlys,'" he said angrily. "All you have to do is say yes. One little word. Why is it so hard for you?"

"You know why," she said, her voice thick with tears.

"Then come with me, come home with me and let me show you that there is nothing, *nothing,* standing in our way."

Jenny's eyes were shining, her lips trembling, when she finally whispered, "Yes. I'll come with you."

He caressed her cheek, his thumb moving over the lush curve of her lower lip as his heart slammed into his ribs. Anticipation rushed through him, hot and sweet and urgent. Along with it came a faint anxiety that he was certain mirrored hers.

"You won't be sorry," he vowed to reassure them both. "You will never be sorry."

Chapter Eleven

Regrets and doubts rioted deep inside Jenny the instant she agreed to go home with Frank. But the temptation had proved too strong, the illusion too powerful. Caught up in it, she'd been unable to say no. She would give anything for this one night to be perfect. She didn't doubt, not for a second, that Frank would try to make it so. She didn't doubt that he loved her. Every considerate action spoke of the depth of his feelings.

But was love the only thing that mattered? She had doubts enough about that for the both of them.

Even so, there could be no backing out now, no second thoughts leading to a tearful withdrawal. When she had said yes, she had made a commitment, to him and to herself. It might last no longer than this one night, but it was a commitment just the same. And, like Frank, she believed in honoring her vows.

Inside his house, she caught him studying her, his expression thoughtful, worried. "Nervous?" he said.

Jenny nodded.

"Me, too."

It had never occurred to her that he might be every bit as scared as she was. His nervousness and his admission of it both charmed and reassured her.

"You can change your mind anytime," he said, his blue eyes serious. *"Anytime."*

Feeling stronger with each reassurance, she shook her head. "I won't change my mind," she said with absolute conviction. "I want to be with you more than I've ever wanted anything in my life."

He nodded and held out his hand. When she placed her hand in his, he rubbed the pad of his thumb across her knuckles, then lifted her hand to his lips, his gaze fastened on hers. Inside, she trembled with the magic of that tender gesture.

"Would you like a drink?" he offered. "I think I have some wine."

"Yes. Wine would be good," she said, though she wanted time more than she wanted the drink. She needed to accustom herself to being here, to the prospect of an almost-forgotten kind of intimacy. She needed to steel herself to the possibility of rejection. Though her heart told her that Frank would never ever hurt her intentionally, she knew that the faintest hint of revulsion in his eyes, the least sign of disappointment would be devastating. She had to prepare herself for that, had to be ready not to cast blame for something over which he might have no control.

As she waited for the wine, she walked down the hall to his workroom and flipped on the light. She breathed in the clean scent of the various woods, rubbed her fingers over the textures of his finished carvings. When she came to the unfinished blue jay, she recalled how she had guided his inept fingers in this very room, how she had badgered him until he began fighting back against his injury, fighting to regain his skill. Unless she was mistaken, there were fresh details on the piece, less delicate perhaps, but evidence that he was trying.

She sensed that Frank was standing in the doorway. Glancing over her shoulder, she smiled at him. "I hope you don't mind that I'm in here," she said, suddenly realizing that he might consider this an invasion of his privacy, a claim to intimacy that she didn't rightfully have.

"Of course not," he said, though his uneasiness contradicted the words. He came closer and handed her the wine.

"You've been working." She gestured toward the blue jay.

He shrugged, his expression unexpectedly vulnerable. "I'm trying."

"It's very good."

He shook his head and regarded the carving critically. "Not yet," he said, but there was a trace of hope even in the denial.

"I'm proud of you."

"I'm proud of you, too."

Startled, she stared at him. "Why?"

"For daring to take this step, for trusting me."

"It was time," she said simply, and knew it was true. She might have put off the action for a week or a month or a year, but emotionally she was as ready now as she was ever likely to be. No man was ever likely to be more right for her than this kind, gentle man who waited patiently for her to set the pace. She put down the glass he'd given her. "Frank, would you hold me?"

A slow smile trembled on his lips as he put aside his own glass. "I thought you'd never ask," he murmured, opening his arms then folding them around her.

Jenny rested her head against his chest, listening to the quickened beat of his heart and breathing in the faintly woodsy masculine scent of him. There was such comfort in his embrace, such a sense of coming home at last. And yet...

And yet there was the lightning-quick racing of her pulse. Warmth that had nothing to do with the comfort and everything to do with rising passion stole over her. When his lips finally, inevitably settled on hers, the lightning added thunder, the warmth became white-hot urgency. There was no rush to the kiss, no hurry to the slow exploration by his tongue, but deep inside her, need built feverishly, demanding more, demanding a more passionate pace. She appreciated the care he was taking, the gentle advances, but she hungered for desperate loving, loving that would carry her beyond thought to pure sensation, passion able to overshadow doubts.

Her fingers tangled in the dark midnight of his hair as she pressed him closer. Her now-sensitive lips brushed across stubbled cheeks, seeking, again, the velvet fire of his mouth. When one arm braced her back and the other tucked beneath her knees, she gasped in startled astonishment, then settled against his chest as he carried her down the hall and into his bedroom.

For a few seconds she registered the room's details, the clean, masculine lines, the cheerful colors, the clutter of framed family pictures crowded on the dresser, the haphazard toss of clothes scattered about by a man always in a rush…until now. Then Frank captured all of her attention, his eyes smoky blue with desire, his expression still anxious.

"You're sure," he said one last time.

Though her heart raced with something very much like sheer panic, Jenny nodded. "I'm sure," she whispered. Then, more loudly, "Very sure."

He stepped closer, his gaze locked with hers. With fingers that trembled, he traced the neckline of her blouse, leaving a trail of goose bumps along her neck. Scared as she had never been scared before, filled with a yearning deeper than any she had ever known, Jenny allowed him to slowly, carefully, unbutton her blouse. With the release of the first button, she stilled, but the press of his lips against the newly exposed flesh had her quivering with need. His touch was so deft, his kisses so potent that she forgot to watch for the revulsion in his eyes as first her blouse, and then her specially designed bra fell away. All she remembered were the nights she'd lain awake imagining being cherished like this.

When she first felt his lips against the scar, a cry of dismay gathered in her throat, but before she could utter a single sound, she was lost in the sensations he aroused, the fierce tug deep in her belly, the sweet, aching hunger below. She wanted nothing more than to go on feeling, but she had to know. She had to.

At last she opened her eyes. With a mixture of awe and dread, she observed him as he gently traced the line of the scar. With her breath caught in her throat, she waited for him to back away, but the only sign of emotion was the tear that tracked down his cheek and the faint trembling of his hand as he touched her. He lifted his head, though his hand continued to stroke and caress and inflame.

"I love you, Jenny Michaels," he said, his gaze locked on hers.

"I love you," he whispered again, as his gaze slid lower to the scar and lingered there. There was an instant when he seemed to freeze, and Jenny felt her heart go still. Then she realized that he was staring at his own fresh scars, seeing the cruelly reddened skin against the whiteness of her flesh. She captured his hand in hers and kissed each finger until he, too, believed in the healing power of love.

Her own tears falling, mingling with his, Jenny heard the tender endearments, felt the powerful stirring of her body responding to his touch. Eyes closed, she gave herself over to the feelings, savoring them as a treasure she would hold always. Even after he'd gone.

That these wonderful, wild sensations couldn't last seemed a certainty. She wouldn't dare to hope beyond tonight, beyond this sweet, thrilling moment. With the fascination of a woman capturing dreams enough for a lifetime, she studied the magnificent lines of his body, the sculpted flesh with its richness of texture. No wonder that he created perfection with his carving knife, when he'd been given such an example. She traced each hardened muscle, each curve and indentation until she knew him as well as she knew herself, until his body tensed with need.

When their touches grew more frenzied, when their blood flowed like warm honey, when their thoughts had given way to pure sensation, they came together at last. Years of pain and hurt and doubting vanished in one shuddering moment of exultation. Love, as fresh and new as springtime, flowered in Jenny's heart.

As she curved her body against his, she told herself that forever was within reach. With his hands curved gently over her disfigured flesh, she could believe that she was beautiful and that anything was possible.

Awakening to find Jenny still in his arms filled Frank with a joy so profound it was as if he'd been reborn. He stretched cautiously, trying not to disturb her, then settled back to study the perfect silk of her skin, the tumble of curls with highlights the color of amber caught in the muted rays of morning sun. She was even tinier than he'd realized. His hands could probably span her waist. He rested one hand just above the curve of her hip to prove his point.

Beneath his touch, her flesh warmed and she began to stir. As she rolled onto her back, his fingers moved from hip to belly in a slow, sensual caress that changed the pattern of her breathing from restful to hurried. Hesitant to touch her breast, fearful that she would perceive the touch as a need she couldn't amply fulfill, he stroked the scar instead. Jenny whimpered, then sighed, then came slowly awake.

Frank smiled down at her, her sleepy sensuality an incredible turn-on that had him instantly hard and wanting. For an instant she remained open to him, then as if realizing her vulnerability, the exposure in daylight that hadn't existed the night before, she grabbed for the sheet. He reached out to stay her hands.

"Don't," he whispered, trying to quiet the panic in her eyes. Meeting that fearful gaze straight on, he said, "You are beautiful, a beautiful, desirable woman. Inside and out. And I could not possibly love you any more than I do right now."

Her lower lip quivered, and he wanted desperately to cover that faint trembling with his own lips, but he held back, knowing that the best proof was in not looking away. She would only believe him if he acknowledged the defect and showed her time and again that it didn't matter. It would take words and actions and time.

"You must believe me, Jenny," he said. "You are all the woman I need, and I will spend the rest of my life proving it to you."

Tears gathered in her eyes, then spilled down her face. She captured his scarred hand in hers and held it to her damp cheek. "I know that," she said with a sigh.

There was a hesitation in her voice, a shadow of doubt. "But you don't entirely trust what we have, do you? Why not? How can a woman who spends her life teaching others to look beyond scars, not see beyond her own?''

She drew away from him then, both physically and emotionally. He could read the distance in her sudden stiffness, the dullness that took the lively sparks from her eyes.

''Frank, it's not just the scars. If it was, don't you think I would throw myself into your arms and never let go? Last night was the most perfect night of my life. I felt fulfilled and complete and desirable. You did that for me. But I won't be one of those people you gather in and protect. You've already raised five brothers and a sister. You deserve a life that is carefree and filled with happiness.''

Frank struggled to follow what she was saying. It made no sense. How could she equate herself with his family? It sounded as if she viewed herself as a burden, rather than an incredible woman to be treasured. It sounded as if she planned to end things just as they were beginning.

''Jenny, this is crazy. I love you. I certainly don't think of you as some stray I have to take in and care for.''

''But that could happen and I won't have it.''

''Won't have what?'' In his frustration, his voice rose to an irritated shout. ''Dammit, talk to me. Make me see why you're willing to throw away what we have.''

She turned pale at the thunder of his voice, but her voice was steady and bleak. ''Because I don't trust it to last.''

If she'd used the excuse that the sky might fall in a million years, he would have been no more confused. ''Sweetheart, I know there are no guarantees, but why give up what we have now because of something that might never happen?''

''I don't like the odds.''

''Odds? What odds? The fifty-percent divorce rate? What?''

''Stop yelling.''

''I'm sorry. It's just that you're making me crazy,'' he said impatiently.

Her look quelled him. He took a deep breath. ''Okay, talk to me. Make me understand. Are you worried about the way we met? Are you afraid that I've just grown dependent on you?''

Her expression softened. "No," she said, taking his hand and pressing a kiss to the knuckles. "You're strong now, and I know exactly what your feelings for me are. And I won't take advantage of that."

"Take advantage how?"

She did grab the sheet then and tug it around her. When it was snug, when there was nothing for him to see below her bare shoulders, she said quietly, "What scares me more than anything is the possibility that I might become dependent on you."

"Jenny..."

She touched a silencing finger to his lips. "No, listen to me. It's been just about four years since the surgery. Five years seems to be the magic number in cancer survival. I'm still a long way from that. Every day I live with the reality that the cancer could come back. I won't burden you with that, I won't ask you to live each day with the possibility of a death sentence hanging over us." Her gaze met his. "I won't," she said with finality.

Frank struggled with the horrible possibility of losing her to a disease he thought she had conquered. His heart ached for her as he tried to imagine living with that fear of recurrence. And, yet, weren't they losing even more by living now as if the merely possible were certain? He had to make her see that.

Gently he brushed the tendrils of hair back from her face. He searched his heart for words that would be convincing. "Jenny, my love, haven't you ever listened to the wedding ceremony? In sickness and in health, remember that? You're healthy now. We have this moment in our lives. We'll take each tomorrow as it comes. If we don't, Jenny, if we turn our backs on this, what sort of memories will we have? Loneliness? Fear? Longing? I don't want that for myself. I don't want it for you. Maybe we'll never quite stop being afraid, but we certainly don't have to be alone."

"It's not fair to you," she said stubbornly.

"It wasn't fair for you to get this disease. It wasn't fair for me to get burned. We both have to go on. It was your cancer and my burns that brought us together. Maybe we should concentrate on that and count our blessings."

"I'm scared, Frank."

"Of dying?"

"Of leaving you."

"Then don't do it now, not while you have a choice in the matter."

It was the most eloquent Frank had ever been, and he waited to see the effect of his words. For a moment as Jenny's arms slid around his waist, he thought he'd won. But then she rose, found the clothes they had tossed aside last night in their haste and, after sorting through them for hers, took them into the bathroom.

Frank wanted to throw something. He wanted to grab her by the shoulders and shout until she not only listened, but heard him. Instead he could only sit by helplessly as she did what she thought was right, what she thought was the noble thing.

When she came out of the bathroom, he held out his hand. "Jenny, don't go. I'll fix breakfast. We'll talk this out."

Swallowing hard, she shook her head. Then she kissed him one last time, with tears in her eyes, and left.

Chapter Twelve

Letting Jenny go, admitting that he didn't know how to help her grapple with her fears that obviously tormented her, was the most difficult thing Frank had ever done. He'd wanted to fold her in his arms, to hold her and love her until she couldn't walk away, but something told him that would only make the leaving harder, not impossible. He, better than anyone, knew just how stubborn and determined she could be. Yet knowing that he'd done the right thing didn't make the days any easier.

Boredom, worse than anything he'd faced in the hospital, set in and, combined with the loneliness, made him cranky. By the end of the week, he was snapping at anyone who dared to set foot near him. He tried carving again, but one slip of the knife had marred the blue jay he'd been struggling to complete and he'd tossed wood and knives into the trash. A day later he dug them out and tried again.

When Sunday rolled around, he begged off from the family dinner. He felt as though a lifetime had passed since the previous week, and he wasn't up to the questions and teasing innuendoes about a relationship that no longer existed. As soon as the excuses were out of his mouth, though, he knew it had been a mistake. By four, instead of gathering at his mother's, the whole clan began descending on him. Tim and Jared were the first to arrive.

"You look okay to me," Jared said after a close inspection.

"I'm fine."

"You told Ma you were sick," Tim reminded him.

"I think I'm coming down with something," he amended hurriedly. "I'm sure it's not serious, but it could be catching. You two go over to Ma's."

"We can't," Jared said.

"Why not? She'll be expecting you."

"No, she won't," Tim said, just as the doorbell rang. "That should be her now." He glanced at Jared. "I'm betting on chicken soup. How about you?"

"Broth. Beef broth and custard."

Frank groaned. "This is ridiculous. I am not that sick."

"Then you shouldn't have told her you were. Now we're all going to have to eat wimp food," Tim complained grumpily. "Do you have any idea how much I detest custard?"

There was a deeply offended gasp from the doorway. "What do you mean, Timothy Chambers? You've always said you loved my custard."

"Cripes, Ma, you weren't supposed to hear that."

"Then you shouldn't have said it, should you?" she said, hiding a grin. "Go out to the car and get the rest of the dinner."

"Real food?" Jared inquired hopefully.

"Soup and custard are real food. Now, go." Once they'd gone, she observed Frank closely and, with her finely tuned maternal radar, zeroed in on the real crux of his problem. "You and Jenny have a fight?"

"Why on earth would you ask that?"

"Otherwise, she'd be here nursing you."

"Ma, I think you've gotten the wrong idea about Jenny and me."

She shook her head. "I don't think so. What was the fight about?"

"It wasn't a fight exactly."

"What was it then *exactly?*"

"It's private."

She nodded slowly. "Okay. You do what you think is best, but, Son, don't turn your back on your feelings just because things aren't so smooth. If you love her, then you owe it to both of you to fight. Don't let it slip away because of false pride."

Frank didn't think pride had anything to do with letting Jenny leave, letting her make her own choices, but maybe it did. Maybe it had hurt, thinking that she didn't love him enough to try to save what they had. On the chance that his mother might be right, he made up his mind to go by the hospital on Monday, to talk to her and pester her until she saw that they could face the future and whatever it held—good or bad—a thousand times better together than they possibly could apart.

Energized by a stubborn determination of his own, and filled with hope, he strode through the hospital the next day, poked his head into Pam's room to say hello, then marched on to the therapy room like Sherman taking on Georgia. He pushed open the door and stepped inside, glancing first at Jenny's desk, then around the room. It was empty. The desk was ominously neat. He was still standing there trying to decide what to make of it, when Carolanne returned. She looked puzzled at finding him there.

"You here for a treatment?" she asked. "I don't recall seeing your name on the list for today."

"No. I'm here to see Jenny."

Her friendly expression closed down. "She's not in," she said, her tone cautiously neutral.

"I see that. Where is she?"

"She took a few days off."

Frank's heart began to thud dully in his chest. "Why? Is she okay?"

Carolanne studied him with serious gray eyes. "Come on in and sit down," she said finally. "I think it's time we had a talk."

Frank's pulse began to race. "Dammit, tell me where she is. What's happened?"

With the same spunkiness he'd encountered in Jenny, Carolanne pointed toward a chair. "Sit. You want some coffee?"

"Fine. Whatever," he said impatiently, but he sat.

A lifetime seemed to pass before she handed him a cup of coffee, then pulled up a chair and sat opposite him. "Are you in love with her?" she asked bluntly.

"Yes."

"Does she know it?"

"Yes," he said, oddly disquieted by the personal questions, yet sensing that Carolanne really needed to know if she was to be equally honest with him. "I've told her."

She nodded thoughtfully. "That makes sense then."

"What makes sense? Dammit, would you stop hedging and spit it out? Is she okay?"

"I don't know."

Frank felt as though the air were being squeezed out of his chest. Before he could say a word, Carolanne looked contrite and held up her hand apologetically. "Sorry. I didn't mean to alarm you. I just mean that she's undergoing some tests. Bone scans, liver scans, blood tests, the works. It's routine in cases like hers, but that doesn't mean it doesn't scare the dickens out of her, out of all of us who love her. I don't know if you can imagine what it's like waiting out the results, waiting to find out if your life is hanging in the balance, if you're okay or doomed to undergo more surgery, more radiation, more chemotherapy, more hell."

Suddenly Frank made the connection between these annual tests and Jenny's departure from his house. "Did she know these tests were scheduled a week ago?"

Carolanne nodded. "I think she scheduled them three or four weeks back."

"Is she here in the hospital?"

"No, these are outpatient tests."

"Who's with her?"

"I'm not sure. I think Otis probably took the day off to drive her. He usually does, despite her arguments that she can do just fine on her own."

"What's her doctor's name?"

The therapist balked at that. "If she didn't tell you about the tests herself, then she won't want you turning up there."

"Don't you see? I have to be with her."

Carolanne continued to hesitate, then finally seemed to reach a decision. "Go to her apartment. She doesn't need you with her for the tests, but she will need you after. It's the waiting that's agonizing. She needs all the support she can get then." She dug in her purse and handed him a key. "Thank goodness I still have this from the first time I watered her plants, while she was back East. You know the address, right?"

"Yes. Thanks, Carolanne. I owe you."

"No. If you can make Jenny happy, that's all that matters. No one deserves a little happiness more than she does."

"I'm going to try like hell."

"You'd better. Otherwise, she'll kill me for giving out her key."

His first stop wasn't a florist, though that had been his first instinct. He'd dismissed the idea of filling the apartment with flowers as both too ordinary and too funereal. Frank opted instead for balloons, dozens of them in every color imaginable. Filled with helium, they floated in Jenny's living room like a rainbow sky. He ordered dinner from the finest restaurant in San Francisco and wine from the best Napa Valley vineyard. And, after determining that the test results would take days, he called a travel agent and ordered tickets for Hawaii to be delivered immediately by messenger. The impulsive, expensive vacation would dent his savings, but he couldn't imagine any gesture that would be a better use of his money. This was no time for caution. A little extravagance was called for.

With the tickets ordered, he sat back to wait, fully aware that his nervous anticipation was nothing compared to the dread that was likely to occupy Jenny's mind unless he could distract her. It was nearly five o'clock when he finally heard her key turning in the lock.

As the door swung open, setting a wave of balloons bobbing, an expression of delighted surprise spread across her face, wiping away the most obvious signs of weariness.

"Welcome home," he said softly, hiding his dismay at the shadows under her eyes, the slump of her shoulders that she couldn't hide.

"You did all this?"

Otis stood behind her, nodding in satisfaction. He gave Frank an approving thumbs-up gesture, then said, "Guess I'm not needed around here anymore. I'll just be on my way." When Jenny didn't even turn to look at him, his grin widened. "Tell her I said goodbye," he told Frank, feigning irritation. "If she happens to notice I'm gone."

"Bye," she murmured distractedly, apparently having caught just enough of Otis's words to realize he was leaving. Her gaze was riveted on Frank. "Why?"

"Because it's time you and I came to an understanding," he said matter-of-factly.

She stared at him in obvious confusion. "About what?"

"About the way things are going to be from now on. You were there for me when I needed help, when I was facing the toughest days of my life. From now on I'm going to be here for you. That's just the way it is. Like sunrise and birds singing and tides changing. Don't fight it, Jenny. I can't let you win this one."

There was a spark of fire in her eyes, then a flicker of acceptance. She sighed heavily and sank onto the sofa. Her whole body seemed to slump with exhaustion. "I'm so tired. I don't think I could battle a feather and come out on top right now."

Sensing victory, though not especially happy about the cause of her token protest, Frank pressed. "Does that mean you accept this as a done deal? You and me? Together, always?"

"We'll see," she said weakly, her eyes drifting shut as she curled into a more comfortable position.

It wasn't the commitment he'd hoped for, but at least she wasn't fighting him. Worried by her lack of energy, by her pale complexion, Frank settled beside her and pulled her into his arms. With a quiet sigh, she rested against him. "Oh, Jenny," he whispered as he listened to the even rise and fall of her breath. "Don't you dare leave me."

She murmured something in her sleep, then was quiet. Holding her in his arms filled Frank with the greatest contentment he'd ever known, even as his heart ached with the uncertainty of the future.

Jenny only dimly remembered coming home from the day of medical tests. Nerves, rather than the tests themselves, always took everything out of her. By the time she got home she felt limp as a dishrag. She remembered coming in. She remembered collapsing onto the sofa. She remembered... A puzzled frown knit her brow. Had Frank been there? Had he issued some sort of crazy ultimatum or had that been a lovely dream? She drew in a deep breath and slowly opened her eyes. Then she blinked and blinked again. One part of the dream at least had been real.

Jenny had never seen so many balloons before in her life. Laughter bubbled up as she stared at the reds and greens, blues and yellows bobbing above her, trailing curls of matching ribbon. She reached for one and drew it down, then caught another and another until she held an entire bouquet of vibrant colors.

"Careful or you'll float away," Frank teased from somewhere just beyond the balloons. He ducked beneath them to sit beside her. So it hadn't been a dream at all. He was here. She was glad enough to see him not to ask how he'd gotten in. She could guess anyway. Carolanne had the only other key to her apartment, and Carolanne thought she'd been wrong to cut herself off from Frank, from a chance at love.

"How do you feel, sleepyhead?" he asked.

"Better. What time is it?"

"Nearly eight. Are you hungry?"

"Starved, but there's nothing in the house for dinner."

He grinned. "Ah, but there is. Veal piccata, pasta and a chocolate mousse cake that will make you weep."

Her mouth watered at the tempting descriptions. "If you prepared all that, maybe we do have something to talk about after all."

"Meaning?"

"Meaning that I will reconsider on the spot marrying a man who can make a chocolate mousse cake."

Frank didn't seem especially pleased by the concession. Either he hadn't made the cake or she was missing something. "You're going to marry me, cake or no cake," he reminded her. "That's been decided."

Her gaze narrowed. "Since when?"

"Since three hours ago, when you swore to stop fighting me."

"I don't remember that conversation."

"Then let me remind you. You and me. Together, always. Those were the exact words."

"Yours or mine?"

"Mine, but you agreed. How can I take you on a honeymoon to Hawaii if you don't say yes?"

"Honeymoon?" she repeated weakly. "Did I agree to that, too? I must have been more out of it than I thought."

"Just sensible, for a change."

"Frank, I can't get married and I can't go to Hawaii. I have to wait here."

"For the test results," he said matter-of-factly. "No problem. They can call us in Hawaii. I hear the phone lines are very modern. No more tin cans or drums."

"No," she said, feeling the pressure build in her chest. "I will not marry you. Not until I know for sure."

He waved the tickets under her nose. "Nonrefundable. For tomorrow. We're going, Jenny Michaels, if I have to sling you across my shoulder and carry you onto that plane. You deserve a break, you need a rest and I'm going to see that you get it. If you want to wait to get married until after the honeymoon, that's a little weird, but it's something we can talk about."

She stared at him. "You want to take the honeymoon first?"

"I don't want to do it that way, but I'm willing to compromise. Just to prove what an agreeable sort of guy I am, what a catch."

She touched a hand to his cheek. "You are a catch. Any woman would be proud to marry you."

"I don't want any woman. I want you and I mean to have you."

"By bullying me into it?"

He grinned and taunted, "I learned from a master."

Jenny saw her own tactics coming back to haunt her. But even as she fought the idea of marrying Frank or even taking this idiotic trip he'd planned without consulting her, she couldn't deny that Hawaii with Frank sounded like heaven. Would it be selfish of her to go? Would it be cruel to start something they might not be able to finish?

As if he'd read her mind, Frank said, "We are going to live every single day as if it's the only one we've got. We are not going to put our lives on hold for 'what ifs.' I won't have either one of us waking up one day with regrets."

He kissed her then, stealing away her breath, teasing her senses until her spirits were soaring every bit as high as the balloons she'd allowed to drift away. "I'll go," she said, when she could finally catch her breath. It might be wrong, it might be selfish, but oh how she longed for a few more days of magic.

A triumphant smile broke across his rugged face. "The wedding?"

"One step at a time," she pleaded. "I can't take any more than that."

He nodded slowly. "One step at a time. We start with the honeymoon of a lifetime."

Less than twenty-four hours later they were on the beach in Maui where the breezes smelled of frangipani and the sun caressed almost as seductively as Frank. For three days they rested and swam and made sweet and tender love. There was no forbidden talk of the future, only the here and now and the delicious thrill of Frank's most persuasive touches, the joy of being together. Jenny felt healthier, more alive and more desperately in love than she ever had before.

On the fourth day when they came back to their cottage, the message light was blinking red. The sight of that impatient light was like a punch in her midsection. All of the energy and hope seemed to drain out of Jenny in the scant thirty seconds it took her to cross the room and call the desk.

As the operator read the name of her doctor and his number in San Francisco, Jenny reached instinctively for Frank's hand. Instead of taking her outstretched hand, though, he came up behind her and wrapped his arms around her waist. He pressed a kiss to the back of her neck, sending shivers down her spine, reminding her of all that was at stake. It was no longer simply her own existence that hung in the balance, but their future.

"I love you," he said urgently. "Marry me, Jenny. Say yes."

She turned in his arms and met his gaze. Her heart thundered in her chest, nearly breaking with despair. Oh, how she wanted to say yes, wanted to believe in the future, but she couldn't. It wouldn't be fair. "I can't answer you now," she said, but the words were an uncertain, breathless tremble.

He shook his head. "I want it settled before you make the call. I don't want there to be a single doubt that I'm asking because I love you or you're answering because of what's in your heart. Tell me now, Jenny. Do you love me?"

She wanted to do the right thing, the fair thing and deny it, but she couldn't. "More than life itself."

"Then that's our answer, isn't it?"

With a wobbly smile, she touched his lips. "Frank, are you sure? Really sure?"

"Absolutely. In sickness or in health."

She read the certainty in his eyes, heard the conviction in his voice, felt the love in his touch. "Then I guess that's our answer. I'll marry you."

Holding her tighter, giving her his strength, he said, "Now make the call."

When the nurse answered, Jenny had trouble even getting her name out. Her voice shook, but she took courage from Frank's embrace, from the commitment they had made only seconds before.

"Jenny," Dr. Hadley said in that low, soothing, bedside voice he had. "We have your results."

"And?"

"Everything looks good."

Hope, radiant and joyous, spilled over her like sunshine. "Everything?" she repeated.

"Not a sign of a recurrence. I'll want you in here a year from now, but I think there's every reason to be optimistic."

"Thank you," she whispered, her eyes locked with Frank's. Only one more year until that fateful fifth anniversary. One more. "You can't know how much this means to me."

"To both of us," Frank murmured huskily.

He took the phone from her grasp and replaced it in its cradle. With a sigh, he slanted his mouth over hers, filling her with an incredible sense of euphoria.

They had a chance, a real chance at a future, she thought as he tugged at the buttons on her beach coverup. When the gauzy material caught and tangled, he ripped it away with a fierce urgency that matched the rising tide of her own need. His hands were rough as he stripped her of her bathing suit, but the heated look in his eyes had her body shivering with the need for speed far more than finesse.

At the first daring touch of his tongue to her breast, excitement streaked through her like lightning. The last shred of self-consciousness between them shimmered, then disintegrated in a hot whirlwind of magical feelings. When he lifted his head to look in her eyes, cautiously seeking her reaction, she arched her back and drew him to her, wanting that exquisite, all-but-forgotten tug of need to go on forever. As pleasure built deep inside, she savored the bold strokes that told her again and again that she was woman enough for him. When his fingers sought the scar on her chest and his gaze locked with hers, she closed her hand over his and showed him the gentle caresses that inflamed and delighted.

There was no time to revel in each delicious sensation, because there were always more. Her body demanded and Frank gave, his lovemaking totally selfless. He reaffirmed the depth of his commitment again and again, building the aching hunger inside her.

With his kisses, slow, deep, passionate kisses that set her senses spinning.

With his caresses, the tenderest of touches, the boldest of claimings.

With his heart, his enduring love evident in his eyes, with the way he responded to her needs time and time again.

In moments, naked and filled with a wicked hunger, they tumbled together on the bed, a tangle of arms and legs, slick with perspiration, alive with desire.

"I love you," Frank said as he stilled above her, fulfillment an anxious heartbeat away. "I love you, Jenny."

"No more than I love you," she said fervently as their bodies at last joined together in a chaotic rhythm as old as time.

Never had Jenny been more aware of the rough and satin textures of his body, of the scent of saltwater and sweet air that surrounded them, of the way he tasted against her tongue or the way her body ached with need until the moment he slid inside her, making her whole, mending her dreams, reaffirming the sheer joy of living.

They were married on the beach a day later. She wore a white Hawaiian wedding dress, and he wore an impossibly loud shirt. She had a bright yellow flower tucked behind her ear and orchids for a bouquet. When they said their vows, Jenny stumbled over the words, but the commitment was etched forever in her heart.

When the brief ceremony was over and they were alone again, giddy on champagne and passion, Frank said, "You realize we're going to have to do this all over again in San Francisco?"

"Your family?"

"You bet. And it's our family now. Don't ever forget that."

"Don't you think with all those sons, your mother wouldn't mind missing this one wedding? My parents will be satisfied with a phone call."

"Not Ma. She'll be convinced we're living in sin unless she hears the vows for herself."

Jenny snuggled closer. "Could be fun," she teased. "It would add an element of danger, when things get too predictable."

"Things won't have a chance of getting predictable," Frank

warned. "She's liable to move in with us until she's certain we've done the right thing."

"In that case, call ahead and line up the church. I am not going to give this up for a single night."

"I promise you, Jennifer Michaels Chambers, we will never be separated again. Never."

* * * * *

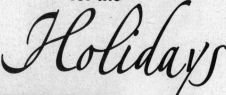

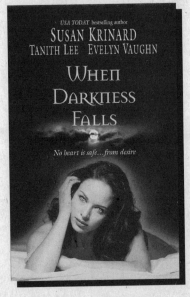

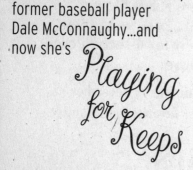

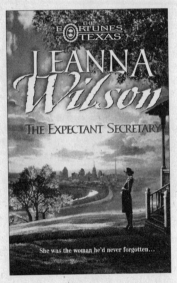

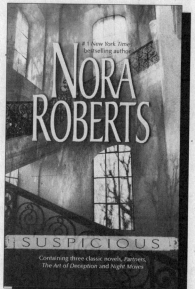

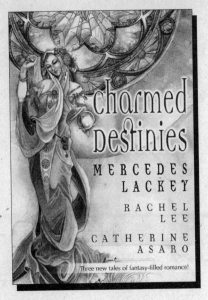